Kimberley CHAMBERS

The Traitor

HARPER

HarperCollins
PUBLISHERS
Since 1817

Harper
An imprint of HarperCollins*Publishers*
The News Building
1 London Bridge Street
London SE1 9GF

www.harpercollins.co.uk

This paperback edition 2017
2

First published in Great Britain by
Preface Publishing 2010
Published by Arrow Books 2013

Copyright © Kimberley Chambers 2010

Kimberley Chambers asserts the moral right to be identified as the author of this work

A catalogue record for this book is available from the British Library

ISBN: 978-0-00-822867-5

Set in Times New Roman by Palimpsest Book Production Limited, Falkirk, Stirlingshire

Printed and bound in Great Britain by Clays Ltd, St Ives plc

MIX
Paper from
responsible sources
FSC
www.fsc.org
FSC™ C007454

FSC™ is a non-profit international organisation established to promote
the responsible management of the world's forests. Products carrying the
FSC label are independently certified to assure consumers that they come
from forests that are managed to meet the social, economic and
ecological needs of present and future generations,
and other controlled sources.

Find out more about HarperCollins and the environment at
www.harpercollins.co.uk/green

In memory of Alf Roberts
(703 legend)

ACKNOWLEDGEMENTS

As always, I would like to thank my agent Tim Bates, my editor Rosie de Courcy and my typist Sue Cox. I am also extremely grateful to everybody at Cornerstone for all the hard work they have put in on my behalf.

A big thank you to cousin Simon for all his help on law and order. Best I don't mention your surname, mate, as being related to me is hardly going to further your career!

Farewell, ungrateful traitor!
Farewell, my perjured swain!
Let never injured woman
Believe a man again.
The pleasure of possessing
Surpasses all expressing,
But 'tis too short a blessing,
And love too long a pain.

John Dryden

PROLOGUE

1988

Eddie Mitchell stared at the handwriting on the envelope. He knew who it was from but, unable to take any more pain, he couldn't face opening it.

Ever since that fateful night in Tilbury, Eddie had shed enough tears to fill a swimming pool. Nothing was going to bring her back, so what was the point of crying any more?

Stuffing the letter under his mattress, Eddie lay back on his bunk and stared at the ceiling. He'd give anything to turn the clock back, fucking anything.

The bullets he had fired had been meant for somebody else, not his beautiful wife. To make matters worse, Jessica had been pregnant at the time with their third child. The unborn baby hadn't stood a chance, God rest its soul. The newspapers had had a field day writing about Eddie's faux pas, the headlines screaming 'Gangland boss in double slaying'.

As soon as Eddie had realised his fatal mistake, he'd immediately tried to take his own life. Unfortunately for him, Jessica's brother Raymond had lunged at him and knocked the gun away. Eddie had still managed to pull the trigger, but the bullet had whizzed through his shoulder, not his brains, as he'd intended it to.

Waking up in hospital and realising he was still alive was the worst moment of Eddie's life. Jessica was his world and he just couldn't live without her.

Consumed by grief and guilt, Eddie immediately admitted

1

what he'd done to the filth. Seven days he'd then spent in hospital under police guard. Once well enough to leave, he'd been carted off to Wandsworth nick.

Eddie was shoved into a cell with an Indian guy who introduced himself as Raj Malik. Company was the last thing Ed needed or wanted. He couldn't even eat, let alone talk.

The screws must have read Eddie's mind when they put him on suicide watch. The pain caused by his blunder was unbearable, and if he could have found something to top himself with, he'd have done it without a second thought.

Eddie had been with Jessica for over seventeen years, and from the moment he first clapped eyes on her, he'd known she was destined to become the love of his life. She was everything a man could want in a woman. She was beautiful on the outside and had a soul to match.

Overall, their marriage was an extremely happy one. Like most contented couples, they'd had their ups and downs over the years, but their love for one another had always remained intact.

Tall, with dark hair and a rugged complexion, Eddie had looked like a scar-faced giant beside his pretty, petite wife. They'd looked good together, though. Everybody used to comment on what a striking couple they made.

Jessica had fallen pregnant within months of them meeting. Eddie married her weeks later, and even though he already had two sons from a previous relationship, he had never felt as content as the day Jess had given birth to their twins.

Frankie and Joey were sixteen now and Eddie knew that he'd lost their love and respect for ever. How could he even consider contacting them when he'd so brutally wiped out their mother's life?

Feeling a shiver go down his spine, Ed sat bolt upright, hugged his knees and laid his head against them. He was forty-eight years old, his life was all but over, and he wished he was fucking dead.

That fateful night would haunt him for ever. It was on his

mind every second of every day. Even sleep didn't release him from his burden, because his nightmares replayed the tragedy over and over again.

As the screw opened the flap to check on him again, Eddie snapped out of his trance. Knowing the letter was under the mattress was doing his head in. He ripped open the envelope and began to digest the words.

Hi Ed,

This is probably the hardest thing that I'll ever have to write and you'll ever have to read.

Before I begin, I just want you to know that I don't blame or hate you for what happened. If anyone knew how much you loved Jessica, that person was me.

Anyway, I thought it only right to inform you that the police have now agreed to release Jessica's body. All the funeral arrangements are now in place, and Jess will be laid to rest at 2.30 p.m. next Wednesday in Upminster Cemetery.

Dad wanted Jess to be buried next to his father over in Plaistow, but Mum didn't want her to go there. She insisted that the happiest days of Jessica's life were spent in Rainham, so her resting place should be as near to there as possible.

I know with everything that's happened, it's impossible for you to attend the service, but I want you to know that I've ordered a beautiful wreath on your behalf. I've enclosed the card, in case you wanted to write it personally. Don't worry if you're not up to it, as I can write one for you.

Mum and Dad have temporarily moved into your house. I hope this is OK with you. Let me know if it isn't. It was Mum's idea. She said that her house wasn't roomy enough for the kids and they'd had enough upheaval without moving them away from their friends. She also

3

said that living at yours makes her feel closer to Jessica.

I've been keeping an eye on Frankie and Joey and both seem to be coping in their own way. They've barely left the house, so hopefully Frankie might be tiring of Jed.

I hope you don't think badly of me, but I really ain't up to visiting you at the moment. I know Gary and Ricky have been to see you and they're coming again next week, so I know you've got visitors. What I'll do is wait till all the press interest dies down, and then I'll pop up and see you.

I know what happened is awful for you, but you must try and be strong for Jessica's sake. My sister loved you very much, and she'd want you to hold it together for the sake of the twins, Ed.

I know it must seem impossible, but try to keep your chin up, mate.

Thinking of you, Raymondo

As he stared at the condolence card, Ed was overcome by grief. 'In deepest sympathy' it said. Screwing the card and the letter up, he let out a painful sob.

With visions of his wife's mutilated body firmly in his mind, he leaped off the bed and, overcome by grief, repeatedly smashed his head against the cell wall.

'Jessica, Jessica' he shouted, as blood began to trickle down his forehead.

As two prison officers ran in, Eddie lashed out at them. He didn't want to be restrained, he wanted to end his misery once and for all.

Two more screws suddenly appeared out of nowhere and, finally overpowered, Eddie sank to his knees.

'I don't wanna live any more. Please just let me fucking top meself,' he screamed.

CHAPTER ONE

Joycie Smith finished off her outfit by adding the black netted hat, then studied her appearance in the full-length mirror. She was so glad she'd bought the new black dress and jacket. It looked very smart and she was determined to do her daughter proud. Moving closer, Joyce noticed how red raw and puffy her eyes looked. She'd had a good old cry this morning – in private, of course. There'd be no tears in front of Stanley and the twins. She had to be brave for their sake.

Joyce put on her tinted glasses and headed downstairs. The flowers had just started to arrive, and she wanted to arrange them neatly. She had to keep herself busy, it was the only way. Not only that, she was determined that her daughter would have the best send-off ever.

Stanley sat in his newly built pigeon shed and stared at his beloved birds. He was all ready – he even had his new suit on – but he'd rather leave Joyce to deal with the tributes.

Putting his head in his hands, Stanley broke down for the third time that morning. The flowers arriving made everything seem so final.

Jessica's death had torn a huge hole in all of their lives. What had happened that night was nigh on impossible to understand, and living hell were the only words Stanley could find to describe life since. There wasn't a parent in the world who imagined outliving their children, and he was no different.

Stanley had disliked Eddie Mitchell from the word go, but

now he despised him with a resentful passion. Living in his house was a constant reminder of the murdering bastard, but it was Joycie's decision and he'd had very little say in the matter.

As his two favourite pigeons, Ernie and Ethel, both cooed at him, Stanley lifted his head, wiped his eyes and smiled sadly. Seconds later, he heard his wife's dulcet tones.

'Stanley! Get your arse out that shed. Raymond and Polly have just arrived.'

Taking a deep breath, Stanley stood up. He was literally dreading the day ahead and it would be a miracle if he got through it at all.

Frankie was sitting on Joey's bed. As her brother offered her a cigarette, she gratefully snatched it out of his hand. Being a couple of months pregnant, Frankie knew she shouldn't really be smoking, but the sound of people arriving downstairs filled her with dread.

Her mother's death and the circumstances surrounding it had created the biggest underworld talking point since the Brinks Mat robbery. The press had had a ball, they'd milked it for all it was worth.

'Gangland boss kills wife in jealous rage', 'Gangster finds wife in bed with daughter's boyfriend', 'Mitchell's moment of madness' were just some of the headlines Frankie had seen.

Most of what had been written was just awful, vicious lies. A couple of the more sensible papers had got the story right, but the ones at the lower end of the scale had written absolute trash just to sell their papers.

Both Frankie and Joey had barely left the house since their mother's death. Frankie had sneaked out a few times to meet up with Jed, but on the last occasion the press had seen her climbing over the back fence and plastered her picture all over the papers.

'Picture of innocence' had been the sarcastic headline.

Frankie was mortified. All her friends had seen it and had

called her on her mobile. Instead of being a victim, Frankie felt like the accused.

Things at home had been no better. Her nan and grandad had moved in to look after her and Joey. Jed wasn't allowed anywhere near the house and every time Frankie mentioned his name, everyone in the room went quiet.

Frankie missed her mother dreadfully, but what had happened was neither her nor Jed's fault. She hadn't asked her father to turn up at Tilbury with a gun, had she now?

As her brother dissolved into tears yet again, Frankie hugged him. Joey wasn't as strong as her, and he wasn't coping very well at all.

'Listen, Joey, in a minute we've got to go downstairs and face everyone. You've got to be brave for Mum's sake.'

Joey threw himself on his bed. 'I can't go to Mum's funeral. I just can't face it. Let me stay here, Frankie. Tell Nan and Grandad I'm not well.'

Frankie stroked her brother's back. Joey had been as close to her mum as anyone had. That's why Frankie hadn't already moved in with Jed: she couldn't have lived with her guilt if she had left Joey at home with her grandparents. They were twins, had been inseparable, even in the womb; no one could look after him like she could.

'Come on, Joey. Put your suit on, and we'll go downstairs. You'll never forgive yourself if you don't go. You'll regret it for the rest of your life.'

Joey sat up. 'It's all right for you. You've got Jed to look after you. Mum's dead, Dad's in prison and Nan and Grandad do my head in. I've got nothing and no one, Frankie, and I know you're gonna be moving out soon. What am I gonna do then, eh?'

Frankie squeezed his hand. 'I'll only be living down the road, Joey. And what about when I have the baby? You'll be an uncle for the first time, and I know you'll be the best uncle ever. All you have to do is stop blaming Jed for everything, then you can be part of our lives.'

As she finally persuaded Joey to get dressed, Frankie made a mental note to ring Dominic the following day. Her brother had barely spoken to his ex since their father had found out Joey was gay and threatened Dom, but now Eddie was banged up, he could ruin her brother's relationship no more. Joey was desperate for love and support and Frankie needed him to be OK before she could move on with her own life.

Downstairs, Joycie was keeping herself busy. She'd chatted to all the mourners, kept their drinks topped up, and managed to convince herself that she was over the worst. No amount of sobbing would bring her beautiful Jessica back from the dead, so she just had to get on with things.

It had been kind of her friends, Rita and Hilda, to come to the house, instead of just turning up at the service. They'd been her neighbours at her old house in Upney for over thirty years, and had known Jessica since she was knee-high.

'So, what do you think of the house?' Joyce asked them brightly.

Rita and Hilda glanced at one another. Joyce liked to act as if she was as tough as old boots, but they both knew that she wasn't. Her behaviour today, considering what had befallen her, was strange, to say the least.

Gary and Ricky, Eddie's sons from his previous marriage, had just turned up and, seeing them in deep conversation with Raymond, Stanley eyed his son suspiciously. Joyce might have forgotten about Raymond's involvement on the night of Jessica's murder, but Stanley most certainly hadn't. If it wasn't for Joyce, he could have quite easily washed his hands of the boy, but his wife had given him a lecture.

'Now, you listen to me, Stanley, and you listen bloody carefully. I've lost one child and if you think I'm having the other banished from our lives, you can think again. Our son had nothing to do with what happened. He wouldn't hurt a fly, that boy. He was just in the wrong place at the wrong time. He loved every hair on our Jessica's head, did our Raymond.'

Joycie wasn't one to argue with, and Stanley had little choice other than to agree and reluctantly forgive his son. Trouble was, deep down he hadn't – it was all pretence.

As the twins appeared, there were lots of emotional condolences. Vicki, Jessica's heavily pregnant best friend, sobbed as she clung to Frankie. 'I loved your mum so much. She was such a wonderful woman. I've already told Dougie, if we have a little girl, I want to name her Jessica.'

Tears were streaming down her face, but Frankie forced a smile. 'Mum would have been honoured,' she whispered.

As more and more people arrived, Stanley became increasingly anxious. All he'd wanted was a quiet send-off for his daughter and already it was turning into a bloody circus. The driveway was packed with people he didn't know and Stan was furious that Eddie's brothers had shown their faces. It would have been bad enough if they had turned up at the church, let alone coming to the house beforehand. Surely they were aware of what Eddie had done? Didn't they have any remorse or guilt whatsoever?

By the time the hearse arrived, the driveway was a mass of beautiful flowers.

As she cuddled her grandchildren, one on either side, Joyce couldn't bear to look at the coffin she'd so carefully chosen. It just didn't seem possible for Jessica to be inside that box. Trying to suppress her emotions, Joyce took a deep breath. She had to keep it together in front of all these people. Stanley was in a terrible state and somebody had to look after the twins. Aware that the undertaker was ready to take Jessica on her final journey, Joyce led Frankie and Joey outside.

Seeing his father almost collapse with grief, Raymond held Stanley's arm to support him. 'I've got you, Dad. Just hold my arm and walk with me,' he told him.

Joyce had insisted they just have the one family car. She'd never got on with her parents – she hadn't even seen them for years – and they were going straight to the service. Jessica's other grandparents, on Stanley's side, were both dead.

Joyce, Stanley, Frankie, Joey, Raymond and Polly sat in the

hearse behind the coffin. Everybody else was to make their own way to the cemetery. In normal circumstances there would have been at least three or four cars laid on for Eddie's sons, brothers and family. However, the circumstances surrounding Jessica's death were anything but normal.

As the chief undertaker walked in front of the hearse, the cars crawled along behind him.

Stanley was furious as he saw how many reporters were taking pictures on the road outside. 'Couldn't they have left us alone for just one day?' he mumbled.

Raymond put a comforting arm around his father's shoulder who, but it was quickly brushed away.

Noticing the young reporter who had given her a wonderful write-up in the *Daily Mirror*, Joyce gave a solemn wave. Stanley went apeshit. 'Our daughter is lying in that coffin in front of us. Show some respect, you stupid woman. Fucking parasites, they are.'

Raymond put his other arm around his mother. This was as hard a day for her as anyone and acting normal was just her way of coping.

Frankie and Joey clung to one another throughout the short journey through the lanes. Neither could believe that they would never see or hear their mother again. As she stared at the coffin, Frankie thought of her father. Throughout her childhood, Frankie had always been a daddy's girl. She had his dark features, fiery temper and impulsive nature. Joey looked nothing like Frankie or their dad. He was blond, mild-mannered and a clone of their mum.

'Do you think Dad knows that Mum is being buried today?' she whispered to her brother.

Joey looked at her in horror. 'Don't mention his name. How could you Frankie, today of all days?'

As the rest of the journey continued in silence, Polly studied Raymond's family. They were a funny bunch, to say the least, especially his parents. Polly's own parents had been horrified when Jessica's murder had made all the nationals. They'd known

10

that Raymond worked with Eddie and they were worried about what she'd got herself involved with.

'I know you're very keen on Raymond, but there's plenty more fish in the sea. Why don't you walk away while you still can?' her father had urged her.

Polly had taken no notice of her mum or dad. They weren't exactly whiter than white themselves. She was besotted by Raymond, in a way that a woman could only dream of. She wasn't stupid – she'd always known that he was a bit of a rogue, but even so, the circumstances of Jessica's murder had frightened the life out of her.

Raymond had recently made a promise to her. He'd sworn that he would give up the job he was doing and find a normal nine-to-five number.

'Are you OK, Ray?' Polly asked, squeezing his hand.

Raymond nodded, but said nothing. Obviously, working with Eddie over the years, they'd seen and been responsible for many a dead body. Remembering how Jessica had looked, Raymond felt physically sick as he stared out of the window. The sight of his sister's bullet-torn corpse would prey on him for the rest of his life. There wasn't an hour that went by when the death of Jessica didn't enter his thoughts. His sister had been one of life's beautiful people. Thinking back to when they were kids, Raymond nervously bit his lip. Life without her was pretty much unbearable, and he was dreading doing his speech.

When Joyce stepped out of the hearse, she was surprised by the number of people already at the church. They'd tried to keep the funeral small and private, and she was thrown by the crowd of mourners that had turned up. Grabbing the distraught Joey and Frankie, Joycie bowed her head as she led them into the church.

Raymond had instructed all of Eddie's family to sit well away from his parents. 'I know none of this is your fault, lads, but because Eddie did what he did, it ain't appropriate for you to sit near the front.'

11

Eddie's sons from his first marriage, Gary and Ricky, were devastated by Jessica's death. They'd loved her immensely, and over the years she'd been a better mother to them than their own. Seeing their dad in prison had broken both boys' hearts. They knew how much Jess had meant to their old man, and what had happened was the tragedy of all tragedies.

Eddie had only agreed to see them the once. He was a broken man, a shadow of his charismatic former self, and had sat opposite them in bits. Neither Gary nor Ricky had known what to say or do. It was a surreal situation that had devastated everybody. The only words of comfort they could offer their father were to promise to continue the family business and do him proud.

'All right, Gal? Packed innit?' their uncle Ronny said in a loud voice, as the boys now entered the church.

Seeing that Ronny's eyes were already glazed, Gary put his finger to his lips. The service was about to start, and a drunken Ronny causing havoc in his wheelchair was the last thing the vicar needed.

The vicar cleared his throat. He was a seasoned professional, but this particular service was difficult, even for him. 'Today we are here to commemorate the life of Jessica Anne Mitchell,' he said.

There wasn't a dry eye in the house as parts of Jessica's life were remembered. The twins and Stanley were inconsolable. Joyce couldn't look at them; if she did, she'd break down, so she ignored their sobs and stared at the vicar.

'Can we open our hymn books at page twenty-one?'

As the congregation stood up, Raymond had to once again physically support his father.

> All things bright and beautiful,
> All creatures great and small,
> All things wise and wonderful:
> The Lord God made them all.

Jed O'Hara entered the church and stood quietly at the back. He held the hymn book in his hands, but couldn't sing because he couldn't read properly.

Jimmy O'Hara put an arm around his son's shoulder. Jed was a good boy and had been determined to attend Jessica's funeral, so he could keep an eye on Frankie. Not wanting his son to become raw meat in a starving lion's cage, Jimmy had insisted on coming with him. Jed was worried about Frankie; she was carrying his child and he had every right to be there in her hour of need.

Jimmy knew what losing a child was like. His wife, Alice, had been pregnant up until a couple of weeks ago, when she'd suddenly miscarried.

As the hymn came to an end, Ronny Mitchell decided he was busting for the toilet. Being stuck in a wheelchair, he was unable to hold himself like other people could. Nudging his brother, Paulie, he urged him to take him outside.

'I need a shit. I've gotta find a bog,' he said in an extremely loud tone.

As Raymond stood up to give his speech, an embarrassed Paulie also stood up. Ronny was a nuisance with a capital N at times.

'Jessica was the most wonderful sister a brother could wish for,' Raymond began.

While Paulie wheeled his brother towards the exit, a nosy Ronny scanned the mourners. The church was full of villains, most of them mates of Eddie, his father and his uncle Reg. Spotting Jimmy O'Hara's ugly mush, Ronny did a double take and slammed the brake on his wheelchair.

Because he was staring at the piece of paper he'd so carefully written, Raymond didn't notice what was happening at the other end of the church and, with tears rolling down his face, carried on with his speech.

'The day Jessica gave birth to her twins, Frankie and Joey, was the happiest of her life. Even though she was no more than a child herself, she quickly adapted to become the most wonderful . . .'

Raymond's speech was stopped in its tracks by Ronny's drunken voice. 'Get out of here, you pikey cunts! Hit 'em, Paulie. Go on, fucking do 'em,' he yelled.

Shocked by the commotion, every mourner turned around to see what was happening.

Jimmy O'Hara held his hands up. 'Look, we don't want no trouble. I've only come here to support my Jed. He has every right to be here. Jessica was his future mother-in-law and would have been grandmother to his chavvie.'

When Paulie lunged at Jimmy O'Hara, the vicar pleaded for order. 'Can we stop this awful nonsense? Please respect the deceased and also the house of God,' he shouted over the loud-speaker.

Uncle Reg eventually broke up the fracas and, with the help of Paulie and a couple of Eddie's pals, they threw both Jed and Jimmy out of the church.

'Frankie's having my chavvie – we're getting married. Tell 'em Frankie, tell 'em,' Jed screamed, as he was roughly pushed out of the door.

Frankie went to run to her boyfriend's aid, but Raymond put his arm out and stopped her. 'You stay there. It's your mother's funeral, and you're partly to blame for all this,' he reminded her coldly.

Traumatised, Stanley and Joey clung to one another and, seeing their anguish, Joyce was unable to keep it together any more. Bursting into tears, she fell to her knees. 'The least my baby deserved was a good send-off. Why us, God? Why?' she screamed.

CHAPTER TWO

As a distraught Joyce was led from the church by Stanley, Raymond urged the vicar to round the service up. Jessica's funeral had been completely ruined and the quicker it was over, the better.

Raymond sadly shook his head. Like most men, he was sceptical about the idea of life after death, but if by any chance it did exist, his sister would be horrified by what had just happened.

The vicar quickly wrapped up his speech with a prayer, then led the mourners outside for the burial.

Joyce had all but collapsed and was now sitting on a chair, sipping water and being comforted by friends and the curate. 'I can't watch my baby being put into that grave, I just can't face it,' she wept.

Urging Stanley to walk on ahead, Hilda and Rita crouched down either side of her. 'You don't have to do anything you don't want to, Joycie. Jess knows you're here and that's all that matters,' Rita said kindly.

Jimmy and Jed had now disappeared, but Ronny was still there. Ray caught up with him and gave him a sharp dig in his shoulder. 'Did you have to kick off in the middle of my speech? Ain't you got no fucking sense? Why didn't you wait till we all got outside?'

Looking remorseful, Ronny shrugged. 'I know me and Paulie fell out with Ed, but he's still me brother, Ray. When I saw them pikey shitbags there, I just lost it. How dare they fucking turn up?'

Raymond sighed. He felt the same as Ronny did himself. The difference was, he had a brain, so would have handled things better.

As Ronny held out his right hand, Raymond unwillingly shook it. 'Look, no hard feelings, but I think it might be best if you don't come back to the house afterwards. Me mum's proper upset by what happened in the church and it ain't fair on her.'

Ronny glanced at Paulie. He hated missing out on a free funeral piss-up. 'I ain't gonna upset your mum,' he slurred.

Realising Polly had now caught up with him, Raymond linked arms with her and said no more. Ronny could have a full-scale argument with an ant, and Ray just wasn't in the mood to row with him.

Joey broke down completely as his mother's coffin was lowered into the ground. 'I want her back, Frankie, I really want her back,' he sobbed.

With tears streaming down her own face, Frankie cuddled him. 'I want her back as well, Joey.'

Overcome by grief himself, Stanley led the twins away. 'Let's go and find your nan,' he told them gently.

The mood in the hearse on the journey back to the house was extremely sombre. Annoyed with herself for breaking down inside the church, Joyce was the first to pull herself together. 'Look, I know the service never went as well as we planned, but let's see if we can give Jessica a good send-off back at home. It's what she would have wanted, I know it is,' she said brightly.

Admiring his mother's strength, Raymond squeezed her hand. 'I'll second that. Let's do our Jessica proud.'

Over in south London, Eddie Mitchell was also having an extremely difficult day. The knowledge that his wife was being buried and that he wasn't able to attend had torn his heart to shreds. He had been in solitary confinement for five days now, serving his punishment for lashing out at the screws. In solitary, Ed had had very little contact with anyone, and the silence suited him just fine.

The other prisoners did his head in and he couldn't give a shit about exercising or watching the telly. Nothing mattered any more, his life had all but ended. Chewing his lip, Eddie guessed what the time was. The funeral must be all over now, it had to be. Wondering how the service had gone, Ed wiped the sweat from his brow. His Jessica, his beautiful wife, was probably now lying six foot under and it was all his bloody fault. Hearing the jangle of keys, Eddie looked up as two screws walked in.

'Up you get, Mitchell, you're being moved early,' the tall one said.

Eddie looked at the two guards in amazement. He had another two days to do in solitary yet. 'Why am I being moved?' he mumbled.

As the two guards grinned at one another, Eddie knew that his already awful day was about to take another turn for the worse.

Over in Rainham, the house had become packed to the rafters, so Stanley escaped to the serenity of his pigeon shed. Fifty per cent of the mourners were probably villains and he couldn't be doing with any of the dodgy bastards, he'd rather be sitting on his own.

'You in there, Stan?'

Recognising his best pal Jock's voice, Stanley opened the door. 'Come in, mate. I've stocked up with bitter; let's have a beer in here, eh?'

Jock followed him in and sat on the wooden bench. His heart went out to his pal, Stanley and, having a daughter himself, he couldn't begin to imagine how the poor bastard must be feeling. Cracking open a can, Jock studied the pigeons.

'I think you should breed Ethel with Willie rather than Ernie next time,' he said, trying to cheer Stan up.

Stanley shook his head. 'Ethel hates Willie! Her and Ernie are inseparable, he'd be heartbroken, like I am now,' he replied, bursting into tears.

Jock moved towards his pal and awkwardly put an arm round his shoulder. 'Go on, Stan. Let it all out, mate.'

'I miss Jess so much, Jock. What am I gonna do without her, eh?'

Jock had no answer to Stanley's question. 'I don't know, mate.'

Inside the house, Joyce was knocking back yet another glass of brandy. She studied the people in the living room. She'd been so distressed at the cemetery earlier that she'd barely recognised anyone. Mary, Ginny and Linda, who had been friends with Jessica since childhood, were all there, and lots of the twins' friends had come to pay their respects as well.

As she stared at the three older ladies with Gary and Ricky, Joycie suddenly remembered who they were. Ed's auntie Joan, his aunt Vi, and his father Harry's lady friend, Sylvie. Most families would have been appalled by the heavy presence of the Mitchell clan, but Joycie wasn't. Being old school, she saw it as a mark of respect, not a fucking liberty.

Feeling smothered by people's condolences, Joey and Frankie went out in the garden with their friends. Joey was pissed, but Jed had insisted that Frankie only had a couple of drinks. 'I really fancy another vodka,' she said to her pals.

Stacey smiled at her. 'I'll go and get you one. I'm sure another weak one won't hurt the baby, Frankie.'

As Demi and Paige followed Stacey into the house, Frankie pretended to Joey that she was going to the toilet.

'I'm busting to go meself, so I'll come with you,' he said.

Frankie was annoyed. 'For fuck's sake, Joey, leave me alone for five minutes, will ya?'

Running up the stairs, Frankie shut her bedroom door. She was desperate to ring Jed, to make sure he was OK.

Jed answered immediately, and then launched into a torrent

of abuse. 'I swear on our chavvie's life, Frankie, if you don't get your arse down to my trailer in the next hour, I'm gonna come round to yours and fucking drag you down the road,' he ended.

Not for the first time that day, Frankie began to cry. 'Please Jed, it's my mum's funeral and I can't leave, not yet. I promise, as soon as today's over, I'll sort things out with my family and then we can be together. I'm sorry for what happened earlier with my uncles, but that's not my fault. Please be patient, Jed. I can't leave Joey on his own, not tonight. He's not ready.'

Jed seldom lost his temper, but when he did, he lost it big style. 'I've had enough of this now, Frankie. I know what happened to your old girl was awful, but don't treat me like a fucking dinlo. I know you've had a drink, I can hear it in your voice, and I ain't having it, not when you're carrying my chavvie. I'm telling you again, if you ain't back within the hour, I'm coming round there. I've had a gutful of your family and, as far as I'm concerned, all of 'em can go fuck their grandmother.'

As he cut her off, Frankie slumped onto her bed. Joey, who had followed her upstairs anyway and heard her side of the conversation, opened her bedroom door. 'When are you going to realise that Jed's an arsehole and he's no good, eh?' he said, as he held her close.

'What am I gonna do if he turns up here? Raymond will kill him, I know he will,' Frankie sobbed.

For once, Joey was the strong one out of the two of them. 'Listen to me. There's Raymond, Paulie, Uncle Reg, Uncle Albert and all Dad's mates here. Jed won't turn up here today, trust me. He's bluffing.'

As he dried her eyes with his handkerchief, Frankie forced a smile. Jed had never spoken to her like that before and she was furious with him. How could he treat her like that, today of all days?

Joey held his sister's hand. 'Come on, let's go back downstairs, and you can sort things out with Jed tomorrow.'

*   *   *

Having finally been enticed out of his pigeon shed by Jock, Stanley was horrified to see his wife not only inebriated, but also laughing and joking with Eddie's aunts and uncles. Spotting Joycie's parents, whom he had always liked immensely, Stan sidled towards them. Ivy and Bill were both well into their eighties now and neither looked the picture of health.

'I'm so sorry I never got much of a chance to talk to you earlier. It was just such a difficult day and I didn't really know if I was coming or going,' Stan apologised.

Ivy hugged her son-in-law. Stanley was a lovely man, but her Joycie had never truly appreciated him. That's why she and her daughter had never really seen eye to eye. Joycie had always blamed her mother for encouraging her to marry Stanley; the silly little cow had always thought she was worth more.

'I'm so sorry, Stan. Me and you knew all along what that Eddie was capable of, didn't we? Do you remember Jessica getting married to the bastard? I told you at the reception that he had them eyes – you know, cold and calculating. I'll never forget it, that man sent shivers down my spine and I just knew he'd ruin her bleeding life.'

Keeping half an eye on his wife, Stanley nodded. 'I remember that conversation, Ivy. I told you that his eyes reminded me of dead fish.'

Hearing his old woman screech with laughter, Stanley decided enough was enough. Storming over to where she was standing, he roughly grabbed her arm and yanked her into the kitchen.

'What do you think you're doing? You senile old bastard!' Joyce yelled at him.

For once in his downtrodden life, Stanley had the bottle to give her what for. 'How can you stand there laughing and joking with Eddie's relations when we've just buried our daughter? What is the matter with you, eh? Your parents are disgusted by your behaviour and so am I, and I'll tell you something else, shall I? If you think I'm living in that murdering bastard's house one day longer than I need to, you can think again, Joycie.'

Shocked by Stanley's outburst, Joyce did her best not to show it. 'Move, then, if you don't like it. You go back to that pokey council house of ours, see if I care. I'm staying here, 'cause it makes me feel close to my Jessica.'

Aware of Eddie's sons, Gary and Ricky, staring at them, Stan led Joyce out on to the front drive.

'You must think I've just stepped off the banana boat, Joycie. When we first found out Jessica had been murdered, you couldn't agree with me enough about Eddie and his family. You soon changed your mind when you moved in 'ere though, didn't you? All you've ever wanted is a nice, big house so you can show it off to your friends. I'm not as shallow as you, Joycie. I know exactly what you think of me and the home I've worked my bollocks off for over the years. I even bought it for you off that right-to-buy scheme 'cause you begged me to and I've bought you new furniture at your every whim. Well, I've had enough of it now, and tomorrow I'm going back home. You can do as you please. Stay 'ere on your own, for all I care.'

Joyce was gobsmacked. Stanley had rarely raised his voice to her throughout the whole of their marriage. As he walked away, she stood open-mouthed, and for once she said nothing.

Eddie Mitchell was agitated as he sat on the bunk in his cell. He'd known by the attitude of the two prison guards that he was in for a nasty surprise. They'd been laughing and joking as they took him down a corridor he'd never seen before. 'Ain't I going back to me old cell?' Ed asked, bewildered.

The shorter guard grinned at the taller one. 'No, Mitchell. The guvnor decided you and Malik weren't suited and you needed better company, so he's found you a new home with a nice friendly English cellmate.'

Ed had been in the cell for what seemed like four hours now and he still didn't have a clue who he was sharing with. Apart from a few belongings, there was no sign of the geezer.

When he heard the key slot into the lock, Eddie picked up his book and pretended to read it. Glancing out of the corner of his eye, he felt his heart leap into his chest as he recognised his new cellmate.

After her argument with Jed, Frankie had necked at least four more vodkas. Her hormones were having a field day, and she was tired, depressed, lonely and tearful. She and Jed rarely argued. On the odd occasion when they'd had a lovers' tiff, it had always been immediately resolved.

Seeing Dougie and Vicki, her parents' friends, heading her way to say goodbye, Frankie forced herself to be polite. About to get Vicki to take her mobile number so when she gave birth they could swap baby talk, Frankie heard a commotion coming from her left.

'Get out of here, before I kill yer,' she heard somebody yell.

Looking around, Frankie dropped Vicki's pen in shock. Jed was sitting on a nearby wall, telling her uncle Reg where to get off.

Reg hobbled towards Jed. 'Do yourself a favour, son, and get the fuck out of here, before you get hurt,' he warned, his eyes bulging.

'I'm going nowhere without my wife-to-be. You do whatever you have to, you senile old grunter. Frankie belongs to me and she's coming with me right now.'

Aware that Gary, Ricky and Raymond had all run out of the house, Frankie began to scream. 'Don't hurt him. Please don't hurt Jed,' she begged.

Jumping off the wall, Jed showed no fear as Raymond went for him. 'Frankie's my woman,' he screamed, as Raymond caught him straight on the chin.

Watching Jed fall to the grass, Frankie intervened and chucked herself on top of him. Seeing his uncle trying to manhandle his sister, Joey also joined in the fracas.

'Leave Frankie alone,' he shouted, as his weak punches landed nowhere.

Having been told that it was all kicking off in the garden,

Joyce flew into action. 'Oi, whaddya think you're doing?' she screamed, as she lost her footing and stacked it in one of the flowerbeds.

As all hell broke loose, Frankie decided enough was enough. She needed to make a decision, and if she was ever going to leave home, that moment was definitely now.

CHAPTER THREE

Stanley's alarm clock went off at eight the following morning and he immediately got out of bed.

After the mass brawl in the garden the previous evening, he'd sodded off upstairs without saying goodnight to a single soul. Jessica's funeral had been a catastrophe from start to finish, and Stanley would never forgive the bastards that had ruined it. Animals, that's what the Mitchells were, and he was just glad that Jock had already left when the whole wake kicked off.

Pulling his suitcase out from under the bed, Stanley began to pack his clothes. The quicker he got out of this cursed house with its awful memories, the better.

Hearing her husband banging about in the room next door, Joyce lifted her head off the pillow. She felt as sick as a parrot, and as she burped, she heaved. All she could taste and smell was brandy, and she vowed there and then never to touch the poxy drink again.

Joyce got up and put on her dressing gown. Her recollection of the previous evening was vague, to say the least, but she could sort of remember a big fight happening. Noticing a large bruise and cut on her leg, she winced as she touched it. Surely she hadn't fallen over in front of all the mourners? Desperate to get rid of the taste of brandy, Joyce made her way downstairs to make herself a coffee. Gagging for some fresh air and to rid the house of the smell of stale smoke, Joyce opened the conservatory door.

'Christ almighty,' she mumbled in complete astonishment.

Jessica's once-perfect garden looked as if a bomb had hit it. All the furniture was smashed to pieces. The wooden table was lying upside down and the chairs had no legs left on them.

Shuffling outside, Joyce put her hand over her mouth as she noticed that all the beautiful flowerbeds had been trampled on. Seeing shards of glass by her feet, she turned to her left. The three smashed windows were the final straw for Joyce, and she ran back into the house.

'Stanley! Stanley!' she screamed.

When Stanley marched down the stairs with a suitcase in his hand, Joyce looked at him in bewilderment. 'What are you doing? What's with the case? You seen the state of the garden? Everything's smashed to smithereens.'

Dropping his case, Stanley ran out the back. He'd locked the pigeon shed, but what if it had been smashed or the birds had died of fright? Fearful for the safety of his babies, Stanley shook as he put the key in the door.

'Thank God,' he said, as all four cooed at him. 'Daddy's here now and he's taking you back home, away from this loony bin.'

'What are you gonna do about cleaning this mess up, Stanley? I think I'll ring Raymond, he'll know a glazier. The twins can help an' all. I mean, we don't ask 'em to do much, do we?'

For once in his life, Stanley felt like a man as he spoke. 'You ask who you like, Joycie. I won't be here. I told you yesterday, I'm moving back home.'

Joyce remembered bits of what Stanley had said the previous day about leaving, but she thought it had been one of his little tantrums. 'Don't be silly, Stanley. You can't leave me here on my own.'

'Come with me then, Joycie. I told you last night, I cannot live in this house one minute longer, and I meant it. There's too many memories, and it's making me ill.'

Joyce had waited all her life to live in a luxury property and she wasn't about to walk away from it without a fight. Turning on the tears, she begged her husband to stay. 'Please don't go, Stanley. It makes me feel close to Jessica, living here. I can almost feel her presence at times. And what about the twins? You can't leave them. They need both of us.'

Stanley shook his head. It was obvious Joyce didn't remember that Frankie had done a runner last night. 'Cor, you must have been well gone, love. Frankie left home last night. Don't you remember the gypsy boy turning up here for her? That's what started the fight. I bet you don't even recall falling arse over tit in the flowerbeds, do you, dear? No, well you wouldn't, would you? I'm off, Joycie. Jock's coming round in an hour with the van. He's gonna take the pigeons back for me.'

As he walked back out to the garden, Joyce glared at him. Stanley had always done just as she had wanted throughout their entire marriage, and she couldn't understand what had suddenly got into him. Remembering what he'd said about Frankie, she went up the stairs and knocked on Joey's bedroom door.

'Joey, it's Nan. Can I come in?'

'Just leave me alone. Go away,' Joey shouted.

Desperate to know exactly what had happened the night before, Joyce tried the handle. The door was locked. After the morning she'd had, Joyce quickly lost her temper and screamed at her grandson.

'Open this door now, Joey, else Raymond will kick the bastard thing down. He's on his way over, you know. He'll be here in five minutes,' she lied.

Her fib worked, and as Joey unlocked the door, Joyce stormed in. As she clocked the state of her grandson's bruised face, Joycie's temper melted.

'Oh my God! What happened, love?' she asked, as she sat on the edge of his bed.

Joey just burst into tears. 'I tried to help Frankie, and Raymond caught me with his elbow. It was an accident, he didn't mean it. Frankie's gone, Nan. What am I gonna do without her? We've never been apart before.'

26

Joyce held him tightly. 'You listen to me, Joey. That won't last with that gypsy boy. Different breed, that mob are. Wicked bastards, I should know. One of 'em put a curse on me years ago. Frankie's young, headstrong, but that boy'll show his true colours, and when he does she'll come back.'

'I don't think she will, Nan. She loves him. It's as though he's cast a spell on her. And what about the baby? She won't leave him if she's got his kid, will she? I hate him, Nan. He's wrecked our entire family. I mean if it weren't for Frankie getting with Jed, Mum would still be alive, wouldn't she?'

Desperately wanting to put a smile back on Joey's face, Joyce thought of the dogs. Buster and Bruno, the twins' Rottweilers, had been living at Pat Murphy's since the night Jessica died. Joyce didn't like dogs very much. Bleeding nuisance they were, pissing and shitting all over the place. 'I tell you what. Why don't you get yourself dressed and go and pick Buster and Bruno up? I'm sure they'd love to come home and they'll be a bit of company for you, Joey.'

Joey sighed. Buster and Bruno were no replacement for his sister, but at least they'd give him something to focus on.

As he got out of bed, Joycie played her ace card. 'Before you trot off to Pat Murphy's, I need you to do me a favour. Your grandad's having one of his funny turns, says he's moving back into our old house. Go and talk to him, love. Don't tell him I sent you, but beg him to stay. If he says no, start crying, Joey.'

'OK,' Joey said sadly. He really didn't want his grandad to leave. The house would feel so empty with just him and his nan rattling about.

Stanley was sitting on the sofa drinking a mug of tea. As Joey walked into the room, Stan put his mug on the table and stood up.

'Please don't go, Grandad. I don't want you to leave. I love you,' Joey begged.

Joyce smiled as she stood earwigging in the hallway. Joey was that good an actor, he should have gone to drama school,

27

and as for Stanley, the silly old goat, he certainly wouldn't have the guts to walk away from his distressed grandson.

When the doorbell rang, Joyce nigh on jumped out of her skin. 'Oh, it's you. I don't think he's leaving now,' she confidently told Jock.

About to tell him to go back home, Joyce was shocked to see Stanley walking towards her with his case in his hand.

'Put that in the van, Jock, while I sort out the pigeons. We'll dismantle the shed and take it at the weekend,' he said.

Joyce gawped at him. 'You can't go now, Stanley. Look how upset Joey is. You can't leave him like that – you'll break the boy's heart. And how would Jessica feel? If she's looking down, that girl would be disgusted by your behaviour.'

Stanley had no intention of changing his mind. How dare she use their dead daughter as blackmail? 'I've spent my whole life doing things to please other people, Joycie, and it's about time I started looking out for myself. Joey can come and stop with me whenever he wants, I've told him that.'

Aware that nothing and no one was going to change her husband's mind, Joyce let rip at him. 'You nasty, selfish old bastard. Go on then, get out and take them disease-ridden fucking birds with ya. I should have divorced you years ago, Stanley Smith. You're nothing but a waste of space that's dragged me down all my life and I'll be better off without ya.'

While Jock stood open-mouthed, Stanley went off to the shed to collect his babies. He didn't want Joycie to see him cry; he wouldn't give her the satisfaction.

As Barry Macarthy was let back into the cell, Eddie tried to shut out the sound of his droning voice.

Macarthy, better known as Big Bald Baz, was a total head case and Eddie had had ructions with him years ago, when they were just teenagers. He had been about eighteen at the time and had been enjoying a quiet drink in a boozer in Mile End one evening. All of a sudden there was a fracas a few feet away, and Eddie had watched in horror as Baz smashed a glass straight into some girl's face, ripping her cheek in half. Ed had always hated blokes who roughed up women, so, being a gentleman, he'd immediately intervened and got a damn good hiding for his troubles.

Eddie had stood no chance that night. Big Bald Baz was at least eighteen stone back then, and two of his mates had joined in as well. Even at the tender age of eighteen, Eddie wasn't one to forgive and forget. Six weeks later, he'd returned to the same boozer with his dad, brothers and uncle and they'd given Big Bald Baz and his pals the hiding of their lives.

From that day onwards, Baz and his mates had given the Mitchells a wide berth. Ed had seen him about and heard plenty of stories about the fat bastard over the years, but they'd never spoken since.

Ed now knew why the screws had been laughing at him. Big Bald Baz was looking at a life sentence for murdering his old woman. Eddie had read all about it in the newspapers. The evil scumbag had even chopped off her hands and pulled out her teeth to hide her identity. The police had enough evidence to charge Baz, even though they didn't have him bang to rights, and the case had made front-page news.

'You're quiet, Mitchell. I ain't gonna lamp you one again, if that's what you're worried about,' Baz said, laughing.

Eddie ignored him. He hadn't spoken to the fat, arrogant prick since he'd first entered the cell yesterday and he wasn't about to start now. Turning the pages of his book, Ed pretended to be engrossed. He wasn't, of course. All he could think about was Jessica.

As Stanley slammed the front door, Joycie glanced at Joey. 'Go on, love, go and pick the dogs up,' she urged him.

As soon as her grandson had left the house, Joyce ran to the kitchen and poured herself a large brandy. 'So much for not drinking it again,' she mumbled when the sickly taste hit the back of her throat.

Taking the bottle into the lounge with her, Joyce slumped

29

on the sofa and topped up her glass. She had to tidy up at some point. The house was still littered with dirty glasses, cans and overflowing ashtrays, but for once she didn't know where to start. Knowing she'd be ill if she didn't eat something, Joyce walked over to the table where the half-eaten food lay. She grabbed a sausage roll and heaved as she nigh on swallowed it whole. Two more brandies later, the realisation of what had just happened suddenly sunk in.

'How could you be so callous, Stanley? How could you leave me at a time like this?' she said between sobs.

By the time Joey returned with Buster and Bruno, Joyce had drunk half a litre and was screaming the house down. Wary of the nutty old woman, the dogs immediately flew out to the garden to get away from her.

'You sound ever so drunk, Nan. Don't drink no more,' Joey said worriedly.

Joyce rarely showed her emotions, but when she did, there was no stopping her. 'Thirty-six years of my life I gave to your grandad, and this is how he treats me,' she screamed.

Joey felt uncomfortable as he tried to hug her. 'Why don't you go and have a lie down? You might feel better if you get some sleep, Nan.'

'Sleep? Sleep? I want revenge. Revenge for all them years I wasted on that bastard.'

As his nan stood up and staggered towards the kitchen, Joey sat frozen to the spot. He could hear her rummaging about in the big cupboard, but didn't have the guts to ask what she was looking for. Hearing the kitchen door slam, he crept over to the window. He gasped as he saw his nan zigzagging down the garden with his dad's big hammer in her hand.

'Shit!' he shouted as he ran outside. Surely she wasn't going to hurt the dogs.

Joyce had had little to smile about for weeks, but as she lifted the hammer and smashed it through the side of Stanley's beloved pigeon shed, she began to laugh. 'You fucking bald-headed old bastard,' she shrieked, as she let fly again.

Wishing they were back at Pat Murphy's, Buster and Bruno cowered next to the fence.

'Nan, stop it. What are you doing?' Joey yelled.

'Your grandfather deserves all he gets. Shame he's took them pigeons home with him. I could have killed 'em and cooked 'em in a nice pie,' Joyce cackled.

Petrified by the look of madness on his nan's face, Joey ran back into the house. If only Frankie was here, she'd know what to do. At the sound of more wood splintering, Joey knew he had to do something. Dashing upstairs, he grabbed his phone. 'Please answer, please answer,' he said out loud.

Thankfully, his wishes were answered. 'Uncle Raymond, you need to come to the house quickly. Nanny's gone loopy, she's smashing Grandad's pigeon shed up with a big hammer. I don't know how to stop her. Please hurry up. Please.'

CHAPTER FOUR

Frankie felt nervous as she followed Jed into his parents' house. She'd spent many a night in Jed's trailer but, apart from a few hellos and goodbyes, she'd had very little contact with his parents, Jimmy and Alice.

'Hello Frankie, you come and sit down 'ere next to me,' Alice told her warmly. 'You know what these men are like, all they wanna do is talk business,' she said, laughing.

Frankie was surprised to see the table laid.

Noticing her expression, Alice smiled. 'Didn't Jed tell you? We're having a nice family meal. Billy and Marky, Jed's brothers, will be here soon with their wives and chavvies. Now you're living here and having my grandchild, we gotta introduce you to the family, ain't we?'

Frankie felt like a fish out of water. She had been nervous enough officially meeting Jed's parents, let alone his brothers and their wives.

While Alice waffled on about baby names, Frankie studied the decor in the house. It was decked out in china and some of the ornaments were like those Jed had in his trailer.

'What are you looking at – the china? Or my Jimmy's brass collection?'

'Both,' Frankie said, embarrassed.

'I'll take you upstairs later and show you me handmade dollies. Beautiful they are, Frankie. All we need now is for you to have a little girl, so we got someone in the family to appreciate 'em. Did Jed tell you that I was pregnant and recently lost a baby?'

Frankie nodded. 'I'm sorry, Alice.'

Alice's eyes filled with tears. 'Rushed to hospital bleeding to fuck I was, and do you know the worst thing about it?'

Incredibly uncomfortable, Frankie wished Jed would re-appear. He'd gone into the other room with his dad. 'What?' Frankie asked awkwardly.

'The nurse asked me if I wanted to know the sex of it. I said yes and she told me it was a girl. All I ever wanted was a daughter, and although I was blessed with three beautiful boys, I still crave one. Billy and Marky have got three kids between 'em and they're all boys as well. The doctors say it's too dangerous for me to have another one now, so I need you to produce me a little granddaughter, Frankie. Do you think you can do that for me?'

Frankie nodded dumbly. She wasn't usually lost for words, but Alice was very loud and overpowering.

As soon as Jed and Jimmy returned, Alice went off to prepare the dinner. Jed was engrossed in deep conversation with his father, so Frankie amused herself by studying her new family.

Jimmy was tall and very broad-shouldered. He had dark brown hair that was greying round the edges and his nose was flat and was squashed towards the right side of his face. He was certainly no looker – Jed didn't resemble him one little bit, thank God. Glancing towards the kitchen, Frankie watched Alice peel the potatoes. Apart from their eye colour, Jed didn't really look like his mum either, as she was plump and short with long black hair. Alice had always considered herself to have a sixth sense, and without even turning around, she knew Frankie was watching her.

'If you're that interested in what I'm doing, come out here and peel these carrots,' she chuckled.

Frankie was mortified as she slunk towards her. 'I was just looking at your kitchen. It's very pretty,' she said apologetically.

33

Alice handed her a strange-looking object. 'Peel from the top downwards,' she ordered.

Frankie had rarely prepared or cooked anything in her life. Her mum had been the boss in the kitchen, and Frankie barely knew how to boil an egg.

Alice snatched the scraper out of her hand and showed her exactly how to use it. 'One golden rule, Frankie. You need to be a good cook to keep your mush happy. A good-looking boy like my Jed could have any filly he wanted. You don't wanna lose him now, do you?'

'No,' Frankie whispered.

Alice smiled. 'Well, that's settled then. From tomorrow while Jed's out grafting, you come to me and I'll teach you how to cook.'

The doorbell saved Frankie from replying.

'Go back and sit at the table. That'll be one of Jed's brothers, and his wife will need some female company.'

Like a scolded puppy, Frankie sidled into her seat.

Sitting at the table alone, Jed smiled at her. 'How you getting on with me mum?' he asked.

'Great,' Frankie lied. She could hardly tell Jed that his mother frightened the living daylights out of her.

Jimmy reappeared with a fattish lad, who had the same piercing green eyes as Jed, and a tarty-looking blonde girl. Jed nudged Frankie and urged her to stand up.

'Frankie, this is my brother Billy and his wife, Shannon.'

Frankie politely shook hands, disliking both Billy and Shannon on sight. Billy had a slobbery kind of look about him and Frankie noticed him staring at her breasts. Shannon was just hideous. Her hair was dyed a yellowish blonde, showing at least two inches of dark brown roots. She was dripping in gold jewellery and her outfit consisted of a denim skirt so short that it barely covered her buttocks, a pink boob tube that looked far too small, and knee-length white plastic boots. Considering she was obviously about five months pregnant, she didn't look good, to say the least.

34

A sulky-looking dark-haired boy ran into the room and Shannon grabbed him. 'This is Billy Junior, but everyone calls him Mush.'

Frankie smiled politely as little Mush kicked his mother in the shins. 'He's lovely,' she lied. 'When is your other one due?'

As soon as the room fell silent, Frankie knew she'd said the wrong thing.

'Shannon isn't pregnant, Frankie,' Jed said, embarrassed.

Frankie was mortified. 'I'm so sorry.'

Shannon glared at her, then at Jed. 'Trust you to end up with some dinlo gorjer,' she said nastily.

In a huff, Shannon stomped out to the kitchen to see Alice. 'I'm sorry, Jed, you know what Shannon's like, she didn't mean what she said,' Billy mumbled, as he followed his wife out of the room.

'Don't worry, she'll be OK in a minute,' Jed soothingly told Frankie.

'What's a gorjer? I'm sure you told me once before, but I've forgotten,' Frankie asked. She already knew from Jed's expressions that dinlo meant stupid.

'It just means a non-gypsy girl. You sit 'ere a minute while I go and sort it out,' Jed said.

As Frankie sat alone in the dining room, she put her head in her hands. Apart from Jimmy, who didn't say very much, Jed's family were just awful, and for the first time since she'd met Jed, Frankie had doubts as to what she'd let herself in for.

Another person in the middle of a crisis was Raymond, who was currently pacing up and down his deceased sister's living room. It was Polly's mum's birthday that night, and he was meant to be taking them to a select West End restaurant.

'You ain't gonna leave me here on my own with Nan, are you, Ray?' Joey asked solemnly.

Shaking his head, Raymond sat on the sofa. His fucked-up family were doing his head in lately, and all their dramas certainly weren't doing his relationship any good. Ray picked up his mobile. Polly was sure to be well pissed off when he told her he had to cancel yet again.

Desperate for a bit of privacy, Raymond told Joey to take the dogs out for a quick walk. As soon as the door slammed, he made the call.

'I'm sorry, babe, but I don't think I can get there tonight. Me mum's ill; I'm round there at the moment. The doctor's upstairs with her as we speak.'

'Oh Raymond, you must come. It doesn't matter if you get there late. What's wrong with your mum? Is she really ill or is it just flu or something?'

Raymond rubbed his tired eyes. He loved Polly and would be devastated if she grew sick of his problems and binned him. He debated whether to tell his girlfriend the truth, but quickly decided against it. How could he tell her that his father had fucked off and his mother had taken a hammer to the old man's pigeon shed? Polly's parents had their faults. Her mum was a big drinker and her dad was a bit of a know-all but, compared to his own parents, they were reasonably normal.

'I think it's all the grief caught up with her. She had a funny turn today and fainted. Joey's here on his own with her. I can't leave him, Polly.'

'Where's your dad?' Polly asked. 'Can't he look after her?'

'No, he's got a few problems of his own, so he's had to go away for a few days. I'm so sorry, Polly. I'll make it up to you, I promise, babe.'

Polly, for once, wasn't so understanding. 'I'm furious, Raymond, absolutely furious,' she screamed, as she slammed the phone down.

Pissed off with events, Raymond went into the kitchen and poured himself a large Scotch. To say his life had been difficult recently was a huge understatement. Polly was the only thing that even got him through the days, and he knew it was time to reward her patience and perhaps propose.

Ray took a swig of his drink as he heard the doctor coming down the stairs. 'Well?' he asked hopefully.

'I've sedated your mother and she seems comfortable. She's probably just suffering from a mixture of stress and grief. Losing a child affects people in different ways and it might have caused a minor breakdown. I suggest we see how she is in the morning and go from there. I've done all I can for now, but she might need to be hospitalised for a short period. I know a very good psychiatrist and I'll leave you his card just in case you need to contact him.'

Raymond thanked the doc and showed him to the door. Polly and her parents would be well impressed if they knew that his mother was on the verge of being shoved in a loony bin.

When Joey returned with Bruno and Buster, Raymond spoke to him gently. 'Listen, mate, Nanny's fine. The doctor's given her something to calm her down. Now I think the best thing I can do is shoot over to your grandad's and see if I can sort things out between them. You don't wanna be stuck here with your nan and neither do I. If Grandad comes back, he can take care of her.'

Joey looked scared. 'What if she wakes up while you're gone? You've seen what she's done to the shed, Ray. What if she goes off her head again?'

'She won't,' Raymond said confidently.

Approximately half a mile down the road, Frankie's night was going from bad to worse. Shannon was now extremely drunk and kept throwing nasty little digs her way. Jed was oblivious to what his sister-in-law was up to. He was too wrapped up discussing business with his dad and brother. As the three men stood up to leave the table, Frankie's heart lurched. Surely he wasn't going to leave her alone with his mum and Shannon.

Noticing her look of despair, Jed called her into the hallway. 'What's a matter, babe?'

'Where you going?' Frankie asked him fearfully.

Jed put his arms around her and squeezed her buttocks against his groin. 'I won't be long. I'm only going in the lounge to have a game of cards with me dad and Bill.'

'Please don't leave me on my own, Jed. Your sister-in-law really doesn't like me. Ever since I said I thought she was pregnant, she's been saying horrible stuff and giving me daggers. I feel like a gooseberry with her and your mum. I don't really know 'em that well, so can't I just go back to the trailer?'

Jed pulled away from her. 'No, you can't, Frankie. Me mum's just cooked you dinner and if you fuck off, it's rude. We're living together now, so you're gonna have to get used to our way of life. It's the norm in travelling families for the women to sit chatting and the men to go off and do other stuff. You've gotta learn to mix better. If Shannon gives you a hard time, then give it to her back.'

Frankie's eyes welled up, but in seconds tears were replaced by fire. 'OK, I'll be polite, but if she keeps getting on my case, then I'll tell her her fortune. And as for your mum telling me she needs to give me cooking lessons otherwise you'll leave me, if she starts again, I'll tell her an' all.'

Frankie went to walk away, but Jed violently yanked her back by the arm. 'Say what you like to Shannon, but don't you ever disrespect my mum, else you'll have me to deal with.'

Shocked by the way he'd grabbed her and the look on his face, Frankie lowered her eyes. 'Of course I won't, Jed. I'm sorry.'

As Jed kissed her and went off to play cards, Frankie wandered back into the kitchen.

'There you are,' Alice said, patting the seat next to her.

Shannon glared at Frankie. 'Now you're back, gorjer girl, I'm going outside for a smoke.'

Alice smiled as Shannon left the room. 'Between me and you, I've never liked Shannon that much. Old shitty drawers is my nickname for her. Jimmy's great-great-grandfather was Irish, but why my Billy married an Irish tinker, I'll never know. They ain't decent travellers like us English ones. Scum, they are. Take no notice of her behaviour. She's just jealous because you're prettier than her,' she whispered to Frankie.

Shocked by Jed's mother's kindness, Frankie was lost for

words. She didn't want to involve herself too much in family business she knew nothing about, and Alice had been all over Shannon like a rash earlier.

'Where's Jed's other brother, Marky?' she asked Alice.

'Oh, Marky can't make it. Rang up over an hour a go, he did. His youngest chavvie, Teddy boy, fell over. Got a big gash down his leg, he has, and they've taken him up the hospital.'

Frankie didn't know how to react. 'Will he be OK?' she whispered.

Alice laughed. 'Teddy's a tough kid. He'll be fine. You just worry about yourself and that grandchild of mine, Frankie. I dunno if Jed's told you, but I can see the future. My grandma was the same, and her mum before her. It's a gift that's been passed down through the generations. You know I told you earlier that the nurse asked me if I wanted to know the sex of my child when I miscarried. Well, I already knew it was a girl. Jimmy didn't believe me – that's why I wanted 'em to confirm it. I also knew that my pregnancy was cursed. I kept telling my Jimmy, but he wouldn't listen.'

Alice smiled sadly and held Frankie's hand. 'I know you're having a little girl, Frankie. I can sense it, in fact I've never been so sure of anything in me life.'

Frankie's eyes were as big as flying saucers. 'But, how do you know?' she asked. Alice was staring at her and completely freaking her out.

Alice chuckled. 'Because I do. Now listen to me, I know you ain't got your own mum to help out, but I want you to know I'll be there for you every step of the way. I'll teach you everything you need to know, and between me and you, that little girl will want for nothing.'

Frankie nodded dumbly.

Alice took another gulp of wine, then continued. 'If you ever wanna talk to your mum, you just ask me, and I'll sort it. I speak to the dead on a regular basis, you know. People come from all over to see me. It's a gift, Frankie, a special gift.'

When Shannon walked back in, Frankie was actually pleased

to see her. 'I won't be a minute, I'm just going to the toilet,' she said as she ran out the room.

Frankie locked the bathroom door and put her head in her hands. Alice had given her the heebies. Thinking of her own mother, Frankie began to cry. She had never truly appreciated her when she was alive, but she did now. Feeling extremely disturbed by Alice's comments, Frankie stared at the ceiling. 'Mum, if you're up there and you can see or hear me, I just want you to know that I miss you and I love you very much,' she whispered.

Jed's arrival stopped her from saying any more. 'You in there, Frankie? Are you OK?' he shouted.

'Won't be a sec,' Frankie replied.

Wiping her eyes with toilet paper, Frankie quickly pulled herself together. Her mum was dead, her dad was in prison, and there wasn't anything she could do to change that. As she unlocked the bathroom door, Jed took her in his arms.

'I've finished playing cards now, so shall we go back to the trailer?'

Frankie clung to him. The whole get-together had been horrific from start to finish. The company, the conversation, and even Alice's lamb stew had all left a bitter taste in her mouth. Jed's family were not her type of people and, to put it bluntly, Frankie couldn't get away from them quickly enough.

Raymond checked his watch as he sat in the restaurant with Polly and her family. He couldn't be too long, it wasn't fair on Joey. He had popped in to see his dad earlier and had begged him to return to the house in Rainham, but Stanley was having none of it.

'You should have heard the things she said to me, Raymond. I hate to say it, but your mother is a wicked, vicious woman, with a tongue like acid. I want no more to do with her. She's never supported me, all she's ever done is put me down, and if it weren't for her encouraging Jess to marry Eddie in the first place, your sister would still be alive.'

Surprised by the change in his usually mild-mannered father, Raymond had left shortly afterwards. Polly was ignoring his calls, and he needed to make things OK with her. His girlfriend had been delighted when he'd turned up unexpectedly at the restaurant. He'd been too late for the meal – they'd already eaten – but even so, Polly had made a real fuss of him.

Squeezing Polly's hand now, Raymond smiled at her. 'I'm gonna have to make a move soon, babe. I can't leave Joey alone with Mum for too long.'

Polly was well over her earlier strop. 'I understand, but thanks for coming, Ray. It means such a lot to me.'

Raymond said his goodbyes to her family and urged Polly to follow him outside, where he kissed her tenderly. 'Keep Saturday free. I've got a nice surprise for you,' he whispered.

Polly smiled. She just loved Raymond's surprises.

Aware of his nan screaming obscenities and her footsteps plodding down the stairs, Joey was frozen to the armchair. His uncle Raymond said he wouldn't be long, but he'd been gone for almost three hours.

As Joyce threw open the living-room door, Buster and Bruno cowered in the corner. They might be Rottweilers, but they were no match for Joyce.

Seeing the look on his nan's face, Joey's voice shook. 'Are you OK, Nan?' he stuttered. 'What's the matter?'

'OK? OK? Do I look fucking OK?' Joyce screamed.

Petrified, the dogs legged it out of the room, quickly followed by Joey. His hands were shaking as he dialled his uncle Raymond's number. Unfortunately, for Joey, Raymond's mobile was switched off.

'Stop it, Nan, stop it,' he screamed, as he heard the glass and china being smashed.

Joey peeped round the door and saw that she was trashing the room. 'Please don't do that, Nan. You're really frightening me,' he begged.

Joyce took no notice. Her eyes were glazed and she was

41

away with the fairies. 'Look at this photo, with your grandad and your father in it. Both arseholes!' she screamed, jumping up and down on the frame.

Worried for his own safety and that of the dogs, Joey picked up the phone and dialled 999.

'You have to help me. My nan's smashing the house up, she's gone loopy,' he cried.

CHAPTER FIVE

Eddie Mitchell sat alone in the prison canteen. He was fully aware that he was the centre of attention and that a lot of the lags were gossiping about him. He didn't care, though, they could say what they liked, as long as they left him alone.

'Do you mind if I sit 'ere, Ed?'

Ed looked up and nodded at Bertie Simms to sit down. Bertie had been good friends with Ed's dad, Harry, and Eddie remembered him coming to the house regularly when he was a kid.

'How you doing, Ed? I'm so sorry to hear about what happened.'

Eddie nodded and carried on eating his breakfast.

'How's Gary and Ricky doing?' Bertie asked, not knowing what else to say.

'All right. They're coming up to see me later today. They've took over the business for me. They'll do a good job, they're good lads.'

Seeing Big Bald Baz and his cronies sniggering at them two tables away, Bertie leaned forward and spoke in a whisper. 'Listen, Ed, I think you should know that Baz, your cellmate, has been taking the right piss out of ya behind your back. He's been telling everyone that you've lost the plot, mate. Reckon's he's gonna do you in the shower room with a tool, he does. I heard him saying some terrible stuff about your Jessica the other day, and he was also taking the piss about your old man being murdered.'

43

Eddie digested the information, but said nothing. Inside he was fuming. How dare anyone say stuff about his beautiful wife, or his poor old dad? Couldn't people just let them rest in peace?

'We go back years me and you, Ed. I know what happened must be fucking awful for ya, but I also know you're no man's fool. Don't let some shitbag like Baz mug you off. If you do, we both know that there's many others in here waiting to jump on the bandwagon. Take my advice – sort it out before it's too late.'

Eddie's eyes wandered to the table where the laughter was coming from. He briefly locked eyes with Big Bald Baz, then quickly looked away. It was in that split second that Ed felt the fire return to his belly. He'd get through his stretch – he had to. He was Eddie Mitchell, for fuck's sake.

Frankie sat nervously in the Albion pub. She hadn't seen Joey since the night she'd left home, and she was both anxious and excited. She'd rung the house this morning praying that her brother would answer and, as luck would have it, he had.

'Can you talk? It's me,' she'd asked cautiously.

At the sound of his sister's voice, Joey had burst into tears. 'It's been awful here without you, Frankie. Nanny's gone off her rocker and I'm so unhappy.'

Frankie told him to meet her at the pub at one o'clock and to pack some of her clothes in a sports bag. She also told him to charge up her mobile and bring the phone and her charger with him. 'Oh, and Joey, don't forget my new trainers, the Adidas ones.'

Because his uncle Raymond had come into the room, Joey abruptly ended the phone call. 'I'll see you at one then, Wesley,' he'd lied. Raymond would have gone apeshit if he had known Joey was helping Frankie out. He blamed her and Jed for Jessica's death and everything else that had happened since.

As soon as Joey walked into the boozer, Jed stood up.

'I'll leave yous two to it. Ring me when you want picking up,' he told Frankie.

*   *   *

44

As Jed left, Frankie and Joey clung to each other.

'I've missed you so much,' Joey said, his eyes brimming with tears.

Aware that some of the pub regulars were staring their way, Frankie pulled away from her brother and sat down.

'Did you bring everything I asked for?' she asked, nodding towards the sports bag.

'The only thing I couldn't find was your Fila tracksuit top. I brought everything else, though.'

Frankie thanked him and went to get them both a drink. 'Where's my phone?' she asked, as she handed Joey his vodka.

Joey found it for her, then launched into the story of their nan. 'She just went bananas, Frankie. You wanna see what she did to Grandad's pigeon shed. The doctor came and sedated her, but while Raymond was out she woke up again. She started smashing up the house and I was petrified.'

'How is she now?' Frankie asked genuinely concerned.

'I don't really know. I rang the police and they rang an ambulance. Ray had come back by the time the paramedics arrived. She was like a woman possessed, lashing out at everyone. She wouldn't get in the ambulance, and I think they had to hold her down and give her an injection. I wasn't there when they took her. I got a bit upset, so Ray sent me upstairs with the dogs.'

'So, who's staying with you now?' Frankie asked. She was feeling more guilty by the minute for leaving Joey.

'Ray and Grandad have been taking it in turns to stay at the house with me. Grandad wants me to live in Upney with him, but I don't wanna leave the house. I hate Upney and I've got no friends over that way.'

Frankie nodded understandingly. She couldn't believe that her grandparents had split up after all these years and, as for her nan going mad, the whole situation felt surreal. 'Go and order us some more drinks and some food. I'll have a quarter pounder with cheese and chips,' she told her brother, handing him one of the twenty-pound notes Jed had given her.

As he walked away, Frankie grabbed her phone. Joey needed help and support, and if she couldn't be there for him, maybe Dominic could. She punched in Dom's number and held the phone to her ear. He answered on the second ring.

'I read what happened to your mum in the papers. I'm so sorry, Frankie. I was going to call Joey, but I was afraid he wouldn't want to talk to me,' Dominic said.

'Joey still loves you, Dominic, and he needs you. I know what my dad did to you was awful, but you haven't got to worry about him now, he'll be locked up for years to come.'

Dominic didn't know what to do for the best. He still loved Joey, but was petrified of his father, even though he was inside. Eddie Mitchell had given him many a nightmare. Suppose he had spies on the outside and they tried to finish off what Eddie had begun? 'I'm not sure, Frankie. Say your dad gets someone to finish off the job he started the last time?'

'He won't,' Frankie replied confidently. 'My dad's life is in tatters, Dom. You and Joey's relationship are the least of his problems right now.'

Aware that Joey was being served at the bar, Frankie knew she had to hurry things up. 'Listen Dom, Joey and I are having lunch in the Albion as we speak. Can you meet up with us?'

Dominic's feelings for Joey were far too strong for him to decline. 'OK, I'll order a cab and be there within the hour.'

Raymond and Stanley sat in a relatives' room at Warley Hospital. The name of the place made it sound normal, but both Ray and Stan knew it was anything but. The wails and screams coming from different directions were enough to let anybody know that the place was actually a nuthouse.

Joyce had been admitted only yesterday. She'd originally been taken to Oldchurch Hospital in Romford, but the nurses hadn't been able to control her mood swings. In the middle of the night, Joyce started shouting and bawling and, after numerous complaints from the other patients and their families, she had been moved over to Warley.

As Ray and Stan sat opposite one another, neither of them spoke. Both were deep in thought and neither had much to say to the other.

'Mr Smith, the doctors have examined your wife now, so you can go and sit with her if you want. If she's woozy, don't worry, it will just be the medication she's been prescribed.'

Stanley walked into the room where Joyce lay, and was immediately consumed with both anger and guilt. His Joycie was usually glammed up to the nines, and would never be seen dead without her lippy on. Today she looked old, pale and thin, a shadow of the woman he knew so well. Leaning towards her, Stanley clocked her vacant expression.

'Hello Joycie. Raymond and I have brought you some fruit and some chocolates,' he said.

Joyce stared at the ceiling. Her body was OK, but her mind had drifted off to another planet. Turning her head, she looked blankly at Stanley, then turned away again. With one tear running down her cheek, Joyce shut her eyes and went back to sleep.

Eddie walked into the visiting room and spotted Gary and Ricky at once. 'All right? How's tricks?' he asked them.

Both Gary and Ricky immediately noticed an improvement in their father's manner and appearance.

'We're fine, Dad. Business is booming. What about you?' Ricky asked.

Eddie shrugged. 'I'm OK. Just gotta get on with it, ain't I? How did the funeral go?'

Ricky nudged Gary. 'Yeah, OK. Ray sent some lovely flowers from you and a lot of your old pals showed up to pay their respects. All in all, Jessica had a lovely send-off,' Gary lied. He could hardly tell his old man that Jed and Jimmy O'Hara had turned up, causing Ronny to kick off and the service to be cut short. That would do his father's improvement no good at all.

'How's Joey and Frankie?' Eddie asked.

Ricky glanced at Gary. They'd already decided to come clean

about Frankie moving in with Jed. Gary looked at the floor as he spoke. 'Frankie's gone, Dad. She's living down on O'Hara's land with Jed. Do you want us to have a chat with her? See if we can make her see sense?'

Eddie shook his head. Everything that had happened was down to his daughter's stupidity. Frankie had made her own bed, so let her fucking lie in it. 'Leave her be. She'll realise her mistake one day and come crawling up here to visit me with her tail between her legs.'

'Joycie ain't well. Ray rang up last night. She's gone off her rocker, by all accounts,' Ricky said.

'Whaddya mean?' Ed asked, surprised. He'd always liked poor old Joycie. She'd stuck up for him over the years, especially to Stanley, who had always despised him.

'Apparently, she just went loopy all of a sudden. It all started on the day of the funeral, I think. Ray said Stanley left her the following day and that was when she lost it completely,' Gary chipped in.

Eddie felt terrible. There was nothing he could do to bring Jessica back, but he had to try and make amends to Joycie somehow.

'Listen boys, I want you to do me a favour. I want you to go and see Joycie and tell her how sorry I am for what has happened. I know she's been stopping at the house and I'm gonna sign it over to her as a way of apology. Tell her I'll sort a solicitor out, I'll have a word with Larry. He'll deal with the legal stuff and I'll sign the deeds over to her.'

'Are you sure, Dad? The house is worth a fortune,' Ricky asked him, perplexed.

'What about the twins?' Gary said agitated.

Ed couldn't even bring himself to think about the twins. Frankie was now shacked up with O'Hara's scumbag son, and Joey liked sucking men's cocks.

'Fuck the pair of 'em,' Eddie said bluntly. 'And so what if the house is worth an arm and a leg? I've got all your grandfather's money for when I get out, ain't I? I ain't mucking about,

48

lads. I've made my mind up and I want Joycie to have that house.'

Back in Rainham, Frankie had just eaten dessert and her eyes were firmly fixed on the door.

'Whaddya keep looking at? Jed ain't coming back yet, is he?' Joey asked, annoyed. He hadn't seen his sister for Christ knows how long and she wasn't even listening to him properly.

'No, Jed's not coming back. I promised you that he wouldn't be here with us and I meant it,' Frankie said honestly.

Joey smiled. 'So, how are you getting on, living together? Have you met all of his family yet?' Joey pried.

'I'm happy living with Jed, he treats me really well. As for his family, his dad's OK, but I'm not sure about the rest of them. His mum's very overpowering – she does my head in. I met one of his brothers the other night and I didn't like him at all. His name's Billy, and he's married to this girl called Shannon, who was just awful. I put me foot right in it, Joey. She had this massive fat gut, and I only asked her when the baby was due.'

'So?' Joey said, urging her to carry on.

'Well, it turns out that she was just fat and wasn't even pregnant. She hated me from that moment onwards.'

'So, why don't you like his mum? What's overpowering about her?'

Frankie was about to answer, when she clocked Dominic and waved.

'Who you bloody waving to? Frankie, I'm talking to you,' Joey said, annoyed.

As soon as Dominic arrived at the table, Frankie excused herself. 'I think yous two have stuff to talk about, so I'm going outside to make a few phone calls.'

Joey looked up and immediately felt his body shake. Dominic was gorgeous, even sexier than he'd remembered. 'All right? Let me get you a drink, Dom,' he said awkwardly.

Noticing that Joey's hands were unsteady. Dominic offered

to do the honours for him. 'You sit there. I'll order us a bottle of wine.'

Outside the pub, Frankie was an interested spectator. The boys had been laughing and joking for over half an hour now. Frankie smiled as she ended the phone call to her friend Stacey. Dominic had just held Joey's hand, which meant her plan was obviously working.

Back inside the pub, Dominic stared into Joey's innocent eyes. 'It can't be like before, Joey. If we're gonna make a go of this, I'd like us to move in together.'

Joey was ecstatic. Dominic was the only person in the world who could help him recover from the trauma of his mum's death. 'I'll move in with you tomorrow if you want me to,' he told Dom.

Dominic suddenly remembered Eddie Mitchell again. 'What about your dad though, Joey? I know he's in prison, but say he sends one of his henchmen around the flat? He might even send your uncle or your brothers round to finish off what he tried to do last time.'

Joey clenched Dominic's hand. 'I'm finished with my dad and so is Frankie. I can come out now he's locked up. Everything about us can be out in the open. My dad won't bother us again, I just know he won't. How could he even say or do anything, after what he did to my mum?'

'Are you sure? I really don't want any more trouble,' Dominic said cautiously.

'I'm absolutely positive.'

Dominic leaned forward and, not caring about anybody else in the pub, gently kissed Joey on the lips. 'I've missed you so much,' he said to the beautiful blond boy who had stolen his heart.

Over at Warley Hospital, Stanley was sitting alone with his wife. Raymond had left a couple of hours ago, which had given him plenty of thinking time. Joycie was still fast asleep, and as Stanley checked her breathing yet again, he smiled to see her chest rise in a steady rhythm.

Deep down, Stanley knew that he would always love his wife, whether she loved him or not. As she opened her eyes, Stanley gently held her hand. 'How are you feeling, Joycie? You've had a nice long sleep, my love.'

Joyce indicated that her throat was dry, so Stanley held the paper cup to her mouth and urged her to sip some water. As she laid her head back on the pillow and stared at the ceiling, Stanley spoke honestly and kindly to her.

'I'm so sorry for leaving you, Joycie. This is all my fault, darling, but I want you to know that I still love you and from now on, whatever happens, I'll look after you and help you get better.'

Joyce turned towards him. She was too weak to sit up properly. 'Thank you,' she whispered. 'I'm ever so sorry for smashing up your pigeon shed, and even though I don't always show it, I do love you too, Stanley Smith.'

CHAPTER SIX

Joycie seemed to recover quickly after her reconciliation with Stanley, and a month later the doctors gave her the go-ahead to return home. She had suffered some kind of nervous breakdown, which the doctors said wasn't uncommon after the death of a child.

Joyce spent her last morning at the hospital sitting on an armchair by the window reading the *Daily Mail*. Stanley and Raymond were coming to collect her and were due to arrive soon. As the sun beat down through the glass, Joyce put down her paper and sat deep in thought. She still missed her daughter dreadfully, but after her recent illness, she knew that her own life had to go on. She felt much better mentally and physically since the doctors had taken her off those awful bloody tablets. They had turned her into a zombie, and the more her dosage was reduced, the better she had started to feel.

Watching two sparrows splashing about in a bird bath, Joycie smiled. She couldn't wait to get back to the house in Rainham and its beautiful garden, soon to be her own. Gary and Ricky had come to visit her last week, explaining Eddie's wishes.

'Me dad is in bits and he can't apologise enough for what happened, Joycie. He loved your Jess and he'll never forgive himself for the awful mistake he made. Anyway, he wants you to have the house. He said signing it over to you is the least he can do,' Gary told her.

Joyce had been stunned and hadn't known what to say or

do. 'I need to discuss this with my Stanley and Raymond. Can you pop back tomorrow, boys? And I'll let you know my decision then,' she said.

Stanley had gone apeshit. 'Can't you see what the bastard's trying to do, Joycie? He's trying to ease his own guilt by buying us. Tell him to stick his house where the sun don't shine.'

Keen for his parents to have a better life, Raymond disagreed and had a long chat with his father. 'Look, Dad, your ex-council house must be worth a fair old lump sum. If you take Ed up on his offer, you can sell that and live the life of Riley. I know how you feel about Eddie, but for once you wanna think about your own well-being. For all Ed's faults, we both know that he adored Jessica, and he didn't mean to do what he did. If you let him sign the house over to Mum, you and her will be set up for the rest of your lives. You'll never have to worry about money again. Even though you don't agree, you've gotta think of Mum. She loves that house and it makes her feel close to Jessica. Knowing that she owns it will help her recovery no end.'

'But what about all the memories, Raymond? Every time I walk in the kitchen, I picture Jessica standing at that cooker.'

Raymond put a comforting arm around his father's shoulder. 'Decorate the place so it don't look the same. Take my advice, Dad, take Eddie up on the offer.'

Joycie was snapped out of her daydream by the arrival of her husband and son. 'There you are. I've been ready and waiting for you for over an hour.'

Stanley smiled. Joycie's moaning only proved to him that his wife was on the mend. 'Hold me arm, Joycie,' he ordered her.

Joyce glared at him. 'I'm not an invalid, you silly old goat. I'm quite capable of walking, you know. Now pick up that case, Stanley, and hurry up and get me out of this godforsaken loony bin.'

Eddie Mitchell smiled as he placed the file in his sock. Tomorrow was the big day, and he couldn't wait to wipe the smiles off the faces of Big Bald Baz and his dickhead mates.

Ed had found an inner strength over the last few weeks, and had eased himself into the prison system. He'd even made friends with a young screw called Johnny, who was easily won over.

Obviously, he never stopped thinking of his beautiful wife, but as the weeks had passed, the tears and pain had now turned into anger and a stomach full of revenge. One day Jed O'Hara would pay for what he had made him do, Eddie would make sure of it.

Ed didn't allow himself to think of Jessica's murder at all any more; instead he concentrated on all the good times that they'd had. Holidays, Christmases, parties, that kind of stuff, but most of all he pictured himself and Jessica lying in bed together. Those were the very special times, when no one else in the world, not even the kids, had existed.

As soon as Big Bald Baz stopped snoring, Eddie prepared himself for the usual claptrap out of the fat prick's mouth.

'All right, Mitchell? You're not thinking of that night you did your wife in again, are you?'

While Baz chuckled, Eddie did his best to keep hold of his temper. He'd been desperate for weeks to shut the ponce up, but he wasn't about to do it in the cell. Eddie loved a bit of impact, so to have Baz in front of his cronies was the only way forward.

Pretending to scratch his foot, Eddie smirked as he ran his fingers along the file that Johnny had managed to smuggle in. He'd doctored the thing himself by rubbing it endlessly against the brick wall. Sharp as a razor the fucker was now, with a point like the Eiffel Tower.

When Baz let out one almighty fart, Eddie picked up his book. The geezer was filth, an utter animal, and Ed couldn't wait to get rid of his oversized carcass once and for all.

Unaware that her dad was up to his old tricks again, Frankie stood awkwardly in Alice O'Hara's kitchen. Unfortunately for her, it was time for another cooking lesson.

'Now, don't stand there doing nothing. You're never gonna learn how to be a good wife if you don't do stuff with your own hands. Wash that liver under the cold tap, then roll it in the flour,' Alice ordered.

Frankie had been relatively lucky with sickness during her pregnancy. She'd had a couple of bouts of it in the first few weeks, but since then she'd been OK. Until now, that was.

Picking up the liver, Frankie quickly slung it back down on the worktop. 'I can't do it. It feels horrible,' she said.

'Don't be such a dinlo,' Alice said, picking the liver up and waving it in front of her nose.

Feeling under duress, Frankie tried to touch it again. Without warning, she immediately heaved and slung her guts up all over the kitchen floor. Feeling embarrassed and scared of Alice's reaction, Frankie began to cry.

'Now, stop all that. You can't help it, you're pregnant,' Alice said kindly, as she led her into the lounge.

While Alice went off to clear up the mess, Frankie felt extremely sorry for herself. She missed her own family terribly. Joey, her mum, Nan, Grandad and, even though he'd done a dreadful thing, she even missed her dad.

Living with Jed was turning out to be not as much fun as Frankie had hoped. She loved the evenings when they were alone and all cosied up in the trailer, but when Jed was out grafting, she hated it. Alice taking a special interest in her potential homemaking skills wasn't exactly helping matters, either.

Frankie spoke to Joey virtually every day and she knew that her nan was much better and was moving back into the house with her grandad. The trouble was, Jed had made her promise that she would have no more to do with her family, and, each day that passed, Frankie missed them that little bit more.

'When we get wed, you'll be an O'Hara, Frankie. Look at the way they've treated you and me. You're my girl now, we're having a chavvie together, so you've just got to forget about 'em.'

Although Frankie had originally agreed with Jed, she didn't now. She wanted to go and see her grandparents, try to build some bridges. Knowing Jed would strongly disagree, Frankie decided that if and when she went, she wouldn't tell him. Hopefully, if she was careful, he would never find out anyway.

Joey punched the air in delight as he spotted Dominic waiting for him in reception. Dom had got him an interview in the building where he worked and Joey had just been offered the position. It was nothing special. He'd be working as a post boy/courier, and would spend half of his day in the post room and the other half delivering mail and parcels in and around the City.

Dominic hugged him. 'I take it you got it, then?'

Joey dragged him into a nearby pub. 'Of course I did. Let's celebrate.'

Dom ordered a bottle of champagne and they sat down at a quiet table. 'Is everything still OK for tomorrow?'

Joey nodded. His nan had come out of hospital only this morning and insisted that he bring his new friend round for one of her special roasts the following day. Ever since they'd got back together, Joey had spent most of his time staying at Dominic's flat. Dom had been keeping him financially, as since his mum had died and his dad had got locked up, he'd been completely brassic.

'Once I get my first wage packet, I'll pay you back all that money I borrowed,' Joey said happily.

Dom shook his head. He had a high-powered job and certainly wasn't short of a few quid. 'I didn't lend it to you, Joey, I gave it to you. I tell you what you can do though, when you get that first pay packet – you can take me out for a nice slap-up meal. The works, I want.'

As Dom left the table to answer a business call, Joey grinned. His boyfriend was one in a million, and the only downside to his life was that his mum wasn't able to share his happiness with him.

Joey rarely thought consciously of his dad any more. Now and again he dreamed about him, but other than that, he'd completely erased him from his mind and his life.

When he saw Dom walk back inside the pub, Joey smiled. Uncle Raymond and Polly were also going to his grandparents' for dinner tomorrow and Joey felt that perhaps the time was right to tell his family about his and Dom's relationship.

It might come as a shock to them at first, but the quicker he and Dominic were accepted as a couple, the happier Joey could be.

Joycie felt content as she sat on the bench in the garden. Raymond and Stanley had worked wonders while she had been in hospital. They'd repaired the broken furniture, assembled a new pigeon shed, replaced the trampled flowers, and the house itself was absolutely spotless. As Stanley handed her a cuppa, Joyce urged him to sit down next to her.

'Where's Joey?' she asked.

Stanley shrugged. 'I think he said he had an interview or something. To be honest, Joycie, the last few weeks he's hardly been here. He's got that mate, Dominic, ain't he, who lives in Islington, and he's been stopping over at his. He did pop in the other day, mind, and he seems much brighter and happier.'

'Well, who exactly is this mate? I'm sure I ain't met no Dominic,' Joycie said suspiciously.

'Joey says we have met him before. He said he came to his and Frankie's birthday party earlier this year. You gotta remember he's sixteen, Joycie. If Joey wants to stop at his mate's flat, we can't do much to stop him.'

Joyce pursed her lips. 'Well, good job he's bringing this Dominic around for dinner tomorrow. At least we can check him out, make sure he comes from a good home. For all we know, he could be a druggie, Stanley.'

Just a short distance down the road, Frankie had felt tired and depressed all day, so had taken herself off to the bedroom for a catnap. On awakening, still bleary-eyed, she stumbled into the lounge. The reek of aftershave hit her nostrils immediately, and she was shocked to see Jed spruced up in a shirt and trousers.

'What's happening? Why you all dressed up? Are we meant to be going out?'

Jed kissed her on the forehead and laughed. 'I'm going out, you're staying 'ere, Frankie. I told you the other day I was going to a stag night. You know my cousin, Sammy? Well, his mate Donny's getting married at the weekend.'

'You never told me anything,' Frankie said stubbornly.

'I did. Your mind's all over the place at the moment. It's because you're borey – that means "pregnant" in Romany – before you ask. Anyway, you don't have to feel left out, 'cause I'm taking you to their wedding reception over in Kent.'

Frankie moved away from him and flopped onto the sofa. 'Do you have to go to his stag night, Jed? I've been stuck here on my own all day and I'm so bored.'

Sitting down next to her, Jed squeezed her hand. 'Of course I have to go. You don't want me to look like a dinlo, do ya? Why don't you go next door and watch telly with me mum and dad?'

At the mention of Jed's mother, Frankie burst into tears. 'I want my own mum, not someone else's,' she sobbed.

Making sure that her tears didn't ruin his Ralph Lauren shirt, Jed put an arm around her. 'Look, no one can bring your mum back, Frankie. I know what happened was rotten, but you've got your cuntsmouth of a father to blame for that. We're gonna be parents ourself soon, so you gotta pull yourself together. How you gonna take care of our chavvie properly if you're upset all the poxy time?'

Frankie stared at him in horror. Her mum had only been dead for two months, so surely she was allowed to grieve. 'Just go, Jed,' she said angrily.

Jed stood up. He was gagging for a good night out and he wasn't going to let Frankie spoil it for him. 'I'll try not to be late. Why don't you have an early night? You look ever so tired,' he said gently.

Frankie wanted to tell him to fuck off, but didn't have the guts to. If she was still living back at home, she would have told him where to go, but what was the point now when she was so reliant on him?

'Love you,' Jed said, as he slammed the trailer door.

Over in South London, Eddie Mitchell reread the letter he'd received today from Paulie. He didn't usually receive a lot of post, but today he'd had mail from Raymond, his Uncle Reg and his eldest brother.

Raymond's letter was pretty brief, but he'd asked for a visiting order to be sent, which had pleased Ed no end.

Reggie's letter had been pleasant, but long-winded. He'd spoken in detail about Auntie Joan, Auntie Vi, Uncle Albert, but had said very little else of interest.

It had been Paulie's letter that had been the real eye-opener. A, Ed hadn't expected to ever hear from him again after the fall-out they'd had earlier this year, and B, no other fucker had told him that Jed and Jimmy O'Hara had turned up and ruined Jessica's funeral.

To say Ed was livid was the understatement of the century. It wasn't just the fact that the bastards had had the front to turn up, it was also because no one had felt fit or brave enough to tell him about it. Eddie was especially annoyed with Gary and Ricky. He could understand people not wanting to tell him what had happened by letter, but his sons had been to visit him week in, week out.

Folding up Paulie's letter, Ed shoved it under his pillow. Even his own flesh and blood obviously believed he'd lost the plot that fucking much he couldn't handle any more bad news.

Turning on his side, Eddie stared at his vulgar cellmate. Big Bald Baz was in his usual position, lying flat on his stomach, snoring and farting like an unadulterated pig. Ed didn't smile much lately, but tonight he couldn't help but grin. All them arseholes that thought he was a sunken ship would think differently after tomorrow. He had mourned as much as he could mourn, cried as many tears as he could cry, and now he couldn't wait to prove his doubters wrong. From tomorrow onwards, Eddie Mitchell was back with a bang.

CHAPTER SEVEN

At 6 a.m. the following day, Frankie got out of bed. Jed still wasn't home and she had barely slept a wink all night.

She debated whether to go and wake his parents, but decided against it. She was worried that he'd got drunk and had an accident in his truck, but his mum and dad would probably accuse her of overreacting. She tried Jed's mobile again, but the phone was still switched off. About to ring her brother for advice, she heard an engine nearing and ran over to the window.

When the headlights turned into the drive, Frankie was relieved, but also angry as she spotted Jed's truck. Hearing loud voices, Frankie peeped through a gap in the curtains. Recognising Jed's cousin Sammy, she ran back into the bedroom.

Eddie Mitchell took a slow walk towards the shower room. He knew Big Bald Baz and his cronies were already in there, as his pal, Johnny the screw, had given him the nod.

Johnny was a good lad and Ed had noticed, within weeks of arriving at the prison, that he had little respect for the many scumbags residing there. Today Johnny was on duty with another screw called Fred. Fred hated Big Bald Baz, because on many occasions the fat bastard had tried to terrorise him. Baz could sense weakness in people and Fred wasn't like most of the other screws. He was meek and a bit of a loner and people like Baz tended to cause him no end of aggravation.

Nearing his destination, Eddie smiled as he heard Big Bald Baz laughing. He bent down, took the file out of his sock and slipped it up his sleeve. The dirty stinking animal wouldn't be laughing for much longer, that was for sure.

Frankie darted into the bedroom, curled back up under the quilt cover and turned off the light.

Jed and Sammy were obviously slaughtered and she was fuming that Jed had driven home in such a state. She knew they were still drinking, because she could hear the cans being opened. She could also smell cannabis wafting through the crack in the door. She listened intently. They were giggling about some girls they'd met. She heard Jed mention the name Sally, but he then lowered his voice and she heard footsteps heading her way.

As the bedroom door opened, Frankie shut her eyes and pretended to be asleep. She couldn't wait to give Jed a piece of her mind, but she wasn't going to show herself up in front of his cousin, Sammy.

Jed sat on the edge of the bed and kissed her on the cheek. 'How's my girl? Been looking after that chavvie for me, have yer?'

Frankie ignored him. Jed stank of booze, fags, and his clothes smelt sweaty and stale. She was livid with him and didn't want him anywhere near her.

'I know you're awake,' he said cockily.

Frankie opened her eyes. 'Leave me alone, Jed, I'm tired,' she said angrily. 'Go and have fun with your cousin. You can talk about what girls you pulled.'

'We never pulled no girls, Frankie. Me and Sammy knew you were awake, we saw the light go off as we drove in. We've been winding you up, you dinlo.'

Unable to stop her eyes welling up, Frankie turned away from him. 'I was worried sick. I thought you'd had an accident. Why was your phone switched off all night?'

Jed lay down next to her. ''Cause me battery ran out. Don't

have the hump, Frankie. Stag nights go on for hours and I ain't had a night out with the boys for ages, have I? Surely you don't begrudge me a good time once in a while?'

As his arms went around her waist, Frankie moved away from him. She could feel his hard-on, but he smelt like a tramp and sex was the last thing she fancied, especially with Sammy in the next room. 'I need to get some sleep, Jed.'

Annoyed, Jed stood up. 'I'll speak to you later,' he said, as he slammed the bedroom door.

Over in South London, Eddie was ready to strike like a viper. As a grinning Baz put the towel around his extra-large midriff, Eddie made his move.

'You fucking fat cunt, take that,' he shouted, as he came at Baz from the side and aimed the file straight at his right eye.

As luck would have it, Eddie had taken Baz completely by surprise. His aim was spot on and as the big man fell to the floor in agony, Ed pulled the file out of one eye and aimed straight for the other. 'That's what you get for slagging off my family, you fat piece of shit.'

As Baz's three mates ran towards him, Ed stood up with the file pointing their way.

'Help me! I can't see. I'm blind, I'm fucking blind!' Baz screamed hysterically.

Baz's mates saw the state of his face and stopped, rooted to the spot. There was blood pouring from both his eyes, and it looked as if he was crying red tears.

As Eddie walked towards them, all three of Baz's friends took a step backwards. 'You saw nothing, you mugs, and I swear if you say one word, you'll have no fucking eyes left as well.'

The three men all held their hands up. 'We didn't see anything,' they repeated one after the other.

Knowing that it was time to leave, Ed couldn't resist a closer look at the bleeding, screaming mess he'd just attacked. He lifted his foot and kicked Big Bald Baz as hard in the bollocks

63

as he could. 'You grass me up, or ever say one more word about my wife or dad, I'll cut your fucking heart out next time, got me?'

'I can't see. For fuck's sake get me some help,' Baz screamed in agony.

Eddie washed the blood off his hands, smirked, and sauntered out of the shower room.

Joey was a bundle of nerves as he and Dominic headed towards Rainham in a taxi.

'You haven't got to tell them tonight if you don't want to,' Dominic said kindly.

'I want to. If me and you are gonna be truly happy, we can't live a lie.'

Admiring his boyfriend's strength of character, Dominic squeezed his hand. 'Why don't we stop off and get a couple of drinks inside us first.'

Joey shook his head. 'No. My nan's expecting us at six and we don't wanna be late. I won't tell them straight away. We can eat our dinner, have a few drinks, and I'll break the news towards the end of the evening.'

Dominic nodded. It was Joey's family, so the decision was entirely up to him.

Raymond and Polly had just arrived at Joycie's house.

'Take Polly's coat and pour our guests some drinks,' Joyce said to her husband in her posh voice.

Stanley smiled as he obeyed his wife's orders. Joyce was properly back to her old self; so much so, it was hard to believe that she had ever been ill in the first place.

Raymond thanked his father for their drinks and politely asked about his pigeons. Their relationship had been difficult after Jessica's death, but his mother's illness had helped to heal the rift between them.

Joyce checked on the roast potatoes, shut the oven door, then made her way into the lounge.

'So lovely to see you again, Polly,' she said, kissing her son's girlfriend.

As the dogs ran into the living room, Joyce shushed them out. Buster, the slightly bigger of the two, was having none of it. He'd taken a shine to Joyce since she had come out of hospital and rid herself of her madness. As Buster clung to her leg and tried to hump her, Joyce screamed in mortification.

Realising that the dog was very excited and rubbing his masterpiece against Joycie's best dress, both Stanley and Raymond burst out laughing.

Joyce was furious. Talk about embarrass her in front of Polly. 'Get this dog away from me now. Put them out the back,' she yelled at Stanley.

Trying to stifle his laughter, Stanley ushered Bruno out, then managed to untangle Buster from Joycie's leg.

'I feel grubby now, so I'm going to get changed again. Now that Joey's rarely here, I'm sending them slobbering, filthy creatures back round to Pat Murphy's,' Joyce said haughtily.

Once she left the room even Polly started to laugh. Joycie's face when Buster had got a hard-on had been an absolute picture.

Joyce quickly changed her dress and when the doorbell rang, ran downstairs to answer it.

'You must be Dominic?' she said to the tall dark-haired lad who stood next to her grandson.

Naturally polite, Dominic handed Joyce the bouquet of flowers he'd bought. 'Thank you for asking me for dinner. These are for you.'

Joyce immediately liked the look of Dominic. He was obviously older than Joey, but seemed polite and sophisticated.

'Thank you so much – they're beautiful. Take Dominic into the living room, Joey. Your grandad will get you both a drink while I put these in water.'

Raymond shook Dominic's hand and was immediately aware of Joey's nervousness. Ray still remembered clearly the night in the Flag earlier this year, when Ronny had blurted to Ed that Joey had a boyfriend.

65

While Dominic chatted away happily to Polly, Raymond studied him. Ed had never mentioned the incident again, or said anything about Joey's sexuality since that day, but Raymond was now in no doubt that Ronny had been telling the truth.

Less than a mile away, Frankie was bored stiff. After rejecting Jed's advances this morning, her fiancé had gone out again with his cousin Sammy and still hadn't returned. Knowing that her family were having a get-together down the road was hardly helping matters. If she had known that Jed was going to do a disappearing act, she could have sneaked off to see them.

Frankie felt incredibly sorry for herself as she sat down to watch *Coronation Street*. To say she felt lonely was putting it mildly – she felt utterly desolate.

Jed finally arrived home during the commercial break and when she heard the door open, Frankie kept her eyes glued to the telly.

'I got us a takeaway. Cheered up now, have we?' Jed said, slamming the trailer door.

Frankie could see immediately that he'd been drinking again. Full of pent-up emotion, she spoke clearly, but with venom. 'I've had a lot of time to think today, Jed. I'm not happy living here, so I'm going to move back in with my grandparents.'

Jed threw the Chinese on the side and walked over to her. 'You can't do that. We're meant to be getting married, and what about our chavvie?'

He sat down next to her and Frankie was glad that he looked upset. 'I won't be treated like shit, Jed. You was out on the piss all night and again today, while I'm sitting here like some idiot. I wasn't brought up to be treated like a fool.'

'I'm sorry, Frankie. It won't happen again. Don't leave – I love you, you know I do.'

Knowing she had him by the gonads, Frankie carried on. 'It's not just about you going out last night and today, Jed. There's other stuff that I'm unhappy about as well.'

Holding both her hands, Jed knelt in front of her. 'What? Just tell me and I'll sort it.'

'Your mum, for a start. I'm sick of the cooking lessons every day. I know she's only trying to help, but some days I don't feel well and I don't fancy bloody cooking.'

'I'll have a word with me mum. Leave it with me.'

Frankie nodded then continued. 'I also want to be able to visit my nan and grandad as well. I ain't got me mum and dad now and I miss having no family.'

'You've got your brother, ain't ya? I worry about you going to that house because I don't trust your uncle Raymond,' Jed argued.

Frankie shrugged. She was determined to get her own way. 'How about if I see my nan and grandad away from the house? I could meet 'em for lunch, or go shopping with me nan.'

Jed wasn't happy, but was desperate not to show it. 'Look, we'll work something out, I promise ya. Why don't me and you take your grandparents out for a meal next weekend? Tell 'em it's my treat.'

Frankie smiled. She was getting somewhere now. 'There's one more thing, Jed.'

'Go on,' Jed said sarcastically. He was getting bored with this shit now.

'I know if we have a son you're desperate to name him after your grandad, but I really hate the name Butch. Can't we choose a name that we both like, instead of just you deciding?'

Jed stood up before he lost his temper. She was really beginning to get on his nerves, the silly tart. 'Our dinner's getting cold. Let's eat that and we can discuss names later,' he said coldly.

As he began to dish the Chinese up, Frankie smiled. She'd said her piece, stood up to him and her threat to leave – seemed to have worked.

Unaware that Frankie was missing her so much, Joycie had just cleared away the dinner plates and was now sitting back at the table sipping a glass of wine. Her roast chicken had gone down a treat. Everybody had cleared their plates and there wasn't so much as a baked parsnip left.

Raymond held his glass aloft. 'That was lovely, Mum. Cheers, everybody,' he said.

Joycie cleared her throat. Obviously Raymond knew that Eddie was signing the house over to her, but she was yet to tell Joey. Frankie wasn't even in touch, so she could hardly tell her.

'Joey, there's something I need to tell you which I hope you won't be upset about.'

Joey looked up in shock. He wanted to announce that he was gay himself, surely she hadn't clocked his sexuality and was about to do it for him?

'When I was in hospital, Gary and Ricky came to see me. They said that your dad was devastated by what had happened and that he wanted to sign the house over to me.'

'I don't understand. You haven't forgiven him, have you, Nan?'

Joyce shook her head. 'No, I haven't, darling, but I do think in his own way your dad is very sorry and he's trying to make amends.'

Seeing that his mum was struggling, Raymond took over. 'To put it bluntly, Joey, your dad has given the house to Nan and Grandad. None of this will affect any inheritance due to you in the future, as you're gonna outlive your grandparents and when anything happens to them, you will get the house.'

'What about Frankie?' Joey asked immediately.

Raymond shrugged. 'Well, obviously, your sister will get left something, too.'

'Even if she's still with that pikey toerag, we won't leave Frankie out, Joey. I'll make my will according to what your mum would have wanted,' Joyce assured him.

Joey eyed his grandad suspiciously. 'You ain't all gonna forgive my dad, are you?'

Stanley shook his head. 'Don't look at me, Joey, I wanted to tell your father to shove his offer up his arse.'

'So will you sell the house, or live here?' Joey asked his nan.

Aiming a kick at Stanley under the table, Joyce carried on. 'We're staying here until we die. I will never sell the house, because of your mum. She loved it here and while I live here, I can still feel close to her.'

Joey nodded. 'OK, so do you and Grandad actually own it now?'

Joyce shook her head. 'Your grandad doesn't want his name on the deeds, so it will be signed over to me. Your dad's solicitor is coming round tomorrow to finalise all the paperwork.'

Joey looked at Dominic for support. He wasn't very good at anything formal.

'Well, it all sounds OK to me. Now, who fancies a top-up?' Dom said, cleverly changing the subject.

As the drinks flowed and the mood lifted, Raymond decided the time was right for his own announcement. 'Well, I've got some good news for once. After all that's happened this year, I decided it was time I got myself an honest career. Polly's dad came up trumps and I'm gonna go and work with him in the jewellery business. I dunno exactly what I'll be doing yet, but I'm sure he won't make me sweep the floors.'

Stanley was the first to leap up and shake Raymond's hand. For once, his son had done the right thing. 'Good on you. I'm proud of you,' Stanley said, choked up.

Raymond turned to Polly. 'And,' he continued, 'last Saturday, I decided that the time was right to ask this beautiful woman here to marry me.'

Joyce jumped up from her seat and clapped her hands together. 'Go on, don't keep us in suspense,' she yelled.

Raymond winked at Polly. 'Well, after kneeling on the floor for what seemed like an hour, Polly said I was such a catch there was no way she could refuse.'

Joyce was ecstatic. A wedding to organise was just what she needed. 'Now Polly, you must invite your parents over to the house to meet me and Stanley. We need to start making arrangements.'

'Hold your horses, Mum, we ain't even set a date yet,' Raymond said, laughing.

Polly smiled politely. She had always found Raymond's family quite strange, so said very little in their company.

Grinning at Dominic, Joey stood up. Everybody was so happy and jolly, it was perfect timing to give his own speech. 'I've got some news as well. Nan, Grandad, are you listening?'

Joyce was feeling a bit light-headed. It was the first proper drink she'd had since she had fallen ill and the wine had gone straight to her head. Staring at Polly, she was too busy picturing how she would look in a wedding dress to listen to Joey.

Stanley poked her in the arm. 'Joycie, Joey's talking to you.'

Snapping out of her trance, Joyce smiled at her grandson. 'Sorry, darling,' she said.

'Well, yesterday I got my first job. I'll be working as a courier-type of post boy in an office in the City.'

'That's fantastic,' Stanley said proudly.

'Well done,' Joyce said, giving him a hug.

Feeling confident, Joey continued. 'And I've got something else to tell everyone.'

'Go on, don't keep us waiting,' Joyce said laughing.

Glancing at Dominic, Joey took a deep breath. 'Well, you know I've been staying at Dominic's flat?'

Raymond nudged Polly. He sort of knew what was coming next.

'Spit it out, Joey,' Stanley urged him.

'I think it's time you all knew the truth. Dominic isn't my friend – he's my boyfriend.'

Stanley and Joyce glanced at one another. Whatever was the boy trying to say?

'Whaddya mean, boyfriend?' Joyce said, frowning.

'I'm gay, Nan. Dominic and I are a couple like you and Grandad are.'

'Oh my gawd,' Joyce said, feeling faint.

Not knowing what to say or do, Stanley stood up. 'Excuse me. The pigeons need feeding.'

Unaware that her brother had just come out of the closet, Frankie was snuggled up to Jed, discussing baby names. After her earlier outburst, Frankie had enjoyed the rest of the evening. Jed had been really attentive, had got himself showered and then made passionate love to her.

'What about Rocky? That sounds well cool, Rocky O'Hara,' Jed suggested.

Frankie screwed her nose up. Girls' names, they could agree on, but Jed had the most awful taste in boys' names.

Yawning, Jed shut his eyes. Frankie had got on his nerves today, so he pictured what he'd done to her grandfather and smiled.

'What you looking so happy about?' Frankie asked him.

Jed opened his eyes and propped himself up on one elbow. 'How 'bout if we have a boy, we call it Harry in memory of your grandad? At least then the name's got meaning.'

Frankie had never been particularly close to her grandfather, so was initially unsure. 'Harry O'Hara,' she repeated over and over again.

She smiled at Jed. 'Actually, I quite like it. It has a certain ring to it.'

Jed winked at her. 'Well, that's decided, then. If it's a boy, Harry O'Hara it is.'

Thrilled by Jed's thoughtfulness, Frankie kissed him gently.

'Night, babe,' Jed said, as he turned the light out.

Picturing Sammy's face when he told him the choice of name for his unborn child, Jed struggled not to giggle. If Frankie ever found out what he'd done to her grandad, she'd muller him.

There was little chance of that, though. Jed was far too clever for even the Old Bill, let alone some simpleton like Frankie.

71

CHAPTER EIGHT

Joyce and Stanley sat in silence over the breakfast table. Both were still in shock over Joey's revelation the previous evening and neither knew what to say to one another.

Knowing that it was usually her job to break the ice, Joyce swallowed the last mouthful of her beans on toast, then broached the subject. 'We need to talk about Joey, Stanley.'

Stanley threw his knife and fork down onto his plate. 'I've nothing to say going the boy, Joycie.'

Joyce sighed. Her husband could be such a stubborn man at times. She wasn't exactly thrilled about the situation herself, but she wasn't going to lose her grandson over it.

As Stanley stood up, Joyce ordered him to sit back down. 'I need to see to me pigeons, they'll be starving,' Stanley said sullenly.

'Them poxy birds will have to bloody well wait for their grub for once. They eat more than I bleedin' well do. They're getting that fat, I'm surprised they can even bastard well fly!'

Stanley sighed as Joyce continued. 'Now, you listen to me. When you stormed off last night, like you always do in a crisis, our Joey carried on talking. He told me and Raymond that Jessica knew all about his relationship with Dominic. He said that she was happy that he'd found love and she fully supported his sexuality. If that's the case, and I believe Joey was telling the truth, then we have to support him, too. He's not a nonce or a murderer, Stanley, he just likes boys rather than girls. If

72

our Jess is looking down, she would want us to accept him for what he is.'

Stanley averted his eyes from his wife. He'd never really known any homosexuals before and the subject made him feel extremely uncomfortable. 'I know what you're saying, Joycie, but a bloke fancying a bloke ain't natural, is it? Can't you have a chat with Joey, see if you can try and fix him up with a girl or something? I mean, imagine Jock and me mates at the pigeon club finding out? It's embarrassing.'

Joyce pursed her lips. 'Ain't natural, ain't fucking natural! What about you and them bleedin' mates of yours? Spend half your life talking about your hens and playing with your cocks. Love them poxy birds more than anything, the lot of yous do, and that ain't bloody natural. Like it or not, Stanley, I'm gonna support that boy. Joey's my grandson and I love him dearly.'

Stanley nodded, got up and opened the back door. If Joycie had decided to stand by Joey, he knew he had little choice other than to agree with her decision.

Flanked by a prison guard on either side, Eddie Mitchell walked confidently towards the guvnor's office. He didn't know either of the two screws who had summoned him there. As for Johnny and old Fred, Ed still hadn't seen either of them since yesterday morning.

The taller screw out of the two tapped on the guvnor's door and shoved Eddie inside.

'Ah, Mr Mitchell,' the guvnor said sarcastically.

The guvnor was a lot older and shorter than Eddie had imagined him to be. He had grey, curly hair, was probably in his late fifties and had the look of a judge or a magistrate.

Eddie stood tall, arched his shoulders back and made strong eye contact with him.

'Yesterday morning, at approximately 7 a.m., your cellmate, Barry Macarthy, was viciously attacked in the shower room. You were seen within the vicinity, Mitchell, so what can you tell me about this unfortunate incident?'

73

Eddie didn't flinch as he stared the guvnor straight in the eye. 'Nothing whatsoever, sir. I do remember seeing Barry Macarthy in the shower room, but I left before him. There was certainly nothing wrong with him while I was there, as I remember hearing him laughing and joking with his mates.'

When the guvnor started to pace up and down the room, Ed knew he had nothing on him. The mug was just fishing, that's all he was doing.

'This is a very serious offence, Mitchell. The doctors have already had to remove one of Macarthy's eyes and at this precise moment they're desperately trying to save his sight in the other.'

Eddie shrugged. 'I'll be honest with you, sir, I was no fan of Barry Macarthy, but what happened to him was nothing to do with me. The best thing you can do is ask him who's responsible.'

The guvnor eyed him suspiciously. 'Barry Macarthy was attacked from behind, so he says. Whether that is true, Mitchell, is for him to know and me to find out.'

'Well, if I hear any rumours, I promise I'll let you know, sir,' Eddie said calmly.

As he was led away from the office, Ed wanted to laugh. For blatantly obvious reasons, he suppressed his urge to do so.

Jed O'Hara had been on his best behaviour all morning. Firstly, he had cooked Frankie breakfast and now he'd just suggested that he take a day off work so they could go out and buy some stuff for the baby.

'Oh Jed, that's wonderful. If we buy any clothes we'll have to get white though, won't we? Shall we look for a cot and a pushchair as well?' Frankie asked excitedly.

Jed smiled. Frankie might have forgotten about yesterday, but he most certainly hadn't. He hadn't been put on this earth to be pushed around by a woman and he wasn't tolerating Frankie's demanding ways for much longer. He'd have to play things cleverly, of course. He'd let her think she had him under the thumb, the silly girl.

'Can you speak to your mum before we go shopping, Jed? You know, to tell her what I said about the cooking lessons and stuff.'

Jed nodded. 'I'll go and talk to her now.'

Alice O'Hara was mopping the kitchen floor as her son strolled in. 'Don't walk in 'ere with them muddy boots on,' she screamed at him.

Telling her to put the mop down as he needed to talk to her, Jed removed his boots and gave her a big hug. 'I need to have a chat with you about Frankie, Mum.'

'What's a matter? Is she OK? It ain't the baby, is it?' Alice asked, concerned.

Jed shook his head. He loved his mum more than anything and was desperate not to hurt her feelings. 'It's just that Frankie's tired a lot lately. I dunno if she's up to all these cooking lessons.'

Alice snorted. 'She's having a chavvie, not dying of cancer. Anyway, I'm only trying to help her, Jed. She's one lazy little whore at times.'

Jed decided to try a different tactic. 'It ain't just that, Mum. She's been a bit upset over her mother again. I think she needs time to grieve and stuff, if you know what I mean?'

'I was only trying to help,' Alice said, obviously hurt.

Jed smiled. 'I know you were, Mum, but do me a favour, leave her be for now. Once the baby's born, she'll be crying out for your help.'

'Do you think so? I know it's a little girl, Jed, I do,' Alice said excitedly.

Jed laughed. 'Well if it is, I'm relying on you to bring it up for us, Mum. My Frankie's only young, she won't have a clue.'

Watching her son walk away, Alice beamed. Sod the cookery lessons, they meant nothing compared to bringing up a child, especially when that child was a beautiful little girl.

As Jed walked back inside the trailer, Frankie smiled at him.

'Well?' she asked expectantly.

'Sorted. Now why don't you give your grandparents a ring and tell 'em about the meal next weekend? Don't forget to tell 'em I'm paying,' Jed said.

'I'll ring me nan tomorrow,' Frankie said immediately. She wanted to speak to her alone, not with Jed listening to her conversation.

Jed handed her her mobile. 'I've just spoken to me mum for you, so now I want you to ring your grandparents for me.'

Frankie felt awkward as she dialled her old home number. She hadn't spoken to either her nan or grandad since the night of her mum's funeral.

It was Joyce who picked up the phone. 'Oh, it's you,' she said as she heard Frankie's voice.

'How are you, Nan?' Frankie said nervously.

'I'm fine now, thank you. And to what do we owe this pleasure?' Joyce asked sarcastically.

Frankie took a deep breath. 'I'm sorry I never visited you in hospital, Nan. I've really missed you and Grandad and I was wondering if we could meet up?'

Joyce's voice softened. 'That would be nice, Frankie. Have you spoken to your brother today? Has he told you about the house being signed over to me?'

Frankie hadn't spoken to Joey since yesterday, so had no idea what her nan was on about. 'What do you mean the house has been signed over?'

Annoyed with herself for presuming that Joey had spoken to Frankie, Joyce explained what had happened. 'So it was all your dad's idea, Frankie. But as Raymond told your brother, when anything happens to me and your grandad, you and Joey won't go short of a few bob. Anyway, forget all that. When are you coming to see us?'

'Actually, I wasn't going to come to the house. Jed wants you and Grandad to come out for a meal with us. Jed's paying, of course. We was thinking maybe next weekend, if that's OK with you?'

Joyce felt her blood start to boil. In her eyes the little bastard

76

Frankie was with was the cause of Jessica's death. 'That won't be possible, Frankie. Your mother would still be alive if it weren't for that boy. Me and your grandad want nothing to do with him.'

Frankie looked at her boyfriend. She could sense he knew that the conversation wasn't going too well and it was her duty to stick up for him. 'How can you say stuff like that, Nan? It was Dad that murdered Mum, Jed ain't done nothing wrong.'

As Joyce slammed the phone down on her, Frankie burst into tears.

Jed took his girlfriend in his arms and rocked her from side to side. 'See what I mean, Frankie? You've gotta forget about your family. They're not nice people and we don't want our chavvie getting involved with the likes of them, do we? I love you, you know that. I'll always look after you. You don't need anybody else.'

Frankie clung to him. Jed was right, her family were no good. Wiping away her tears, Jed kissed her on the nose. 'What was your nan saying about the house, babe?'

Still snivelling, Frankie shrugged. 'It's nothing important. She just said that my dad felt guilty about what had happened, so he signed the house over to my nan. Her and grandad can stay there for ever now, I suppose.'

Jed laughed. 'You're so naive, Frankie. That's your family's way of erasing you out of their lives. Can't you see that?'

As Frankie shook her head, Jed continued. 'They hate you, Frankie. That's your dad, nan and grandad's way of telling you to fuck off. It's obvious they blame me and you for everything, ain't it?'

'I suppose so,' Frankie agreed. She hadn't really thought of it that way.

'Now I want you to promise me something. I want you to promise me that you'll never contact them arseholes again. I'm not having you upset like this, Frankie, it ain't good for your pregnancy.'

Frankie clung to her hero. 'I promise, Jed. I'll still speak to

Joey, but other than that, it's just me, you and the baby from now on.'

Jed held her tightly. 'How do you know you can trust your brother? He might be in on it with 'em. I bet that cunt of an uncle of yours is something to do with it as well.'

Shocked, Frankie pulled away. 'My brother would never betray me. You don't know Joey like I do, Jed, he's not like them. Anyway, he's not even living there any more.'

'Where's he living then?'

'With his friend, Dominic. He's living in Islington,' Frankie replied.

Jed chuckled. 'Why don't you just admit to me that he's gay? I ain't no dinlo. The first time I met Joey I knew he was as queer as a nine-bob note.'

'So what if he is? It don't make him a bad person, does it, Jed?'

Deciding it was time to be nice again, Jed reverted to the softly-softly approach. 'Why don't we invite your brother and his boyfriend round for dinner one night, eh? Or if you'd prefer, we can take 'em out. I'll pay, of course.'

Wiping her eyes with her sleeve, Frankie managed a smile. 'I'd love that, Jed. I promise I won't have no more to do with the others, but if I still see Joey at least I've got some family left.'

Jed pushed her hair out of her eyes. 'Go and sort your face out, then let's do that shopping. I'll take you out for a meal when we're done, then tomorrow you can ring your brother and arrange a night for us to see him.'

As Frankie started to walk away, she glanced back at him. 'I love you, Jed.'

Winking at her, Jed smiled as she disappeared into their bedroom. From his point of view, the conversation she'd had with her nan couldn't have ended any better.

Yesterday, when she'd threatened to leave him, Jed had seen the fire in her eyes. He hadn't liked it, not one little bit. Now she had nowhere to go once more and that suited Jed O'Hara down to the ground.

*   *   *

Eddie Mitchell acted like cock of the walk as he strutted into the canteen. Clocking Baz's friends, he ordered his food and sat on the end of their table.

'All right, lads?' he asked boldly.

The three petrified men nodded simultaneously. They'd all seen what Eddie Mitchell was capable of and were truly shit-scared of him. As Ed munched away on the dry bit of bread-crumbed cardboard that the authorities had the cheek to call fish, he decided to mutter a few special words.

'Get word to your mate, if he grasses me, I'll kill him, then I'll kill you,' he said threateningly.

Seeing a screw clocking him, Eddie smiled.

'He won't say a word. We'll make sure of it,' the shortest guy insisted.

When the three men hurriedly made their excuses and left the table, Eddie began picking at their dinners. All the more cardboard for him. For the first time in ages Ed felt incredibly hungry and he was thrilled that his appetite had finally returned. If he was to make a success of his time in nick, he needed every ounce of strength he could muster.

With her anguish from earlier now long forgotten, Frankie felt extremely happy as Jed pulled up outside the trailer. Their shopping trip had been a great success. They'd bought babygros, toys, a highchair, a pushchair and Jed had insisted on buying her some ultra-modern maternity clothes for when she got bigger.

'Choose what you want, Frankie. You're showing now and, another couple of weeks your clothes won't even fit you,' he told her.

Frankie giggled as Jed struggled to unload all the bags from the truck.

'Shall I make us a cup of tea?' she asked.

Jed dropped the bags, grabbed her hand and pulled her close. 'Why don't we go in me mum and dad's for a cup of tea? Me mum would love to see all the baby stuff we've bought.'

Frankie agreed. She knew that she had to start making more of an effort, for Jed's sake.

Alice O'Hara was in her element as she pawed over the purchases for her unborn grandchild. 'Look at that little suit, Jimmy. Ain't it pretty?' she said to her husband.

Jimmy nodded, cracked open a couple of cans and handed one to Jed.

With his mother and Frankie sitting on the carpet rabbiting about babies, Jed couldn't help but smile. Once his mum and girlfriend bonded properly, his life would be a damn sight easier and he could go out partying more.

Just lately Frankie had become too clingy for his liking. He loved her and all that, but hated feeling trapped, and that's how Frankie had made him feel recently. He felt like a poxy bird stuck in a wire cage. It was for that reason and that reason only that he'd copped off with that pretty little filly the other night.

Sally was her name. She was twenty-one years old, a right little goer and, as Jed thought about her, he could feel his cock rising to attention in his trousers.

Watching his mum look at his dad like a lovesick teenager, Jed smiled. He'd only been a nipper when his mother had caught his dad knobbing some bird in his salvage yard, but he remembered it like it was yesterday. At the time he was too young to understand, so he'd sided with his mum, but years later his dad had explained the situation and given him a good man-to-man talking-to.

'Jed, take my advice. Find yourself a good woman, a loyal one. Once you're sure she's the one for you, chain her to the cooker and the bedroom. Whatever she cooks for you, even if it tastes like shit, tell her how nice it is, then, once she gives birth to your chavvies, that woman is yours for life. Never forget to enjoy yourself though, son. Us men are grafters: we put the food on the table, therefore we're entitled to have some fun. A travelling man will always be a travelling man, in more ways than one, boy.'

80

As his dad handed him another can of beer, Jed again clocked his mother looking adoringly at his father.

'Cheers, Dad,' Jed said, clicking cans with him.

'To you and Frankie,' Jimmy said.

As Frankie squeezed his hand, Jed smiled. 'To me and Frankie,' he repeated.

CHAPTER NINE

As visiting time approached, Eddie felt his stomach start to churn. He hadn't seen Raymond since the night he'd murdered Jessica, and even though he was desperate to see him, he was also incredibly nervous. Ed knew that Raymond understood what had happened was a pure accident. Ray had sent him quite a few letters and there was no sign of anger or blame in his words.

'You OK, Ed?'

Eddie smiled at his young cellmate. 'Not bad, Stu. I'm a bit apprehensive, I suppose.'

'Don't worry. Ray'll be fine with you, mate, I just know he will.'

It had been just over two weeks since Eddie had attacked Big Bald Baz and got away with it. Five days after that, young Stuart Howells had become his new cellmate. Ed hadn't particularly wanted to share with anybody, but he'd somehow taken to Stuart immediately.

At twenty-two years old, Stuart was only a nipper compared to Eddie. He was from Hackney and was awaiting trial for stabbing a black lad who had later died.

Within days of Stuart's arrival, both cellmates had opened up to one another.

'The police tried to make out it was racial, but I ain't like that, Ed. Jonesy had it coming to him and there was no way I was letting him get away with it. I had him as soon as the police released him on bail,' Stuart admitted.

Eddie admired the kid's morals, attitude and bravery. Stuart had been with his girlfriend, Carly, for two years when she had been dragged into a block of flats on the way home from a night out and brutally raped.

It had taken the police six months to find the culprit. They finally arrested and charged a local lad called Michael Jones, whom they later released on bail.

Stuart's girlfriend, Carly, had been petrified when she found out that her attacker was back on the streets. She was afraid to go out of the door, and she couldn't bear Stuart coming anywhere near her. Sex was a definite no-go. The rape had been so violent it had left Carly with severe internal injuries.

With their relationship inevitably breaking down, Stuart decided to get his own back for his girlfriend. It had taken him two weeks to find out exactly who Michael Jones was and where he hung out of a night.

Armed with a six-inch blade, Stuart headed to the bar on a Friday night with his pal, Dan. The bar was small inside, played reggae music, was full of black guys, and Stuart didn't have a clue if he'd be able to spot his girlfriend's attacker amongst the crowd.

As luck would have it, he recognised him within minutes. Michael Jones was standing with another black guy talking to two white girls on the edge of a very small dancefloor.

Telling his mate Dan to stay at the bar, Stuart approached Jones from behind. Overcome by the need for revenge, Stu pulled the knife out of the inside of his jacket and repeatedly stabbed the bastard in the back.

'That's for my Carly, you cunt,' he screamed, as her rapist fell to the floor in a pool of blood.

Stuart had tried to run away from the bar, but was held on to by a crowd of black geezers until the police arrived. They kicked and punched him and called him every white motherfucker under the sun. He was badly beaten by the time he was arrested, and if the police had arrived any later, he'd have probably been killed himself. Dan had tried to help him, but Stuart had told him to leg it. He didn't want his pal getting banged up as well. This was his problem and he wanted to sort it alone.

Michael Jones had clung to life for almost a week. He had many internal injuries and was rushed straight into intensive care. Stu was informed eight days later by a police officer that he had died. He felt no remorse whatsoever.

After Stuart had opened up about his arrest, Eddie told him his own story. He explained in detail about that fateful night in Tilbury, leaving no stone unturned.

The two cellmates had somehow formed a bond for life. Ed adored Stu – he was like another son to him – and Stuart adored Eddie. Stuart had never had the pleasure of having a father figure around, his own dad had fucked off when he was a toddler and he'd never seen him since.

As soon as the screw unlocked the cell door, both Eddie and Stuart stood up. Stu's mate, Dan, was coming to visit him and he hoped that Ed would be sitting nearby so he could introduce them.

Stuart slapped Eddie on the back. 'Good luck, mate,' he whispered.

Over in Rainham, Frankie had just heard a car pull up. Full of excitement, she flung open the trailer door and ran outside to greet her brother and Dominic. She couldn't wait to show Joey how happy she and Jed were. She'd got all the baby stuff out to show him and Jed had promised that he would take them for a ride on the horse and cart later.

It had been Jed's idea that they visit her at home. 'You want your brother to see where you're living, Frankie. He needs to know that I'm looking after you properly. Let him come here, then later on we'll all go out for a nice slap-up meal. My treat, of course.'

Joey hugged his twin sister tightly. He'd missed her immensely and it was great to see her again.

'Look at you! The baby's really showing now,' he said, patting her tummy.

Frankie giggled. She was now almost five months gone and had put on tons of weight since she'd last seen Joey. While Frankie turned her attention to Dominic, Jed stepped outside the trailer. He held his right hand out to Joey.

'Good to see you again. It's cold out 'ere – come inside and we'll have a beer,' he said awkwardly as they shook hands.

Glancing around the land surrounding the mobile home, Joey clocked a goat staring at him and heard some dogs barking. 'Look at all these animals. It won't be safe to bring a kid up here, will it?' he whispered to Dom.

Dominic shrugged. His boyfriend's father had once attacked him and nearly cut off his manhood, and since that had happened he tried to keep his nose out of any business that involved Joey's family.

When Joey sat down he was surprised but pleased by how clean the trailer was inside. 'Do you do all the housework yourself, Frankie?' he asked, impressed.

Jed answered the question for her. 'Don't be silly – me muvver does it,' he said laughing.

Frankie squeezed her brother's hand. Joey looked so well, he was almost glowing. 'So how are things going? What's it like living together? Do you two ever argue?'

Dominic put an arm around Joey's shoulder. 'No, not at all. We get on really well, don't we?' he said lovingly.

Jed smirked as he took in the scene in front of him. He considered himself to be a red-blooded male and he found the whole situation highly amusing.

While Frankie chatted to Joey about his new job, Jed looked at his watch. He'd ordered Sammy to ring him at two on the dot and he hoped his cousin hadn't forgotten. Jed wasn't silly, of course. He had already got himself spruced up earlier.

'You look lovely. Why have you put your good clothes on in the daytime?' Frankie asked suspiciously.

Telling her how much he loved her, Jed had taken her into his arms. 'I did it for you, babe. This is the first time your brother has come to our home. I know how important it is to you, so I wanted to make an effort.'

Frankie clung to him like a leech. 'I really do love you, Jed O'Hara,' she whispered.

Willing his phone to ring, Jed was relieved when it finally did. He spoke loudly so everyone could hear him. 'Whaddya mean he's had a bad accident? Is he OK? What happened?'

On the other end of the phone, Sammy was pissing himself laughing.

'OK, Sammy, give me half-hour,' Jed said, pretending to be upset.

'Was that Sammy? What's up?' Frankie asked as Jed snatched his truck keys off the table.

'Me little cousin Billy, Sammy's brother, has been involved in a bad car accident. It's touch and go, apparently. I'm gonna have to go and see him, Frankie.'

Frankie's eyes welled up. 'Oh, Jed, that's awful. Shall I come with you?'

Jed shook his head. 'You stay 'ere with your brother and Dominic. I don't want you getting upset, not in your condition. I also don't want to spoil your day.'

'Take your phone, Jed, so you can let me know how he is,' Frankie urged.

Jed picked up his mobile. 'If Billy's really bad, I might have to stay with Sammy tonight. I'll call you and let you know the score. Bye Joey, Dominic. Sorry about all this.'

'It's not your fault, babe,' Frankie shouted, as he bolted out of the trailer.

Jed started up his truck and drove away at top speed. Smiling, he then punched in Sammy's number.

'Well, did she fall for it?' his cousin asked.

Jed burst out laughing. 'Of course she fucking did.'

Eddie was a bundle of nerves as he sat down opposite Raymond.

Raymond guessed how he must be feeling, so quickly tried

86

to thaw the situation. 'Good to see you, mate. You're looking well. Gary and Ricky said you'd lost a load of weight the last time they saw you, but I can't notice it.'

Ed took a deep breath. Seeing Raymond brought everything back to him and he could feel his heart pounding through his chest. 'I did lose a lot of weight at first, but I've put some back on now. I've been going to the gym, I was losing all me muscle and, well, there's fuck all else to do in here but read or get fit.'

Raymond didn't know how he felt, looking at Eddie. The crime Eddie had committed was, in most people's eyes, despicable, but even though he was Jessica's brother, Ray couldn't hate Ed. They'd been through too much together.

Unbeknown to Ed, Raymond had also been nervous about the visit. He had no idea how he would react to seeing Eddie again, but however bad he might have felt, he knew he had to take the chance and come. 'Shall I get us a drink?' Ray asked.

Ed smiled. 'Get us a coffee and a Mars bar as well.'

Watching Raymond walk away, Eddie relaxed a bit. Because he was on remand, he was allowed more visits than a convicted inmate. It was the old cliché of being innocent until proved guilty.

Raymond sat back down and handed Eddie his coffee. 'So, what's going on with Gary and Ricky? They're really upset, Ed, 'cause you won't let 'em visit you at the moment.'

Eddie shrugged. 'They never told me about the O'Haras turning up at Jessica's funeral. I'm fuming with 'em, Raymondo. What do they think I am? Some mug? I'd rather have heard it from their mouths than in a letter from cunting Paulie.'

Knowing how much the boys thought of Eddie, Raymond stuck up for Gary and Ricky. 'They thought you was in a bad way, Ed. Them boys both worship the ground you walk on and they thought by not telling you, they were doing the right thing at the time. You've gotta send 'em a VO. They're devastated, mate.'

Eddie rubbed his hands over his short hair. For some reason,

Raymond always had the ability to make him see sense. What a tragedy he hadn't listened to him on the night that Jessica had died.

'OK, I'll write to 'em tomorrow and send 'em a VO,' he mumbled.

Ray nodded. 'Have you heard my news?'

Ed laughed. 'Yeah, someone told me you're now a jeweller.'

Raymond felt embarrassed. He hated his new job with a passion. 'I hate it, Ed. I did it for Polly. Her dad offered me the job, but it ain't me, mate. It's so fucking boring and I'm surrounded by pricks all day long. Whaddya think I should do?'

Feeling sorry for his pal, Eddie spoke seriously. 'I know you wanna go straight, Ray, and I don't blame you for that, but you've gotta find something that suits ya. You've got dough: why don't you set up a business and let some mug run it for you?'

Raymond shrugged. 'Like what? Apart from being a butcher when I was a kid and working in your salvage yard, I've never had a normal job.'

Eddie had no idea what to suggest. Pub protection and loan-sharking was all he really knew and that was all he'd taught Raymond. 'Look, Ray, I know what happened that night was all my fault, but it was nothing to do with our work, was it? It was family stuff that went wrong. I know the old sharking can get a bit violent at times, but why don't you go back to work with Gary and Ricky? Let them do the dirty work, you can take a step back.'

Raymond shook his head. 'I've proposed to Polly. We're getting married. I can't go back to that life, not if we're gonna have a family.'

'Congratulations,' Eddie said, his eyes welling up. He could remember the day he'd proposed to Jessica in his gold Merc, as if it was only five minutes ago.

'You must have some idea of something I can get into, Ed?' Ray asked, obviously worried.

Eddie shook his head. 'I really don't know, mate. The trouble with men like me and you is we ain't led a normal life. From working with me to selling fucking jewellery is nigh on impossible. I don't know what to advise you to do, Ray. The only thing I can say is that Polly must have known what sort of bloke you were when you met her and if she loves you, she'll stand by you whatever career path you take.'

Raymond nodded. Eddie was right, as per usual.

'What you should do is go home and have a long, hard think about things. I can have a word with Gary and Ricky. If you go back to the firm, I'll guarantee you, you won't have to get your hands dirty no more.'

Raymond said nothing. He'd loved his old job, but needed to speak to Polly before he could even think of going back to it.

Eddie pointed out his new pal, Stuart, and spoke highly about what he'd done to get revenge for his girlfriend. With neither man wanting to be reminded of that awful night in Tilbury, they stuck to general chitchat for the rest of the visit. As the bell rang, Ed leaned forward. 'There's something I need to ask you, something important. My dad's old brief, Larry, has taken over my case. He reckons he can get my murder charge dropped to manslaughter. I won't let him do it unless you agree, Ray. I loved Jess, you know I did and I'm willing to do life for what I did, if that's what you and your family want.'

'Come on, Mitchell, move,' shouted a prison guard.

Raymond didn't particularly understand the situation. Eddie hadn't meant to kill Jessica, but had owned up to it, so how could he not be convicted of murder?

Aware that a screw was approaching, Ray stared at Eddie. What had happened was a case of mistaken identity, so why should his pal do life if he didn't have to? 'Go for it, Ed. Tell your brief to go for it. I'll speak to Mum and Dad,' he said.

Over in Tilbury, Jed O'Hara and his cousin Sammy were having the time of their lives. They were in the salvage yard where

Jessica had been murdered, doing a bit of entertaining in the new trailer Jimmy O'Hara had recently bought.

'Does that feel good? You like it rough, don't ya?' Jed asked, as he thrust his cock forcefully into Sally's arse.

'Oh yeah, I love it, Jed. When you gonna leave Frankie?' Sally replied, groaning.

Jed winced, then smiled as he shot his load up her harris. Sally was a good fuck, a dirty little whore, but he had no intention of leaving Frankie for her.

As he pulled his manhood out of her anus, Sally turned over and repeated her question. 'Are you gonna leave her, Jed?'

Taking a plastic bag out of his pocket, Jed opened it and handed Sally another ecstasy pill. 'Get that down your neck. I'll leave her soon, I promise,' he lied.

Jed stood up, zipped up his trousers and went in search of his cousin. 'Oi, oi, saveloy,' he shouted, as he saw Sammy's bare arse bouncing up and down on Sally's best friend, Julie.

Sammy laughed as Jed walked over and handed them both an E. Jed took a swig of water and swallowed another himself. He'd had two earlier, so already felt out of his nut.

When his phone burst into life once again, Jed suddenly thought it would be funny to answer the bloody thing. Frankie had been ringing for the past couple of hours and he, Sammy, Julie and Sally had had a right old laugh over the story he'd told his girlfriend earlier.

'Sssh, shut up a sec,' he said, as he put the phone to his ear.

'Jed, is everything OK? I've been so worried. How's your cousin?' Frankie asked in a panicky voice.

Drugged up to the eyeballs, Jed wanted to laugh, but somehow managed to stop himself. Turning away from the others, who were all giggling, he spoke seriously. 'Billy ain't too good, Frankie. He's in intensive care now. The doctors reckon they might have to take his leg off.'

With her hormones all over the place, Frankie burst into tears. 'Oh Jed, that's terrible. Whereabouts are you? Joey and

Dominic are still here and they said they'll bring me up in a cab if you need me there.'

'No, Frankie. You stay there with your brother and his boyfriend. I'm fine, honest, all my family are here. I might not get home tonight, but I'll see you tomorrow, babe.'

Usually Jed would make a reference to the baby, but on this occasion he couldn't, as he hadn't told Sally that Frankie was pregnant.

'Take care, Jed. I love you,' Frankie said solemnly.

'I can't hear you. The battery's going now,' Jed said, switching the phone off.

Turning back to the others, Jed burst out laughing. He picked up his mobile, opened the door and threw the phone outside.

'Come on then, let's party,' he screamed.

CHAPTER TEN

Eddie sat down opposite Larry Peters, his brief. Larry had represented Ed's father many times over the years and was an expert at swinging a jury.

'So, have you thought about what I said?' Larry asked.

Ed nodded. 'I had a chat with Raymondo. I needed his approval, Lal. Jess was his sister, after all. Anyway, he told me to go for it.'

Larry smiled. He had been great friends with Eddie's dad, Harry, and had been devastated when poor old H had been murdered. The police had never found the bastards who'd killed him and Larry was forever trying to uncover new information on the case. The Old Bill might have put Harry's death on the back burner by now, but he most certainly hadn't.

Larry leaned forward and lowered his tone. 'I went over all the paperwork again yesterday. Don't get me wrong, Ed, this isn't going to be easy, but I know that with the right judge and jury you can get acquitted of murder and instead be charged with manslaughter.'

'What about my original statement, though? I admitted what I'd done when I woke up in hospital. I told the filth that I'd gone there to shoot Jed and I admitted I'd shot Jess by mistake.'

Larry waved his hands in the air. He had a habit of doing this when he got overexcited about something. 'Forget about that original statement. You were ill, in shock, drugged up on medication. You didn't know what you were saying, that will be my argument. The positive thing, Ed, is that apart from that one admission, in every other interview you said, "No comment." Now, we can't get out of the fact that you went to Tilbury with a gun. But what we can say is that all you wanted to do was put the frighteners on Jed. You said in your statement that you didn't know Jessica was there. My argument will be that Jed did a runner as soon as you got there. You wanted to scare the lad, so you sprayed bullets round the trailer. You had no idea that your wife was there, which is true, and you were heartbroken when Raymond turned up and you found out what you'd done, which is also true.'

Even though none of it was funny, Ed gave a slight chuckle. 'It sounds a bit far-fetched, Lal. I wouldn't believe that bollocks if I was on the jury. Would you?'

Larry waved his hands in the air once more. 'Look, there isn't going to be many people as cute as you and me on that jury. At least fifty per cent of the general public are a sixpence short of a shilling. What you need is a few middle-aged women that take a shine to you. Give them the eye and that killer smile of yours. Once they hear what a good husband and father you were, you'll have them eating out the palm of your hand. We need to pray that we get some blokes on the jury who have daughters themselves. Many a man has gone apeshit because some awful chap has knocked up his teenage daughter and that would earn you the valuable sympathy vote.'

Larry's enthusiasm was contagious and Eddie found himself believing, for the first time, that he could get away with murder. 'If I only get a guilty for manslaughter, how long do you think I'll get?'

Larry shrugged. 'Six, eight, ten. It all depends on the judge. You're bound to cop a separate lump for being in possession of a firearm. I'm no mind-reader, Ed, but at a guess, I reckon put the two charges together and you're looking at a twelve to fourteen stretch. You'll then do two thirds of that, providing you behave yourself, of course, and your time spent on remand will also be taken off.'

Ed worked the figures out. 'So, if I'm lucky, I could be looking at as little as a seven?'

'If you're lucky,' Larry said bluntly.

It was two o'clock the following afternoon when Jed finally arrived back home. He'd had a great night over in Tilbury. Sex, drugs and acid house – what more could a man want?

Sammy, Julie, Sally and himself had been up all night shagging and dancing, but he'd managed to get his nut down for a couple of hours this morning.

'All right, Jed? How's your cousin?' Frankie asked, rushing out of the trailer towards him.

'Not too bad. He's better than he was. They managed to save his leg,' Jed lied, remembering his fable.

Noticing how tired and deathly white her boyfriend looked, Frankie decided he needed some pampering. 'Why don't you jump in the shower and freshen up? I went to Tesco with your mum and dad earlier and I bought sausages, bacon, eggs, mushrooms and a crusty loaf. I'll cook you a nice breakfast, if you like.'

Jed grabbed her arse and pulled her towards him. 'Don't burn it like the last one you cooked, will ya?' he said, laughing.

As Frankie hugged him, she could smell perfume on his shirt. She said nothing. It would be awful to make a scene when his cousin was so ill.

Jed stripped off, left his clothes in a heap on the bedroom floor, then jumped into the shower.

Frankie waited until she heard the water running, then crept into the bedroom. His shirt was staring her in the face. Unable to stop herself, she picked it up to inspect it. She held it to her nose and breathed in deeply. It was definitely a feminine scent and not aftershave. Jed only ever wore Kouros and it certainly wasn't that. As Frankie looked closely, she could see signs of lipstick and possible foundation. Her heart turned over. Surely Jed wouldn't be unfaithful to her. How could he have been up to no good when he'd been stuck at the hospital all night?

Realising the water had stopped running, Frankie threw the shirt back onto the floor and dashed into the kitchen area to make a start on the breakfast.

'You ain't ate much. What's a matter?' Jed asked, as he finished his last mouthful. Frankie knew she had to say something. She wasn't the type to stay schtum and brush things under the carpet. She needed peace of mind.

'I need to ask you something, Jed, and please don't lie to me.'

'What?' Jed asked, as he leaned across her and nicked the sausage off her plate.

'I know you were at the hospital last night, but did you go out afterwards?'

'Whaddya mean? I had a beer back at Sammy's with my family. Spit it out, what's the problem, Frankie?' Jed said, acting annoyed.

Frankie began to cry. 'I was going to put your clothes in the washing machine, when I noticed your shirt smelt of women's perfume. It's covered in lipstick and make-up as well.'

As bright as a spark, Jed had an answer within seconds. 'You silly cow. I told you all my family were at the hospital last night, didn't I? There was loads of me aunts and girl cousins there that I ain't seen for years. Because Billy was in such a bad way, everybody was hugging one another and crying. The lipstick and whatever else you thought you saw or smelt obviously belongs to either an aunt, a cousin or both.'

Frankie felt incredibly stupid as Jed took her into his arms. He'd been sitting at his sick cousin's bedside all night and she felt awful for doubting him. 'I'm sorry, Jed. I think because I feel so fat and ugly at the moment, I'm worried you'll go off with someone else.'

Jed smiled. The baby weight didn't suit Frankie, but even though she looked far less attractive than when they'd first met, he still fancied her.

Feeling himself harden, he unzipped his jeans and unleashed his penis. He put Frankie's hand on it and spoke gently to her.

'I love you Frankie, but you can't go around accusing me of stuff I ain't done. My cousin nearly died last night. Watching Billy suffer like that was awful, really awful.'

Frankie sank to her knees. Jed loved her sucking him off and she had some serious grovelling to do. Jed held Frankie's head and thrust himself as far as he could down the back of her throat. As she began to choke, he grinned. That'd teach her to fucking snoop.

Joyce took the last of the sausage rolls off the baking tray and carefully arranged them on the silver platter. She had been cooking, baking and preparing all day and at last she was finally finished. Joyce prided herself on her homemaking and culinary skills. Today she had made a special effort because her friends, Rita and Hilda, were coming over.

The house had now been officially signed over to Joyce. Even though the circumstances were horrific, Joyce was thrilled finally to own such a wonderful property. Of course, she'd swap it for her old house in Upney tomorrow if it brought her Jessica back, but Joyce had to face facts: Jessica was gone for good, bless her soul.

Joyce had added her own touches to the property in the last couple of weeks. She had painted the hallway a different colour, replaced the kitchen table for a smaller one and she'd had a beautiful picture of Jessica blown up and framed, which now took centre stage on the main wall in the lounge.

Glancing at the kitchen clock, Joyce decided it was time she started getting ready. Not only were her friends coming tonight, but also Joey, Dominic and Stan's mate, Jock.

After the initial shock of discovering that her grandson was gay, Joyce had now embraced the fact. So what if Joey was different? There were many actors, singers and politicians who were the same way, and even one of the Kray twins was rumoured to be gay.

Joyce had purchased a book, read up on the subject, then digested and accepted homosexual culture. She hadn't told

96

Stanley that Joey and Dominic were coming tonight. Her husband was an old-fashioned old fart and if he'd known their grandson was bringing his boyfriend over, he wouldn't have invited Jock.

Joyce smiled as she admired her new red frock. Tonight she would show off her new house and also tell everybody that Joey and Dominic were a couple. Being open was the only way forward and Joyce was sure that once her friends accepted the boys' sexuality, then so would Stanley.

Eddie, Stuart and Bertie Simms were glued to the screen. An old western was on the telly and the film was the bollocks. Bertie nudged Ed as he spotted one of Barry Macarthy's mates heading their way.

It was now common knowledge among the lags that Big Bald Baz had completely lost his eyesight. It was also common knowledge that he was seriously depressed and suicidal.

Annoyed that he'd been interrupted while watching such a good movie, Eddie glared at Baz's mate. 'What?' he asked sarcastically.

'I thought you should know – Baz's dead. He slit his wrists this morning with a razor blade.'

Eddie nodded, then casually looked back at the telly. As Baz's mate left the room, Ed turned to Stuart and Bert. 'It's a miracle the fat cunt could find the razor blade or his fucking wrists. I thought he was meant to be as blind as a bat,' he said in a deadpan voice.

Tickled by Ed's comments, both Stuart and Bertie Simms burst out laughing.

Frankie smiled politely at Jimmy O'Hara as he explained to her that he was breaking in a new horse. She didn't have a clue what he was talking about so, rather than be rude or come across as thick, she decided to nod her head at appropriate moments.

'You need to be brutal with 'em, Frankie. Show 'em who's

97

boss. Did you know that a horse has a brain the size of a pea?'

When Alice and Jed walked into the room, Frankie was relieved. It was obvious that Jimmy had had a couple of beers too many and he was nigh on boring her to death.

Alice smiled as she put the plate of sandwiches in front of Frankie. 'Help yourself, darling.'

'Oh, I'm fine thanks, Alice. Me and Jed went to Pizza Hut this afternoon. I still feel stuffed.'

'You're eating for two, Frankie. You need to keep your strength up for that chavvie of yours. Now, eat,' she demanded, as she lifted the plate off the table and thrust it in front of Frankie's nose.

Not at all hungry, Frankie felt obliged to take a couple of sandwiches and nibble at them. Even though Alice had stopped the cookery lessons, Frankie still found her very domineering and scary. She hadn't mentioned this to Jed. At the end of the day, Alice was his mum and she would hate to hurt his feelings.

Jed and Jimmy were now deep in conversation so, swallowing a mouthful of her sandwich, Frankie desperately tried to think of something to say to Alice. Not having much in common with the woman, she decided to concentrate on the terrible car accident that Jed's cousin had been involved in the day before.

'Terrible news about Billy, wasn't it, Alice? Jed's been so upset,' she said.

Alice was confused. 'What, my Billy? What you on about?'

Frankie shook her head. Names were very confusing in travelling families, as they always seemed to call their children by the same few. Billy, Tommy, Stevie, Jack and Sammy seemed to be the most common. Jed had at least twenty members of his family with those names.

'Sammy's brother, Billy. You know, the one who's in intensive care, who nearly lost his leg,' Frankie said innocently.

Clocking the words 'Billy', 'leg' and 'intensive care', Jed grabbed Frankie's arm and quickly dragged her from the room.

'Jed, you're hurting me. What's the matter?' Frankie asked bemused.

Away from his parents' eyes and ears, Jed turned to her. 'Me mum and dad don't know about me cousin Billy, Frankie.'

'What do you mean they don't know? I thought you said that all your family were up the hospital with you. I knew your mum and dad weren't, as I saw their lights on last night, but surely someone must have told them.'

Jed paused. He was good at making up stories and quickly thought of his answer. 'Me cousin Billy ain't on me mum's side of the family. We wanted to tell her and Dad, but because we thought that Billy might die last night, we decided it was best not to. You gotta remember, Frankie, it weren't long ago that me mum miscarried and lost the chavvie. You weren't living here at the time, but her and me dad were distraught. Billy being at death's door would have brought it all back to them and I love my parents, Frankie, I can't have 'em upset again.'

Frankie couldn't apologise enough. Jed was the most thoughtful person she had ever met and she had such a big mouth. 'I am so sorry,' she said, as she clung to him.

Jed kissed her on the forehead. 'It ain't your fault, babe. I should have explained the situation to you. Don't worry, I'll make up some story to me mum, she won't be none the wiser.'

'Are you sure she won't know, Jed? I'd feel terrible if I've put my big foot in it. I wouldn't upset your mum or dad for the world.'

Jed looked at Frankie's worried expression and smiled. When they'd first met, Frankie had thought she was a match for his cleverness. She'd obviously rated herself far too highly, bless her.

Joycie had had a wonderful evening. Joey and Dominic had both been entertaining and charismatic. Hilda and Rita were gobsmacked when she'd given them a full guided tour of the house, then told them it was now all hers. They'd seen the house on the day of Jessica's funeral, but they'd never seen the upstairs before and they were really impressed with the size of the bedrooms.

Jock and Stanley had talked pigeons most of the night, but this didn't bother Joyce for once. She was a bit tiddly, happy in a strange sort of way, and decided it was each to their own. The words hen or cock usually grated on her, but they didn't seem to bother her at all this evening.

Returning from the lavatory, Joyce sat back down in her chair. Joey and Dominic looked really happy together and now she'd got her head around their unusual situation, she was thrilled for them. She topped up her glass and stood up.

'I have an announcement to make, everybody,' she said, tapping her glass with a spoon.

Stanley, who had been busy talking to Jock, quickly realised that his wife was drunk. 'Sit down, Joycie. Don't make a show of yourself,' he said, tugging the sleeve of her dress.

Joycie ignored him. She'd read up on homosexuality and she was ready to give her speech on the matter. 'I want to tell you about my grandson, Joey,' she said proudly.

Hilda, Rita and Jock all nodded. Guessing what was coming, Dominic squeezed Joey's hand under the table.

Stanley stood up. 'Come on, Joyce, let's get you to bed, love,' he said, thoroughly embarrassed. It was obvious where this conversation was leading.

Joyce pushed his hand away. She smiled at Joey and Dominic before continuing. 'Last week, or was it the week before – I can't remember? – but my grandson Joey brought Dominic over here for a meal.'

As his nan paused to slurp some more wine, Joey looked nervously at his grandad. Joey was extremely proud of what he was, but he hadn't expected this showcase.

With her glass now empty, Joyce poured a refill and carried on. 'I want everybody here tonight to know something very important. My grandson Joey is a gay man and I couldn't be happier about it.'

Hilda, Rita and Jock sat open-mouthed as Joycie ordered

both Joey and Dominic to stand up. 'Tell 'em you're gay, Joey. Go on Dominic, tell 'em you're both homosexuals,' she ordered.

Extremely embarrassed, Joey and Dominic looked at one another in horror.

'Go on tell 'em. I've been reading up on the subject and there's nothing to be ashamed of. One of the Krays was gay and so was that John Inman, you know, he was in that programme, *Are You Being Served?* Then there was Larry Grayson and Rock Hudson. You tell 'em, boys; there's nothing to be embarrassed about.'

Dominic was the first to speak. 'Yes, I am gay,' he said awkwardly, not knowing where to look.

Joyce patted Joey on the arm. 'Come on, love. Stand up and be proud. Tell 'em you like a bit of willy.'

'For fuck's sake, Joycie,' Stanley shouted. How could she show him up like this in front of Jock?

Joyce ignored her husband's pleas and began to cackle. She'd just thought of something extremely funny. She pointed at both Stanley and Jock.

'Yous two have more in common with these boys than you think. All you ever do is talk about your cocks. And you're always playing with one another's.'

As Stanley bolted from the room, Joycie pulled her grandson out of his chair. 'Now that miserable old goat's sodded off, you can tell everyone, Joey.'

By this time Joey was as red as a beetroot. 'I'm gay,' he whispered.

Clapping her hands with delight, Joyce broke into song. 'Congratulations and celebrations,' she sang gleefully.

CHAPTER ELEVEN

'You're popular, Mitchell,' the screw said as he waved a pile of letters in front of Eddie.

The post had been up the creek for well over a week now and all the inmates had been up in arms about it. At a time like Christmas, receiving cards and letters was the only thing to keep some of the lags going. One poor sod had hung himself two days ago because he hadn't heard a word from his wife.

Ed snatched at the letters. 'Now, now, Mitchell. Where's your manners? Say thank you.'

Desperate for some correspondence with the outside world, Eddie begrudgingly mumbled the word 'thanks'. He hated Carter, the new screw on his wing. He was a cocky fucker and seemed to get a kick out of winding the inmates up. Unfortunately for Ed, he hadn't seen young Johnny or Fred since the day he'd attacked Big Baz. Word had it that both had been suspended, then moved to another wing.

Eddie had the cell all to himself as Stuart was at a meeting with his brief. Feeling excited, Ed studied the envelopes and put the letters in order. He knew who most of them were from by the handwriting or postcode, but there were two or three he didn't recognise at all.

He read the two sent from his uncles first. Neither Reg nor Albert ever seemed to have much of interest to say, but he still enjoyed receiving their letters. In prison, any contact with the outside world was better than none.

Eddie immediately recognised the handwriting on the next two he opened. Both his Aunts, Vi and Joan, had become a bit shaky in their old age and their writing stood out like a sore thumb. Ed laughed out loud as he read what Joan had written about her recent visit. Reg had brought her up to see him last week and Eddie had happened to mention how much he hated Carter, the new screw on his wing.

When the bell rang, Carter had picked on Eddie first.

'Come on, say goodbye, Mitchell. Visiting time's over,' he yelled.

'Why don't you fuck off? I ain't going nowhere until everyone else has gone,' Auntie Joan shouted back.

Furious, Carter tried to grab her arm and march her out. Auntie Joan was having none of it. 'Don't you dare touch me! Get off me, you fucking nonce-case,' she screamed, as she booted him in the shin.

'You keep your chin up, Ed, don't let these bastards grind you down,' Joan yelled, as she marched out of the building with her head held high.

All the other lags had pissed themselves laughing. None of them liked Carter and they thought Eddie's Auntie Joan was the bollocks. Joan had been the talk of the prison for the next few days. Ed was only a nipper when his mum died, and his aunt had all but brought him up. Joanie had always been a real card, and Eddie had great pleasure entertaining the other lags with stories of his childhood.

Putting Joan's letter back in its envelope, Ed opened the next one. It was from his pal, Dougie.

Hi Ed,

I hope you're doing OK, mate. Sorry I haven't been in touch for a while, but as you can imagine, life gets pretty hectic this time of year. Anyway, I wanted to be the first to tell you that Vicki gave birth to a little girl last weekend. She was adamant we call her Jessica – I didn't get a say in the matter.

As Ed's eyes welled up, he screwed up the letter. He couldn't read the rest; it was far too upsetting for him. Jessica would have been blooming herself by now and they would have had a wonderful Christmas this year. Jess was so full of plans for the new baby, God rest her soul. Overcome by emotion, Ed turned over, lay flat on his mattress and sobbed his heart out.

Over in icy Rainham, Joyce was all of a fluster as she prepared for the arrival of Polly's parents.

Raymond and Polly had arranged their wedding for June next year and, with the parents not having yet met, Raymond had reluctantly agreed to Joyce inviting her soon-to-be in-laws over on Christmas Eve.

As soon as her husband walked into the room, Joyce put her hands on her hips. 'What have you got on? You're not wearing that, Stanley. I thought I told you to put your nice grey suit on. Polly's parents are upper class, for goodness' sake!'

Stanley for once argued his point. 'This is my best shirt and trousers, Joycie. I feel ridiculous wearing a suit indoors. Can't I just wear this?'

Joyce shook her head vehemently. 'I won't have you embarrassing me in front of Polly's parents. Now go and put that suit on. I've bought you a new red tie, so make sure you wear that as well.'

Annoyed, Stanley punched the wall as he trudged upstairs. 'I preferred you when you were ill, you fucking old bat,' he mumbled.

A few hundred yards down the road, Frankie's day was going from bad to worse. Jed's father always threw a big party on Christmas Eve and Frankie was absolutely dreading it.

'Frankie, take these sandwiches into the other room and then you can help me prepare the meat platters,' Alice ordered.

Aware that his girlfriend had barely said a word all day, Jed followed her into the lounge. 'What's up? You've had a face like a smacked arse since you woke up this morning.'

'I don't feel up to this party, Jed. Do you mind if I go back to the trailer and have an early night?'

Jed grabbed her arm roughly. He was getting sick of Frankie's black moods. 'You're my girlfriend and you'll stay 'ere and make an effort with my family and friends. My mum and dad have fallen over backwards to make you feel welcome and all you do is throw their kindness back in their faces. Well, I ain't putting up with it no more, so you'd best start pulling your fucking socks up.'

As Jed let go of her arm and stormed from the room, Frankie ran to the toilet and locked the door. She felt so lonely. She couldn't even ring Joey, because he was at his work's Christmas party. Frankie sat on the toilet seat and cried. Memories of Christmases with her mum and dad came flooding back and she wished she could go back in time.

Her mum had always made such a big fuss about Christmas. Frankie used to love it as a child, but over the years she'd felt too old and cool to bother with the preparation or the big day itself.

Frankie guiltily put her head in her hands. Last year, her mum had asked her and Joey to help her with the Christmas shopping and she'd begged them to decorate the tree and the house with her. Both she and Joey had laughed in Jessica's face. Neither had known it would be their mum's last Christmas and Frankie now felt full of remorse. She hadn't appreciated her family life at the time, but after living with Jed's parents, she bloody well did now.

Her reminiscing was ended by her boyfriend's angry voice. 'Frankie, get out 'ere now. You're meant to be helping my mum,' he yelled.

Frankie took a deep breath. 'I'll be out in five minutes. I've just been sick, Jed,' she lied, as she pulled the chain.

Hearing his footsteps walk away, Frankie checked her eyes in the mirror. They weren't red and there were no signs that she had been crying. She unlocked the bathroom door. The guests had started to arrive, and their loud, coarse voices could be heard a mile off.

Determined to make Jed happy, Frankie plastered a smile on her face and walked into the kitchen. 'Sorry about that, Alice, I came over a bit queasy. Now, what can I do to help you?'

Alice patted her arm. 'You go and sit yourself down with Jed,' she said kindly. 'I'm all done here now.'

Jed was sitting in the lounge talking to a couple Frankie had never seen before. 'You all right, babe?' he asked, nodding at her to sit down on the sofa next to him.

Frankie smiled and sidled up to him. 'I feel much better now.'

Jed cuddled her. 'About time too,' he whispered sarcastically.

As the Bentley pulled on to the gravel, Joyce clapped her hands in glee. 'They're here! Oh, my God, look at the car, Stanley. Thank Christ I made you hide yours.'

Stanley said nothing while Joyce first checked her appearance in the mirror, then ran to answer the door. She looked ridiculous in the full-length blue dress she was wearing. She looked like she was going to a fucking ball. As for making him leave his car at Dougie and Vicki's house, Stanley was lost for words.

'We can't have Polly's parents thinking that we have no money, Stanley,' she said. 'That Sierra of yours is an utter embarrassment, you'll have to get rid of it for the day.'

As his mother opened the front door, Raymond looked at her in horror. Not only was she speaking like she had a plum in her mouth, she was also dressed as though she was going to a film premiere.

'Welcome to my home. Do come in,' Joyce said, adding a little curtsey.

'Hello. Pleased to meet you,' Polly's mum said.

'All right, sweetheart,' said Polly's dad.

Overcome by her own self-importance, it wasn't until Polly's parents stepped inside the house that Joyce noticed their clothes. Polly's dad, Dickie, was the spitting image of the character Boycie out of *Only Fools and Horses*.

Dickie was wearing blue jeans, tan shoes and a tan leather jacket and instead of sounding extremely upper class, which Joyce had imagined, his voice had a strong south London lilt to it.

Jenny, his wife, also had jeans on. With her knee-high boots, short fur jacket and short blonde hair, she reminded Joycie of the famous singer, Lulu.

Joycie was mortified. She and Stanley were all done up to the nines and Polly's parents were dressed as if they were off to some seedy strip club.

'Now, would you like a drink or something?' Joyce asked in her ultra-posh voice.

Dickie slapped Joyce on the arse and winked at Jenny. 'I'll have whatever's on offer, you little raver!'

Back in south London, Eddie waited until he heard Stuart snoring before he opened the rest of his letters.

It was Johnny, his little mate the screw, who had got hold of a torch for him. Ed wasn't a great sleeper at the best of times and the torch had proved to be a lifeline for him, because he sometimes read under the covers well into the early hours.

The letter from Dougie earlier had upset Eddie immensely. Doug's wife, Vicki, had been Jessica's best friend. Ed had introduced them years ago at a party and they'd been inseparable ever since.

Truth be known, Eddie was honoured that Vicki was naming her child in memory of his wife, but seeing it written in black and white brought everything back that he'd tried so hard to move on from. Over the last couple of months, he'd hardly thought about Jessica's death, but reading that letter had done him up like a kipper.

Eddie put his hand under his bunk. He'd Sellotaped the torch underneath, so nosy screws like Carter couldn't find it. He could see that one of the envelopes contained a Christmas card, so he opened that first.

Hello Ed.
Hope you're doing OK, bruv? I hate the fact we've fallen out. We went through so much together and I want to make things right between us. Please send me a VO so I can visit you in the New Year.
Happy Christmas,
Ronny

Ed looked at the front of the card and smiled. Ronny had always had the brains of a rocking horse and only he could send a card with the words 'May your Christmas be jolly' scrawled across the front whilst Eddie was sitting in clink for murdering his wife.

Everybody else had just sent letters, apart from two, who had sent cards inscribed 'Thinking of you'.

Eddie was down to his last two letters now. He knew from the writing and the air-mail sticker that one was from Gary and Ricky, who were currently on holiday, and he decided to save that until last. He loved hearing from his sons. He'd had a right go at them for not telling him that the O'Haras had turned up at Jessica's funeral. Raymond had made him see sense and Ed had soon after made it up with both of them.

In prison, lots of things got blown out of proportion. Living your life in a goldfish bowl wasn't exactly easy and lags had far too much time on their hands to mull things over and get paranoid. That's why that poor sod had hung himself recently when he hadn't heard from his old woman. The unfortunate bastard had convinced himself that she was having an affair with his brother.

Ed put Gary and Ricky's envelope to one side and studied the other. The handwriting was kind of unique and professional and the postmark was from Southend-on-Sea. Eddie ripped it open. He had no idea who the letter was from, but guessed by the handwriting that it had to be a woman.

Hi Eddie,

I hope you don't mind me writing to you, but I just felt that I had to.

Firstly, I would like to say how upset I am by what has happened to you. I understand your predicament more than most as, in a way, I obviously played a big part in it. I have read all the press coverage and I would really like to help you. I am willing to stand up in court on your behalf. I would love to come and visit you so that we can have a proper discussion about this. If you do not want my help and do not reply, I will not think any less of you.

My thoughts are constantly with you.

Take care,

Mrs Smith x

Eddie knew immediately who the letter was from. He'd called himself Mr Smith when he'd hired Gina, the private detective, and he knew that by using the same name, she was talking in code.

He read the letter again. Gina had fancied him rotten – he had known that at the time.

Eddie lay back on his bed and smiled. He couldn't wait to ring Larry, his solicitor. Gina had been, and obviously still was, under his spell and if Ed could keep her sweet, she could be the difference between him doing fifteen years or seven.

Frankie stood in the corner of the O'Hara's living room. Apart from her dad's old friend Patrick Murphy, she didn't know a soul and she felt as out of place as a cat in a dogs' home.

Even though she loved Jed, Frankie wasn't at all comfortable with the gypsy culture. In her opinion, the women were rough and common, spoke in a language of their own and there had already been one big punch-up. One youngish mum had accused another bird of stealing her gold and, seconds later, had started walloping her with her baby buggy.

As the argument between the two women started up again, Frankie's eyes scanned the room for Jed. He was nowhere to be seen, as usual.

Suddenly all hell broke loose and, frightened for her own safety and that of her unborn baby, Frankie ducked a flying glass and ran from the room, screaming. Visibly shaken, she finally found Jed in the garden. He was talking to his cousin Sammy and two scantily dressed girls.

'What's up?' he asked as she fell into his arms.

'Everybody's fighting in the lounge, Jed. I nearly got hit in the face by a glass.'

Winking at Sammy and the two birds, Jed led Frankie towards the trailer. 'Let's get you to bed, babe. I'm sorry for shouting at you earlier. This Christmas must be really difficult for you and sometimes I'm such a dinlo, as I forget what you've been through this year.'

Frankie put her pyjamas on and smiled as Jed handed her a cup of hot chocolate. 'Thanks,' she said gratefully.

Jed insisted that Frankie got into bed and then sat on the edge as he tucked her in. 'You don't mind if I go back to the party, do ya?'

Frankie shook her head. Just because she didn't feel part of the gypsy way of life, it didn't mean to say that Jed shouldn't enjoy himself. Frankie kissed him on the lips. 'You go and have fun,' she told him.

As Jed shut the trailer door, he smirked. Have fun he most certainly would.

Still unable to sleep, Eddie switched on his torch again. He'd wanted to save Gary and Ricky's letter, so he had something to look forward to on Christmas morning, but his insomnia had made him change his mind. Ripping open the envelope, Eddie grinned. Now he had banished the twins from his world, Gary and Ricky were his life.

As much as Ed had loved Jess, what Frankie and Joey had done was unforgivable in his fragile mind, and even though they were all he had left of his beloved deceased wife, he no longer cared about either of them. One had turned out to be a poof and the other had fallen in love with the gypsy son of his biggest enemy, so the pair of them were now history as far as he was concerned.

Ed chuckled as he began to read the letter. Both Ricky and Gary were fuckers for the birds and they always filled him in on their escapades.

The paragraph at the bottom was the moment Ed's smile turned into an angry snarl:

PS You told us not to keep anything from you, so here goes. Rumour has it that Joey is gay and he has a boyfriend called Dominic. He turned up at . . .

Eddie's pride wouldn't allow him to read the last line. If the lags found out about Joey, he'd be the laughing stock of the poxy prison.

Ripping the letter into shreds, Ed turned off his torch. His son repulsed him, and as for that fucking Dominic, if he ever saw him again, he wouldn't just threaten him, he would bastard well kill him.

Back in Rainham, Joyce had a look of disappointment etched across her face.

Polly's parents were nothing like she had envisaged at all. Dickie was flash, loud and loved the sound of his own voice, and his wife Jenny was bordering on alcoholic, and was drinking her and Stanley out of house and home.

As Jenny stood up and started dancing around the room, holding her glass aloft, Stanley nudged Joyce.

'I can't believe you made us dress up like a pair of prized pricks to meet these two,' he hissed.

'I didn't know they were going to behave like this, did I?' Joyce hissed back.

'I think it's time for a toast to the happy couple. Have you got any champagne in the house?' Dickie said in a loud, annoying voice. He didn't just look like Boycie, he sounded like him as well.

Joyce scuttled out into the kitchen. She had been so desperate to impress the in-laws, that she'd spent over fifty quid yesterday on just two bottles of champagne.

'Here we are,' she said proudly, handing one to Dickie.

Dickie looked at the label on the bottle and laughed. 'We can't drink rubbish like this. I had to drink this shit at a party recently and it tasted like bloody antifreeze. Jenny, go to the car and get the champagne we brought out of the boot.'

Extremely drunk, Jenny picked up her husband's keys, lost her balance and fell straight on top of the coffee table.

'Are you OK, Mum?' Polly asked in an unconcerned voice. She was used to her mother getting in these states. The falling over was nothing she hadn't seen a hundred times before.

Raymond stood up. 'Let me help you, Jenny,' he said politely, as he picked her up off the table.

Joyce was mortified. She looked at Stanley. 'I don't fucking like 'em one little bit,' she whispered.

Stanley squeezed his wife's hand. 'My sentiments exactly, dear.'

Less than a mile down the road from Joyce and Stanley, Frankie was unable to get off to sleep, due to the loudness of the music. She wasn't that bothered she was just glad to be in the safety of the trailer, away from the brawling guests.

As Tammy Wynette's, 'Stand by your Man' was played for about the tenth time, Frankie smiled. She had known very little about country and western music until she met Jed. 'Stand by your Man' was their favourite song and they'd agreed that when they finally got married, they would choose it as their first dance.

As the song came to an end once more, Frankie pulled the quilt over her head. She and Jed had certainly had their ups and downs, but she still couldn't wait to become his wife.

112

Frankie O'Hara had a certain ring to it, and with a bit of luck once they got married, they could buy their own place and get away from his parents.

Deciding to speak to Jed about setting a date very soon, Frankie shut her eyes. Within minutes, she drifted off into a contented sleep.

Jed O'Hara grunted and groaned with ecstasy. He was in the stables having his cock sucked by a forward little filly called Mary.

Seeing his cousin Sammy shafting her mate just a few feet away, Jed smiled. 'Do you remember what we were doing this time last year, Sammy boy?' he shouted out.

Sammy paused, then laughed. 'Yeah, we were terrorising that old shitcunt, weren't we?'

Grabbing Mary's hair, Jed ordered her to turn over. He spread the cheeks of her arse and rammed himself into her anus. Pumping away, Jed ignored Mary's gasps of pain. All he could think of was Harry Mitchell's battered corpse.

'Ahh, you slut, fucking hell!' Jed screamed, as he shot his seed.

Jed's orgasm was so intense that it seemed to go on for ages. Releasing his cock from Mary's arse, Jed stood up and grinned. He couldn't wait to fuck Frankie while thinking of what he'd done to her grandfather. Now, that orgasm would be mind-blowing.

CHAPTER TWELVE

1989

It was ten o'clock on a wet, cold Friday night in March when Frankie felt her first real contraction. She had experienced slight stomach pains that afternoon and had begged Jed not to go out and leave her again.

'I've gotta take a chordy motor down to Norfolk, Frankie. You'll be OK. You ain't due for another couple of weeks.'

'Please, Jed. I keep getting these funny twinges and I'm scared. Can't you deliver the car another day?' she'd pleaded.

Jed hugged her. 'I can't, babe. It's gotta be done tonight. Mum and Dad are only next door and I'll have me phone with me. Now we've got a chavvie on the way, we need the money, don't we?'

As another contraction ripped through her, Frankie screamed in pain. If only her mum were still alive, she would have known exactly what to do. Absolutely terrified, Frankie rang Jed's mobile. It was switched off.

Holding her swollen stomach, she staggered towards his parents' place and banged on their door. 'Alice, open up, I think the baby's coming,' she sobbed.

Alice took one look at her and told Jimmy to go and find his keys. 'We'll go in the Land Cruiser, not that poxy truck,' she ordered.

Alice sat in the back with Frankie and did her best to comfort her. 'There's no need to be frit to death, everything will be fine,' she said soothingly.

Still clutching her mobile phone, Frankie handed it to Alice. 'Ring Jed again for me. I couldn't get through when I tried,' she said tearfully.

Alice was annoyed as she tried her son's number. How could Jed have his phone switched off when he knew his girlfriend could go into labour any minute? 'Typical bloody man,' she mumbled as she handed the phone back to Frankie.

Jimmy, who had barely said a word so far on the journey, immediately stuck up for his son. 'Give the boy a break, Alice. He's out grafting to support his family. Them phone batteries don't last long, you know.'

Missing her own family more than ever, Frankie scrolled down the names and rang Joey. As luck would have it, he answered immediately.

'Oh, Joey, thank God you answered. I think the baby's coming. I'm on the way to Oldchurch Hospital with Jed's parents.'

Joey gasped and whispered the words 'Frankie' and 'baby' to Dominic. 'We'll get a taxi,' Dominic said, nudging him.

'Frankie, hold tight. Me and Dom are in a bar up in Liverpool Street. We're leaving right now and it should only take us half-hour or so to get to the hospital.'

Frankie ended the call and screamed as another contraction ripped through her.

Alice sat in silence as they continued the journey. She was fuming that Frankie had invited that brother of hers. In her eyes all homosexuals were disgusting creatures, and Alice was thankful that they didn't exist in the travelling community. She glared at Frankie.

'He ain't bringing that boyfriend of his with him, is he?' she asked nastily.

'Yes, he is, actually. Dominic's a lovely bloke,' Frankie said, silently cursing Jed. Alice had only found out about Joey's sexuality a few weeks ago, when her drunken boyfriend had made a joke of it after dinner one evening.

As Jimmy drove at speed through a large puddle and splashed some people at a bus stop, he smiled to himself.

When he'd heard that Eddie Mitchell's son batted the other way, he'd felt like throwing a party. Even though Frankie was now part of his own family, Jimmy still despised her father and every kick in the teeth that Mitchell received made Jimmy that little bit happier. Eddie killing his old woman by accident with a machine gun had been the funniest story Jimmy had ever heard.

Unbeknown to his girlfriend, Jed and his cousin Sammy were in the Berwick Manor in Rainham. Although Jed and Sammy were currently earning a bundle by selling hooky motors, they had decided to take this weekend off to go out and party.

As the ecstasy tablet he'd just taken began to take effect, Jed smiled as he nudged Sammy and pointed out the two little birds that were giggling and staring their way.

'I love this tune and them birds are well fit,' Sammy said as the DJ put on Richie Rich's 'Salsa House'.

About to bowl over to where they were dancing, Sammy grabbed Jed's arm. ''Ere, cacker, Sally and Julie have just walked in. Dordie, they're heading this way.'

Jed took a deep breath. He knew he was probably about to receive a barrage of abuse and he really couldn't give a fuck.

He and Sammy had stopped seeing Sally and Julie a good few months ago. Both girls had got too serious, so the lads had shagged them one last time just before Christmas, then ignored their numerous phone calls.

Sammy had recently moved his girlfriend, Kerry, into his trailer so, for obvious reasons, both Jed and Sammy had recently changed their mobile numbers.

Having now come up properly on his E, Jed was in the mood for taking the piss. 'All right, Sally? You've put on a bit of weight, ain't ya, girl?' he said laughing.

Sammy nodded politely at Julie. He wasn't quite as brazen as his cousin. 'How you doing?' he asked her awkwardly.

Julie ignored Sammy and nudged her best friend. 'Tell him then, Sal.'

116

Sally was physically shaking as she turned back towards Jed. 'I'm pregnant,' she said bluntly.

'Congratulations! I ain't been near them old shitty drawers of yours for months, so what's that got to do with me?' Jed asked cockily.

Sally looked him in the eye. Jed was so good looking that he turned her to jelly. 'It's definitely yours,' she told him bluntly.

Being pilled up and being told that you were about to become a father by a bird you had no interest in wasn't the best mixture in the world. Grabbing Sally's arm, Jed marched her outside. The music in the club was blaring and he needed to get this sorted.

Once out in the cold, crisp air, Jed quickly came to his senses. He dug deep into the pocket of his jeans and pulled out a large wad of money. 'You told me you were on the pill,' he said angrily, as he handed her five fifty-pound notes.

'I was on the pill, but something obviously went wrong. Why are you giving me money?' Sally asked, bemused.

'To get rid of it, you dinlo. You're lucky I'm giving you anything. I don't even know if the chavvie's mine,' Jed said sarcastically.

Sally threw the money back at him. 'I don't want your money, Jed. I'm keeping this baby whether you like it or not.'

Getting angrier by the second, Jed grabbed her roughly by the arm and dragged her around the side of the building. He pushed her up against the wall and squeezed her face between his thumb and fingers.

'You do as I say and get rid of it. If you don't, I'm telling you, I'll get rid of it for ya.'

'What's going on? Are you OK?' Julie screamed, as she ran over to her friend.

As Jed let go of her face, Sally slid down the wall, sobbing.

'Get away from her, you bastard,' Julie screamed.

Realising that Jed was probably only seconds away from clumping Sally, Sammy waded in and dragged him away. 'Come on, let's get back inside,' Sammy said.

117

Unable to resist a parting shot, Jed turned around, slung the fifty-pound notes on the ground, then pointed his finger at Sally. 'I meant what I said, you silly fucking slag,' he screamed.

As Jed and Sammy disappeared out of sight, Sally and Julie clung to one another. Both girls had thought they had hit the jackpot when they'd met Jed and Sammy but, as they watched the fifty-pound notes blow off in the wind, they realised that they didn't really know the boys at all.

Inside the hospital, Alice O'Hara was doing Frankie's head in. 'Pant – you're not panting properly,' Alice yelled at her.

'You're doing fine. The baby's not quite ready yet,' the midwife said kindly.

'I want my brother. Get Joey for me,' Frankie shouted. She had never felt pain like this in her life and, with only Alice by her side, she was incredibly frightened.

'You can't have a mush in 'ere, especially one like your bleedin' brother,' Alice said spitefully.

'Please get my brother. I think he's outside,' Frankie pleaded with one of the nurses.

The blonde-haired nurse felt extremely sorry for Frankie. She was only young and the rough older lady with her wasn't exactly sensitive.

Joey had tears in his eyes as he entered the room. He walked around the other side of the bed, opposite where Alice was standing, and grasped his sister's hand. 'How you doing?' he asked awkwardly. He could sense Alice glaring at him.

'It don't half hurt, Joey,' Frankie sobbed.

'Where's Jed?' Joey asked. He'd been fully expecting to see him.

'He's out earning money,' Alice said coldly.

Joey smiled. 'I'm Joey, Frankie's brother. It's nice to meet you.'

Alice ignored him and stood up. 'I'm popping out to see my Jimmy for a bit. We need to get in touch with family, let 'em know the chavvie's on its way.'

As Alice left the room, both Frankie and Joey were relieved.

'She's been driving me mad,' Frankie said quietly.

'Sod your luck having her as a mother-in-law,' Joey replied jokingly.

The midwife winked at Joey. 'My sentiments exactly,' she said.

Back in the Berwick Manor, Jed had forgotten about the earlier incident with Sally. He and Sammy had just dropped another E each and they had also blagged the two little birds they'd had their eye on earlier. They'd even persuaded them to come back to the trailer in Tilbury with them.

'We fit then?' Jed asked, as Dawn, the one he was sweet on, finished the last of her drink. The other girl was called Lisa, and Jed and Sammy had already discussed who was having who.

Dawn and Lisa giggled as they followed the lads out of the club. Both girls had only got into the rave scene recently and the tablets Jed and Sammy had given them had kind of knocked them for six.

Outside the club, Jed grabbed Dawn and pushed her against the wall. He kissed her passionately, shoved his hand up her miniskirt and teased her by putting his hand inside her knickers. 'You want me, don't ya?' he asked, unaware that he had three very interested spectators.

When Jed grabbed Dawn's hand and nigh on dragged her across the car park, Stacey, Paige and Demi stayed hidden behind the wall.

'Are you sure it was Jed? It is dark out here,' Demi asked, puzzled.

Seeing Jed clamber into his pick-up truck, Stacey nodded. 'That's his motor. I've seen Frankie in it with him.'

Paige agreed. 'That's definitely him. I'd recognise his swagger anywhere.'

Paige, Demi and Stacey had all been friends with Frankie for years. They'd even been with her on the night she'd first met Jed in the Berwick Manor.

'What we gonna do? She's due to have his baby soon,' Stacey asked the other two.

Paige shrugged. None of them had seen much of Frankie since she'd moved in with Jed. 'I don't think we should get involved. My dad used to work with gypsies and he reckons they shouldn't be crossed,' Demi said.

'Sod that – I don't wanna get involved, then,' Paige agreed.

Stacey was still in shock as she followed the other two girls into the club. She had known Frankie a lot longer than the others – since infants' school. They had always been very close until recently and Stacey knew, as a good friend, it should be her duty to tell Frankie.

As she paid her entrance fee, Stacey shivered. She didn't like the look of that Jed, there was something about him that gave her the creeps.

Back at the hospital, Frankie was in the final stages of her labour.

'Push, just fucking push,' Alice yelled.

Insisting that Alice move out of her way, the midwife spoke gently to Frankie. 'I can see the baby's head. We need you to push again, Frankie. Take deep breaths, my love.'

Frankie was petrified. Joey had passed out ten minutes ago and had to be carried out of the room. 'I can't push any more,' she screamed tearfully.

'Yes, you can. Come on, you can do it,' the midwife urged her kindly.

'For fuck's sake, Frankie, push,' Alice shouted.

The midwife turned to Alice. 'You are not helping me or Frankie by shouting and swearing. One more word and I shall have to ask you to leave the room.'

Wishing more than anything in the world that her own mum or Jed was by her side, Frankie shut her eyes and pushed as hard as she could.

'That's it, Frankie, you're doing great. Now take a deep breath and see if you can push one more time.'

Frankie screamed blue murder as she strained and pushed with all her might.

As the midwife grabbed the baby and tapped it on the back, it immediately let out its first cry.

'What sex is it?' Alice asked, trying to get a closer look at the child.

The midwife ignored Alice and smiled at Frankie. 'You have a beautiful little girl, Frankie,' she said.

Unable to control her emotions, Alice leaped up and down with excitement. 'Thank you, God. Thank you so much.' Finally, after years of want and heartbreak, Alice had got her baby girl.

Over in Tilbury, Jed had just been given a blinding blow-job by the insatiable Dawn. He'd already shagged her twice and she still couldn't keep her hands off him. Taking a breather, he zipped up his jeans and walked over to Sammy.

'Did ya shag yours? That Dawn's a right little goer,' he whispered in his cousin's ear.

Sammy nodded and laughed. 'Where's ya phone, Jed? My battery's dead and I'd better phone home, make some excuse.'

Dawn and Lisa were both inside the dirty toilet, probably swapping stories.

Seeing them reappear, Sammy went outside to call his bird. 'Sorry I never rang you earlier, Kerry. Me and Jed only fucking broke down in that motor. We didn't want the gavvers on our tail, so we did a runner from it and we've just found a B&B back in Norfolk,' he lied.

'As long as you're OK, that's all that matters. I'm cooking us a nice piece of roast beef for when you get home,' Kerry replied.

Sammy smiled as he ended the phone call. He'd moved in a gorjer girl, just like Jed had. Travelling girls were too much grief, but choose a gorjer girl and you can get away with murder. Jed and he always stuck to the same stories, so unless they were caught red-handed, there was little chance of either of them getting rumbled.

When the phone started to ring, Sammy automatically answered it, thinking it was Kerry again. 'What's up?' he asked, as he recognised Jimmy O'Hara's voice.

As Jimmy waffled on, Sammy ran into the trailer and urged his cousin to come outside.

'What?' Jed shouted, as Sammy handed him the phone.

'Jed, I dunno where you are, but you'd better get your arse up Oldchurch. Frankie's had the chavvie. Your mother's over the moon, son, you've got a baby girl.'

Jimmy ended the call and laughed. He was a man of few words, but showed his emotions in other ways. The little girl that had just been born was an O'Hara and, with Eddie Mitchell looking at a life sentence, Jimmy would be its only grandad.

CHAPTER THIRTEEN

Jed drove like a lunatic as he made his way towards Oldchurch Hospital. Sammy was sitting beside him and they'd just dumped the two girls at an all-night cab office in Dagenham.

'I'll give you a call,' Jed told Dawn, slinging a tenner at her for the fare. She'd already written her number down for him earlier.

'Good luck. I hope your dad's OK,' Dawn shouted as Jed drove off.

Obviously, Jed had had to lie to her. He'd told her that his dad had been involved in a bad car accident. Telling her his fiancée had just given birth to their first child would have gone down like a sack of spuds.

Sammy turned down the volume on the radio. Now the girls were out of the way, they could talk properly. 'Congratulations, Jeddy boy. I bet you're excited, ain't ya? What did you say you were gonna call her?'

Jed smiled. He couldn't wait to meet his daughter. 'Georgie. Me mum chose it. You remember her sister, don't ya, the one that died of cancer? Her name was Georgina. Frankie didn't like it at first, so we made a deal. We put Georgina on the birth certificate for me mum's sake, then we shorten it to Georgie.'

Remembering Jed's choice of name if the baby had been born a boy, Sammy laughed. 'Bet you're hoping for a mush next time, ain't ya?'

Jed grinned. 'Yeah, I'll have to knock Frankie up again. Little Harry boy'll be running about before you know it.'

With the effects of the ecstasy tablets still firmly in their system, both Jed and Sammy burst out laughing.

Even though it was now the early hours of the morning, Frankie was still wide awake. She'd just been moved into a little room and Jed's family had been told by the midwife to let her and the baby get some rest. They still hadn't gone home – Frankie could hear Alice's voice in the corridor. Jed's mother had driven Frankie bonkers; she hadn't left the baby alone. All Frankie had wanted was some time on her own with Joey and Dom, but Alice refused to budge.

'We'll come back tomorrow, sis,' Joey promised as he and Dominic had left.

Frankie felt sorry for her brother. The O'Haras were a loud, overpowering family and Joey had obviously felt like a fish out of water among them.

Staring at her beautiful daughter lying in the cot next to her, Frankie took in her features. She had a mop of dark hair, a cute button nose and long eyelashes like Jed's.

Frankie thought of her own family and the odd tear ran down her cheek. Her mum would have been ecstatic and so proud. Little Georgie was exceptionally beautiful and Frankie was sure that her dad would have accepted her in time, even though he hated Jed. Frankie thought of her nan and grandad. Her nan, especially, used to drive her mad at times, but Frankie wished she could be here now.

As baby Georgie began to cry, so did Frankie. Her whole family had been ripped to shreds and the thought of bringing her baby up with Alice and Jimmy O'Hara's parental guidance filled Frankie with dread.

Jed spotted his family immediately as he ran towards the maternity ward. His mum, dad, brothers, aunts, uncles, cousins – they were all there.

Alice grabbed her son in a bear hug. 'Chucked us out, the old rabbit's crotch of a nurse did. Oh, Jed, go and see Georgie girl. She's the most beautiful little chavvie I've ever seen in my life. Looks just like you, she does. Thank you boy, you've made me the happiest mother alive.'

Filled with emotion, Jed went off in search of Frankie.

'They're both asleep,' the nurse on duty told him bluntly. She'd had enough of this particular family earlier and felt incredibly sorry for Frankie, whom she liked immensely.

Jed had never taken no for an answer in his life and he wasn't about to start now. 'I'm the child's father. I have every right to see my woman and my daughter and if you try to stop me, I promise you'll regret it.'

Desperate to avoid a scene, the nurse led him to Frankie's room. It had been her idea to put Frankie in a side room, as she didn't want the O'Haras upsetting all the other families on the maternity ward. 'Wait here,' she ordered, as she opened the door.

Frankie had her eyes shut, but was still awake. Her body felt battered and bruised, but the nurses had told her she'd had a relatively easy labour compared to most first-time mothers.

'Your boyfriend's here, Frankie. Are you awake?' the nurse asked.

Frankie opened her eyes and smiled. She wished Jed had been there for the birth, but she wasn't particularly angry with him. He'd only been out working, and Georgie was so gorgeous that any earlier annoyance had now evaporated.

As Jed strolled into the room, he felt his chest swell with pride. Tears filled his eyes as he stared at his perfect daughter. 'Can I hold her?' he whispered.

Frankie nodded. 'I'm your dad, Georgie girl,' Jed said, as he tenderly lifted his daughter out of her cot and planted a kiss on her forehead.

The scene was an emotional one. Jed kissed Frankie, handed her the baby and sat on the edge of the bed. 'I'm really sorry you had to go through it on your own, babe. I'll never forgive meself for not being here with ya. I'll make it up to ya though, I promise.'

As baby Georgie gurgled, Frankie handed her back to Jed. 'Why wasn't your phone on? You promised me that it would be.'

'Sammy and I had murders, Frankie. The chordy motor broke down and we had to do a runner and leave it in the middle of the road. I had so many phone calls to make to sort stuff, then the battery went dead on me. I'll tell you what I'll do, I'll buy another phone. If I've got two, you'll always be able to get me on one of the numbers. You and little Georgie girl are my life, Frankie, and I promise I will never let either of you down ever again.'

Joey turned up at his grandparents' house at nine o'clock the following morning. He was on his way to the hospital with Dominic, but had decided to deliver the news of Frankie's baby in person. It had been too late to ring them last night, so Joey decided to pop in while he waited for Mothercare to open.

'Hello boys, what a lovely surprise,' Joyce exclaimed, as she opened the front door.

Ushering them into the living room, she went off to the pigeon shed to locate her husband. Ordering Stanley to get his arse indoors and make polite conversation, Joycie made a brew.

'How's the driving lessons going, Dominic?' she shouted from the kitchen.

'Not great, Mrs Smith. I ran over a cat last week. I think the instructor is losing patience with me,' Dom replied honestly.

Joey laughed. Dominic had promised to buy a nice sports car when he finally passed. Trouble was, he was no Stirling Moss, and had already failed five tests. His inability to pass had since become a standing joke between the pair of them.

'Hello, nice weather, isn't it?' Stanley said politely, as he plonked himself in the armchair.

Joyce scowled at her husband as she brought the tea tray in. 'You've got pigeon shit all over them trousers, Stanley. Go and change 'em,' she shouted.

Joey grabbed Stanley's arm. 'Stay there, Grandad. Dom and I can't stay long. We've got a cab waiting outside. I only popped in because I really need to tell you both something.'

'What's up?' Joyce asked.

'Frankie had a little girl early hours of this morning. Beautiful she is. Six pound, seven ounces and she's called her Georgie.'

Joyce pursed her lips. 'Frankie made her choice, Joey. Everything that's happened is partly her fault and I'll never forgive her for ruining her own mother's funeral. We want nothing more to do with her, do we, Stanley?'

Stanley nodded automatically. There was no point in him saying anything, nobody ever listened to him.

Desperate to bridge the gap between his grandparents and sister, Joey tried a different tactic. 'Look, Nan, I was up that hospital last night and I met Jed's family properly for the first time. Jed weren't even there, no one could get hold of him. His mum is awful, really common, and if we don't do something, I'm worried what will happen to Frankie and the kid.'

Joyce wasn't in the mood for sob stories. 'Silly little cow made her own bed, let her bleedin' well lie in it,' she said coldly.

Joey stood up and urged Dom to do the same. His nan was so obstinate at times, there was no reasoning with her.

Stanley said goodbye to the lads and was relieved when they left. Ever since he'd found out Joey and Dominic were lovers, he was at a loss knowing what to say to them.

Joycie hugged both Joey and Dom. As they got into the cab, she waved and slammed the front door.

Aware that Joyce was crying, Stanley ran into the hallway. 'What's the matter?' he asked.

'Frankie, the baby, everything, Stanley. If our Jess was here, she would know how to handle all this. If only she could give us a sign or something.'

Stanley took his wife into his arms. 'Life's a funny old game, but one thing you can guarantee is I'll always be here for you, darling.'

*   *   *

127

Frankie wasn't having a very good morning. She felt sore, tired and had had more visitors than a female knocking shop in a men's prison.

As Jed showed out yet another eight people she'd never met before or ever wanted to see again, Frankie started to cry.

'What's up?' Jed asked, rushing over to her bed.

'I'm tired, Jed. I don't want no more visitors,' she sobbed.

Jed held Frankie in his arms. 'Leave us alone for five minutes, Mum,' he ordered.

Alice had sat in the room all morning. She was besotted with her granddaughter and it was unbearable to be parted from her for even five minutes.

'Why don't me and your dad sit outside and look after Georgie girl, while you and Frankie have some time to yourselves?' Alice offered.

'No, leave her here,' Frankie said abruptly.

Gesticulating for his mum to leave them alone, Jed waited for the door to shut before he spoke. 'Are you OK, babe? Let me know what's wrong and I'll sort it.'

Frankie clung to him. 'All these people coming in and out. I feel like shit and I hate it, Jed. Your mum won't leave me or the baby alone. I know everybody has brought nice presents for us and I do appreciate it, but I need to get some sleep and rest now. Please tell them all to go home, Jed, please.'

Jed sighed. 'No one means to be a nuisance, babe. Travelling families are like this and you're part of one now. Everyone gathers when a baby is born, it's the way we're brought up.'

'But I ain't got no family of me own here,' Frankie sobbed.

Seeing how distressed she was, Jed knew he had no choice other than to go and speak to his family. 'Listen, I'll go and get rid of everyone. I might even pop home and have a shower meself. I'll take some of these presents home, shall I? And I'll come back later when you've had some sleep.'

Frankie nodded. 'Come back on your own though, Jed. I want to spend some time with just you and Georgie.'

Jed nodded, kissed her and left the room. His mother was not going to be happy, that was for sure.

As Jed shut the door, Frankie lay back on the bed and shut her eyes. She'd had to put up with Jed's cousins, aunts, uncles, brothers; even that horrible Shannon had sat beside her bed for ages.

They'd brought nice presents, mainly gold, and Frankie had been given loads of money. The clothes they'd got for Georgie were a bit over the top, but Frankie had been polite and thanked them.

As the door opened, Frankie's heart went over. If it was Alice, she would scream.

'All right, sis?'

Frankie immediately sat bolt upright. She cried as she hugged both Joey and Dominic. 'I'm so pleased to see you. I've been lumbered with Jed's family all day and they've done my head in.'

Joey handed her two big sacks. 'These are from me and Dom,' he said.

As Georgie started to cry, Frankie urged Joey to pick her up. Joey rocked Georgie, rubbed her back and spoke gently to her. 'I'm your uncle Joey, your mummy's twin brother,' he whispered in her ear.

Dominic smiled as the baby stopped crying. 'You're a natural, Joey. Don't you leave me and go straight, will you?' he said jokingly.

Frankie was thrilled with the presents Joey and Dominic had brought with them. Babygros, rattles, dummies, a little ski-jacket, booties, a massive teddy bear, they had literally thought of everything. Their presents were so much more practical than any of the others she'd received.

'Thanks so much for all this,' Frankie said gratefully.

'What did Jed's family buy for the baby?' Joey asked, still staring at Georgie. He was unable to take his eyes off his niece; she was the cutest little thing he'd ever seen in his life and he was so proud to be her uncle.

129

'Most of 'em gave money and gold. Jed's dad gave us a thousand pounds, and other people brought necklaces, bracelets and earrings. Georgie even got a sovereign off Jed's brother, Billy.'

Joey looked at Frankie in amazement. 'Strange presents for a baby. How's she meant to wear a sovereign and earrings?'

Frankie laughed. 'I think they're meant to be for when she's older. She got some clothes as well, but I don't like the dresses. They're way too frilly and she'll look ridiculous in them.'

Joey handed the baby to Dominic and sat down on the bed next to Frankie. 'I popped round Nan and Grandad's earlier and told them.'

'What did they say?' Frankie asked hopefully. She was secretly hoping for a reconciliation.

Joey shrugged. 'You know what Nan's like, but I reckon she'll come round in time.'

Dominic handed the baby back to Frankie. 'I'm busting for a wee and a coffee. I'll be back in a bit,' he said diplomatically. He wanted Frankie and Joey to spend some time alone together.

Frankie lay Georgie back in the cot, sat back on the bed and held Joey's hand. It was like old times, just the two of them. Joey immediately took the mickey out of Frankie's not-so-fashionable nightdress and Frankie returned the compliment by slating her brother's new red leather jacket.

'I don't half miss you, Joey,' Frankie said honestly.

'I miss you, too, and I'm really worried about you, Frankie.'

'Why? I'm OK,' Frankie replied abruptly.

Joey had tears in his eyes as he held both of her hands. 'I'm worried about the situation you've got yourself into. I was horrified when I met Jed's family. They're not like us, Frankie, they're a different race. I'm not slagging off Jed, so please don't think that, but his mum's really awful and the way she was speaking about Georgie was as though she belonged to her, not you.'

Frankie explained Alice's predicament. 'She miscarried a

daughter herself recently and she's always craved a little girl. All the other kids in the family are boys. Georgie's the first girl, so she's bound to be a bit over the top with her.'

Joey shrugged. 'It's not just that, Frankie. It's the way they speak, the way they live. Truth be known, I've always wanted better for you. Look at me and Dom, we're living in a nice flat in Islington, we're both working up town, we have a great social life. These are the things you should be doing. I know you've got Georgie now, and she's absolutely gorgeous, but you can always leave Jed and come and live with me. I've already spoken to Dominic; he knows how worried I am and he said you and the baby can live with us for as long as you want. You can't bring your child up around them people, Frankie, you just can't.'

'But I love Jed. I can't leave him, Joey. He's my life, he's all I've got.'

As they hugged one another, both twins wept.

'I hope it works out for you, Frankie, I really do, but if it don't, you know where I am,' Joey said.

'Be honest with me, Joey. You don't like Jed, do you?'

Joey looked at his feet. He didn't want to upset Frankie, but he loved her so much, he couldn't lie to her. 'No, I don't like Jed, Frankie. Call it brotherly intuition if you like, but I don't trust him and I'm positive that one day you'll agree with me.'

Frankie shook her head vehemently. 'You're so wrong, Joey. Jed's a good person. He's generous, he'll make a fantastic father and he loves me, I know he does.'

As Dominic reappeared, Joey lowered his tone. 'For your sake, I hope you're right, sis.'

CHAPTER FOURTEEN

As Eddie was driven to the Old Bailey for the first day of his trial, his mood wasn't a good one. He'd found out only yesterday, via Raymond, that Frankie had given birth to a daughter the previous week, and the thought of that made him feel sick to the stomach.

Eddie had said a silent prayer many a time that Frankie would miscarry the child. God hadn't listened and now his beautiful daughter was tied to that O'Hara mob for life.

Eddie had tried to banish good memories of Frankie and Joey from his mind. Frankie had given him the ultimate kick in the teeth by shacking up with Jed O'Hara. As for Joey parading around town with his boyfriend, he'd caused Eddie humiliation beyond belief.

Ed wasn't completely heartless and deep down he missed Frankie and Joey something rotten. They were half of him and half of Jessica and, as much as he would never let himself admit it, a part of him would love them whatever they did or became.

In prison, the only way to cope was by distancing yourself, therefore Eddie would never allow himself to remember the twins' childhood. The happy times he'd spent with the kids and Jess together were locked away in a box in his heart, a box that would only be reopened on his release. The same applied to his father. He tried not to think of the brutal way his dad had been murdered. If he did, he'd drive himself doolally.

Eddie wasn't stupid. Whatever happened at this trial, he

knew he was looking at a lengthy stretch. The one thing he was sure of was that he'd sort things in his own way once he was released.

As the meat wagon came to a standstill, Eddie took a deep breath. His whole future depended on this trial. Larry, his solicitor, had found him the best QC money could buy and between the three of them, he hoped they had the power to get the jury on their side.

Little Georgie O'Hara had been living in Rainham for just over a week now. She was a contented baby and only cried when she was hungry. Frankie, on the other hand, felt like crying constantly. Visitors came and went on a regular basis and Alice was stuck to Frankie and the baby like a leech.

Jed had taken a week off work. He hadn't left Frankie's side, but even this was making her unhappy. Between him and his mother, she felt as if she was being slowly and surely suffocated. All Frankie wanted was some time alone with her daughter. She wanted to nurture and bond with her child, but whenever Georgie wanted feeding, changing or comforting, Alice took over and Jed encouraged her to do so.

'We're only young ourselves, Frankie, we need me mum's help,' he insisted.

Frankie felt differently. She might only be seventeen, but she sensed what her baby wanted and needed. She was Georgie's mother, for Christ's sake, but no matter how much she complained, she didn't get a look in.

Breast-feeding had been totally out of the question from the start. Frankie had always been shy when it came to flashing her bits, and because the hospital and now the trailer were always packed out with Jed's family, she'd opted to bottle-feed instead.

'It's not natural. The best milk for that chavvie is your own milk,' Alice insisted daily.

Frankie ignored her. The nurses at the hospital fully understood and told her to feed her child however she felt most comfortable. 'I wouldn't fancy getting my boobs out in front of your in-laws either,' one of the nurses joked.

Jed was going back to work later today and Frankie couldn't wait to have her freedom back. Obviously, Alice would still be stuck to her like glue, but Frankie had some plans of her own.

She was going to get back in contact with her old friends, for a start. She had hardly spoken to Stacey, Demi or Paige since her mum's funeral and she wanted them to be part of her life with Georgie.

Frankie also planned to pay her grandparents a visit in the near future. She wasn't going to tell Jed. They were only down the road, living in her old house, and she was going to turn up there unannounced with the baby. If they turned her away, there was little Frankie could do, but she was positive that once her nan and grandad laid eyes on baby Georgie, they would want to be part of her life.

Driving lessons was another idea Frankie had come up with. She hadn't mentioned this to Jed yet, but planned to ask him today. He controlled the purse strings and would obviously have to pay for them.

The trailer door opened and, as Jed walked in, Frankie decided to take the plunge. Alice had popped back to her own house to make Jimmy some lunch and she wanted to ask Jed before his mother returned and intervened.

'How's my two favourite girls?' Jed said sitting down on the sofa next to Frankie.

Frankie handed him the baby. 'Get us a beer out the fridge, Frankie,' Jed ordered, his eyes firmly on his beautiful daughter.

Frankie leaped up, got him his lager and decided to have one herself. She hadn't had any alcohol for ages and was hoping a can would give her the courage to ask the all-important question.

As she drank the lager in record time, Jed tore his eyes away from his daughter and stared at her. 'Fucking hell! You thirsty or what? Don't start drinking like that while you're looking after the baby, Frankie.'

'It's only one can, and you're drinking,' Frankie said stubbornly.

'Yeah, but you're Georgie's mother. It's different for men.'

Frankie ignored his chauvinistic comments, took a deep breath and started her speech. She'd already devised what she was going to say. 'I was thinking, Jed. It's so remote here and if you're going back to work and I'm here alone, I'm gonna need a way to get out and about. As Georgie gets older, it's not good for her to be stuck here all day with just me and your mum, so I was wondering if you would pay for me to have driving lessons.'

Jed looked at Frankie in amazement. If she thought she was going out gallivanting while he was out grafting, she could fucking think again. Trying to be as diplomatic as possible, Jed kept the annoyance out of his voice as he answered. 'I don't think that's a very good idea, Frankie. There's so many nutty drivers out there and these lanes are well dodgy. If you and the baby had an accident, it would break my heart, babe.'

Frankie was determined to argue her point. 'But Jed, when Georgie's older I want her to go to a nursery and stuff. She has to mix with other children her own age. I also want to be able to go out shopping. I'm sick of having to ask you or your dad to drive me to Tesco's; I need some independence.'

Jed wasn't silly. Frankie was going nowhere, but he had to be tactful and he'd always been a master with words. 'I tell you what, babe. Wait till Georgie's a bit older, then I'll give you driving lessons meself. I'm the bollocks behind the wheel and if I teach ya, it'll put me mind at ease.'

'Why can't you just pay for me to have lessons, Jed? I know you're a good driver, but you haven't even got a licence.'

Jed laughed. 'Never had an accident though, have I?' he said cockily.

Frankie sighed. She knew when she was beaten. 'When can you start teaching me, then? I mean, why do I have to wait until Georgie's older?'

Jed smiled as he handed the baby back to her. 'Because it's sensible, Frankie. Look, I promise I'll teach ya, right? But don't get on me case, because if you do I might change my mind. Right, I'm off to earn us some wonga now. Me and the old man have gotta pick up a motor in Grays.'

Frankie felt deflated as he slammed the door. She felt like a prisoner in her own home and she hated it.

Jed hid behind the trailer and peeped through the net curtains. He could see that Frankie was crying and he was glad. She was going nowhere on her own, the silly little cow. How dare she even have the cheek to ask? As he strolled towards his parents' place, Jed smiled. Now Frankie had his kid, she was his property for life and the quicker she realised that, the better.

As Eddie stood in the dock, he was surprised by the number of familiar faces he could see. He'd fallen out with his two brothers, Paulie and Ronny, a good few months before he'd been imprisoned and even though they'd written to him, he hadn't expected them to attend his trial.

Reg and Albert, his uncles, were there, along with Joan and Violet, his two favourite aunts. He'd known Gary and Ricky, his boys, couldn't sit in the gallery until they'd stood as character witnesses for him, but he hadn't expected Pat Murphy or Flatnose Freddie to turn up. Raymond, obviously, wasn't in court, as he was also giving evidence. The same applied to his old pals Dougie and John, the old guvnor of the Flag in Canning Town, who had offered to stand as character witnesses for him.

The biggest relief for Eddie was that Frankie hadn't been called up. She'd been there on the night of the murder but, thanks to Raymond's intervention, she'd given a statement saying she knew nothing. At one point, Ed had fully expected Frankie to be issued with a subpoena, but his solicitor, Larry, had worked wonders in keeping Frankie out of it. A letter a couple of months ago from a top doctor had confirmed that Frankie was so traumatised by the death of her mother that she was contemplating suicide, and as she was also pregnant, it would be best for the well-being of herself, as well as that of the baby, if she did not give evidence.

Eddie would always be indebted to Larry for this, whatever the outcome of the trial. Facing his daughter in a packed courtroom while having to speak about her mother's death was something he could not have dealt with.

As the jury were ushered in, Eddie felt the beginnings of nervousness. Three looked like total nutters and if they were picked to decide his fate, he'd need a fucking miracle.

In a pub in the Essex countryside, Stanley and Joyce sat opposite one another in silence. They had ordered lunch, but barely even nibbled at it. Neither was hungry; both were well aware that today was the start of Eddie's trial.

It had been Stanley's idea to go out for the day. 'Let's take our minds off things, Joycie. We'll go to a nice pub in the country and have a bite to eat, shall we?'

Joyce had agreed, but wished now that she hadn't. Not only could she not eat a morsel, she didn't even feel like talking. Neither Stanley nor she had felt up to attending the trial. If Jessica had been murdered by some maniac, they might have felt differently, but what had happened was a terrible accident, so what was the point? There was no way in the world that Eddie had meant to kill Jessica. Their beautiful daughter had just been in the wrong place at the wrong time.

Raymond had told them that Eddie was pleading not guilty to murder. Stanley had been extremely upset, but Joyce fully understood. Joyce knew she should hate Eddie, but she didn't and couldn't. Stanley was bound to feel differently. He'd never liked Jessica's choice of husband in the first place.

Desperate to go home, Joyce broke the silence. 'Neither of us is hungry, Stanley, so why are we sitting 'ere like two of eels?'

Stanley shrugged. 'I thought it would do us good to go for a drive and get out for the day.'

137

Joyce stood up and held out her hand. 'Let's just go home, eh, love?'

Sick of the sight of Alice O'Hara, Frankie stood up. 'I'm going for a walk. You'll be OK looking after Georgie for ten minutes, won't you?'

A besotted Alice rocked the baby and nodded. 'Take as long as you like,' she mumbled.

Grabbing her mobile phone, Frankie opened the door of the trailer. She was desperate not only to get away from Alice, but to also make some phone calls in private. She needed to speak to normal people and have some familiarity back in her life.

She called Joey first.

'You OK, sis? How's Georgie? I can't talk for long, I'm at work,' he told her.

'Yeah, me and Georgie are both fine,' Frankie lied. Joey had never liked Jed and she was too embarrassed to tell him how she was really feeling.

'What's up? You don't sound yourself. Is Alice driving you mad again?' Joey asked.

'A bit. She means well, though, I think. How's Dom, and when you gonna come and see me next?'

Joey sighed. Both he and Dominic were sick of Jed's family spouting homophobic innuendo and had come to a joint decision. 'Look, sis, me and Dom will come and see you whenever you want, but we ain't coming to the trailer any more. It's obvious that Alice has a problem with what me and Dominic are, and Jimmy and Jed both take the piss out of us in their own way. Me and Dom feel really uncomfortable around them, so we'd rather pick you and Georgie up in a cab and spend some time alone with you. Or, if that's a problem, we can always meet you somewhere.'

'OK, I understand,' Frankie replied. She felt too choked up to say anything else.

'Frankie, I don't know if you know, but Nan told me yesterday that Dad's up in court today. It's the start of the trial. Listen,

I've got to go, my guvnor's just walked in. I'll call you back later, yeah?'

Frankie sat on a bale of hay and put her head in her hands. She hadn't known that it was her dad's trial and the thought of it made her feel sick. She forced herself not to cry. Perhaps she just had the baby blues or something.

Frankie stared at her phone. What she needed were her friends back in her life. Since she'd moved in with Jed she had hardly spoken to Stacey, Paige or Demi. She decided to ring Stacey first. None of them had mobiles and she hoped at least one of them was at home.

'Hello. Is Stacey there?' she asked as her friend's mum answered the phone.

'No, love. Is that you, Frankie?'

'Yeah.'

'She's at work, darling. Staccy's got a job in Topshop in Romford. How's things with you? Have you had the baby yet?'

'Yeah, I had a little girl. I've called her Georgie. When's the best time to contact Stacey? Is she around in the evenings?'

Stacey's mum laughed. 'She's rarely in, Frankie. She's always out pubbing and clubbing with Demi and Paige. They've all got jobs now and they've just booked a holiday. Going to Lloret de Mar in Spain, they are. Me and her dad are worried sick, but hopefully they'll all come back unscathed.'

Frankie forced a laugh. 'I've got to go now, the baby's crying,' she lied.

As she ended the call, Frankie sank to her knees. She would have loved to still have a mum who cared about her, a dad who wasn't in prison, a job in Topshop and a holiday to look forward to. As Frankie cried, her sobs were raw and pure. Everybody else was getting on with their lives, including Joey, and hers seemed like a living hell.

With the jury now whittled down to twelve, Ed was finally satisfied with those chosen. He had always prided himself on having a sixth sense when it came to people's characters – that's why he'd had the cocky-looking dark-haired geezer removed earlier.

'I'm sure I know that bloke. I think I had a tear-up with him in a boozer in East Ham years ago,' Ed had told his solicitor. He was lying, of course. Eddie had never seen the geezer before in his life, he just hadn't liked the man's persona or his smarmy face. The bloke had 'wrong 'un' stamped all over him.

The judge cleared his throat. 'Would the defendant please stand.'

As the charges, along with his wife's name, were read out, Eddie stared the judge straight in the eye without flinching.

He had been through enough suffering over what had happened to Jessica, and he was determined to get away with her murder, however many lies he had to tell.

CHAPTER FIFTEEN

DI Blyth was not a happy woman. She had been on maternity leave for the past six months and things had gone to pot in her absence. Reading over the papers and statements of Eddie Mitchell's court case, Blyth scratched her head.

On the night of Jessica's murder, Eddie had apparently confessed to killing her, claiming it was a case of mistaken identity because he'd gone to Tilbury to shoot his daughter's boyfriend, Jed O'Hara. DS Lineker had taken a short statement, but after being told by a doctor that Eddie was too ill to be properly interrogated, had arranged to come back the following day.

Eddie later denied giving his original statement and because there was no solicitor or tape recorder present, it was just Lineker's word against Mitchell's. The police had originally thought that because Eddie was badly injured himself, he was also a victim, but that was not the case. By the time the police returned the following day, Eddie had his solicitor present and said, 'No comment,' in answer to every question.

As DI Blyth studied Lineker's report of the evening in question, she shook her head in disbelief. Frankie, Eddie's daughter, had been there on the night of her mother's murder, therefore should automatically be a key witness in the case.

Blyth almost laughed out loud as she read the doctor's report on why Frankie was unfit to be a witness. 'What a load of old bollocks,' Blyth mumbled as she threw the papers on the table and grabbed her handbag. Frankie Mitchell should be testifying against her father and if anyone could make that happen, she could.

Eddie Mitchell was now into the fourth day of his trial and it was a case of so far so good. The prosecution had tried to slate him as a person and slander his name, but Ed was as cute as a button when it came to digging himself out of a hole. When he was a kid, his father used to tell him he had an answer for everything, and over the years Eddie had honed this talent. His brain was as sharp as a razor and it would take more than some dumb-arsed coppers and a wanky prosecution team to catch him out.

Eddie was thrilled by the performance of the QC that Larry had found him. James Fitzgerald Smythe was worth his weight in gold. He had just finished questioning the prosecution and not only had he picked massive holes in their version of events, he had also managed to portray Eddie himself as some kind of saint.

While Smythe addressed the jury, Eddie stared at their faces. Their expressions gave nothing away and, not for the first time in his life, Eddie wished that he could read people's minds.

Alice O'Hara had had a terrible fear of coppers ever since she was a young child. She'd been nine years old when the police had raided the gypsy site and arrested her father. She had never seen her dad again. He had died of a heart attack while in police custody and Alice swore to this day that the bastards had killed him and covered up his death.

Alice was listening to her Patsy Cline tape and doing the washing up when she heard the sound of tyres on the gravel. She ran over to the window. Jimmy had gone to visit one of his brothers in hospital and Frankie and Jed were in their trailer with the baby.

As the woman stepped out of the burgundy Ford Granada, Alice knew exactly who she was. She and Jimmy rarely had

142

visitors during the day and Alice could spot a copper a mile away.

She ran to the phone and dialled Jed's mobile number. 'Dordie, boy. The gavvers are 'ere, send 'em away,' she screamed.

Telling Frankie to stay put, Jed composed himself and opened the trailer door. He, Sammy and his dad had been making a mint for months now by ringing stolen vans, lorries, horse-boxes, trailers and anything else they could get their thieving hands on. Whatever they nicked, they would get rid of the chassis number, then mould two similar vehicles into one to hide the stolen one's identity. They would then sell it on with false or no paperwork depending on who was buying it. They kept nothing locally. Anything they chored was kept in a couple of yards belonging to a friend of an uncle up in Norfolk. Praying that their profitable little scam hadn't come on top, Jed held his composure and walked towards the tall, dark-haired woman.

'I live here. Can I help you?'

DI Blyth smiled. She was an expert at playing the softly-softly approach. She held out her right hand. 'Hello. You must be Jed. I'm Detective Inspector Blyth and I'm here to have a little chat with Francesca Mitchell. It's about her father's court case.'

Relieved that he and his old man were in the clear, Jed shook DI Blyth's hand and invited her inside his trailer. 'She hates being called Francesca – she prefers Frankie,' he said.

Frankie was feeding Georgie as the woman appeared beside Jed. 'What's wrong?' she asked, her voice sounding edgy.

Jed urged Frankie to hand him the baby. 'This lady wants to have a chat with you about your dad's court case, Frankie.'

As DI Blyth formally introduced herself, Frankie nervously shook her hand. Feeling awkward, Jed excused himself. 'I'll take Georgie into Mum's for a bit. She can finish feeding her,' he said.

'What a beautiful baby, Frankie. Your boyfriend seems like a lovely lad as well,' DI Blyth said, smiling. She could sense

143

that Frankie was nervous and was eager to calm her down before she asked her any difficult questions.

Frankie nodded. 'Georgie's adorable, everybody loves her and Jed's brilliant with her. He's my fiancé; we're hoping to get married in the next couple of years.'

'Congratulations. What sort of wedding are you planning?'

Frankie shrugged. 'To be honest, we haven't really discussed it in detail. We're ever so young. Jed's only just turned seventeen and I'll be eighteen this summer.'

DI Blyth nodded understandingly. Noticing that Frankie's hands had now stopped shaking, she cleared her throat. 'Frankie, your dad's court case is going on at the moment and I'm afraid I need you to appear as a witness. I know you haven't been well and I can't begin to imagine what you've been through, but you need to stand up in court and tell the truth about the way your dad felt about your relationship with Jed.'

Startled, Frankie shook her head. 'I can't face my dad. I can't go to court.'

DI Blyth sat next to the distraught girl and put a comforting arm around her. 'Your dad is denying that he went to Tilbury to hurt Jed that night. We know that he didn't mean to kill your mother, but you and I both know that what happened to your poor mum was meant to happen to your boyfriend. Now, I don't expect you to say that in court, Frankie. All I want you to do is tell the jury the truth about the way your dad felt about you and Jed being together and how upset he was when he found out that you were pregnant by Jed.'

'But I haven't been well. I can't leave my baby. I don't want to think about my mum being killed. I can't, I won't,' Frankie sobbed.

As Jed walked back inside the trailer, Frankie rushed towards him and threw herself at him. Jed had thrust the baby at his mother and had been earwigging outside for the past couple of minutes.

'Whatever's the matter, babe?' he asked innocently.

Frankie clung to him like a limpet. 'The lady wants me to face my dad in court, Jed. I can't do it, I know I can't.'

Even though he played about with other birds, Jed still had extremely strong feelings for Frankie. He knew her inside out and this was a perfect opportunity for him to secure their future together and ensure that her father got his comeuppance.

'Can you give us five minutes alone?' he asked DI Blyth.

Blyth stood up. She was well aware that Jed had been earwigging outside, she'd seen him through the window, and she could see through his caring persona as clearly as she could see through a recently cleaned pane of glass. 'I've got to make a few phone calls, so I'll wait in the car,' she said tactfully.

Jed sat Frankie down on the sofa. He took two cans of lager out of the fridge and urged Frankie to drink one.

'I'm not thirsty,' Frankie wept.

'You've had a shock, just drink it,' Jed ordered.

Jed sat down next to her, sipped his own lager and spoke in a soft, comforting voice. 'You have to do as the gavvers say, Frankie. If you don't, they'll force you to go to court anyway. You gotta remember, they know you were at Tilbury that night, so in their eyes you're a star witness.'

Frankie felt sick to the stomach. 'But you were there that night. Can't you offer to go to court in my place? Please Jed, I beg you to do this one thing for me. Tell that woman you'll stand up and speak and then I won't have to go.'

Jed shook his head. He'd been long gone that night by the time the Old Bill had arrived and as much as he hated Eddie Mitchell, he had no intention of testifying against him, or anyone else for that matter. Grasses were classed as the lowest of the low in the travelling community and Jed would rather blow Eddie Mitchell's brains out with a shotgun than stand in a courtroom and put him inside by snitching on him.

Jed held his girlfriend tightly. Now if Frankie put her old man inside, that was a different matter. 'I think you're gonna have to go through with it, Frankie. Now the gavvers have come 'ere for ya, you ain't got a lot of choice, babe.'

'I can't, Jed. I know what my dad did was wrong, but he's still my dad. I can't say bad things in court about him. I won't do it.'

Jed decided to try a different tactic. 'Listen, say the jury believes your old man and he gets away with it. He might come back and finish me off or something. And what about your poor mum? You can't let your dad get away with that, Frankie, it ain't on. I love my dad, but if he fucking killed my mum, I'd wanna see him strung up by his bollocks.'

Frankie knew in her heart that Jed was right, but she still had strong feelings for her dad. He'd been a good father for many years and it was impossible to wipe out so many happy memories. 'If I do it, Jed, I ain't saying nothing bad about my dad. All I'll say is that he never got on with your dad, so he wasn't happy when I got with you.'

'That's all you've gotta say. The DI ain't asked ya to say any more than that, has she?'

DI Blyth sat patiently in her car. She'd finished her phone calls, checked the messages on her pager and was now thinking about Frankie Mitchell. As an experienced member of the police force, Blyth had seen a lot of bad things over the years. Murders, rapes, muggings: she'd dealt with them all. She had hardened up over the last decade especially, but even so, her heart went out to young Frankie.

Eddie Mitchell's case was very unusual, to say the least. Blyth had dealt with husbands murdering their wives before, but it was usually premeditated, not accidental.

Blyth had remarried only two years ago, and Frankie reminded her of her stepdaughter, Sophie, who had also recently fallen pregnant at a young age. Her own husband, Keith, had hit the roof at the time, even though the boy was a decent lad with good prospects and a good family.

Blyth didn't like Jed O'Hara one little bit. His politeness hadn't fooled her an inch and she could guess what was happening inside that trailer right this very moment. Over the years, Blyth had arrested and dealt with at least a dozen or so travellers. They were always cute when it came to dealing with the police, very wily, she thought, but considering he was only a young lad, Jed came across as the most cunning of the lot.

Blyth sighed. She didn't really know Eddie Mitchell as a person, but she could understand the man being upset over his daughter's involvement with the likes of Jed.

As the trailer door opened, Blyth pretended not to notice Jed approach her. She had her sunglasses on and as she pretended to read the newspaper, she could see the smirk on the little shit's face.

When Jed tapped on her window, Blyth immediately opened her car door. 'Is Frankie OK now?' she asked in a businesslike manner.

Jed looked extremely pleased with himself, but Blyth could sense he was trying not to show it. 'I've had a chat with Frankie and I've made her see sense. I told her she needs to abide by the law and she's ready to speak to you again now. She'll stand up in court, I'll make sure of it,' Jed said cockily.

Blyth stepped out of her car. Her opinion of Jed, Eddie, Frankie or anybody else, for that matter, was unimportant in a case like this. Conviction was the key, the end result was crucial.

Throughout her career as a dectective, Blyth was and always had been the ultimate professional. Personal feelings had to be put to one side, no matter what the circumstances were. She hadn't climbed the ladder and got to where she was today by getting to like and dislike people.

Blyth entered the trailer and sat down next to Frankie. Eddie Mitchell was a cold-blooded killer; he'd murdered his own wife, therefore the bastard deserved to be locked up for life.

CHAPTER SIXTEEN

The following morning, Jed was up at the crack of dawn. He, Sammy, his dad and two other blokes were off to Norfolk for the weekend. It was work, not pleasure, as they had two lorries and two caravans to cut and shut.

As Jed filled the kettle with water, he was surprised to see Frankie appear by his side. 'What you doing up this early, babe?'

Frankie had barely slept a wink. The visit from the DI had completely unnerved her and she was dreading having to appear in court. She threw her arms around Jed's neck. 'Do you have to go to Norfolk today, Jed? Can't your dad just go with Sammy? I feel really down in the dumps and I need you here with me.'

Jed shook his head. As much as he cared for Frankie and enjoyed her being reliant on him, she could be overbearingly clingy at times. That's why he messed about with other girls. He was a travelling lad, who hated being smothered, and dipping his wick in other places gave him the sense of freedom that he sometimes craved.

As he hugged Frankie, Jed glanced at his watch over her shoulder. If he skipped breakfast, he had just about enough time to dip his wick in her. He slipped his hand inside her dressing gown and into her knickers.

'I have to go up to Norfolk, babe. We need the money. We'll never save up enough to get married and buy our own piece of land unless I work hard, will we?'

Needing to feel loved and wanted, Frankie nodded and allowed Jed to lead her back into the bedroom. Since the birth of the baby they hadn't had full intercourse, because Frankie had felt too sore down below.

She winced as Jed entered her. 'Are you OK?' he asked, concerned.

Frankie nodded. It hurt like hell, but she would rather suffer the pain than risk Jed going off with other girls. Men had needs and Frankie was determined to satisfy Jed's herself.

Jed bounced up and down on top of Frankie as quickly as he could. Time was knocking on and he needed to shoot his load quickly, else his old man would be on his case. Determined to hurry things up, he shut his eyes and pictured the prostitute he'd fucked the last time he'd worked away. Remembering how she'd expertly sucked his cock, Jed groaned with ecstasy as he came. As he rolled off her, Frankie propped herself up on one elbow.

'I think I might ring Joey and Dominic. If they're not busy, they can take me and the baby out somewhere for the day.'

Jed felt the hairs rise on the back of his neck. 'Invite 'em over 'ere if you want to see 'em. You can't go partying while I'm out working, Frankie.'

'I'm not going out bloody partying. I only want to go out for lunch or something,' Frankie replied indignantly.

Jed shook his head. 'I'd rather you didn't. What about me mum? She was looking forward to spending the day with you and Georgie.'

Frankie was annoyed. She didn't want to tell Jed that Joey and Dominic had refused to come to their trailer any more in case it caused a big argument. 'Look, Jed. Joey's my brother and if I want to go for lunch with him, then I will.'

Jed got out of bed and put his jeans back on. He picked up his keys and glared at Frankie. 'If you wanna go out with the gay boys, then go, but you ain't taking my chavvie with you. You leave Georgie with me mum, do you hear me?'

Upset by his attitude, Frankie ignored him and pulled the quilt over her head.

Jed could hear his dad calling him outside, but he ignored him and angrily ripped the quilt off her. 'I'm going now. I'll ring you later and if I find you've taken my daughter out without my permission, I swear, Frankie, you'll pay for it.'

As the trailer door slammed shut, Frankie felt herself and the walls shake simultaneously.

Over in Wandsworth, Eddie Mitchell was in a reasonably good mood. His court case seemed to be going quite well and although being reminded of Jessica was gut-wrenching, he had somehow managed to hold his emotions together.

The prosecution had continually tried to trip him and his QC up, but so far they had had very little joy. The witnesses would be called next Monday and Eddie was especially looking forward to this.

His defence team had arranged for both his sons, Gary and Ricky, to speak on his behalf. Dougie and John, his pals, were going to do the same, and when Raymond was questioned, he was going to tell the jury what a dedicated husband and father Eddie had been.

Eddie was looking forward to Gina, the private detective he'd once hired, giving her evidence. Gina was as cool as a cucumber and Ed knew that she wouldn't let him down.

Ed and Stuart laughed and joked while they waited patiently in the queue to make their daily phone calls. Larry, Eddie's brief, had all but blackmailed the now retired Chief Inspector Dickens to stand up on his behalf and Ed was desperate to know if Larry's plan had worked.

In his day, Dickens had been as bent as a nine-bob note. Eddie's dad, Harry, had lined the Inspector's pockets for years and now it was time for the bastard to give something in return.

When they reached the front of the queue, Eddie urged Stuart to use the phone first. It was Stu's mum's birthday today and Ed knew how desperate the boy was to speak to her.

As the other phone became vacant, Eddie said a silent prayer that Larry had twisted Dickens' arm. An experienced retired chief inspector singing his praises would surely help swing the jury in his favour.

'Lal, it's me. Well, is he gonna do it?' Ed asked. Mentioning names on prison phones was a definite no-go, because you never knew who could be listening in.

Larry took a deep breath. He had good news and also some bad news for Eddie and was dreading telling him the latter. 'The good news is yes, he's going to do it, Eddie. But I also have some bad news for you.'

'Spit it out then,' Eddie said, immediately agitated. He hated bad news and he'd had enough in the past year to last him a lifetime.

Larry sighed. He was scared of Eddie's reaction. 'The prosecution have informed me that Frankie has to stand up in court next week,' he said bluntly.

'What! No, she can't,' Ed yelled.

'Listen, Eddie. This was always a possibility. I know it's extremely unfortunate, but there's very little I can do about it, I'm afraid.'

'I can't have her face me in court. Do something Lal, anything,' Eddie pleaded.

Larry spoke calmly but firmly. 'It's out of my hands now, Eddie. I can wangle most things, but not this. My advice to you is just be strong. I know it's an awkward situation, but you have to face it head on. If you don't, it could spell disaster for all of us.'

Overcome by the horror of what he'd just been told, Eddie slammed down the receiver and punched the wall in temper.

Back in Rainham, Frankie's initial shock over Jed's behaviour had now turned into wrath. How dare he tell her that she wasn't allowed to take her own baby out with her brother? Frankie decided enough was enough. She loved Jed immensely, but she needed to start standing up to him. If she didn't, she would regret it in the future when he started treating her like some kind of doormat.

For the past few weeks, Frankie had felt like a prisoner in her own home. Alice hovering around constantly didn't help matters. It was almost as though Jed had ordered his mother to keep an eye on her in his absence.

Frankie checked on the sleeping Georgie and then stared at herself in the full-length mirror. Since her pregnancy and her mother's death, she had let herself go somewhat and she didn't like what she saw in her reflection.

With fire in her belly for the first time in ages, Frankie put on her faded jeans, black ankle boots and black leather jacket. Jed had fallen in love with the girl she once was, not the girl she was now. She hadn't worn make-up for months because Jed preferred her without it, but today she decided to put on some blue eyeshadow, black mascara and red lipstick. Sod Jed, she was sick of dancing to his tune. Let him dance to hers, for once.

Just about to finish her outfit off by putting on the gold sovereign earrings that Jed had bought her for Christmas, Frankie was disturbed by the sound of Alice's coarse voice.

'Frankie. What you doing? You in there?'

Frankie grimaced and unlocked the trailer door. Joey was picking her up in a taxi at twelve and she still had stuff to do yet. 'Hi Alice. Do you want a cup of tea?'

Alice looked at her future daughter-in-law in horror. She was dressed and made up like a fucking tart and was obviously going out gallivanting somewhere.

'What you got all that make-up on your face for? You're not going out whoring while my Jed's out working, I won't put up with it.'

Determined not to rise to the bait, Frankie kept her cool. 'My brother and Dominic are picking me up at twelve. They're taking me and Georgie out for the afternoon.'

Alice shook her head in disbelief. Jed had given her strict instructions to look after her granddaughter and Alice was determined to do just that. 'Now, you listen to me, you can go where you fucking well like, but that chavvie stays here with her nan,' she said bluntly.

152

Frankie couldn't believe what she was hearing. Georgie was her baby and she would decide what was best for her child. Struggling to be diplomatic, Frankie tried to keep the fury out of her voice.

'Look, Alice, I don't want to argue with you, but I'm taking Georgie out with my brother whether you like it or not. She's my baby. I gave birth to her, remember?'

Alice's lip began to curl with hatred. She'd always told her Jed to find himself a nice travelling girl – and look what he'd ended up with. Gorjer girls like Frankie had far too much to say for themselves and Alice silently cursed her son for not listening to her advice in the first place.

Georgie let out a wail and, quick as a flash, Alice ran over to the cot and picked her up. 'I'm taking her indoors with me,' she said, with a face like a rabid Alsatian.

As Georgie started screaming, Frankie began to lose the plot. 'Give me my baby or I'll call the fucking police,' she yelled as Alice opened the trailer door.

As the taxi approached the bend, Joey told the driver to slow down. 'It's about fifty yards up on your right, mate.'

Dominic squeezed Joey's hand. Baby Georgie had become one of their main topics of conversation recently and both Joey and Dom were thrilled when Frankie had rung them this morning. They had cancelled their original plans, which were to go to a gay bar in Greenwich with their friends, Lee and Cliff. The opportunity to spend the day with baby Georgie was just too good an offer to refuse.

As the taxi pulled onto the drive, Joey's mouth fell open. 'Oh my God, Dom, do something,' he shouted. Alice was holding the baby with one arm and pushing Frankie with the other.

Dominic jumped out of the taxi and ran towards Frankie. 'Leave her alone. What's going on?'

Frankie was hysterical. 'She won't give me Georgie back,' she screamed.

Joey had never been one for confrontation, but seeing the

state of his sister, he felt his blood boil. He marched over to Alice. 'Give me the baby now,' he yelled.

As Alice's brazen manner momentarily faltered, Frankie snatched the sobbing child out of her grandmother's hands.

'Go into the trailer and get Georgie's carrycot, baby bag, my black handbag and phone. They should all be in the bedroom,' she ordered Joey.

Dominic put an arm around Frankie's shoulder and led her over to the taxi. 'You're OK now. Me and Joey will take care of you and Georgie,' he said comfortingly.

Alice was livid. She loved her granddaughter more than anything else in the world, but she hated her bloody mother. 'Gertcha, you fucking old rabbit's crotch. I'm ringing my Jed right this minute to tell him what you're up to. You don't deserve a good boy like him,' she screamed.

As Joey ran over to the taxi with Frankie's belongings, he glared at Alice. 'You leave my sister alone, you horrible cow.'

Alice burst out laughing. 'And what are you gonna do, you big poof? It ain't natural what you are. God made Adam and Eve, not Adam and Steve, you fucking bumboy.'

Frankie was distraught. 'Just drive, will you,' she screamed, as Alice approached the car.

The taxi driver was an elderly man in his sixties. To say he was petrified was an understatement. Desperate to escape the woman who was now pummelling against his window with her large fists, he swung the car around and drove off like Ayrton Senna.

Joey told the driver to head towards the Albion pub.

'I think we all need a drink after that, don't you?' he said to Frankie.

Frankie handed Georgie to Dom and clung to her brother. 'What am I gonna do, Joey? I hate Alice, I'm so unhappy living there with her breathing down my neck all the time. And next week, I've gotta face Dad in court. I wish I was dead sometimes; I wish I could be with my mum.'

Joey glanced at Dominic. Frankie's predicament was way

beyond his control and as much as he wanted to help her, apart from offering her a place to stay, there was very little else he could do.

A few hundred yards down the road, Joyce and Stanley were having one of their usual little tiffs.

'You silly, bald-headed old tosspot. I told you you'd took the wrong turn off, didn't I?' Joyce yelled.

Stanley sighed. Joycie had driven him mad this morning. He'd planned to meet Jock for a beer, but she'd insisted he drive her to the garden centre in Aveley. She'd then cost him over a hundred quid on plants, gnomes and accessories.

'Can't we do it tomorrow, Joycie? Jock wants me to go and look at a pigeon with him this afternoon,' he'd pleaded with her earlier.

Joyce had been adamant that she wanted to go today. 'I want to get started on that garden as soon as possible. I want it to be a tribute to our Jessica this summer. You and Jock can discuss pigeons tomorrow. Today you're taking me to the garden centre, Stanley.'

Seeing a rabbit run across the road, Stanley winced as he slammed his foot on the brakes to avoid it. 'What the bloody hell are you doing? You trying to kill me or what?' Joyce shouted.

Stanley ignored her. There were times when he would gladly love to run over Joycie, but not some poor defenceless little rabbit.

'I'm starving and I need a drink. Your driving makes me nervous, Stanley. Drive to that pub – you know, the one on the roundabout along the A13.'

Stanley nodded. 'You mean the Albion, my dear.'

Watching Dominic and Joey fuss over the baby, Frankie flinched as her phone rang yet again. Jed had been ringing her constantly for the past half an hour and she knew that Alice had told him every little detail of their argument.

155

'Leave it,' Joey said, as Frankie debated whether or not to answer it.

Frankie sighed. 'I can't exactly ignore him. I'm gonna have to talk to him at some point, aren't I?'

Joey studied the menu, chose what he wanted and handed it to Dom. 'Go up the bar and order for us.'

As Frankie cradled Georgie, Joey leaned towards her. 'What you gonna say in court? You know, about Dad?'

Frankie shrugged. 'I don't know, I don't want to think about it. The detective that came to see me was a nice lady and she said I don't have to say anything bad. All she wants me to do is tell the jury that Dad never liked Jed's family and was unhappy when me and him got together.'

Deep in thought, Joey sipped his lager. He knew what he should do, but he didn't know if he was brave enough to go through with it.

Frankie could read her brother like a book. 'What's the matter?'

Joey shrugged. 'I feel I should come to court with you. Do you want me to book a day off work?'

Frankie squeezed his hand. 'Oh, yes please, Joey. I know you can't stand up and speak for me, but even if you were there and I could look at you, it would help me get through it.'

Joey nodded. 'OK, I'll come.'

Joyce punched Stanley on the arm as he pulled into the pub car park. 'You can't park in between those two posh cars with your bleedin' old banger. Park over there, where it's empty.'

Stanley sighed as he reversed his Sierra out from between the Mercedes and BMW. Joycie could be so far shoved up her own arse at times, it was a joke. Anyone would think she was Lady bloody Diana by the way she behaved. Moving over to the empty spaces, Stanley turned the engine off. 'Ready, dear?' he asked, with a hint of sarcasm in his voice.

Joyce waited for him to open her door and stepped out of

the car. She held his arm. 'I do love you, Stanley, you know,' she said fondly.

Inside the pub, Frankie's phone was still ringing.

'Can't you turn that bloody thing off?' Joey asked. He hated Jed; he was frightened of him and Jed's continuous hounding of Frankie was putting him off eating his fish and chips.

Frankie stood up. Unlike Dom and Joey, she hadn't ordered any food. She'd had the morning from hell and didn't feel at all hungry.

'Look after Georgie for a minute. I'm gonna ring Jed back, Joey. I have to.'

Joey shook his head. 'Why don't you come and stay with me and Dom? I worry about you, Frankie, living with that awful family, I really do.'

Frankie touched her brother's arm. 'Jed loves me and I love him. It's his mother that's the problem.'

About to leave the table, Frankie froze with shock. 'Oh my God, Joey. Nan and Grandad have just walked in.'

CHAPTER SEVENTEEN

Jed O'Hara was like a bear with a sore head. He had been trying to ring Frankie for just over an hour now and he was absolutely seething because the bitch wasn't answering his calls.

His mum had been livid when she'd rung him up earlier. 'She's a proper old whore, she is, all tarted up, she was, like a single girl. And the way she spoke to me, Jed! Hurt I was, fucking hurt. You've made a rod for your own back there, son. I told you you should have settled down with a nice travelling girl, didn't I?'

As Jed tried to ring Frankie once again and got no answer, he threw the phone against the passenger seat in temper.

Sammy laughed. 'You wanna give her a right-hander – that'll stop her going out,' he said, as Jimmy tried to calm his son down.

Jed was in no mood to be calmed down. He couldn't believe that Frankie had done exactly what he'd warned her not to. As for shouting at his mother, that was unforgivable. He turned to his dad. 'Listen, when we get to the yard, I'm gonna borrow the motor and drive back home. I'll find Frankie, sort her out and then I'll drive straight back again.'

Jimmy nodded sympathetically. He guessed what Jed might do, turned away and smirked. If Jed was with any other girl, Jimmy would have probably warned him to tread carefully, but seeing as it was Eddie Mitchell's daughter, Jimmy didn't really care how far his son went to teach her a lesson.

*　　*　　*

158

Back in Rainham, Stanley was a bundle of nerves as Joey approached the table. He'd spotted Frankie and not wanting any more aggravation, had begged Joyce to let him drive her to another pub. His wife, unfortunately, had been as obstinate as ever.

'We've got as much right to be in this pub as anyone else,' she'd said, plonking herself at a nearby table.

'Hello Nan, hello Grandad,' Joey said, with a hint of awkwardness. Usually, whenever he was in the vicinity, he would arrange to visit his grandparents, but today's arrangements had been made with such haste, he hadn't even thought of it.

'This is a nice surprise. Planning to visit me and your poor old grandad later, was you?' Joyce asked sarcastically.

Joey sat down at their table. 'Dom and I didn't know we were coming down until this morning. It was a last-minute thing.'

'How very convenient,' Joyce mumbled cynically.

'Don't be like that, Nan. Frankie's really upset, that's why me and Dom rushed down here. The police are making her stand up in court to face Dad next week. In bits, she is.'

Joycie softened slightly. 'That's awful. What has she got to say?'

Joey shrugged. 'Why don't you speak to her, Nan? The baby's over there. Georgie is your great-granddaughter and she's absolutely gorgeous.'

Stanley turned to Joyce. 'Please, Joycie. That baby's our flesh and blood. We can't be in the same place and ignore Frankie or the baby, it ain't right.'

Joycie, who had knocked her first glass of wine back in record time, told Stanley to go up to the bar and get her another.

'Shall I order us something to eat as well?' Stanley asked.

Joyce shook her head. She'd been starving earlier, but the situation she now found herself in had taken away any hunger. As her husband walked away, Joyce turned to Joey. 'How's she getting on with that Jed and his family?'

Joey had always been extremely loyal to his twin sister, but for once he decided not to be. 'Between me and you, not great, Nan. The mother's awful and has been giving Frankie a real hard time. Please try and build some bridges with her. Frankie needs us, I know she does.'

Joyce had always liked to be needed. She was also glad that things weren't that rosy in the O'Hara household. When Stanley returned from the bar, Joyce nudged her grandson. 'You go back over to Frankie. Give us ten minutes or so and me and your grandad will join you.'

Eddie Mitchell sat forlornly on the bunk in his cell. He hadn't felt like talking to anyone since finding out he had to face Frankie in court. The thought of seeing his daughter again made him feel physically sick with guilt.

Stuart, his cellmate, was extremely worried about his pal. Ever since they had shared a cell together, Eddie had been vibrant and full of life, but today he seemed seriously depressed. Knowing there was nothing he could say to make things right, Stuart tried to think of something that might cheer Eddie up and snap him out of the trance he seemed to be in. He jumped off his bunk and smiled. 'Let's go down to the TV room, Ed.'

Ed didn't feel one bit like socialising. 'I dunno if I feel up to it, Stu,' he said honestly.

'Please, Ed. I'm bored shitless and if you don't go, then neither will I,' Stuart said, trying his best to persuade him.

Eddie sat up. Perhaps watching a bit of TV might take his mind off things. He stood up and slung an arm around Stuart's shoulder. 'Come on then, you fucking nuisance.'

Back in Rainham, Frankie had taken her brother's advice and switched her phone off. Joey had told her that her nan and grandad were coming over to the table and Frankie didn't need the added distraction of her phone constantly ringing.

As Joyce and Stanley stood up, Frankie nibbled at her finger-nails. 'What am I gonna say to them, Joey?' she whispered.

160

Joey squeezed her hand. 'Everything will be fine,' he said reassuringly.

Dominic got up. He felt awkward, knowing the situation, and decided to make himself scarce. 'I'm going to pop outside to make some phone calls. I won't be long,' he told Joey.

Joyce felt edgy as she said a quick hello to Dominic and turned to her granddaughter. 'Hello Frankie. How are you?'

As soon as Frankie looked into her nan and grandad's faces, she felt her eyes fill with tears. Seeing them again brought back so many memories of happy times with her mum and dad.

Joycie flinched as Frankie kissed her on the cheek. Stanley was much warmer and hugged his granddaughter tightly. Joyce glanced at the sleeping baby and instantly felt her own eyes well up. The child was a beauty with a massive mop of wavy, dark hair.

'Do you want to hold her?' Frankie asked immediately.

Desperately trying to hold back her tears, Joyce nodded. Joey smiled at his grandad, who winked back. So far so good, they both thought.

As Frankie lifted Georgie out of her cot, she opened her eyes and began to cry. 'Sssh, it's OK. Nanny's here now,' Joyce said, as she took the child in her arms. When Joyce started to rock her, Georgie stopped crying almost immediately. As great-gran and baby stared at one another for the very first time, Joyce melted.

'Oh Frankie, she's adorable. She's got the biggest, most beautiful eyes I've ever seen.'

About to tell her nan that Georgie's eyes were big with long lashes like Jed's, Frankie stopped herself in mid-sentence.

'What did you say?' Joyce asked.

'Oh nothing, Nan. I was just going to say that all the nurses in the hospital said that Georgie's eyes were beautiful, too.'

As Stanley put an arm around his wife's shoulder and stared at the tot, he was overcome by emotion. 'Hello Georgie, I'm Grandad Stanley,' he said in a silly voice.

Joyce smiled at him. 'Do you want to hold her, Stanley?'

161

Stanley nodded dumbly.

With his nan and grandad both besotted with the new addition, Joey sidled over next to Frankie and whispered in her ear. 'Why don't we go back to Nan and Grandad's for a bit? We can have a proper chat there and they can spend some quality time with you and Georgie.'

Frankie felt a bit uneasy. 'After everything that's happened, they might not want me to,' she whispered.

'They will. Ask 'em, Frankie, go on. I bet they say yes.'

Frankie stood up. 'It's a bit smoky in here now. Would you like me and Joey to come round to yours for a bit, Nan? You and Grandad can spend some time getting to know Georgie then.'

Joyce grinned. 'That would be brilliant, Frankie.'

Unaware of the family reunion currently taking place, Eddie Mitchell was getting more and more agitated by the second. Concentrating on the programme he was trying to watch was an impossibility with the loud-mouthed prick sitting behind him.

Johnny Venger was not a popular inmate. Half German and half Scottish, he was built like a brick shit-house and had a mouth like a sewer rat. Venger was serving a five stretch for GBH, but rumour had it, he'd once been arrested for fiddling with little boys. The case was never proven, but in Ed's eyes there was never smoke without fire.

Eddie turned around, his face as black as thunder. 'Will you shut the fuck up? I can't hear the poxy telly.'

Venger looked Ed in the eyes and smirked. He knew most of the inmates were scared of Eddie Mitchell, but he was afraid of no one. 'How's your gay son doing? Still taking it up the rear, is he?'

Eddie's eyes were full of evil as he flew at Venger. No one slagged his kids off, it was an unwritten fucking rule. With both hands grasped around Venger's throat, Eddie spat in his face. 'Got anything else to say, cunt?' he asked, as he pressed tightly against his windpipe.

As all the other lags cheered, Stuart tried desperately to pull Eddie away. 'Leave him, Ed. He ain't worth it,' he yelled.

'Call for assistance,' one of the screws shouted as he was stopped from intervening by the other lags. They were all standing in front of him, so he couldn't see who was fighting whom.

'Nonce, nonce, nonce,' the inmates screamed as Eddie viciously pummelled Venger around the head.

The angst he'd felt over Joey's sexuality was all taken out on his victim and it was only Stuart who finally stopped Eddie from killing the man.

'Ed, listen to me. Don't fuck your case up. Think of your kids!' Stu screamed out.

Satisfied with the damage he'd done, Ed let Stu drag him away. 'Say anything about my kids again, you fucking child molester, and I will kill you,' Eddie spat.

Five minutes later, ten screws ran into the room and were surprised to see an orderly situation. All the inmates were watching the film and apart from Venger, who was covered in blood and writhing in agony on the floor, nothing seemed amiss. Parker, the guvnor's understudy, crouched down. 'Who did this to you?' he asked.

Venger couldn't talk. Mitchell had nearly strangled him, and even if he had been able to speak, he was now too scared to do so. Eddie had battered his face so violently that his teeth had sliced through his tongue and the pain was excruciating.

Parker stood up. 'Who is responsible for this?' he screamed at the other inmates.

The lags stared at the telly as though nothing had happened and not a soul answered. Crossing Eddie Mitchell was something that none of them was prepared to risk.

Back in Essex, Frankie was thrilled to finally be reunited with her grandparents. It was strange being back in her old house and although it was upsetting because of all the wonderful memories it held, Frankie found it almost comforting at the same time. Buster and Bruno were no longer around. They had gone to live with her dad's old mate, Pat Murphy, and the house seemed quiet without them.

As a child Frankie had never really appreciated what she had. She and Joey had obviously been spoilt in a way and it was only now, living in a trailer with Jed, that she appreciated the beautiful home comforts that her parents had given her. Feeling emotional, Frankie went outside into the garden.

'Are you OK?' Joey asked, as he handed her a cigarette.

'Yeah, but I feel sad to be back here, if you know what I mean.'

Joey nodded. 'I know exactly what you mean. Every time I come and visit Nan and Grandad I can see Mum's face. I picture her sitting in the armchair watching the telly, washing up in the kitchen. I sort of picture her everywhere.'

Frankie hugged him. 'Do you ever think of Dad?'

'Sometimes, but I still hate him,' Joey admitted.

'I don't. I know what he did was awful, but it was an accident, Joey. He really loved Mum; we both know he was besotted with her.'

Joey shrugged. 'But look what he did to Dominic? Dad was capable of anything, Frankie.'

'What Dad did to Dom was terrible, but I know he never meant to hurt Mum,' Frankie insisted.

Joey quickly changed the subject. He hated talking about his mum's murder. 'Nan and Grandad haven't left Georgie's side since we've been here. You will bring her to see them on a regular basis from now on, won't you?'

Frankie smiled. 'Of course I will.'

'What about Jed, though?' Joey asked cautiously.

Frankie took a deep breath. 'Talking of Jed, go indoors and get my phone for me, Joey. I have to call him, and don't worry, I'll never let him stop Nan and Grandad from seeing Georgie.'

Joey nodded and went off to get Frankie's phone. He had a feeling that Jed was capable of stopping Frankie doing lots of things, but he wasn't about to cause an argument.

As Joey walked into the living room, he smiled at the scene

164

that greeted him. His nan, grandad and Dom were all sitting on the large sofa fawning over the baby. Georgie was still wide awake and was gurgling happily on Joycie's lap.

'Is Frankie all right?' Stanley asked, concerned.

'She's fine. She just wanted some fresh air. She hasn't been back here for a while, so I think she found it a little bit strange.'

Joyce nodded understandingly. Tickling Georgie's chin, she tore her eyes away from the child. 'Would you like me to have a little chat with her about the court case?'

Joey smiled. 'That would be great, Nan.'

Jed O'Hara was nigh on pulling his hair out. He had been back in Rainham for almost an hour and had searched high and low for his badly behaved girlfriend. As Jed walked out of the Phoenix pub, he kicked the side of a Ford Transit in frustration. He'd been in every bar and restaurant in Rainham and the bitch wasn't anywhere to be seen. Jed got back into his motor. His phone was ringing; he'd left it on the seat.

'Hello, Jed, it's me.'

Having struggled with his temper from infanthood, Jed took a deep breath. If Frankie knew his mood, she might not come home, and he couldn't risk that.

'Jed, are you there?'

'Where are you, Frankie?' he asked, as calmly as he could.

Frankie began to gabble nervously. 'I'm at my nan and grandad's. They love the baby, Jed. They think she's absolutely adorable,' she said.

Frankie had fully expected Jed to be angry because of the argument she'd had with his mum but, surprisingly, he sounded rather calm.

'I'm back in Rainham. Can I come and pick you up?' Jed mumbled.

Frankie was shocked. He was meant to be working away. 'Why are you back in Rainham, Jed?'

Jed bit into his lip as he spoke. He needed to feel some pain to keep himself composed. 'My dad forgot all the important paperwork we needed to sell the lorries and stuff, so I offered to drive back and get it for him,' he lied. 'I ain't gotta go back just yet, Frankie, so I wanna see you and Georgie for a bit while I'm home.'

Frankie sighed. She was enjoying her grandparents' company and wasn't ready to leave just yet. Deciding to compromise, she came up with an idea. 'Why don't you pick me up now, Jed? Don't knock, I'll meet you down the bottom of the drive and when you have to leave you can drop me back here again.'

'I'll be ten minutes, and bring Georgie with you,' Jed retorted, in a false, jolly tone.

Frankie dashed into the living room and urged Joey to follow her into the kitchen. 'I've just spoken to Jed. He's had to pop home and he wants to see me and Georgie for a bit before he goes back to Norfolk. I couldn't say no, so will you and Dom stay here and wait for me to come back?'

Joey felt uneasy. 'Will you be OK, Frankie? Wasn't he angry about the row with his mother?'

Seeing the look of fright on her brother's face, Frankie smiled. 'Jed was fine, honest. And don't worry, he's not gonna knock on the door, I'm meeting him at the end of the drive.'

'Are you sure he ain't come back because you sodded off out, Frankie? How do you know he hasn't got it in for you?' Joey asked suspiciously.

Frankie hugged her brother. 'You worry too much, you always have. I know Jed better than anyone. He's fine with me; he loves me.'

Jed O'Hara tapped his fingers impatiently against the steering wheel of his father's Mercedes. Frankie was already five minutes late and he was getting wilder by the minute. As he saw her finally walking towards him, carrying the baby in the cot, he stared at her. He could see the make-up she was wearing a mile off; she looked like an old slag.

Frankie waved and he forced a wave back. He had to act

166

normal just for five minutes longer. He jumped out of the car, kissed her on the cheek and took the cot from her. 'Get in the car. I'll strap Georgie in the back,' he ordered.

Frankie did as she was told. She wondered why Jed was strapping Georgie in if they were only going down the road.

'Are we not going back to the trailer?' Frankie asked.

Jed started the engine and shook his head. As Frankie glanced at him, expecting him to say where they were going, she felt the first stirrings of fear. His face was flushed and looked angry and his cheeks seemed to be twitching.

'Are you OK, Jed? I'm sorry that I had an argument with your mum. Is that why we're not going home?'

Jed ignored her and drove off like a loony. As he overtook three cars and took a bend at top speed, Frankie started to scream.

'Stop it, Jed! Slow down, you'll kill us all,' she cried.

Jed ignored her. He'd been driving since he was a kid and he was used to driving fast.

Frankie started to sob. She hadn't brought her phone with her and she so wished she had listened to Joey. 'Take your phone with you,' her brother had urged as she'd left.

'No, I won't be long,' she'd insisted.

As Georgie started to scream, Frankie began to scream as well. 'Please Jed, think of Georgie,' she pleaded in an hyster-ical tone.

Jed knew the local area like the back of his hand and, without warning, he skidded onto a dirt track.

'Please don't hurt me, Jed. I love you. I'm sorry for going out and I'm even more sorry for arguing with your mum.'

Jed got out of the car and ordered Frankie to do the same. Frankie did so, but through fear, immediately fell to her knees. Jed dragged her up by her long dark hair. 'Get up, you cunt.'

'Stop it, Jed, you're hurting me.'

'See you, look at ya, all done up like a fucking whore. Been out shagging other men, have ya?'

'No, I only went for lunch in the Albion with Joey and that's where we bumped into my nan and grandad,' Frankie wept.

Jed twisted her hair around his right hand and tugged it as hard as he could. 'Bumped into 'em, my arse. I bet you fucking planned it. Don't lie to me Frankie, I mean it.'

'I'm not lying,' Frankie protested.

Without warning, Jed let go of her hair and grabbed her round the back of the neck. He then smashed her face as hard as he could against the back window of the motor.

'See that chavvie? Look at her, you slag. She's mine, she is, and don't you ever forget that. You ask me first before you take her anywhere in future, do you hear what I'm saying?'

Frankie nodded. She was stunned and also petrified. As Jed held her head against the car window, Frankie could see splashes of her own blood on the glass.

Jed finally let go of her and stood over her as she slumped to the floor. 'And don't even think of leaving me. You'll never get custody, Frankie. Your mother's dead, your father's a murderer, your brother's a poof, there's no court in the land that would let you look after a child with your family history.'

Frankie sat on the floor and put her battered face in her hands. Jed was right; she was trapped and it was all her own stupid fault. Her dad and Joey had been right all along.

CHAPTER EIGHTEEN

'I'm just popping out the back to feed the pigeons, love.'

Joyce nodded at her husband and looked out of the window once more. She was getting impatient now. Frankie still hadn't come back and she was desperate to spend some more time with baby Georgie. 'She ain't half been a long while, Joey. Are you sure she's coming back?'

Joey felt uneasy as he glanced at Dominic. He'd had a bad feeling earlier about Frankie meeting Jed. Jed had seemed too nice, considering Frankie had disobeyed his orders and argued with his mum, and Joey didn't trust him one iota. Being twins, Joey had always believed that he and Frankie were sort of telepathic. Today he felt edgy, and he was sure his sister was in danger.

Not wanting to worry his nan, Joey urged his boyfriend to follow him into the kitchen. Glad to have a couple of minutes together, Dom gave Joey a big hug.

'What's up? I know something's on your mind.'

Dominic was tall and strong and Joey always felt safe in his arms. 'I'm worried about Frankie. Something's wrong, I know it is.'

Back at the trailer, Jed O'Hara was full of remorse. He had meant to teach Frankie a lesson, but he hadn't intended to hurt her as much as he had.

'I'm so sorry, babe. 'Ere, hold this against your face,' he said, handing her a bag of frozen peas.

169

Frankie winced as she held the plastic bag against her sore skin. When her nose had bled profusely, she had originally thought it was broken, but having since looked in the mirror, she was now positive that it was just badly bruised.

When Jed had smashed her face into the car window, it was the right side of it that had taken the brunt. Her right eye and cheek were both swollen and Frankie was positive that she would end up with a big black eye.

Jed sat down next to her. 'Please forgive me, Frankie. I didn't mean to hurt you. I don't know what came over me.'

Frankie had barely spoken to Jed since the attack. He had frightened the life out of her and she certainly wasn't ready to forgive him.

'Please talk to me, Frankie. We have to sort this out. I'm gonna ring me dad and tell him I ain't going back to Norfolk. I'll phone me Uncle Tommy – he can pick the old man's motor up and drive it back down there.'

'Just go, Jed. I need to be alone right now.'

Jed had no intention of going anywhere. He knew he'd overstepped the mark and he was frightened Frankie might do a runner and take the baby with her. He squeezed her hand. 'Please forgive me. I swear on our Georgie girl's life, I'll never hurt you again. When Mum rang me and told me you was all done up with make-up on, I got jealous. I thought you were cheating on me with some other bloke.'

Frankie glared at him. 'Don't you dare swear on our baby's life and don't lie to me, Jed. You knew I was only going out with my brother and Dominic.'

'I swear on my own life, then. Honest, Frankie, I thought you'd met someone else, that's why I lost it. I'm so sorry.'

As Jed leaned towards her and tried to kiss her, Frankie turned her head.

'Do you still love me?' Jed asked, cupping her bruised face gently in his hands.

'I don't know. I can't believe what you did to me,' Frankie replied honestly.

Jed took both her hands in his own and looked pleadingly into her eyes. 'Let me make it up to you. Give me one more chance – I won't let you down, I promise. I'll buy you whatever you want, I'll do whatever you ask, but don't leave me, Frankie, please don't leave me.'

Frankie thought carefully before she answered. 'I'll give you another chance on one condition.'

'What? I'll do anything you want,' Jed said sincerely.

'I don't want to live here any more, Jed. I feel like I'm living with your mum as well as you and it's suffocating me. Can't you find us a place where we can live on our own?'

Jed sighed. His mum wasn't going to be happy with him moving, but he had to keep Frankie sweet. They might not have been getting on well lately, but Jed would hate her to meet another bloke, especially now they had Georgie. 'OK. I can't afford to buy our own plot of land yet, though, but I can find us a place on a site somewhere and we can move our trailer there.'

Frankie smiled. Alice was a troublemaker and once they moved away from her, Frankie was sure that she and Jed would get along much better. 'Another thing: I want to be able to spend time with my brother, Dom, and my nan and grandad. I want them to be a part of Georgie's life.'

Jed wasn't amused, but had no option other than to agree. 'We'll have to still come here and visit my mum and dad, though, Frankie, and they'll wanna visit us. I know you and my mum clash a bit, but she loves Georgie girl, and she's gonna be heartbroken when I tell her we're moving.'

'I don't mind visiting your mum and dad or them visiting us, I just don't want to live with them, Jed. I want us to be a family, just me, you and Georgie, and when you're at work, I want to look after Georgie on my own.'

Relieved that she wasn't taking his daughter away from him, Jed hugged her. 'Now what do you want me to buy ya? I'll buy ya whatever you want to say sorry for what I did today.'

Frankie didn't want presents, all she wanted was to be loved, but suddenly she thought of something that she desperately wanted. 'Driving lessons! I want to have proper lessons with a driving school. Then once I pass my test and you're at work, I can take Georgie out shopping and take her to visit my nan and grandad.'

Jed hated the thought of Frankie being independent. He could imagine other men looking at her at the traffic lights or trying to chat her up as she stopped for petrol and the thought made him feel sick. If she ever left him and another man tried to take over his role as a father, he'd kill the fucking geezer.

'OK. I said I'd buy you anything to make up for what I did and I meant it. I'll find us a place to live first, and then I'll book your driving lessons.'

Frankie threw her arms around his neck. Even though Jed had been violent towards her today, moving away and having driving lessons made her feel happier than she had in ages.

Jed stood up. 'I'd better ring my Uncle Tommy and get him to pick me dad's Merc up.'

'Can I borrow your phone after, Jed? I left mine at my nan's and they're gonna be worried sick. I told them I was going back.'

'What you gonna say to 'em?'

'Don't worry, I ain't gonna tell them what happened. I'll tell 'em that I'll pick my phone up tomorrow. I've got to have it because that policewoman needs to contact me about the court case. I'll just say that you didn't have to go back to Norfolk after all and you wanted to take me out tonight.'

Jed looked concerned. He'd forgotten about the poxy court case and Frankie's eye was looking worse by the second. 'You're gonna have to make up a story, Frankie. Say you tripped down the steps of the trailer and fell flat on your face or something. You won't tell anyone what really happened, will ya? Don't even tell my mum and dad.'

Frankie had no intention of telling a soul. A, she was far too embarrassed and B, she would look a right mug for giving Jed another chance.

'What I'll say is we're going to a party tonight and then tomorrow I'll tell everyone that I got drunk and fell over.'

Jed nodded. He'd tell his cousin Sammy the truth, but he didn't want anyone else to know. He rang his Uncle Tommy, spoke to him, ended the call, and handed the phone to Frankie.

· 'I'm gonna pop over to the house, make sure Mum's all right. I'll only be five minutes and then I'll shoot up the road, get us a takeaway and some booze. What do you want, babe Chinese, Indian or shall I get a Macky D's?'

Frankie wasn't particularly hungry. Her face was hurting like hell and the pain was making her feel queasy. 'I'll just have a little bit of whatever you're having, Jed. I don't fancy McDonald's, though. Can you get me a bottle of vodka and some cartons of orange juice?'

Jed kissed her gently. 'I love you. Won't be long.'

Frankie stared at Jed's phone. She had to plan her story properly before she rang her old home number. Minutes later, she took a deep breath and picked up the phone. Her nan answered.

'Hi, Nan, I'm so sorry I never came back. Jed had to pick up something in Southend and by the time we got back Georgie was grizzly, so I put her straight to bed. Jed's mum's gonna look after her tonight, so me and Jed can go to a party. What I'll do, Nan, is pop round tomorrow and pick my phone and bag up. I'll bring Georgie with me and you and Grandad can spend a bit of time with her.'

Joyce had been annoyed earlier when Frankie hadn't returned, but the thought of seeing baby Georgie the very next day made her happy again. 'What time will you be here, Frankie? Do you want a bit of dinner?'

'No, Nan. I'll pop round about fourish, if that's OK?'

'That's fine. Joey wants to talk to you now, Frankie.'

Frankie's heart went over as the phone was passed to her brother. Her nan she could fool, but Joey knew her too well. 'Are you OK?' Joey asked his voice full of concern.

Frankie began to gabble as she repeated the same story she had told her nan. Joey listened intently. They were twins

173

for Christ's sake – did she think he was stupid? He ended the call, and not wanting to worry his grandparents, urged Dom to accompany him to the garden so he could have a smoke.

Joey shielded his lighter from the wind and lit his cigarette. He took a deep puff and turned to Dominic.

'Frankie's lying. Something's happened, I know it has. I think we should stay here tonight. She's coming round at four tomorrow to pick up her phone and bag and I need to see her, Dom.'

Dominic immediately agreed. He adored Frankie himself and he was obviously well aware of how close Joey was to her.

Joey smoked half his cigarette, stubbed it out, and him and Dominic went back into the house. 'Is it all right if me and Dom stay here tonight, Nan? It's late now and if we stop over we can have a bit of dinner with you and Grandad tomorrow. It will also be nice to spend more time with Frankie and the baby.'

Joyce was thrilled. She loved company. Sometimes it got boring when it was just her and Stanley. 'Yous boys stay as long as you like. I'm cooking a nice leg of lamb tomorrow and we'll have some homemade bread-and-butter pudding for dessert.'

Joey smiled as Dominic yawned. He was so fortunate to have him. Dom was the best boyfriend in the world and so understanding. He turned back to his nan.

'Where do you want us to sleep? Would you rather we slept in separate rooms?'

Joyce stood up. 'Don't be so bloody stupid. You're a gay man now, Joey, and I'm proud of what you are. You and Dom sleep in the spare room with the nice big double bed.'

As Joey and Dominic said their goodnights, Stanley waited until they'd climbed the stairs before he turned to his wife. 'I don't care what they do in their own home, but you shouldn't be encouraging 'em to start fornicating here, Joycie. It ain't right and I don't feel comfortable about it.'

Joyce had had a few glasses of sherry earlier and was in no mood to put up with Stanley's old-fashioned behaviour.

'Stop bleedin' complaining. We're nearly in the 1990s now. Get with it – times have changed, Stanley. Just because our Joey likes a bit of winkle doesn't make him a bad person. I mean, look at me and you, we ain't had sex for donkey's years, but I don't complain, do I?'

The thought and mention of sex with his wife was too much for Stanley to bear. 'Goodnight,' he shouted as he shot up the stairs.

'Gertcha, you old git,' Joyce giggled. She was glad he was gone. She had recorded *Dallas* earlier and fancied another glass of sherry. Shame Stanley didn't resemble JR, Joyce thought mischievously. She'd love to have her wicked way with him.

The following morning Frankie was up at the crack of dawn. She immediately looked in the mirror and gasped. Her right eye was black and blue and she had a lump on her forehead like a table-tennis ball.

Jed got out of bed and stood behind his girlfriend. He put his arms around her waist and kissed the back of her neck. 'I know your face looks bad, but it's only bruised, babe. It'll go down in a couple of days, you'll see.'

Frankie nodded and turned away from the mirror. She felt like the bloody elephant woman and she dreaded facing her grandparents.

Jed gently tilted her chin and planted a kiss on her lips. 'You see to Georgie girl and I'll cook us a nice breakfast. I'm sorry Frankie, really sorry.'

Joyce was in a jovial mood as she washed up the plates from lunch. Her roast and dessert had gone down a storm and she loved having Joey and Dominic around the house. Wiping her hands on the tea towel, she glanced at the clock. The time was quarter to four and Joyce was getting more excited by the minute as she thought of baby Georgie.

*   *   *

175

Jed pulled over at the bottom of the drive. He left the engine running, got out the driver's side and opened Frankie's door for her. 'Now, are you sure you're gonna be OK?' he asked, as he handed her the baby.

'I'll be fine. I know what to say,' Frankie replied.

Jed smiled. 'I'll pick you up here at seven. In the meantime, I'm gonna see if I can find us somewhere to live, babe, and as soon as we move, I'll book your driving lessons for ya.'

Frankie pecked him on the lips and began walking up the driveway.

Joyce, who had been glued to the window for the past ten minutes, saw her granddaughter in the distance.

'She's here,' she yelled excitedly as she ran to the front door.

As the welcome committee ran out to greet her, Frankie was horrified to see Joey and Dom were still there. Pulling the wool over her grandparents' eyes was one thing; trying to pull it over her brother's was a different kettle of fish.

As she clocked Frankie's face, Joyce screamed. 'Oh my God, what have you done to yourself?'

Joey ran over to his sister. 'Did Jed do that to you? I knew it – you ask Dom. I fucking knew he'd hurt you.'

Frankie shook her head furiously. 'Of course Jed never did it. What do you think he is, Joey? We went to a party last night and I haven't really had a proper drink for months, have I? Well, I got so drunk, I don't remember anything. Jed said that I fell down the steps of the trailer. He said that I passed out at the party, he got me home, but I got up in the middle of the night and tried to go outside.'

Joyce and Stanley automatically believed Frankie's story and, not wanting to create a scene or worry his grandparents, Joey pretended to believe it as well.

As soon as Frankie went inside, Joey grabbed Dominic's arm. 'She's lying. I know she's lying. I told you yesterday that something was wrong and I was right. Jed did that to her, I know he did. He's a fucking animal.'

176

Dominic nodded in agreement. 'What are we going to do? How can we help her?'

'There's nothing we can do personally, but I tell you something that I can do: I can ring Gary and Ricky or, even better, I can write to my dad and tell him,' Joey replied.

Dominic shuddered at the mention of Joey's father. 'Do you think that's wise? I mean, what can your dad do if he's locked up?'

Joey shrugged. 'It doesn't matter that he's locked up, my dad will still sort it. I have to do something to help Frankie, and as much as I don't want to contact my old man, with Frankie's safety in question, I have no choice.'

CHAPTER NINETEEN

Frankie Mitchell sat in the trailer and nervously chewed at her fingernails. Realising that her thumb and both index fingers were bleeding, she sat on her hands to stop herself gnawing them down to the bone.

DI Blyth was picking her up at nine o'clock. and every minute that passed felt like an hour. Frankie was dreading going to court and petrified at the thought of seeing her dad again.

Obeying her orders, Jed had gone to Southall horse market this morning. 'I'm gonna sell that mare and foal, Frankie. You know, the mare that's always lame. I won't take 'em this week, though, not with you going to court,' Jed had told her only yesterday.

Frankie had insisted that he went to the market. She had sort of forgiven him for the injuries he'd caused her at the weekend, but seeing as her face was still black and blue, what he had done was proving very hard to forget. Jed had given her a big hug this morning before he left.

'Good luck, babe. All you've gotta do is tell the truth about your dad. Remember to tell the court that he hated me and my family, won't ya?'

With her mind all over the place, Frankie checked the time, then glanced at herself in the mirror. She'd literally caked her face in make-up, but even though the lump on her forehead had gone down, no amount of slap would cover her bruises.

At ten to nine, Frankie heard a car pull up outside. Realising it was DI Blyth, she took a deep breath and picked up her handbag. It was time to face the music.

Eddie Mitchell was sitting on a bench in a cell below the court. He'd insisted on wearing a black suit and tie every single day of his trial. It was in memory of his Jessica, of course.

Nervously twiddling his thumbs, Ed thought of the conversation he'd had on the phone yesterday evening with Gary and Ricky. It was a weird chat, spoken in code, but Eddie had understood the end result.

Neither Gary nor Ricky had had many dealings with Frankie or Joey since Jessica's funeral. In their eyes the twins were equally to blame for the tragedy that had occurred, and also their father's downfall. Joey turning out to be gay had been a knife in their dad's guts; then Frankie, the stupid little cow, had twisted the fucking thing until it would twist no more.

As his solicitor entered the cell, Ed gave a half-smile. His stomach was churning at the thought of facing Frankie, but if Gary and Ricky could get to her first, as they'd promised, maybe things wouldn't be so bad after all.

DI Blyth drove towards central London, glanced at Frankie and smiled. The girl was obviously a bundle of nerves, which was one of the reasons she had insisted on picking her up. Frankie was a key witness and the last thing Blyth wanted was the girl not turning up.

'So, where's that beautiful baby of yours today?' Blyth asked. She needed to keep things as jovial as possible.

'My nan and grandad are looking after her,' Frankie replied, staring out of the window.

Frankie had opted for Joyce to look after Georgie because she had barely spoken to Alice since their argument at the weekend. Jed had told his mum to give him and Frankie some space, and for once the awful woman hadn't been barging in and out of their trailer.

179

'Whatever you do, don't let me mum know that we're planning on moving yet. She'll have a fit and I can't stand the hysterics, so we won't tell her till the day before we leave,' Jed warned Frankie.

Daydreaming, Frankie barely heard DI Blyth's next question. 'Sorry. I was miles away, what did you say?'

'I said is your brother meeting us at the Old Bailey?'

Frankie nodded. 'Joey lives in Islington, so it's not that far from him. He offered to come to Rainham, but I told him there was no point.'

Blyth felt desperately sorry for Frankie. It was unusual for her to get too personally involved with witnesses, but due to the unusual circumstances of this particular case, Blyth couldn't help herself.

'What happened to your face, Frankie? You don't have to tell me if you don't want to.'

Frankie gave a false laugh. 'I got drunk the other night and stacked it. What am I like, eh? Jed reckons I'm the clumsiest person he's ever met.'

DI Blyth gave Frankie a sad smile. She'd made a good career catching out liars and she could spot a bad one a mile off.

'We're nearly there now. The traffic was much better than I anticipated,' the DI said brightly.

Frankie shuddered at the words 'nearly there'. DI Blyth had already run through the set-up and briefed her on the journey as to what she was likely to be asked in court.

Blyth pulled into a car park and turned the engine off. She squeezed Frankie's hand. 'Now, you know what you have to say, don't you? All you need to do is tell the truth.'

Frankie nodded. 'I have to tell the judge and the jury that my dad hated Jed and his family and that he was really angry when he found out about our relationship and my pregnancy.'

Jimmy O'Hara sat opposite Jed in a pub outside Southall horse market. Today had been a very good day. They had got a fair price for the lame mare and its foal and had then purchased a striking sixteen-hand bay trotting mare.

Jed took a sip from his bottle of lager. He had just tried to ring Frankie again, but her phone was still switched off. He smirked and nudged his dad's arm. 'I wonder if she's told the court what a shitcunt her old man is yet?'

Jimmy O'Hara laughed. The thought of Frankie possibly being the one to stick the final nail in her own father's coffin tickled him immensely. 'I still can't believe Mitchell was that much of a dinlo to shoot his own wife. He always thought he was such a big-shot. His old man, Harry, was the same, always punched above his weight. He came a cropper as well, murdered in his own bed. This is what I always try to tell you, Jed: what goes around comes around, son.'

Jed nodded in agreement. His dad had no idea whatsoever that it was he who was responsible for Harry Mitchell's death. Jed's heart wanted to tell his old man the truth, but his head told him not to.

'Whatcha thinking about?' Jimmy said, clicking his fingers.

Jed grinned. 'Eddie "I'm going down for life" Mitchell.'

Appreciating his son's humour, Jimmy burst out laughing.

Frankie wasn't due to give evidence until after lunch. Bored with sitting in the witness-protection room with people she didn't know, she grabbed Joey's arm.

'Where are you going?' DI Blyth asked suspiciously.

'We're going to get a sandwich and a coffee,' Frankie replied.

Blyth immediately stood up. 'OK, I'll come with you.'

Frankie shook her head. 'I need to speak to my brother alone. I won't be long; I promise I'll be back in half an hour.'

DI Blyth wasn't happy. She hadn't planned to let Frankie out of sight for a minute. About to argue her point, she stopped in her tracks. Frankie was clearly agitated and time alone with her brother might help her nerves somewhat. Perhaps she even wanted to talk to him about her facial injuries, tell him what had really happened.

Blyth sat back down on her chair. 'I'll wait here and don't be long, in case they call your name.'

Gary and Ricky Mitchell had been waiting for an opportunity to speak to their sister all morning. They'd toyed with the idea of sending their dad's brief into the witness room to tell Frankie they had an urgent message for her. After much deliberation, they'd decided against it, as if their story wasn't believed, they'd have no chance whatsoever of getting to her.

Gary looked at his watch. 'I think we've had it now. She's due in soon. What are we gonna tell Dad?'

Ricky shrugged. He adored his father, but he and Gary had done their best to help him. 'It ain't our fault, Gal. I mean we've been 'ere since first thing this morning. That pig ain't left Frankie's side, she's been stuck to her like glue. The only hope we had is if she went for a fag or wandered to the canteen with Joey, and she ain't, has she?'

Gary was devastated. Their dad had been relying on him and Ricky to somehow get to Frankie, and they'd let him down. 'Let's give it another half-hour or something. You never know, she might still pop out for a smoke.'

The lads had been taking it in turns to peep around the wall and keep watch.

'I'm just gonna go for a piss,' Ricky told his brother.

As Ricky disappeared into the nearby toilets, Gary peeped around the wall again. His heart immediately started to pound in his chest. Frankie and Joey, minus the cop, were walking his way. Cursing his brother for going to the toilet at just the wrong moment, Gary made a snap decision.

There were too many people milling about for him to drag both Joey and Frankie outside on his own, so the only option he had was to bundle them into the toilet as well.

Gary hid the other side of the wall and took a deep breath.

'What are you doing?' Joey yelled, as Gary put an arm around both him and Frankie.

Seeing a grey-haired woman staring suspiciously their way,

182

Gary smiled at her. 'Smile nicely and do as I say. Scream or shout and I'll fucking kill the pair of ya,' Gary said under his breath as he led the troublesome twins along the corridor.

As Ricky reappeared, Gary nodded to the toilet. 'Is anyone in there?'

Ricky shook his head.

'It's the men's. I ain't going in there,' Frankie said adamantly.

Ignoring her, Gary ordered Ricky to keep watch outside and pushed both twins into a cubicle.

Forever the drama queen, Joey began to cry. 'Let us go or I'll scream,' he said, as Gary squeezed himself in and locked the door.

'Shut up, you fag. It's Frankie I want to talk to, not you.'

Frankie was much calmer than Joey. She guessed that this ambush was something to do with the evidence she was due to give and she certainly wasn't afraid of Gary or bloody Ricky.

'You go outside and stand with Ricky,' she urged Joey.

'I'm not leaving you alone with . . .'

Gary stopped Joey mid-sentence by opening the cubicle and pushing him out. 'Do as your sister says,' he ordered.

As Joey slunk outside, Gary turned to Frankie. 'Sorry, I didn't mean to frighten you, but I had to speak to you.'

'I take it this is about Dad?'

Gary nodded. 'When you stand in the dock you mustn't say anything about Dad hating Jed or any of the O'Haras. I know what Dad did was wrong, Frankie, but me and you both know that it was an accident. He's our flesh and blood and you can't put him away, girl.'

Frankie stared at Gary. 'I've gotta tell the truth. DI Blyth will go mad if I don't.'

Gary moved closer to his sister. 'You can't tell the truth. Dad's statement says that he went to Tilbury just to frighten Jed and I need you to say the same thing. You can say that he was upset because you were pregnant, but you can't say nothing else about Dad hating the O'Haras. If the jury think that Dad meant to kill Jed, then he'll get life. If there's doubt, he might only get manslaughter.'

Frankie ran her hands through her hair. 'I don't think I can do it, Gary.'

Furious, Gary grabbed his half-sister by the shoulders and shook her. 'You're the only one that can help Dad now, Frankie, and seeing as this whole mess is all your fault, it's the least you can bloody well do. What happened to your face? Lover boy been knocking you about already, has he?'

Unable to hold her brother's gaze, Frankie looked at the toilet seat. 'I got drunk on Saturday and fell over.'

Gary made a sarcastic grunt and shook his head. 'You are one silly naive little girl, Frankie, and you need to listen to some home truths. Everyone's lives are fucked up because of you. You killed your mum, no one else. If you hadn't fraternised with the enemy, your poor mum would still be here to tell the tale. And, as for Dad, he was devastated to learn that Joey was queer, then you had to go one further. Well, let me tell you something. I've spoken to Dad and I know for a fact that if he gets life, he's gonna hang himself.'

Frankie looked at Gary in horror. 'No, he won't, will he?'

Knowing his lie had had the effect he had hoped for, Gary elaborated. 'He's even planned how he's gonna do it, Frankie. He said if he gets life, he's gonna kill himself on your mum's birthday with a belt.'

As Frankie began to cry, Gary gave her an awkward hug. 'Look, the ball's in your court. Say the right thing and there's a good chance Dad will get a shorter sentence. Obviously, what you choose to do is up to you, but if you can live with both your parents' deaths on your conscience, you're a better person than I am. I wouldn't be able to sleep at night if I had that much blood on my hands.'

Ricky's voice stopped the conversation from continuing. 'Gal, that pig's looking for Frankie. Joey told her that she's outside having a fag, so you'd better send her out before she comes back again.'

184

Gary unlocked the cubicle. 'Go on, you'd better go.'

Traumatised, Frankie grabbed his arm. 'Dad won't hang himself if he only gets done for manslaughter, will he?'

Gary shook his head. 'Nah, he can handle a short stretch. He said he'd only end his life if he's looking at life.'

Seeing his sister walk towards him, Joey grabbed her arm. 'Quick, DI Blyth is looking everywhere for you. Let's get back to the witness room before she sees us.'

Joey and Frankie ran along the corridor. 'I can't believe Gary called me a fag,' Joey said.

'He said much worse to me. If Dad gets life, he's gonna kill himself, he reckons, and he said it's all my fault.'

Reaching the witness room, the twins stopped outside. 'Why don't you tell DI Blyth about Gary? She saw Ricky standing there, but she didn't know that I knew him.'

Frankie shook her head. 'No, we mustn't say a word, Joey, not to anyone.'

'There you are! Where have you been, I've been looking everywhere for you,' Blyth said running towards them.

Frankie put on a false smile. 'Sorry, I was dying for a fag, then I had the runs. I think it's nerves.'

Blyth nodded understandingly. 'Quick, follow me. They've just called your name out, and don't forget to address the men in the legal teams as "Sir", and the judge as "your Honour".'

185

CHAPTER TWENTY

Frankie took her hand off the Bible and then nervously glanced at the gallery.

Joey was now sitting there, along with many other familiar faces. Her uncles, Paulie and Ronny, stared at her and she quickly averted her eyes. Glancing back, she caught the eye of her dad's auntie, Joan. Seeing Gary glaring at her, she quickly looked away again.

As the prosecution began to cross-examine her, Frankie could barely comprehend the questions. She had just seen her dad and was struggling to breathe properly.

'Could you answer the question please, Miss Mitchell,' the judge said softly.

'I'm sorry, your honour. I didn't hear it properly,' Frankie replied in almost a whisper.

'On the twenty-eighth of August 1988, is it true that you and your uncle, Raymond Smith, drove to Tilbury in search of your mother, Miss Mitchell?'

Frankie glanced at her father again. He looked a bit older than she remembered. He also looked tired and had lost some weight. Tearing her eyes away from him, Frankie cleared her throat. She had never felt so nervous in her life.

'Yes, that's true,' she mumbled.

'Could you please speak up, Miss Mitchell? The jury can't hear you properly,' the judge said, in a much sterner tone than the one he had previously used.

'I said yes, that's true, your Honour,' Frankie repeated, remembering DI Blyth's words about the way she had to address people.

Aware of DI Blyth staring at her, Frankie looked at her feet.

The prosecution addressed her once more. 'Miss Mitchell, how would you describe your father's relationship with your boyfriend, Jed O'Hara?'

'My dad never really met Jed, sir,' Frankie replied honestly.

'So why hadn't you introduced your boyfriend to your father, Miss Mitchell? You were pregnant and planning to marry Mr O'Hara, were you not?'

'Because we hadn't been together for long, sir. I sort of accidently got pregnant and then Jed proposed. It all happened very quickly.'

'So the reason, Miss Mitchell, that you never told your father about your relationship with Jed O'Hara, was not because your father, Eddie Mitchell, passionately hated Mr O'Hara's family?'

'Objection, your Honour,' someone shouted.

'Objection overruled,' the judge stated.

Frankie looked at her dad again. His eyes looked terribly sad, haunted almost. Thinking of what Gary had said to her earlier, she knew what she had to say.

'My dad never hated Jed's family, sir. He never really knew them. If he was upset, it was because I'd got pregnant at such a young age, nothing else.'

The prosecution team looked at Frankie in despair. What was the silly girl doing?

DI Blyth felt defeated. Frankie had been so sure of what she was going to say on the journey here, so what had gone so bloody wrong with her answers? Glancing into the gallery, Blyth saw the man who had been standing outside the toilets with Joey. She knew immediately that Frankie had been got at.

'Shit,' she mumbled under her breath. She knew she should never have let Frankie out of her sight.

The prosecution QC wasn't a happy man. 'Isn't it true, Miss Mitchell, that your father is a well-known gangster, who will stop at nothing to get his own way?'

'Objection, your Honour,' someone shouted again.

Frankie began to cry. Whatever her dad had done, she knew she still loved him.

'Objection sustained,' the judge said.

The prosecuting QC had planned to ask Frankie many more questions, but now decided not to bother. He glared at DI Blyth.

'No more questions, your Honour,' he said, as he sat back down.

Eddie's defence team were thrilled with Frankie's performance. His own QC, James Fitzgerald Smythe, stood up. 'Is it OK to call you Frankie? Miss Mitchell seems too formal for someone so young, don't you think?'

'Yes, sir,' Frankie said. This man seemed much nicer than the last one.

'How would you describe your relationship with your father, Frankie? Were you close?'

'We were very close. I was always a daddy's girl, sir,' Frankie replied honestly.

'And how would you describe your father's relationship with your mother, Frankie? Would you say they were happy? Did they argue much?'

Frankie shook her head. 'They rarely ever argued, sir. My mum and dad were very much in love – so much so, me and my brother used to take the mickey out of them, didn't we Joey?'

As Frankie turned to her brother in the gallery, the judge cleared his throat. 'Can you just answer the questions without involving anybody else please, Miss Mitchell?'

'Sorry, your Honour,' Frankie said meekly.

'Was your father ever violent indoors, Frankie? Did he ever hit you, your mother or your brother?'

Catching her dad's eye again, Frankie took a deep breath. 'No sir, my dad wasn't a violent man. He loved animals and he honestly wouldn't hurt a fly.'

In the gallery, Joey was furious. How could Frankie say that their dad wouldn't hurt a fly, after what he'd done to their mum?

He'd tried to choke Joey with a sandwich once and had even tried to chop Dominic's cock off, for fuck's sake. Unable to listen to any more of his sister's bullshit, Joey stood up and left the courtroom.

Eddie's QC smiled at Frankie. 'No more questions, your Honour.'

Back in Rainham, Joycie and Stanley were in their element. Having baby Georgie to themselves for the day was the tonic both of them had desperately needed. Even though they hadn't attended the court case, it had still taken its toll on them, and babysitting their beautiful granddaughter was a welcome distraction.

Georgie was a happy child, who rarely seemed to cry and was a joy to have around.

'My turn for a cuddle now,' Joyce said to Stanley.

Smiling, Stanley stood up and placed the gurgling baby on Joycie's lap. 'I wasn't sure of her name at first, Joycie, but I like it now. Do you remember that film, *Georgy Girl*?'

Joyce smiled. 'Yeah, it had that song in it, "Hey there! Georgy Girl", didn't it?'

'Weren't it The Seekers that sang that?' Stanley asked.

'I can't remember,' Joyce replied.

Stanley looked at the clock. 'I wonder how Frankie's getting on? Let's hope she's brave enough to get justice for our Jessica.'

Joycie sighed. Unlike Stanley, part of her felt sorry for the predicament Eddie found himself in. She hadn't forgiven him, of course, but she couldn't hate him – not like Stanley did, anyway.

The shrill ring of the phone saved Joyce from answering Stanley's awkward question. 'Get that, love. It might be Frankie.'

Stanley ran to the phone. 'What's a matter, Joey? Calm down, I can't understand you.'

As Joey repeated what had happened in court, Stanley was shell-shocked.

'What's up?' Joyce asked, as her husband slammed the phone down.

'Our Frankie fucked up. Told the court that Eddie wouldn't hurt a fly, apparently. Joey's fuming with her. He walked out and left her. On his way home, he is. How could she do that, Joycie? How can she stick up for that monster after what he did to our Jessica?'

'Maybe she had her reasons,' Joyce said defensively.

'Reasons! What fucking reasons? I want no more to do with her. How can our Jessica have died in vain? It ain't right and I won't stand for it.'

Joyce stood up, put Georgie in her cot and faced her furious husband. Pointing a finger in his face, she gave it to him. 'Now you listen to me, Stanley Smith. What happened was horrendous, but it was a bloody accident. There's not an hour of a day goes past when I don't think of our Jessica, but she's gone and being bitter isn't going to bring her back. Eddie was devastated over what happened. Why do you think he gave us this bloody house?'

'Because he was trying to ease his own bastard guilt,' Stanley yelled.

As her husband tried to leave the room, Joyce grabbed him by the arm. 'Don't you dare kick off with Frankie, 'cause if you do, we will lose contact with the baby and if that happens, I'll never forgive you, Stanley.'

Stanley pulled his arm away. 'Leave me alone, woman.'

DI Blyth collared Frankie as soon as she stepped outside the court-room. She pulled her to one side, away from her villainous family.

'What happened in there, Frankie? Somebody threaten you, did they?'

Frankie could barely look Blyth in the eye. She had been so kind and Frankie felt terribly guilty. 'Nobody threatened me,' she lied.

Blyth shook her head disappointedly. 'I saw the men in the gallery. One of them was with your brother, Joey, when I was searching for you earlier. Did the other one that was with him get to you, Frankie? You were not outside having a cigarette because I looked everywhere for you.'

'Yes, I was. I went round the back of the building as I didn't want to bump into any of my family. Anyway, that was my stepbrother, Ricky, who was with Joey. He's my dad's son from his first marriage.'

After Frankie's failure to produce the goods, Blyth couldn't be arsed to drive her home.

'Your family are waiting for you, I think. Are you OK going home with them?'

Frankie nodded. She couldn't get away from DI Blyth quickly enough. As she went to walk away, she turned around. 'I'm really sorry, but he's my dad and I love him.'

Gary and Ricky Mitchell were standing outside the court having a cigarette as Frankie approached them.

'You did great, sis. Did you see the look in Dad's eyes? Now that he can see you still love him, I know that whatever happens, he won't top himself,' Gary said. His little white lie had worked wonders.

'I don't know how I'm gonna get home. Where's the nearest station?'

Ricky handed Frankie a fag. 'We've got a motor, we'll drop you back.'

'Where's Joey?' Frankie asked.

'I dunno. Gone home I suppose,' Gary replied.

Taking her phone out of her bag, Frankie switched it on and rang her brother. 'It's switched off,' she said dejectedly.

'Bless ya, you angel. You did a great job in there, your dad'll be ever so proud of you,' said a voice.

Frankie hugged her dad's aunt Joan. 'How are you keeping?' she asked politely.

'All the better for your testimony. Your dad's a good man, Frankie, and whatever anyone else tells ya, don't you ever forget that. You remember Vi, don't ya?'

Frankie nodded, kissed both old ladies politely on the cheek, then turned back to Gary and Ricky.

'Can we make a move? I need to get home to the baby.'

Memories came flooding back as Frankie spotted her dad's Land Cruiser. 'I didn't realise you had Dad's car,' she said.

'He told us to use it. Ain't much use to him at the moment, is it?' Ricky replied bluntly.

Frankie sat in the back. Five minutes into the journey the interrogation started.

'So what really happened to your face, sis?' Gary enquired.

'I told you, I fell over.'

Ricky wasn't driving. Positioning himself, he turned around and faced her. 'I know you're lying. While you was in the boy's room with Gary, I was talking to Joey, remember? He's worried about you, Frankie, we all are. He was gonna write to Dad, but I told him not to.'

Frankie was furious with Joey. How dare he involve their father in her relationship after everything that had happened? 'Well, you're all worrying for nothing. I fell over, I swear I did. Jed's good to me, he would never hurt me.'

Ricky turned back round. If Frankie wouldn't admit to anything, then there was sod all they could do.

Gary stared at her in the interior mirror. 'OK, we believe you. But I'm telling you something now, Frankie: if I ever find out that Jed did that to you, I'll break every bone in his puny, pikey body.'

With court adjourned for the day, Eddie was bundled into the back of the meat wagon that would take him back to the prison. Thinking of the day's events, he rested his head against the van's metal interior. He hadn't even been able to bring himself to look at his gay son, but Frankie still loved him, he could see it in her eyes, and just knowing that had lifted his spirits no end.

Eddie knew through Raymond that Frankie was back in touch with Joyce and Stanley. Biting his lip, Ed made a decision. As soon as he got back to his cell, he would write Frankie a letter and send it via her grandparents. Perhaps once the court case was over, Frankie could come and visit him. She might even bring the baby with her, if he was lucky.

For the first time since Frankie had given birth, Eddie thought deeply about his granddaughter. What did she look like? What colour was her hair? Did she look like Frankie? Or did she favour him or Jessica?

Eddie had originally vowed never to have anything to do with the kid. 'It's an O'Hara, not a fucking Mitchell,' he'd said viciously to Raymond.

Seeing Frankie today had changed Ed's mind. Whoever the father was, that kid was still Frankie's and also part of himself and Jessica.

As the meat wagon got stuck in traffic, Eddie felt a serenity within. Whatever the jury decided, his daughter had stuck her neck out for him today and proved her worth not only as his daughter, but also as a Mitchell.

Sitting in his shed with only his pigeons for company, Stanley thought long and hard about Joycie's harsh words.

He'd calmed down a bit now and even though he thought it was awful that Frankie had stuck up for her father, he realised that him kicking off wasn't the answer. Slurping the last of his bitter, Stanley screwed up the can and lobbed it in the bin. He locked the shed and made his way back to the house.

'Frankie's just rung. She'll be here soon,' Joyce told him.

Lifting his granddaughter off Joycie's lap, Stanley held her close. He planted a kiss on the child's forehead.

'I thought about what you said, Joycie, and you're right. Losing contact with this little one would break my heart, so I'll keep me mouth shut and me thoughts to meself.'

Joyce smiled. 'You're a good man, Stanley Smith.'

After the initial awkward conversation about her bruises, Frankie had quite enjoyed the rest of the journey. It was good to catch up with her half-brothers and she'd loved telling them all about Georgie.

As the Land Cruiser pulled on to the drive, Frankie urged Gary and Ricky to come and say hello to her grandparents.

'And you can meet Georgie. She needs to know who her family is,' she told them.

Gary and Ricky felt awkward as they stepped into their dad's old home. They hadn't seen Stanley since the day of Jessica's funeral and they didn't really know what to say to him.

Joyce invited them in and, sensing their awkwardness, was friendly and warm.

'Stanley, make the boys a nice cup of tea,' she ordered.

Gary felt all choked up as Frankie placed Georgie in his arms. 'She's a little darling, bless her,' he said lovingly.

Ricky smiled. 'She definitely looks like a Mitchell, Frankie. She's dark, like Dad.'

Unusually for Gary, his eyes welled up. 'The old man would just love her. You must take her to see him, Frankie.'

Ricky agreed. 'It would cheer him up no end. We'll drive you to Wandsworth if you like. And we'll wait for you and bring you home.'

Frankie smiled. It felt so good to have her family around her once more. 'OK, let's arrange it.'

Less than a mile down the road, Jed O'Hara was seriously annoyed. 'She must be out of court by now. Why ain't the silly cow got her phone on?' he said, as he cracked open another can of lager.

'Because she can't be trusted. I told you you should have never settled down with her. You should always stick with your own, Jed,' Alice piped up.

Ignoring his mother, Jed handed his father another beer and sat on the sofa next to him. Apart from his annoyance over Frankie not having her phone switched on, he and his dad had had a bloody good day today. They'd bought a fine horse, sold a dodgy one, drank loads of beer up in Southall and then continued their drinking session on their return.

'Now, what do yous boys fancy to eat? I've got some nice lamb chops and steak out the freezer,' Alice said.

'Just do us a mixture. We don't want a proper dinner. Just cook us a big plate of meat,' Jimmy replied.

Jed waited for his mother to leave the room, then turned to his father. 'Frankie wants us to move and I've promised her I'll find us a place on a site somewhere.'

Jimmy looked at his son in horror. His Alice had been like a different woman since the baby had come into their lives. She was happy and content. 'Your mother will be devastated, Jed. She adores that chavvie. Why don't you tell Frankie you can't find anywhere? You don't want your mother getting depressed again, do ya?'

Jed felt torn. He loved living close to his parents, but he'd also made a promise to Frankie. 'I'll see what I can do. I'll have a chat with Frankie and see if I can get her to change her mind.'

'You're the man, Jed, the breadwinner. Women are second class to us, you know that, son. You choose where you wanna live – don't let some dinlo woman start ordering you about,' Jimmy retorted.

Hearing a motor pull up outside, Jed ran over to the window. 'It's Frankie, she's back.'

He bolted to the front door just in time to see the motor disappear down the drive. 'Who was that? It weren't the gavver's motor,' he asked, as he ran towards Frankie.

'Gary and Ricky. They dropped me off home.'

Jed grabbed the carrycot. 'Why ain't you had your phone on? How did it go?'

'I couldn't do it.'

Holding the cot with one arm, Jed grabbed Frankie with the other and swung her around to face him. 'Whaddya mean, you couldn't do what?'

Seeing Jed's irate expression, Frankie looked him defiantly in the eye. 'I couldn't say anything bad about my dad. Don't get on my case, Jed, because I'm not in the mood. You wouldn't stand up in court and slag off your dad, would you?'

Jed shook his head in disbelief. 'You stupid cow! If your

dad gets a light sentence, he'll come back to haunt us, and when he does it'll be all your fault. You're a dinlo, Frankie, a proper fucking dinlo.'

CHAPTER TWENTY-ONE

Furious with Frankie, Jed sodded off out the following day. Getting off his face and shagging some old slapper was the only way he could deal with his girlfriend's betrayal, but by Friday morning, he was ready to return home and make things right once again.

As he drove towards Rainham, Jed stopped at a florist, and picked up a bouquet of flowers. He'd spent the previous day with Sammy boy. They'd got well mullered and the two old tarts they'd woken up with in Tilbury this morning were not only old enough to be their mums, but were also haggard and pig ugly.

Jed pulled up outside the trailer and picked up the bouquet. He'd already prepared his lie and, as usual, it was good. He opened the trailer door.

'All right, babe? I got you these.'

Frankie had just bathed and was now dressing baby Georgie. 'Where have you been, Jed? Your phone's been switched off and I've been worried sick about you.'

Jed sat on the edge of the bed and kissed his gorgeous baby on the forehead. Tickling Georgie's chin, he smiled at Frankie. 'I'm sorry, Frankie. I've been everywhere trying to find us somewhere to live. Me battery went dead on me phone and I've been driving around like a blue-arsed fly. There ain't no spaces on any sites at present, but I've put our name on the waiting list in ten different areas,' Jed lied.

Frankie picked up Georgie and sat down next to Jed. She could smell the booze seeping through his pores, but decided not to say anything. She knew he'd been upset by what had happened in court and, as long as they were OK now, she didn't care if he'd got himself pissed and stayed out all night.

'Let me hold her for a bit.'

Frankie placed Georgie on his lap and sighed. 'So what happens now? How long will we have to wait for a place on a site?'

Jed shrugged. After the conversation he'd had with his dad the other evening, he had no intention of upsetting his mum and moving away at the moment. 'It could be weeks, it could be months. The sites are banged out, Frankie, and there's a waiting list on all of 'em.'

'What about if I go up the council? We might be able to get a flat or a house,' Frankie suggested.

Jed immediately shook his head. 'I ain't no gorjer, babe, and I can't live like one. We've got a beautiful trailer and I want us to live in this.'

Frankie had originally enjoyed the novelty of living in a trailer, and had found it exciting, but since Georgie had been born, she no longer liked it as much. She squeezed Jed's hand.

'Please let me go to the council, Jed. If we can get a little house, it'll be lovely for Georgie. She'll be walking before we know it and she needs a garden or somewhere to play.'

Jed had always known how to play women. His sad expression was, and always had been, his ace card. 'I'm a travelling boy, Frankie, and I can't be cooped up in a house or flat. Bear with me, babe, and I promise you faithfully that once I've got enough wonga, I'll buy us the most beautiful piece of land. Georgie will have acres to play in then and, hopefully, by that time she'll have brothers and sisters to play with her.'

Frankie smiled. 'OK, we'll forget the council, but do keep trying to get us a place, Jed. I'm desperate for us to live on our own now.'

Jed kissed her on the lips and tilted her chin. 'You have my word.'

Over at the Old Bailey, Eddie watched with interest as Gina, the private detective, took the stand. The previous day had been a good one for Ed. Dougie and John had each given him a great character reference. The bent, now retired chief inspector they had blackmailed had had no choice but to speak glowingly about him, and Raymond's evidence had been absolutely faultless.

'Jessica was my sister. I loved her more than anyone and I know for a fact that Eddie would never intentionally hurt her. Yes, he was obviously annoyed when he found out his sixteen-year-old daughter was pregnant, but what father wouldn't be?' Ray convincingly told the prosecution. 'He went to Tilbury to pay Jed money to leave Frankie alone. When he wasn't there, he decided to frighten him. I know Eddie Mitchell as well as anyone does and I know that violence isn't part of his nature.'

As Gina began to speak, Eddie thought how attractive she was. He'd known that she had a crush on him when he'd first hired her, but due to his love and loyalty to Jessica, he had never before noticed her beauty. Eddie looked away as he caught her eye. She was fairly well-spoken, obviously intelligent and, with her mass of long, dark, wavy hair, she certainly had the impetus to turn heads. Gina had an English accent, but with a surname like Mulcahy, Eddie realised she had to be of Irish origin. Ed was unsure of her age, but guessed she must be late twenties, early thirties. Gina reminded him of a lawyer and he imagined that most men would find her quite intimidating. She had ball-breaker stamped all over her.

Eddie had ordered Raymond to pay Gina a visit the previous week. The two of them both had to give an account of the evening in question and they needed their answers to be similar.

'So is it true, Miss Mulcahy, that Mr Mitchell paid you to follow his daughter, Francesca, and her boyfriend, Jed O'Hara?' the prosecution asked.

'Yes, sir. Mr Mitchell paid me to find out who his daughter's boyfriend was. Francesca had become extremely secretive and, being a caring father, Mr Mitchell was very worried about her.'

'And were you aware that Mr Mitchell was planning to use violence to get his own way, Miss Mulcahy?' the prosecution asked.

'Objection, your Honour,' the defence QC shouted.

'Objection overruled,' the judge replied.

Gina answered the question professionally and confidently. 'I would never take on any case that I didn't feel totally comfortable with, sir. Mr Mitchell was an absolute gentleman. He adored his wife, his children, and his only worry was his daughter, who had got herself pregnant at such a young age. I do not condone violence of any kind and would never involve myself with a client who was planning on taking the law into their own hands.'

'But Mr Mitchell took the law into his own hands, didn't he? He made you follow Jed O'Hara to find out where he was and he then planned to shoot him. Unfortunately for the defendant, the case of mistaken identity resulted in him shooting his own wife, didn't it, Miss Mulcahy?'

'No, that is untrue, sir.'

Eddie stared at his feet. He could deal with the whole court-case scenario until Jessica's name was mentioned in the same sentence as her murder.

The prosecution carried on. 'Were you aware, Miss Mulcahy, that you were being paid as an accessory to a planned, calculated murder?'

'Mr Mitchell never planned to harm anyone. He was going to Tilbury to frighten Jed and perhaps buy him off, nothing else, sir,' Gina replied calmly.

The prosecution QC did not like Gina one little bit. 'And you're sure of that, are you, Miss Mulcahy?' he asked sarcastically.

'One hundred per cent, sir. Mr Mitchell asked me to wait outside the salvage yard so he could settle my bill. I had another

200

appointment to attend, so I couldn't, but you don't think Mr Mitchell would have wanted my presence if he was planning on murdering someone, do you? Please remember, I barely knew the man.'

'That isn't the case now though, is it, Miss Mulcahy?'

'Objection, your Honour.'

The judge nodded at the defence QC. 'Objection sustained.'

Turning to the prosecution team, the judge spoke to them abruptly. 'Could we stick with asking questions please, instead of insinuating things that might influence the jury?'

'I'm sorry, your Honour. No more questions,' the prosecution QC said, as he flopped back down in his chair.

Back in Rainham, Jed had just harnessed up his new horse and was about to test it out on the road. Seeing his girlfriend standing at the trailer door with the baby in her arms, Jed waved.

'Put some warm clothes on the baby and you can both come with me, babe,' he shouted.

Frankie shook her head. Georgie was far too young to be taken out on a horse and cart. Say it bolted or something?

Jed trotted the horse towards her. 'Let Mum look after Georgie for a bit and you come with me, then. Go on, be a devil. We can stop at a pub and have a few drinks and some lunch.'

Frankie hesitated. She and Jed rarely had any time alone any more and if there was little chance of getting a place on a site just yet, it was best she built some bridges with Alice. 'Wait for me. I'll be five minutes,' she told Jed.

Alice was mopping the kitchen floor when Frankie knocked. 'Who is it?' she shouted.

'It's me, Frankie. I was wondering if you could look after Georgie while me and Jed pop out for a bit.'

Alice was overjoyed. She had missed spending time with her granddaughter and it had broken her heart the other day when Frankie had allowed Georgie to spend the day with her own grandparents, rather than with Alice and Jimmy. Determined to get back in Frankie's good books, Alice plastered a smile on her face and opened the kitchen door.

'I'd love to have her. Be careful if you're coming in 'cause the floor's all wet.'

Frankie handed her the carrycot and her baby bag. 'Everything's in there, I think, but we'll leave the trailer unlocked just in case you need anything else.'

Jimmy had had a good talk to Alice the previous day. 'Frankie's that chavvie's mother. If you can't be nice to her and get on, they'll end up moving away, Alice. You'll lose Jed and the baby then,' he warned her.

Alice hadn't slept. She had lain awake all night thinking about her husband's wise words. She didn't like Frankie – never had, never would – but she was determined to make an effort just so she could be close to Georgie.

'Where are you off to? Anywhere nice?' she asked chirpily.

'We're going out on the horse and cart. Jed wants to take me for lunch and a few drinks.'

As Frankie went to leave, Alice grabbed her arm. 'Can we forget about the argument and be friends again, Frankie? I know me and you clash a bit, but we have to try and get on for Jed and Georgie's sake.'

Frankie smiled. 'I'd like that.'

The second the door was shut, Alice took the child out of the cot and stared at Frankie out of the window. She lifted Georgie's arm up and made her wave.

'Bye, bye Mummy, you old shitcunt,' she cackled.

Terry Baldwin was not a happy man. He had been released from prison in January after serving three years for ABH and now his only daughter, Sally, had just informed him that she was pregnant.

If Sally were in a stable relationship, Terry would have been OK about this, but seeing as the girl was single and moping about indoors, Terry was anything but. Yesterday, he had finally got the truth of the story.

'I love him, Dad. I told him I was pregnant, but he didn't want to know. He promised me he was gonna leave his girlfriend, but I've found out since, she's had his baby as well.'

Terry comforted his beautiful daughter. 'What's his name, love?'

Sally refused to tell him at first, but after a bit of gentle persuasion, she relented. 'His name is Jed, Daddy. Jed O'Hara.'

Terry had heard of the O'Haras and, being in the know, it hadn't taken him long to get an address for Jed.

Finishing his can of lager, Terry picked up his cosh and his car keys. It was time to pay the boy with the wandering cock a visit.

Eddie Mitchell showed little emotion as the judge began summing up his case. He had just tried to give his own evidence, but had failed because his QC had ordered him to do so.

'Show some emotion, these juries love all that. Sob your bloody heart out if you can,' were Fitzgerald Smythe's words of wisdom.

'I loved my wife more than life itself. I went to Tilbury to offer Jed O'Hara money to leave my daughter alone. When he wasn't there, I decided to frighten him by spraying some bullets. I would never intentionally hurt anyone,' Eddie said, before breaking down. He only had to think of what had happened to Jessica to cry real tears.

'From the evidence we have heard throughout this trial, there is little doubt that Mr Mitchell truly loved his wife, Jessica. What you, the jury, have to decide is whether Mr Mitchell intended to kill Jed O'Hara on the evening in question. Do you believe that he arrived in Tilbury with a machine gun just to frighten Mr O'Hara? Or was it a case of mistaken identity?' the judge intoned.

Eddie bowed his head. The jury had felt saddened by his emotional breakdown. He'd glanced at them and seen it written on their faces.

The judge finished his speech, the jury filed out and Eddie

was led back to the cells. This was it, it was now a waiting game, and for once his future wasn't in his own hands.

Unlike her poor father, Frankie had had a brilliant day. She and Jed had had a scream in the pub and it had reminded Frankie of when they'd first got together.

Jed helped her back onto the cart and Frankie giggled as he pinched her bum. 'Let's leave the baby in me mum's. I wanna give you a right good seeing-to when I get you home.'

Frankie blushed. Even though they had a daughter together, Jed still had the ability to make her go all coy.

Jed jumped on the cart and urged Frankie to sit in front of him and take over the reins. 'I can't drive it, I'm drunk,' she protested.

Jed laughed. 'You'll be fine. Trot on,' he yelled, slapping the filly's arse with the reins.

Terry Baldwin sat in the lay-by near Jed's house. He had a clear view of the drive and was waiting for the little bastard who had knocked his daughter up to arrive home. He'd spoken to Alice earlier.

'What do you want? Who you looking for? This is private property, you know,' she shouted, as he pulled up on the drive.

Terry turned on the charm. 'Is Jed about? I've got a couple of horses I wanna sell him.'

Alice softened slightly. 'He's out with his girlfriend at the moment. They won't be long, they're on the horse and cart. Do you know my Jimmy?'

Terry nodded. 'Is he about?'

'He's out with his brothers. One of 'em had a bit of aggro. He won't be back till late tonight.'

Terry smiled. 'Thanks, darling, I'll pop back later.'

He was now waiting in the lay-by outside and he would wait here however long he had to. Resting his bonce on the headrest, Terry sat bolt upright as he heard the clip-clop of horse's hooves. He had no idea what Jed actually looked like, but when the horse and cart came into sight, he knew immediately that the lad on the cart was the culprit.

As Jed and Frankie trotted towards the house, Alice ran out to greet them.

'Georgie's asleep. I've just fed her. Did you have a nice time?' she asked.

Jed laughed. 'Yeah, blinding. Me and Frankie fancy a bit of time alone, so you all right to carry on babysitting, Mum?'

'Yous two enjoy yourselves. Don't you worry about Georgie, she loves being with her Nanna Alice.'

'Go and get undressed, I'll be ten minutes,' Jed whispered seductively to Frankie.

Alice nudged Jed. 'A mush came here looking for you earlier, said he had some grys to sell ya.'

Jed was instantly suspicious. He waited until Frankie was safely inside the trailer, then he turned to face his mother. 'What mush?'

Hearing the conversation, Terry Baldwin leaped out from behind a tree. 'This mush, you dirty little bastard.'

Jed was taken completely by surprise as the thick-set man lunged at him with a cosh.

Alice screamed at the top of her voice as he repeatedly whacked it around her son's head. 'Get off him, leave him alone,' she shouted, as she ran towards the man and jumped on his back.

Hearing a commotion outside, Frankie threw her jeans and T-shirt back on. She opened the trailer door and screamed as she saw a big man hitting her boyfriend with some kind of object.

Patience had never been one of Eddie Mitchell's virtues and today was no different. Waiting for anything did his head in, and here he was sitting alone in a cell waiting to see if twelve complete strangers were about to dish him out a life sentence. Hearing footsteps, Ed looked up. It was his lawyer, Larry.

'What's up?' he asked worriedly.

'The jury haven't been able to make a decision, Ed. The judge has adjourned until Monday.'

Eddie put his head in his hands. The thought of spending the weekend in prison while still awaiting his fate didn't appeal one iota. Thoroughly pissed off, Ed grabbed the cell bars and banged his head against them.

'Fuck, fuck, fuck!' he shouted.

Eddie wasn't the only person shouting; back in Rainham, his daughter was absolutely hysterical.

'Leave him alone. He's my boyfriend,' she screamed, as Jed lay on the floor and curled himself up in a protective ball.

'I'll kill you, you shitcunt,' Alice yelled, as she picked up a broom and clumped Terry Baldwin repeatedly with it.

Jed's face was battered. It was covered in blood, and pain shot through his right leg where he had fallen awkwardly.

Aiming one more kick at Jed, Terry grabbed the broom from Alice and tossed it away.

'You fucking arsehole, my Jimmy'll have you for this. He's only a young mush, look what you've done to him.'

Terry turned to Frankie. He was well aware that she was Eddie Mitchell's daughter. 'I'm sorry you had to see that, love, but you wanna leave that piece of shit while you still can.'

Frankie crouched down and held Jed's battered face in her hands. She turned to Terry. 'You animal. What's he meant to have done to you?'

Terry felt sorry for the innocent-looking young girl, but he had to be brutal, she needed to know the truth. 'My daughter is carrying your scumbag of a boyfriend's child. Told him she was pregnant, my Sally did, and that little shit told her to get rid of it. No one takes the piss out of my little girl, I won't fucking stand for it.'

Seeing Jed looking at him, Terry couldn't resist giving him a sly kick in the bollocks. 'You ain't seen the last of me. You'll be paying maintenance once that baby's born, I'll make damn sure of it.'

As Terry walked away, Frankie stared at his back with her mouth open. It couldn't be true, surely not?

'I ain't done nothing wrong, Frankie. I swear on our baby's life, I ain't cheated on ya,' Jed cried.

Guessing that there was a good chance that the accusation was true, Alice decided to intervene. If Frankie left Jed, then Alice wouldn't see baby Georgie at all and she couldn't risk that happening.

As Frankie went to storm off, Alice grabbed her by the arm. 'Don't believe that nutter, Frankie. I know my own son and I know that he loves you more than he's ever loved anyone. Why would he want a beef burger when he's got fillet steak indoors, eh love?'

Frankie didn't know whether she was coming or going. Little things flashed through her mind. She thought of all the nights Jed had stayed out, the make-up and lipstick she'd seen on his clothes, the distinct smell of women's perfume on that new shirt she'd bought him for his birthday. She'd confronted him at the time, but he had sworn blind that the evidence had been his aunts and cousins making a fuss of him.

Frankie glared at her boyfriend. If he had cheated on her, she would leave him tomorrow, but only if she was one hundred per cent certain. Say she left him, but Jed was telling the truth? If that happened, she would never forgive herself.

As Jed struggled to stand up, Frankie watched him.

'My head hurts,' he whined.

Alice helped her son get up. 'Let's all go inside. That man was a bloody lunatic. We'll ring your dad – he'll know what to do.'

Jed looked at Frankie with pleading eyes. 'I swear Frankie, I ain't got no girl pregnant.'

Frankie started to cry. 'So you don't know no one called Sally?'

As his mum walked away, Jed hugged Frankie. He had to

207

think up a convincing lie and he had to think of one quickly. 'If I tell you something, you have to promise you won't tell anyone.'

'I promise.'

'I know who Sally is. Me old man was knocking her off. It's me dad's baby, not mine.'

CHAPTER TWENTY-TWO

With his lies spiralling out of control, Jed decided that the quicker he and Frankie left Rainham, the better. Telling his mother had been awful. Alice had sobbed her heart out, but had fully understood why he had to go.

Petrified of Sally's father coming back, Jed rang his brother Billy. 'Is that plot still available on your site?'

Billy told him that it was, so Jed arranged for his trailer to be taken to Hainault the following Monday.

Frankie and Jed were up at 6 a.m. on the morning in question. There was so much to do and very little time to get things organised.

'What about your horses? Are you gonna leave them here?' Frankie asked Jed.

'Nah, I'm putting 'em in the field where me brother keeps his. Dad's gonna bring 'em over in the horse-box tomorrow.'

At the mention of Jed's father, Frankie glared at her boyfriend. She was furious that Jimmy had got away scot-free with his infidelities. He should have got a good hiding, not poor Jed, whose head, face and body were still covered in bruises.

'I still think that someone should tell your mum. I know me and her have been known to argue, but she needs to be told that her husband is a pervert and has got some young girl pregnant. I'd wanna know if you ever did anything like that to me.'

Jed put down the box he was holding and gave Frankie a cuddle. He was annoyed with himself for making his dad look

209

like a nonce. He should have told Frankie that his cousin Sammy had got the girl up the duff, but he'd just blurted out the first thing that had come into his head.

'Look, I've spoken to me dad and he promises me it's all over with that girl. It'll break me mum's heart, Frankie, if she ever finds out, so swear you'll never say anything.'

'It should be your job to tell her Jed, not mine. If I'd ever caught my dad messing about with young girls, I'd have told my mum immediately.'

Jed gave Frankie a peck on the nose. 'Maybe I will tell her one day, but not now. She's upset that we're leaving and I don't want her to get all depressed again.'

By the time they had finished packing anything breakable in boxes and had eaten some breakfast, it was gone 9 a.m.

Alice had offered to look after Georgie while Jed and Frankie moved the trailer and got themselves organised. She was devastated they were moving and before they left she wanted to spend as much time with her granddaughter as possible.

As Jimmy walked towards them, Frankie turned away.

'I'm gonna come with ya. I'll give you a hand,' he said brightly.

Disgusted by her soon-to-be father-in-law's appalling behaviour, Frankie urged Jed to go without her. 'I'll wait here with Georgie and your mum,' she hissed, walking towards the house.

Jed ran over and grabbed Frankie's arm. He couldn't risk her saying anything. His dad would kill him if his lie ever came to light. 'I mean it, Frankie, if you say one word to my mum, I'll never forgive you, and me and you will be finished for good.'

Unaware that his daughter was currently moving home, Eddie Mitchell was led into the courtroom. He felt sick with nerves. The jury had spent the weekend holed up in a hotel and he just hoped and prayed that they had come to a decision, because the not knowing was horrendous.

Ed glanced towards the gallery. Gary, Ricky, Auntie Joan, Vi, Paulie, Ronny, Reg and Raymond were all there to support him. So were Dougie, Flatnose Freddie and John, the old guvnor of the Flag in Canning Town.

The judge urged the foreman of the jury to stand up. 'Has the jury reached a decision on all three charges?'

'Yes, your Honour.'

'On the charge of murder, how do you find the defendant: guilty or not guilty?'

Eddie held his breath. He could feel his legs shaking and the sweat dripping down his face.

'Not guilty.'

Gary and Ricky jumped up and hugged one another. Auntie Joan stuck her two fingers up at the devastated prosecution team. 'Bunch of arseholes,' she shouted.

'Silence in court,' the judge yelled, before continuing.

'And on the charge of manslaughter, how do you find the defendant: guilty or not guilty?'

Eddie looked towards Gary and Ricky. They all knew he was going to get found guilty for manslaughter; it was a forgone conclusion.

'Not guilty.'

Eddie gasped. He almost expected Jeremy Beadle to pop up from somewhere; it was like a scene from the TV programme *Beadle's About.*

Neither Larry nor Eddie's QC could quite believe their ears. How could they not find Mitchell guilty of manslaughter? It was a mistake – it had to be.

'Get in there. Well done, Ed. We all love you, boy,' Auntie Joan screamed.

'Silence in court,' the judge ordered sternly.

As the courtroom fell quiet again, he continued.

'And on the charge of being in possession of a firearm, how do you find the defendant: guilty or not guilty?'

'Guilty.'

Stanley and Joyce had been pottering about indoors all day, trying to keep themselves busy. Joey and Dominic had both taken a week off work and had invited themselves over for lunch.

'Go and get changed, Stanley, the boys will be here soon.'

'Why do I have to bloody well get changed to sit in me own bleedin' house?' Stanley snapped.

The shrill ring of the telephone stopped their argument. Raymond had promised he would call as soon as a verdict was announced.

'Answer it then, Stanley,' Joyce yelled.

As Stanley picked up the receiver and heard his son's voice, he felt his hands go like jelly. 'What? I don't believe it!' he yelled.

Without saying goodbye, Stanley slammed down the phone and turned to his wife. 'The bastard got away with it. I hope our Frankie's ashamed of herself. This is all her doing.'

'What do you mean, got away with it? They must have found him guilty of manslaughter.'

With tears in his eyes, Stanley shook his head. 'They found him not guilty. What sort of people do they put on these juries, eh, Joycie?'

Joyce was gobsmacked. 'So has he been let free?'

'He got charged with possessing a firearm. Seven years, he got. The bastard'll be out before you know it. The Devil looks after his own, I've always fucking said that. We've got no justice for our Jessica whatsoever.'

Eddie felt a relief within as he was driven back to the prison. He would never forgive himself for what he had done to Jessica, but at least now he could try to move on with his life.

The whole courtroom had been astounded when he'd got the not guilty for manslaughter verdict. 'That's got to be the biggest travesty I've ever had the misfortune of being part of,' Ed heard the prosecution QC say to one of his team.

James Fitzgerald Smythe, Eddie's QC, and Larry, his brief, had both been totally dumbfounded by the verdict. Both men had told him all along that he had no chance of getting off the manslaughter charge. 'Getting a not guilty for murder is what we have to aim for, Eddie,' they'd insisted.

Eddie wondered if the bent chief inspector or the judge's summing up had swung things in his favour. The bent Inspector had been blackmailed into giving him a glowing reference, but obviously the judge hadn't. Or maybe it was his emotional outburst at the end that had won the jury's hearts.

'What happened was an act of extreme violence, but if there is any doubt in your minds that what Mr Mitchell did was actually a terrible accident, then he should be found not guilty,' the judge had told the jury.

Thinking of how elated his family had been, Eddie grinned. With the time he'd already served, he could be out in as little as four years.

The copper sitting opposite Eddie sneered at him. 'I wouldn't be smiling if I'd just murdered my wife,' he said sarcastically.

Eddie had cried many a tear in private for Jessica, but he wasn't about to let this jumped-up little bastard get the better of him.

Eddie gave him a wink. 'You ain't me though, are you, mate?'

Back in Rainham, Joey had just arrived at his grandparents' and was horrified by his father's lenient sentence. 'If Frankie had told the truth, Dad would have definitely got found guilty. It's all Frankie's fault. I never want to speak to her again,' Joey said, trying desperately not to cry.

As Dominic comforted his partner, Joyce opened a bottle of brandy and poured them all a glass. 'Drink this – it's good for shock,' she urged her grandson.

Two glasses later, Joey's upset had turned to pure anger. 'How can Frankie stick up for Dad when he killed our mum like he did?' he shouted.

Joyce did her best to make her grandson see sense. 'You must make it up with Frankie. You can't let this ruin your relationship. When was the last time you spoke to her?'

'I haven't spoken to her since we went to court. She's been ringing me, but I've got nothing to say to her, Nan.'

'You can't blame him, Joycie,' Stanley piped up.

Throwing her husband a look that could kill, Joyce put an arm around Joey's shoulder. 'If your mum's looking down, she would be so upset that you and Frankie aren't talking. You've always been like two peas in a pod, so you must sort it out, Joey. And what about Georgie? You don't wanna lose contact with her, do you? Say you miss her growing up.'

Joey laid his head on his nan's shoulder. 'If Frankie rings me again, for Mum's sake, I'll answer it, but I'm not ringing her. I feel like I hate her at the moment, Nan, for letting that bastard off the hook, I really do.'

Stuart, Eddie's cellmate, was overjoyed by his pal's stroke of good fortune. 'You're a top geezer, Ed. I'm so pleased for ya, mate,' he said, hugging him. 'That new screw, Leslie, said me and you can go and have a game of cards with Bertie Simms and JD. I asked him earlier, as I thought you might need some cheering up.'

Eddie shook his head. 'It's been a long day, mate. I've got a few letters I need to write. I need to thank people and stuff. Now I'm no longer on remand, I ain't allowed as many visitors, am I? So I'd better start putting pen to paper a bit more.'

'Shall I stay here with ya?' Stu offered.

'Nah, you go and play cards,' Eddie replied. He usually adored Stuart's constant chitchat, but after the trauma of the court case, all he wanted was to be left alone.

When Stuart left the cell, Eddie picked up his pen and writing pad. He wanted to drop a quick line to everyone who had given up their time to support him. He penned letters to Gary and Ricky, his aunts, uncles and brothers. Finishing the last of the family letters, he laid back on his bunk and thought of Gina.

No one would ever replace his wonderful Jessica, but watching Gina perform in court had excited Eddie to some extent. He couldn't put his finger on what attracted him to her.

It wasn't just her looks – she definitely had something else about her. He propped himself up and picked up his pen and pad again.

Dear Gina,

I just wanted to thank you for standing up in court on my behalf. My case ended today and, as you probably know, I got a not guilty for murder and manslaughter, but got a guilty for possession of firearms, what resulted in me getting seven years, of which I'll probably have to serve about four.

I've no idea how busy you are workwise at the moment, but if you fancy popping up to visit me, let me know and I will send you a VO.

Take care of yourself,
Thanks again.
Eddie x

Eddie reread the letter and then dithered over sending it. Perhaps he should take the bit about her visiting him out. Deciding to leave it in, Ed sealed the envelope before he could change his mind again. Part of him felt disloyal to Jessica, but he managed to convince himself that he was doing nothing wrong. If Gina visited, it would be nice to have a bit of female company and, seeing as he was stuck in the clink, it wasn't as if anything untoward could happen.

Over in Essex, Alice was in floods of tears as she clung on to baby Georgie for dear life.

'Anyone would think we were moving to Scotland, not bloody Hainault,' Jed said, laughing.

Alice ignored her son's little joke. She knew exactly why he was moving so quickly – because he'd got that other girl up the duff. He might be able to lie to Frankie and get away with it, but she knew he was as guilty as sin. Alice felt quite sorry for Frankie as she handed her the baby. She'd caught her Jimmy

215

at it once and, after clumping him, had left him immediately. She found it strange that Frankie seemed so laid-back about the whole drama. The girl hadn't said one word about it all day.

Alice kissed her philandering son. 'Me and your dad will pop over and see you tomorrow.'

The journey from Rainham to Hainault took about half an hour. Noticing that her phone was switched off, Frankie turned it on and was surprised when it rang almost instantly.

'Frankie, it's Gary. Just to let you know Dad got seven years, but he won't have to serve all that. He got done for firearms, but got a not guilty to the other two charges. Now, when do you wanna go and visit him?'

Not wanting Jed to know that she was planning to visit her father, Frankie swerved the question. 'I bet you and Ricky are well chuffed. Listen, Gal, I'm a bit busy right now. Jed and I have moved to Hainault today and we're just taking the rest of the stuff over there, so I'll give you a ring tomorrow.'

'Whereabouts in Hainault you moving to?' Gary asked, surprised.

'The gypsy site. It's near Hogg Hill – you know the one I mean.'

As Frankie ended the call, Jed glared at her. 'Do you have to tell everyone where we've moved to? I don't like people knowing my business, Frankie.'

'It's not *everyone* I've told, it's my bloody brother. Surely I'm allowed to tell my family where we're living, Jed? What's the big secret? It's your dad that's in shit street, not you.'

Jed quickly changed the subject. 'What was that about being well chuffed? Has your old mush been sentenced?'

'Yeah, he got seven years,' Frankie replied.

Jed slammed his foot on the brake and mounted a kerb in shock. 'Seven fucking years! Didn't he get a guilty for manslaughter or murder?'

Frankie shook her head. 'He only got a guilty for having the gun.'

Jed shook his head in stunned disbelief. 'Unfuckingbelieveable!

He'll be out in less than four years and then what will happen when he tries to kill me again, Frankie? This is all your fault and I hope you're proud of yourself, you stupid fucking bitch.'

CHAPTER TWENTY-THREE

Waving Jed goodbye, Frankie darted back inside the trailer. Today was the day she was visiting her dad and, seeing as Jed had left later than expected, she had very little time to get ready.

Frankie rarely lied to Jed, but she couldn't chance telling him that she was taking the baby to see her dad in Wandsworth Prison. Jed would have flipped, so Frankie had asked if it was OK for her to take Georgie out with her brothers for lunch. Jed had been reluctant at first but, knowing how unhappy Frankie was living on the site in Hainault, he'd reluctantly agreed.

Since moving, Frankie had never felt so alone in her life. She still wasn't talking to Joey, which was making her miserable, and all the other women who lived on the site were part of the travelling community. Suspicious of outsiders, the travelling girls refused to accept Frankie as one of their own and, apart from the odd insult thrown her way, none of them bothered to speak to her at all. It didn't help that Shannon, Jed's sister-in-law, lived on the same site.

Frankie thought back to her first meeting with Shannon when foolishly she had looked at Shannon's big stomach and asked when the baby was due. By the looks of it, Shannon had never forgiven her, and had now turned the whole of the Hainault site against her.

Over the past couple of weeks Frankie had begged Jed to move them back to his parents' place. Even Alice seemed pass-

218

able compared with some of the women on this site. Jed had flatly refused, but had also been quite sympathetic for a change.

'They ain't used to gorjers, Frankie, but I promise you, they'll soften in time. Leave it with me and I'll have a word with me brother and the other lads. In the meantime, I've booked another batch of lessons for you. Once you pass your test, you can go and visit your nan and stuff.'

Frankie smiled as she thought of her driving lessons. Jed had insisted that she have a female instructor and had found her a lovely lady called Donna. Desperate to have her independence as quickly as possible, Frankie had taken to driving like a duckling takes to water. She was having two lessons a week and she treasured the time she spent with Donna. She was wonderful company and also a very patient instructor.

'You're an absolute natural, Frankie. We'll have you passing that test in no time,' Donna had told her only yesterday.

Hearing a toot outside, Frankie looked through the net curtains. 'Shit,' she mumbled. Gary and Ricky were quarter of an hour early.

She opened the trailer door. 'Do you wanna come in for a cup of tea? I ain't ready yet.'

Gary shook his head. 'I've got a couple of phone calls to make. Just hurry up, sis, or we'll be late,' he shouted.

Ricky looked at his brother. 'What a fucking shit-hole this is,' he said, as he noticed some weedy-looking old geezer glaring at them.

Unable to stop himself, Gary opened his window. 'Got a problem, have ya, mate?'

The geezer in question shook his head and darted back inside his trailer.

Ricky turned to Gary and laughed. 'Pikey cunts – I hate 'em.'

Eddie Mitchell paced nervously up and down his cell. He was desperate to spend some time with Frankie and meet his grandchild, but he was also edgy about what he was going to say to her.

Stuart did his best to put his pal's mind at rest. 'If Frankie hated ya or didn't want nothing to do with ya, then she wouldn't have stuck up for you in court and she wouldn't be schlepping up here today.'

'What am I meant to say to her, Stu? Should I mention Jessica or not?'

Stuart smiled. 'Why don't you just go with the flow? Now, will you sit down for fuck's sake? You're wearing the floor out.'

Eddie sat down and thought about exactly what he should say. He could hardly start the conversation with, 'Sorry for killing your mother,' could he now?

As the screw opened the cell, Stuart patted Eddie on the back. 'Good luck, mate. It'll be fine, I know it will.'

Frankie was shocked when she realised that Gary and Ricky were not going inside the prison with her. 'I can't go in on my own. What am I meant to say to him?' she asked.

Ricky hugged her. 'This visit is just about you and Dad. Talk to him, Frankie, tell him that you still love him. He's so excited and he can't wait to meet Georgie.'

Gary showed her where to go and also hugged her. 'Don't be afraid, Frankie, he's your dad and we'll be right here waiting for ya when you come out.'

Frankie queued up with the other visitors and waited in line to be searched and have her hand stamped. Georgie was also checked over and then they were allowed inside.

Frankie spotted her dad immediately. She felt her heart rate quicken as she walked towards him.

'Hello, Dad,' she said, giving him a light peck on the cheek.

Eddie felt like a complete idiot as his eyes welled up. Overcome by emotion, he stared at his first grandchild in awe. 'Can I hold her?' he croaked.

Frankie placed Georgie in his arms.

Eddie drank in her features and gently stroked the smiling

child's cheeks. 'She's gorgeous, Frankie. I can't believe I'm a grandad, girl.'

Frankie sat down. She didn't know what to say, so said the first thing she thought of. 'How are you doing in here, Dad? What are the other men like?'

'I've got a great cellmate. His name's Stuart. He's only young, but he's a top lad. The rest of the blokes are a mixture: some are OK, but there are some real arseholes in 'ere as well. I ain't allowed out the cell as much, since I was convicted. They offered me a job in the kitchens, but I told 'em to poke it. They've got some real tossers working in there and if I lose me rag with 'em Frankie, I might get time added to me sentence.'

'Gary was saying on the way here that you haven't been moved off the remand wing yet. Why's that then, Dad?'

Eddie smirked. He was positive that the real reason he hadn't been moved was because he was behaving himself at the moment. Apparently, the guvnor was under scrutiny by the authorities and, because of this, Ed was sure that the big boss man wouldn't want him kicking off again. He'd already been involved in two very nasty incidents. There was Big Bald Baz, who was now brown bread and, more recently, Johnny Venger who, since Eddie's attack on him, was currently rocking on a chair over in Broadmoor.

'Dad, I asked you a question.'

Eddie snapped out of his trance and smiled. 'Sorry, babe. Er, the reason I ain't been moved was because I begged the screws to let me stay on the remand wing with Stu. They were gonna move me straight after the trial and they still might at some point, but there's a shortage of room on the other wings at the moment,' he lied.

Frankie nodded understandingly. Being in her dad's company brought back so many fond memories and also made her realise just how much she had missed him.

When Georgie began to cry, Eddie handed her back and concentrated on his daughter. Frankie had always been a beauty, but her face now looked tired and bloated. 'You look worn out, and where's all your nice clothes and make-up?' he asked her.

'The baby had me up twice in the night, then Gary and Ricky turned up early, so I just chucked any old thing on.'

Frankie felt embarrassed that her dad had noticed a change in her appearance. She didn't want to tell him that Jed had barred her from wearing make-up. Her good clothes didn't fit any more, due to her diet of takeaways, and living on a gypsy site was hardly an inspiration to wear your best togs.

Eddie put on a false smile. 'So, how's life with Jed? Is he treating you well?'

Pleased that her dad had asked, Frankie grinned. 'We've just moved to a gypsy site in Hainault and Jed's paying for me to have driving lessons. I don't like the women on the site, but Jed's saving up to buy us a plot of land, so we won't be there for ever. I'm doing really well with my driving, Dad, I've got this woman called Donna teaching me and she said I'm a natural.'

'The big bruise you had on your face in court, where did you get it from, Frankie? Gary said you fell over drunk, but I don't believe that,' Eddie asked bluntly.

Frankie glared at him. How did he have the front to throw accusations at her when it should be the other way round? 'You've got some neck, Dad. For your information, I did fall over drunk, but even if Jed had caused it, which he didn't, it's got nothing to do with you. After what you did to my mum, you've got no right to be talking about anything anybody else does.'

Eddie bowed his head. 'I'll never forgive myself for what I did, Frankie. I loved your mum with all of my heart and most days I struggle to deal with my actions. I'm sorry, I really am.'

Frankie had only ever seen her dad cry once before and that was at her grandad Harry's funeral. 'Please don't get upset, Dad. I'm sorry, I know you didn't mean to kill Mum.'

Aware of a couple of lags looking his way, Eddie wiped his eyes on the cuff of his grey prison sweatshirt. 'How's your Nan and Grandad?' he asked, desperate for a change of subject.

'They're both all right. Nan has made the garden look lovely. She wanted it to be a shrine to Mum.'

Eddie smiled sadly. He was glad he'd given Joyce and Stanley his house. It was the least he could do, considering the circumstances.

'Have you spoken to Joey, Dad?'

Eddie shook his head. 'Why do you ask? Yous two ain't fallen out, have ya?'

Frankie shrugged. 'We didn't have a row or nothing, but I ain't spoken to him since that day I stood up in court and he stormed out. I've tried to ring him a few times since, but he never answered the phone and he didn't get back to me. I was gonna ring him again last week, but Jed said it's up to Joey to call me now.'

Eddie wasn't surprised that Jed didn't want Frankie to have contact with her brother. He knew from past stories what controlling bastards travellers were with their women. In fact, he was surprised the wonderful Jed was even allowing Frankie to have driving lessons.

'Dad, will you do something for me?'

Eddie squeezed Frankie's hand. 'Of course, my little princess.'

'Will you write to Joey and apologise for what you did to Dominic? It would mean such a lot to him if you could accept their relationship, and Dom's such a nice bloke, Dad.'

Eddie held his hands up with his palms facing Frankie. 'Hold your horses a minute, girl.'

Eddie glanced around to make sure nobody was listening to their conversation, then continued. 'I'd do anything for you, Frankie, you know I would, but this ain't about you, is it? If you want me to say it's OK for your brother to go around fornicating with other men, then you've got another think coming.'

Frankie immediately flared up at him. Her dad could be so childish at times. 'But that ain't what he's doing, is it, Dad? Joey's in a stable relationship with someone who loves him very much. Dominic's a terrific guy and if you got to know him, you'd see what I do. Mum accepted Joey for what he was and so did I. Why can't you do the bloody same?'

Noticing a bloke on the next table looking at them, Eddie

glared at his daughter. 'Keep your fucking voice down, will ya? Can you imagine the stick I'd get in here if they all knew what your brother was?'

'Does it matter what other people think? I've stuck up for Joey since the day I first found out about his preferences. Why can't you be grown-up about it like I was? He's still your bloody son.'

'Because I'm a man, Frankie. Anyway, why are you so bothered about all this when you and your brother aren't even speaking?'

Frankie's eyes filled up with tears. 'Because I miss him, I love him and I know how much your acceptance would mean to him.'

Desperate not to see his daughter cry or fall out with her, Eddie squeezed her hand. 'Let's talk about something else, eh? Look, no promises, but I will sit down and think about what you're asking me to do, OK?'

Frankie nodded. 'Do you wanna hold Georgie again?'

Eddie eagerly agreed. He studied his granddaughter once more. She was dead cute, but also had a pikey sort of look about her. Frankie was dark like himself and Ed decided that it must be her piercing green eyes that made her look so Romany. As Georgie clung onto Eddie's thumb, Frankie laughed.

'She likes you, Dad. She keeps smiling at you.'

Eddie liked the compliment. 'She's her grandad's girl, ain't ya, Georgie?' he said, lifting her up above him.

'So, does Jed know that you've come to see me?' he asked.

'He knows I'm out with Gary and Ricky, but I didn't say where we were going. He'd be fine about me coming to see you, Dad, but he might not have wanted me to bring Georgie here.'

Eddie gave a sarcastic chuckle. 'Jed's got you living in a trailer on some shit-hole site in Hainault, yet he don't want his kid visiting her grandad in prison. Where you live is probably running alive with vermin and I bet their Sunday roast is baked hedgehog in clay. I'm sorry Frankie, but I can't stand pikeys, you know I can't. They're a different fucking breed, sweetheart.'

The rest of the visit flew by, and as time was called for it to come to an end, Frankie shuffled awkwardly in her seat. 'Dad, there is something I need to know and I want you to tell me the truth.'

'Go on,' Eddie said.

'That night in Tilbury when Mum died, did you mean to kill Jed?'

'Time's up. Say goodbye now, Mitchell,' one of the screws said, as he hovered next to Eddie.

Ignoring his daughter's question, Eddie gave Frankie a big hug. 'Thanks for what you did for me in court. When you coming to see me again?'

Frankie let go of him and stared him straight in the eyes. 'You haven't answered my question, Dad. Did you or didn't you?'

Eddie shook his head. 'Of course I didn't. What kind of man do you think I am, Frankie? All I wanted to do was pay Jed some cash to stay out of your life and when he wasn't there, I decided to scare him, OK?'

Frankie smiled. He was telling the truth, she was sure of that. She held Georgie towards him so he could kiss her goodbye. 'You're a good man, Dad, and I want you to know that I forgive you for everything that has happened and I will always love you.'

CHAPTER TWENTY-FOUR

Aware that his daughter, Sally, was yet again in floods of tears, Terry Baldwin lifted his grandson out of her arms.

Luke was now three months old and even though Sally had had a difficult birth and had since suffered with depression, Terry was beginning to lose patience with her.

As Sally poured herself another glass of wine, Terry shook his head in disgust. 'You've gotta pull yourself together, girl. The answer to your problems ain't in the bottom of a glass, you know.'

Sally dried her eyes and sipped her drink. She was gagging for Jed to see his son, but nobody knew where he had moved to.

Desperate to have his old daughter back, the happy one, Terry sat down beside her and put a comforting arm around her shoulder. 'Look, babe, I know you loved that pikey lad, but you've just gotta move on with your life. Get yourself dolled up and go out with your mates and find yourself a new bloke. Me and Anne will babysit for you.'

Sally glared at her father. She still loved Jed, even though he had been a bastard to her, and she didn't want any other bloke. Positive that once Jed laid eyes on his beautiful son, he would fall in love with her and they would live happily ever after, Sally decided to beg for her father's help once again.

'Please Dad, I really do need to see Jed, even if it's only for closure. Please find him for me. Do it for Luke's sake. As he gets older he has every right to know who his Daddy is, doesn't he?'

Terry turned away from Sally's pleading expression. It broke his heart to see his daughter so unhappy day in, day out. He stood up. He'd had months of this same conversation and he needed to put an end to it somehow.

'OK, I'll pay someone to find him for you, but I'm warning you, Sally, if Jed treats you like shit or upsets you, then I shall personally break every bone in the little fucker's body. Now, do we understand one another?'

Sally smiled. Her dad had been a hard nut to crack on the subject of Jed, but finally she had got her own way.

Considering he was suffering from a dose of man-flu, Eddie Mitchell was in an extremely upbeat mood. The reason why was obvious – it was because Gina was coming to visit him again today. Thinking of Gina, Eddie grinned. He'd been nervous when she had first visited him, but he needn't have been, as there had been an instant spark between them.

'You've definitely got the look of a man in love, Ed. Book me in to be your best man,' Stuart joked.

Eddie playfully punched Stuart. He and his cellmate often wound one another up. They enjoyed the banter and it also relieved the boredom.

As Eddie was let out of the cell, he briefly thought of Jessica. It was the same every time Gina came to visit; there was always a twinge of guilt.

Eddie sat down in the visiting room and thought of his daughter as he waited for Gina. Frankie had come to visit him again last week and he was becoming increasingly worried about her. Pale and drawn with dark bags under her eyes, Ed was positive that Frankie wasn't happy with her life. Sadness seemed to be written all over her face.

'Don't be silly, Dad, everything's fine at home,' Frankie had insisted.

As Gina walked towards him, Eddie forgot about his daughter

and concentrated on her. She always dressed in a classy way, but today she looked amazing in a black knitted coat, faded jeans, and knee-high black leather boots.

'Wow, you look good enough to eat,' Eddie joked as he kissed her.

Gina hugged him, then sat down. She'd had her fair share of blokes over the years, but none of them could hold a torch to the charismatic Eddie Mitchell.

'So, how have you been?' Eddie asked her.

'I've been fine, thanks. Well, that's apart from wishing every morning that I was waking up with you instead of on my own,' Gina said teasingly.

Eddie held her gaze. Every time Gina had visited, they flirted that little bit more and he got off on tantalising her. Unbeknown to Gina, he'd had the occasional wank while thinking of her recently and his orgasms had been blinding.

'Did you have any joy finding out any more stuff about me dad?' Ed asked her.

Gina shook her head. Eddie had been paying her, via Raymond, to see if she could find out some new information about his father's murder. 'I went everywhere you told me to go, but no one knew anything, Ed. I'll keep trying, but at the moment the trail is as cold as ice.'

As disappointed as he was, Eddie nodded understandingly. Bringing his old man's killer to justice had kind of become an obsession with him, but apart from employing Gina and keeping his eyes and ears open in nick, there was very little he could do about it while he was on the inside.

Deciding to change the subject, Eddie squeezed Gina's hand. 'So, have you decided where you're spending Christmas yet?'

'Yeah, I'm going to my friend Claire's on Christmas Day. She's single, like me, so I'm going to stay there until the day after Boxing Day.'

Ed leaned towards her, tilted her chin and gazed into her eyes. 'Why are you still calling yourself single when you've now got me?'

With the undeniable sexual tension between them, Gina lowered her eyes. 'So are we officially an item then?'

Eddie noted that her hands were shaking and he smiled. She wanted him badly, he knew that. 'It all depends if you'll wait for me,' he replied.

Gina nodded. 'Of course I'll wait.'

Eddie stroked her cheek and, unable to stop himself, leaned towards her and kissed her passionately. As one of the screws told him to calm things down, Ed pulled away and grinned. 'You won't regret waiting for me, babe, I'll promise you that.'

On the day before Christmas Eve, Jed offered to drive Frankie over to her mother's grave to lay some flowers.

'Can't I drive, Jed?' Frankie asked him.

Jed shook his head. 'The truck's too big for you, Frankie. You've only just passed your test, ain't ya?'

Instead of arguing, Frankie accepted his decision. She had passed her test six weeks ago now and she was positive that Jed hadn't got her a car yet because he was planning on surprising her on Christmas Day.

'Please give me a clue about what you've bought me,' Frankie had begged him only yesterday.

'No, it'll spoil the surprise. All I'm telling you is it's something I should have bought you ages ago and it's something you really want.'

Frankie was thrilled by his answer. Georgie was nine months old now and Frankie desperately wanted to be able to take her daughter to visit Joey or her grandparents while Jed was out working and stuff.

Joey and Frankie had called a truce a couple of weeks ago. They hadn't spoken for months after her father's court case but, with Christmas approaching, Frankie had called him again. She hadn't told Jed the truth, she'd told him that Joey had rung her. They hadn't met up yet, but Frankie was planning on spending Boxing Day with Joey and Dominic at her grandparents' house and she was really looking forward to their reunion.

On the journey to Upminster Cemetery, Frankie sat daydreaming about her forthcoming independence. She could just imagine herself going shopping with Georgie in Romford Market or driving to that new Lakeside shopping centre that was to open in Thurrock during the next year.

'You're quiet, babe. You ain't got the hump 'cause I wouldn't let you drive, have ya?'

Frankie snapped out of her trance and smiled. Jed might be surprising her with a car on Christmas Day but, little did he know, she had an even bigger surprise for him.

With the end of visiting time fast approaching, Gina decided to take the bull by the horns. There was one important question she needed to ask Eddie and, after her past experiences with men, she couldn't avoid it any longer.

Gina felt hot under the collar as she began her planned speech. 'Ed, there's one thing I really need to ask you. My ex-boyfriend, Grant, the one I told you about, well, when me and him first got together we never discussed the subject of kids. That's when it all went wrong because, after we'd moved in together, I found out that he'd had a vasectomy and had conveniently forgotten to tell me about it. I blew a fuse, so he had it reversed, but the operation wasn't successful.'

Aware that Gina was having trouble spitting out the actual question, Eddie burst out laughing. 'So you wanna know if I've been gelded, do ya?'

Usually so cool, calm and collected, Gina was annoyed as she felt herself blush. 'I want to be with you whatever the situation, Ed, but I don't want to build my hopes up of us perhaps one day having a family and that's not possible. By the time you get out I'll probably be thirty-five. I just need to know where I stand on this one. I know it's a bit early to ask but, obviously, with you stuck in here, I have no choice.'

Eddie leaned towards Gina. Being in prison made you think strangely and he knew that he had already sort of fallen for

230

her. 'If you want my babies, then you shall have my babies, sweetheart.'

Gina's eyes welled up. She had always dreamed of one day having a family, but until now had struggled to meet Mr Right. 'I know we haven't known one another very long, but I'm sure we can make this work, Ed.'

Eddie agreed. When Jessica had died he had never believed that he would find happiness again, especially this quickly and he was desperate to make things work.

Gina stood up. 'I'd better go now. Will you be able to ring me tomorrow?'

Eddie grinned. 'Only if you promise to keep that bed warm for me.'

Frankie hated visiting her mum's grave. She found it too upsetting, so she only went at Christmas or on her mum's birthday. She never stayed for long; just laid the flowers, said hello, told her mum she loved and missed her, and walked away.

'Christ, that was quick,' Jed said, as she got back in the truck.

Frankie lifted Georgie off her dad's lap. 'Where are we going now? I'm hungry. Shall we stop for some lunch somewhere?' she asked.

'Why don't we go and put some flowers on your grandad's grave first?'

Frankie shook her head. She hated visiting graves of any kind and, even though what had happened to her grandad was awful, she hadn't been particularly close to him. 'I never saw much of my grandad, so I'd rather just go for lunch, Jed, if you don't mind.'

Jed did mind. He had his own reasons for wanting to go. 'Let's just take some flowers over there. You can stay in the motor if you want and I can lay them with Georgie. It'll be nice for your dad. You can write to him and tell him that Georgie's been to the grave.'

Frankie shrugged. Jed had no idea that she had taken Georgie to visit her dad in prison, but he knew that her dad had rung

231

occasionally and that she had written to him. Deciding that her boyfriend was only being thoughtful, she smiled at him.

'OK, but you lay the flowers for me.'

Being quite a deep person, Eddie told Stuart very little of his conversation with Gina.

'You ain't 'arf quiet. Are you OK, Ed? They ain't told you you've gotta move to another wing, have they?'

Eddie cracked a smile. 'Don't worry, I ain't being moved. I've told you before, the guvnor in here is shit-scared of me, and of losing his poxy job, so they ain't ever gonna split us up, Stuie boy. I'm just tired, mate. I'm gonna read me book, see if it makes me fall asleep.'

As he pretended to read, Ed's mind was a whirlwind of emotion. When he was with Gina, he felt no guilt whatsoever, but as soon as she wasn't there, he was consumed by remorse.

Putting his book down beside him, Ed stared at the ceiling. He'd just promised to have kids with a woman he barely knew. They had never even been out on a date or anything, let alone lived together. Wondering if the prison system was fucking with his brain, Ed tried to erase his doubts from his mind. Gina obviously felt the same way as he did and she wasn't banged up, so maybe it was the real deal. His thoughts turned to Frankie. Would she accept him moving on and having kids with another woman? Somehow he doubted it.

Thinking of Gina's fit body, Eddie sighed. By the time he got released, Jessica would have been dead for about five years, so surely no one would begrudge him a bit of happiness, including Frankie?

Jed smiled as he bent down and showed his daughter Harry Mitchell's grave.

'Your great-nan and great-grandad are buried next to one another 'ere, Georgie girl. I never knew your great-nan, but great-grandad Harry was a horrible old shitcunt.'

Georgie looked at him inquisitively. Obviously, she couldn't

232

understand what her dad was saying, but Jed still got a buzz out of telling her.

As a grieving family walked past them, Jed nodded. 'Bit nippy, ain't it?' he said politely.

He waited for them to be far enough away, then took all the flowers and cards that other people had left off Harry's grave. 'Where shall we put these, Georgie girl? Shall we move them to that grave over there that's not got none?' he said in a silly voice.

Jed moved all the tributes, then walked back to Harry's now extremely bare grave. He knelt back down again and gobbed at the headstone.

'Are you enjoying yourself up in the sky, Harry boy? Never caught me, did they, mush? And, do you know why? Because, unlike you, I am one slippery cunt. I killed you, shagged and nailed your granddaughter. Then, to top all that, I got your daughter-in-law murdered and your son banged up for killing her. Life's a bitch, ain't it, you old bastard?'

Aware of an old couple staring oddly at him, Jed stood up. 'Horrible time of the year if you've lost someone, ain't it? I brought me daughter 'ere to see her mum's family.'

The lady smiled at Georgie. 'What a beautiful baby. What's her name?'

'Georgie girl. And she takes after her dad in the looks department, not her mother,' Jed replied cockily.

As the couple carried on asking questions about Georgie, Jed became extremely bored. 'I'd better be going now. Her mum's waiting in the motor for us.'

Jed started to chuckle as he walked away. He had just had a brilliant idea, but it was far too busy, being Christmas time, to do it today.

If he came over here again, he would go to the toilet, shit in a carrier bag, and smear it all over Harry Mitchell's headstone.

CHAPTER TWENTY-FIVE

Terry Baldwin was woken up at 7 a.m. on Christmas morning by somebody ringing his mobile phone.

'Who is it?' he asked, still half-asleep.

Hearing his pal Keith's voice, Terry sat bolt upright. 'One sec, let me get a pen and paper.'

Terry scribbled down the address and listened intently to what Keith was telling him. 'No probs. I'll meet you for a beer tomorrow lunchtime and settle up with you then, if you like.'

Terry ended the call and ran back up the stairs. He entered his daughter's bedroom and gently shook her awake.

'What's up? What's the time?' Sally asked, bleary-eyed. She'd been on the wine again until late last night.

Terry smiled as he waved the piece of paper at her. 'Happy Christmas, darling. Now get your arse out of bed, because me, you and Luke are going to pay Jed O'Hara a little visit.'

Another person up with the larks on Christmas morning was Frankie. She was so excited about receiving her first ever car as a gift, she'd barely been able to sleep.

Jed had gone out the previous evening with his cousin, Sammy, and brother, Billy. Frankie had heard him roll in about two in the morning and she wondered if he'd brought the car home with him.

She flung open the trailer door and walked outside. There was no sign of any new vehicles, just the usual ones that belonged to the people on the site. Feeling disappointed, Frankie went back inside to get herself and the baby ready. Although Jed was reluctant, they were spending the day at his parents' house.

'Why can't we invite them over here, Frankie?' he'd asked her repeatedly.

Frankie had refused. There just wasn't enough room, especially as Shannon, Billy and their monster of a son was joining them. Jed's other brother, Marky, was going to his wife's parents. Jed had never been back to his parents' house since the day they'd left. It had obviously frightened him when he had been beaten up by that awful man, and what annoyed Frankie was that Jimmy, the actual culprit, had got away with it, the womanising arsehole.

Jed got up as Frankie had just finished dressing Georgie. He looked rough, and Frankie guessed that he'd got well pissed the night before.

'Did you have a nice evening? Where did you go?' she asked him.

'The Derby Digger in Wickford. Proper night it was, full of travellers in there. Billy didn't come in the end, he went over Marky's, so it was just me and Sammy boy.'

Frankie nodded. She didn't really care where he'd been or how inebriated he'd got; all she was interested in was getting her hands on her log book and car keys. Guessing that he might have hidden the car down the road, away from her prying eyes, she smiled.

'Shall we open our presents now?'

Jed nodded. He'd hidden Frankie's in his horse-box, so went off to get them.

Frankie sat Georgie on her lap and they opened her presents first. She laughed and clapped her tiny hands, even though she was far too young to understand what Christmas was all about. In fact, she seemed more interested in the wrapping paper than the actual gifts they had bought her.

'Your turn,' Frankie said, handing Jed a big gift bag.

Jed loved the black leather bomber jacket that Frankie had bought him. He studied himself in the mirror. 'Where did ya get it? It's well cool,' he asked.

Unable to get out shopping a lot, Frankie had asked Gary and Ricky to choose a decent leather jacket for her. They had seemed reluctant when they knew it was for Jed, but had done what Frankie had asked them because of what she'd said in court.

'I got the bus into Romford one day,' Frankie lied. Jed didn't like her mentioning either of her half-brothers and if he found out they had chosen the jacket, he probably wouldn't wear it.

As Jed handed her a big sack of gifts, Frankie could barely contain her excitement. Perfume, gold earrings, a pair of leather ankle boots – he'd even bought her a funny-looking machine with a load of disc things to put inside it.

'That's one of them CD players, Frankie. No one plays cassettes any more. You'll love it, trust me. My cousin Sammy's got one and the music sounds so much better on it,' Jed explained.

Frankie left the smallest present until last. Surely this had to be the car keys? As she undid the paper and a pink plastic Swatch watch fell out, she struggled to hide her discontent.

Jed winked at her. 'Your big present is over at me mum and dad's. You can open it later in front of the family.'

Frankie clapped her hands in glee. He'd obviously hidden her car at his parents' house, bless him.

Over in Rainham, Joyce was sipping a large Baileys while indulging in a bit of present-opening herself. Last year, the first Christmas since Jessica's death, had been bloody awful, but this year Joyce was determined that they would all have a fabulous time.

'Who wants another Baileys?' she asked, topping her own glass up to the brim.

Stanley glared at her. 'Take it easy, Joycie. It ain't even twelve o' bleedin' clock yet.'

Joyce poked her tongue out at Stanley. 'Open that one, you miserable old sod,' she said, handing him a present.

Stanley got excited as he tore the paper off and stared at his gift. Joycie had already given him the usual jumper and slippers, but this was a specialist book, all about breeding top-class racing pigeons. Thrilled, he thanked his wife and immediately began flicking through the pages.

'That'll keep the old bastard quiet,' Joyce whispered, as she handed Joey another present. Her grandson had already opened his aftershave and had loved that.

Joey tore off the paper and held the T-shirt up in horror. It was plain black and had the words GAY AND PROUD printed across the front in bright pink letters.

'I can't wear this, Nan,' he said bluntly.

'Why not? What's the matter with it? I told the man in the shop that you were gay and he said you would love it.'

As Dominic burst out laughing, Joey couldn't help but giggle himself. 'You've still got the receipt, ain't ya, Nan? I won't wear it. Take it back and get your money back.'

Joyce was annoyed. 'I can't take it back, I had it printed at one of them T-shirt places where you tell 'em what you want on the front.'

'Well, I'm afraid you've wasted your money then, Nan, 'cause I wouldn't be seen dead wearing this.'

'Give us it 'ere then, if you don't want it. Your grandad can wear it when he's cleaning out the pigeon shed,' Joyce said, tutting.

Picturing Stanley wearing the T-shirt, both Joey and Dominic creased up laughing.

Stanley looked up from his book and shook his head in total disbelief. 'Put it in the bin, you silly old woman. I ain't wearing no T-shirt that says the word "gay" on the front!'

'Does it bloody well matter what's on the front if you're only pottering about in the garden?' Joyce argued.

Stanley shook his head. 'I ain't arguing with you, you senile old bat. Now put the bastard T-shirt in the bin.'

*   *   *

Terry Baldwin was in deep thought as he drove towards the gypsy camp in Hainault. His wife, Anne, had insisted that he and Sally pay Jed a visit after dinner rather than before. Anne wasn't Sally's birth mum and she'd been getting sick of Sally's behaviour of late.

'I am not having my Christmas ruined by that daughter of yours, Terry. The girl's psychotic. She needs help, love, and I'm getting poxed off with our lives being turned upside down by her. I can't believe you're going out today, of all days, and if you're not back within two hours, then don't bother coming back at all.'

'Are you OK, Dad?' Sally asked him.

Terry nodded. Luke was asleep in the back of the car and Sally had a big smile on her face for the first time in ages.

Turning up the radio, Terry hoped for Sally's sake that by taking her to see Jed, he was doing the right thing for her fragile state of mind. With his contacts, he could probably have found Jed yonks ago if he'd have really wanted to. The reason he hadn't was purely selfish. He had become so attached to his grandson that he was happy to provide for Luke himself and have him living at his house for ever.

As Terry drove onto the site, he ordered Sally to stay in the car in case Jed wasn't at home. He knocked at the trailer door. Keith had told him that it was the second one in on the right.

'Can I help you? Whaddya want?' shouted an old woman opposite.

Terry walked towards her. He wouldn't pass as a traveller, so the only option was to pretend he was related to the Mitchells. 'Hello, I wonder if you can? I'm Jed's girlfriend's uncle. I was visiting other relatives over this way, so decided to surprise Frankie and Jed by dropping in. I have their presents in the car.'

The old woman looked at him suspiciously. She didn't trust gorjers, never had done. 'Well, you won't find 'em 'ere. Jed's spending Christmas over at his father's house and don't be asking me where that is, 'cause I won't be telling ya.'

Terry smiled as she slammed the door in his face. The silly, toothless old bat had already given him every little bit of information he needed.

Unaware that a gentleman was on his way over with revelations that would turn her Christmas upside down, Frankie was trying to make the best of a bad situation. Alice had been stuck like glue to Georgie all day, and sitting opposite Shannon at the dinner table was doing Frankie's head in.

As a roast potato was chucked across the table at her by Shannon's horrible son, Frankie was annoyed as everybody erupted with laughter.

'He didn't mean it – he was trying to aim for my plate,' Jed whispered, as he saw the annoyance on his girlfriend's face.

Frankie stood up. She was too excited about her car to be hungry or upset. 'I'm gonna feed Georgie now – she must be starving, Jed.'

Alice leaped up. 'You sit back down. I'll feed Georgie girl.'

'No. I want to feed her myself,' Frankie said indignantly.

Jed pinched his girlfriend's bum. 'Let Mum feed her, babe, she don't see as much of her now. Then, after we've eaten dessert, you can have your surprise present.'

The mention of her present was enough to make Frankie agree and sit back down. Jed might have bought her a car but, little did he know, she had an enormous surprise for him also.

Unable to stand the suffocating smell of shit in such a confined space, Terry Baldwin pulled into a pub car park. 'Me mate Andy owns this boozer. Let's go in there, Sally, and while you're changing the baby, I can have a quick pint.'

'Is it definitely open? It's four o'clock, Dad.'

'Yes, he's having a private party. You don't want Luke to be stinking of shit when he meets his dad for the first time, do you?'

Andy made a real fuss of Terry as he entered the pub. 'Christ, this is a nice surprise. To what do I owe this honour?' he joked.

Watching Sally walk into the toilet, Terry pulled Andy away from his pals.

'What's up?' Andy asked.

Terry shrugged. 'I've got to go round Jimmy O'Hara's place and I was wondering if I could borrow one of your guns.'

Frankie was filled with anticipation as Jed handed her her surprise present to unwrap. She had looked on the way in to see if she could spot the car, but she hadn't seen it. Jed was very clever at hiding stuff and Frankie guessed that he'd probably hidden it at the back of his father's land somewhere.

'Don't keep us all waiting. Open it, then,' Alice urged.

Frankie ripped off the wrapping paper and stared at the box. Jed laughed, as every time she opened one box, there was a smaller one inside. Frankie's heart lurched as she got to the final box. It was a bit small for car keys, but it couldn't be anything else, surely?

Smiling at Jed, Frankie took the top off. 'I didn't want this,' she said as she stared at the ring with revulsion.

Jed ignored her. He knew that Frankie had been expecting a car and he also knew how to play her. He knelt down beside her. 'I never bought you a proper engagement ring, did I, babe? Real diamond, that is, cost me an arm and a leg, it did, but you're more than worth it, Frankie.'

As Jed slipped it on her finger, Frankie began to cry. 'But I thought you was getting me a car. I do like it, Jed, but I need to have a car more than I need a ring.'

Shannon nudged Alice. 'Ungrateful little whore,' she said as she walked out of the room.

Ordering everyone to leave them alone, Jed shut the door. 'I wanted to buy you a proper engagement ring, Frankie. I love you and I want everybody to know that you're gonna be my wife. I can get you a car any time, can't I?'

'But when? If you don't get me one soon, I'll forget how to drive,' Frankie sobbed.

240

Seeing headlights looming through the window, Jed stood up. 'Who the fuck is this?' he mumbled to himself.

As soon as he recognised the unexpected visitor marching towards the house, Jed turned to Frankie in blind panic. 'Stay 'ere and don't move.'

'Who is it, Jed?' Jimmy O'Hara shouted.

Jed ran into the kitchen. 'It's that Sally's dad. Go and answer it, Mum. Tell 'em I ain't 'ere. You stay 'ere with me, Dad, please.'

Furious that the man she'd seen beating up her youngest son had the audacity to come back on Christmas Day, Alice picked up the rolling pin and ran to the front door.

'Whaddya want? Jed ain't 'ere,' she shouted.

When Sally appeared from behind her father with her son in her arms, Alice glanced at the baby and gasped.

Terry immediately took control. Andy didn't keep his guns at the boozer any more, so he had no tool whatsoever on him. He hadn't intended to use the shooter – he wasn't that silly. He'd just wanted to scaremonger and ruffle a few feathers if he needed to. He held his hands up, flat, palms towards Alice.

'Listen, we don't want no grief, I promise you that. This is my daughter, Sally, and this is your grandson, Luke. All we want is to speak to Jed. It's about time he met his son, don't you think? I know that Jed's living in Hainault and if I can't see him today, I'll go there tomorrow.'

Not knowing how to handle the situation, Alice called for Jimmy. She had no doubt that this man was telling the truth. The boy was the spitting image of Jed as a baby.

Frankie opened the lounge door a tad. She wasn't stupid and had guessed who the caller was and what was going on. She had sort of recognised the man's voice.

'You've got no right coming 'ere on Christmas Day. And so what if it is Jed's kid? He's engaged now and he's got another family, ain't he?' Jimmy shouted.

As Terry Baldwin started shouting the odds back, Billy ran to the front door. Jed stayed cowering in the kitchen.

Furious that her boyfriend's name was being dragged through the mud when he hadn't done anything wrong, Frankie laid Georgie on the sofa and marched into the hallway. What sort of man was Jimmy O'Hara, allowing his son to take the blame for his own mistakes and infidelities?

'How dare you accuse my Jed of being unfaithful to me? That dirty old pervert standing there is the father,' she screamed, pointing at Jimmy.

Jed cringed when he heard his mum fly at his dad. 'Fuck, fuck, fuck!' he said, holding his head in his hands.

Jimmy grabbed Alice's arm to stop her from hitting him with the rolling pin. 'I ain't done nothing. I swear Alice, I've never seen that girl before in my life.'

Shannon grabbed Frankie around the throat. 'You lying fucking whore,' she screamed.

Billy ran into the kitchen and tried to drag an ashen-faced Jed into the hallway. 'Sort this out now,' he ordered.

Frankie managed to push Shannon off her. 'I'm not lying. Jed told me it was his dad's baby. Ask him – go on, he'll tell you the truth.'

Terry turned to his daughter. 'Tell 'em who the father is now,' he said, as he shoved her and baby Luke into the hallway.

Frankie stood open-mouthed as she stared at the child. The baby was obviously younger, but it was like looking at Georgie just a few months back.

'It's Jed's baby. I don't even know his dad,' Sally sobbed.

Shoved into the hallway by his brother, Jed slid down the wall, sank to his knees and covered his face with his hands. 'I'm so sorry, Frankie. I love you. It was a mistake, I swear it was.'

Jimmy O'Hara was beside himself with rage. 'You lying little bastard. How dare you get me into trouble with your mother?' he yelled, grabbing Jed by the throat and marching him into the kitchen.

While Alice, Jimmy, Billy, Shannon, Terry and Sally all followed them out there, Frankie ran into the lounge.

'Where's my bag? Where's my bag?' she sobbed.

Spotting it by the side of the sofa, Frankie picked it up, chucked it over her shoulder, then grabbed Georgie.

As she ran down the driveway with the baby in her arms, she caught a glimpse of her engagement ring sparkling on her finger. She stopped, yanked the ring off and threw it as far away as she could.

Hearing Jed shout out her name, Frankie quickened her pace. He couldn't see her – it was far too dark and the outside lights had gone off.

As Georgie began to scream, Frankie stopped briefly to stroke her head and comfort her. 'Sssh, don't cry, Georgie girl. We just need to get away from your daddy and, once we do that, Mummy will take care of you for the rest of your life, I promise.'

CHAPTER TWENTY-SIX

Joyce always prided herself at being a bit of an expert at Scrabble, so a score-sheet showing that Stanley was beating her by fifty points did not fill her with glee. Desperate to stop her husband getting on another triple word score, Joyce chewed her fingernails.

'Ah, I've got something,' she said, as she proudly put her letters on the board.

Stanley looked at her incredulously. 'Poofta! You can't have that, Joycie, it ain't a real word.'

Joyce took a sip of her sherry. 'Of course it's a bloody word. Ask Joey or Dominic; they're both pooftas, so they should know.'

Joey raised his eyes at his boyfriend. His nan really needed a lesson in tact at times. 'It's offensive slang, Nan. You can't use it in Scrabble,' Joey told her.

Furious, Joyce punched Stanley on the arm. 'Pass me that bleedin' dictionary.'

As Stanley stood up, he was surprised to hear the doorbell ring. 'Who the bloody hell's that? We ain't expecting no one, are we, Joycie?'

Pushing her husband out of the way, Joyce stomped off to answer the door. She hoped it was an unexpected visitor, then she could put the board away and keep her unbeaten record.

Joyce was stunned when she opened the front door and saw her granddaughter's tear-stained face.

'Can I stay here please, Nan? I've got nowhere else to go.'

*   *   *

244

Guessing that Frankie must have sneaked out of the house and legged it to her grandparents', Jed was adamant he was going there to bring her back.

Alice and Jimmy both tried to make their son see sense. 'You've done enough damage for one day, boy. Give the girl some space, you dinlo,' Jimmy urged him.

Alice agreed. 'Don't be charging down there like a bull in a china shop. Give it a couple of days to let her cool off a bit.'

Jed flopped back down in the armchair. Christmas had been ruined and it was all Terry fucking Baldwin's fault. If he hadn't come round sticking his oar in, Frankie would be none the wiser about his shenanigans.

Terry, Sally and Luke had eventually left about half an hour ago. Jed had barely glanced at the child, but he'd given Sally a couple of hundred quid and had promised to pay maintenance.

Jed put his head in his hands. He was going to have to pull one out of the hat to get Frankie to forgive him for this. Suddenly an idea came to him. He picked up his phone and rang his cousin.

'Sammy, I need a favour. I don't care how much it costs, but I need you to get hold of a motor for Frankie for me. That mate of yours who sells cars, he must have something. Ring him, Sam, it's urgent, real urgent and I need you to get me one by tomorrow at the latest. I want something decent with a small-size engine, and low mileage on the clock.'

Stanley, Joyce and Dominic all stayed downstairs with baby Georgie while Joey took his distraught sister upstairs to talk to her in private. All Frankie had said so far was that she and Jed had split up and she'd asked if she could move in with her nan and grandad until she sorted out somewhere else to live.

Desperate to know what had really happened, Joey led Frankie into his old bedroom and sat her on the edge of the bed. 'Why have you left him on Christmas Day, Frankie? Something bad must have happened for you to leave, today of all days.'

Desperate to tell at least one person, Frankie fell into her brother's arms. 'You were so right about Jed, Joey. You said he couldn't be trusted and he can't. He's cheated on me with this girl called Sally and she turned up today with his baby.'

Joey could barely believe his ears. 'What, he's had a kid with someone else? How old is it?'

'Just a few months, I think,' Frankie sobbed.

Joey held his sister tightly. Frankie needed him and the row they'd had over their father's court case was now long forgotten.

'You can't go back to him after this, Frankie. He's bound to push the boat out to try and win you back, but you have to be strong. A leopard don't change its spots, and if Jed's cheated on you once, chances are he'll do it again.'

Frankie nodded. 'I know you're right, but what about Georgie? Jed's a good dad and I don't want her to grow up fatherless.'

'He can still see her, Frankie. Georgie is only young, she'll get used to Jed not being there, and when she's older, she can spend weekends with him and stuff.'

Frankie rubbed her sore eyes. They were red raw through crying. 'It's not as simple as that though, is it? I'm pregnant again, Joey.'

Joey shook his head in disbelief. 'But Georgie's only nine months old. How can you be pregnant again this quickly?'

Frankie clung to her brother. 'I am, Joey. I've already done the test. What am I gonna do? Jed doesn't know, I haven't even told him yet. I was gonna tell him today, surprise him, and then that old slag turned up at the door.'

Joey held his sister by the shoulders and stared into her eyes. 'You have to have an abortion, Frankie. You can't have any more kids by him, you just can't. Jed's a traitor, he's scum – can't you see that, Frankie?'

Frankie furiously shook her head. 'I won't have an abortion, Joey. I could never kill my own child.'

*   *   *

246

Jed spent Boxing Day over at Sammy's. Sammy had sorted a car out for him, a bright red Ford Fiesta, but Jed couldn't pick it up until the following morning.

'What am I gonna do if she won't take me back? It would break my heart to be separated from Georgie girl,' Jed asked Sammy.

'Of course she'll take you back. You're gonna have to grovel and shit, promise that you'll never be unfaithful again and all that bollocks, but she'll definitely take you back. Don't worry, Jed, Frankie'll be fine once you've worked your magic on her, and if your charm don't work, the car should do the trick.'

Jed was up bright and early the following morning. He picked the car up from Wickford and, with a heavy heart, drove it towards Frankie's old house, which now belonged to her grandparents.

Praying that Frankie would open the door herself, Jed was horrified when he came face to face with her Uncle Raymond.

'Look, I don't want no grief, I just want to talk to Frankie and see my baby,' Jed mumbled. He had never forgotten the time Raymond had chased him down the road with a baseball bat.

Raymond had no idea why Frankie had fallen out with Jed. He'd asked Joey, but Joey was too loyal to his sister to blab and Joyce and Stanley knew nothing other than that Frankie had turned up at the door sobbing on Christmas Day. He glared at Jed and stepped outside.

'You've got some nerve, coming 'ere. You ain't welcome, so fuck off.'

Jed kept his voice calm. 'Look, I need to speak to Frankie and I have every right to see my daughter.'

As Frankie appeared at the door, Raymond ordered her to go back inside the house. Frankie pulled her uncle to one side. 'I am quite capable of dealing with this myself. I can't avoid him for ever, Ray, we've got a child together.'

Raymond pointed at Jed. 'I'm warning you, you hurt her and I'll hurt you – got it?'

247

Frankie waited until Raymond had gone back inside before she spoke. 'Whaddya want?' she asked abruptly.

'I wanna sort things out. Please give me a chance to explain, Frankie.'

Frankie shook her head. As Jed edged closer to her, Frankie pushed him away. The thought of him even touching her after he had put his penis inside that other girl made her feel physically sick.

'It's over between us, Jed, but I won't stop you from seeing Georgie.'

Jed was devastated. Handing some keys to Frankie, he pointed at the red Fiesta. 'I bought you a car, babe. Let's sit inside it and talk, it's cold out here.'

Frankie stared at the car. It was all shiny and looked brand spanking new. 'It will take more than a car to make up for what you did. I will never forgive you or trust you again, Jed.'

'I know and I don't blame you, but please let me try and make it up to you, Frankie. I went to see my cousin Sammy yesterday. His dad has just bought a bit of land over in Wickford and Sammy and his girlfriend Kerry are going to live there. Sammy said me and you can move our trailer on there, too. You'll like Kerry – she's not a traveller and I know you'll be much happier there than you've been on that Hainault site. Now you've got your car you can come and go as you please while I'm out working. You can visit your nan and grandad, your brother and Dom, you can go shopping, do whatever you want. Your life will be different, I promise you it will.'

'Show me the car,' Frankie said.

As Jed went to hold her hand, Frankie snatched it away. 'Don't you dare touch me, you bastard.'

Jed walked over to the Fiesta. 'It's only a year old and it's barely been used. It belonged to some old grunter apparently. He died and his wife can't drive, so she sold it to one of Sammy's pals. It's only done nine thousand miles, Frankie. It's a real beauty.'

Frankie sat inside the car and studied the interior. It was lovely, just the type of car she had dreamed of owning.

'Why don't you take me for a drive? We can have lunch somewhere and have a proper chat, if you want,' Jed suggested.

'I don't wanna go anywhere with you,' Frankie spat, her voice filled with venom.

'Where's your engagement ring?' Jed asked sheepishly.

'In your garden somewhere. I threw it away.'

Jed looked at her, waiting for her to say something else. Surely she had to be joking? The ring had cost him a fair bit of dough, even though it was knocked off.

'Don't muck about,' he said.

'I'm not. I was so annoyed when I left yours that I took it off and chucked it down the driveway.'

Jed was anything but happy, but he daren't show Frankie his annoyance. He was already treading on thin ice as it was.

Frankie turned to him. 'I wanna know everything, Jed. I wanna know how long you was seeing that tart, where you did it with her, and why you felt the need to do it with the old slapper in the first place.'

Jed averted his eyes. He was dreading answering these questions, but had already planned what he was going to say.

'I slept with her once. It was when you was pregnant and had gone off sex. I took her to the trailer over in Tilbury. It meant nothing, Frankie, honest it didn't. I was drunk, out of me nut and I didn't know what I was doing.'

Frankie looked at him in disgust. She didn't believe for a minute that he had only slept with Sally the once. 'You lying bastard. I know you slept with her more than once, so tell me the fucking truth.'

Jed bit his lip. He'd shagged Sally tons of times, but there was no way Frankie would forgive him if he told her that. 'OK, it happened three times,' he lied.

Unable to stop herself, Frankie punched him in the side of the face. 'How could you take her to where my mum died? I hate you Jed, I fucking hate you,' she sobbed.

'Please don't cry, Frankie. The trailer your mum died in isn't there no more, my dad bought a new one to replace it. I swear to you, babe, this will never happen again. Please, let's give it another try. I know you probably hate me at the moment, but that will ease in time. Think of Georgie. She don't wanna grow up without her dad, does she?'

Frankie stopped crying. 'Where did you meet her?'

'The Berwick Manor,' Jed replied.

'You met her in the same place that we met! Didn't you feel guilty about that? How could you, Jed? How could you do this to me?'

Frankie had never seen Jed cry before, so she didn't know what to do when his eyes glistened with tears.

'I will never go out of a night without you again. I love you, Frankie. I can't live without you, I know I can't.'

Frankie glared at him to see if he was actually crying or acting. She had loved him so much once, but now she despised him. She turned her head and looked out of the car window. She was pregnant again, so how could she manage without him? Perhaps once they moved and she had her own independence with the car, there was a chance she could be happy again.

'When were you thinking of moving the trailer?' she asked.

Jed wiped his eyes. 'As soon as possible. The first week in January is probably the earliest I can get it sorted. Are you up for it, Frankie? Please say you'll move to Wickford with me.'

Frankie knew the ball was firmly in her court for once. 'If I do come back, it won't be until you've moved the trailer. I hate that site we live on and I never want to see them awful women again. Shannon's bound to have told them what happened at Christmas and I'll be a laughing stock if I go back there.'

'OK, that's fine. You can stay at your nan's as long as you like.'

'Also, you're not to go out of a night without me any more. I mean it, Jed, I don't want you working away or nothing.'

'I won't go out of a night, babe, but I've gotta go to work to support us.'

'Not of a night you won't. You can't be trusted, Jed, and if you don't agree to my rules, then I ain't moving back in with ya.'

'OK, I won't work away, but most of me choring is done of a night. I can hardly do it in broad daylight, can I?'

'As long as you're home by ten or something, but no later,' Frankie replied.

Jed sighed. Talk about having his fucking wings clipped. He'd been allowed to stay out after ten when he was six years old. He took a deep breath and smiled at her.

'OK, so if I agree to these rules and move the trailer, are we definitely gonna give it another go?'

'Yeah, but not because I want to, Jed, I'm only doing it because I have no choice.'

'Whaddya mean, you ain't got a choice?'

Frankie turned to face him. 'I'm pregnant again. I was going to surprise you with the news on Christmas Day, but I didn't get the chance to, did I?'

'That's absolutely brilliant news! I can't believe we're gonna be parents again,' Jed said, as he tried to hug her.

'Don't touch me,' Frankie said, pushing him away.

Jed urged her to look him in the eye. He then gave her the melting look that he did so expertly with those bright green eyes of his. 'Frankie, I promise you with all my heart that from this moment on I'll be the best boyfriend and dad ever. We can book the wedding, make things official and go on . . .'

Frankie stopped him in his tracks by slapping him around the face. 'You're a cheat and a fucking liar. I ain't marrying you, Jed. Not now, not ever.'

CHAPTER TWENTY-SEVEN

1993. FOUR YEARS LATER

Frankie heard a scream and ran outside the trailer. Harry was lying spread-eagled on the grass. 'What's the matter?' she asked, as she crouched down to tend to her son.

Harry sat up and pointed at his sister, who was standing nearby with a sheepish expression on her face. 'Georgie drop me.'

Frankie gave her daughter a gentle tap on her bottom and sent her to her bedroom. Georgie would never intentionally hurt her little brother, but she'd been told time and time again not to pick him up in case she dropped him.

As Harry stopped crying and fell asleep in her arms, Frankie put him down for his afternoon nap. She was gasping for a cup of tea and needed to tidy the trailer a bit before Jed got home. Frankie picked up the kids' toys while she waited for the kettle to boil. Satisfied that the place now looked passable, she made herself a cup of tea and sat on the sofa.

Jed had brought their new trailer just over a year ago. It was massive, double the size of their old one, and Frankie adored her new luxurious home. Moving to Wickford had been the best decision they had ever made. At first things had been difficult, due to Jed's affair with Sally, but Jed had kept to his word and, to Frankie's knowledge, he'd had no more contact with either Sally or his son.

Frankie was glad she'd managed to weather the storm. She and Jed got along OK now, and even though Frankie could never completely trust him again, she still loved him.

Frankie smiled as she dunked a biscuit in her tea and stared at her little pot belly. She had only found out that she was pregnant again a few weeks ago, and she was looking forward to caring for a newborn once more. Thinking of the two she already had, Frankie smiled. She adored both Georgie and Harry, but they were hard work at times, especially Georgie, who had just opened her bedroom door and was currently staring at her, with her hands on her hips.

'Can I come out now, Mum?'

Frankie put her cup on the coffee table. 'Only if you promise not to pick your brother up again, Georgie. He's too heavy for you, and you don't want to make him ill, do you?'

'Promise,' Georgie said walking towards her with her arms held out.

Frankie lifted her up, sat her on her lap and stroked her long dark hair. Georgie was such a striking girl. She had piercing green eyes, long dark hair, and was the spitting image of Jed.

As her daughter's eyes shut, Frankie laid her down next to her on the sofa. Georgie was four now and would be starting school in September and Frankie just hoped that she liked it. At times, Georgie could be a boisterous child who loved being outdoors and hated being indoors. She also had some strange eating habits that worried Frankie immensely. Some days Georgie would gorge herself senseless and other days she wouldn't eat a morsel.

Spotting her daughter clutching the doll that Alice had given her at the weekend, Frankie smiled. She hadn't gone anywhere without that doll since she'd come home; she had even slept with the bloody thing.

Frankie's thoughts turned to Alice and Jimmy. She still wasn't a massive fan of Jed's parents, but always tried her best to be polite to them. Alice still had a habit of interfering at times. She spoiled Georgie rotten and was often critical of Frankie's parenting skills. Frankie had learned to let her comments go in one ear and out the other, but it did wind her up when

Georgie came back from visiting Alice and Jimmy and played up something rotten.

Harry usually stayed with her when Georgie went to Alice and Jimmy's. A laid-back, happy child, he looked nothing like either her or Jed, as he had strawberry-blond hair and bright blue eyes. Frankie often wondered if his features favoured her mum and her brother. Harry looked very much like Joey had when he was a baby and there was certainly no one blond in Jed's family.

Thinking of her brother, Frankie smiled. He had been fuming with her when she had originally taken Jed back. 'Being pregnant again, Frankie, is no excuse for staying with that bastard. You can come and live with me and Dominic, we'll help you bring up the kids. I've already spoken to Dom and he's well up for you moving in with us.'

Frankie had thanked Joey for his kind offer, but by that time she had already promised Jed that she would move back in with him once he moved the trailer over to Wickford.

'Don't come crying to me when it all goes wrong again, Frankie. I'm sick of worrying about you, I really am,' Joey had warned her.

They had barely spoken for weeks after that, but were on good terms again now. Joey and Dominic had recently moved themselves. They had bought a town house over in South Woodham Ferrers, which wasn't far from Frankie, and she often visited them with the kids.

All in all, life was pretty good at the moment. Her dad was due to be released from prison soon and Frankie couldn't wait for him to spend some quality time with her, Georgie and Harry. Another reason why Frankie couldn't wait for her dad's homecoming was because she was desperate to organise a reunion between him and her brother. They had had no contact whatsoever since her mum's death and Frankie was determined to change that. It certainly wasn't going to be easy. Joey was still very bitter about their mum's murder. He couldn't accept that it was an accident and he still vowed to this day that he would never forgive their dad for what he had done. Her dad, on the other hand, could still not accept Joey's sexuality, and he swore that he would never forgive Joey for the embarrassment that he had caused Ed and the family name.

Frankie's thoughts were disturbed by the sound of Jed's new motor pulling up outside. He had just bought himself a year old dark-grey Mitsubishi Shogun. It was well flash, with loads of extras on it, including a body kit.

'You're early,' Frankie said, as her boyfriend walked in.

'I've popped home for a bit as me and Sammy have gotta work late again tonight. He's gone to sort out the horses, so I told him I wanted to spend some time with you and the kids.'

Hearing her father's voice, Georgie woke up. 'Daddy,' she squealed, running towards him with her new doll in her hand.

Jed picked her up and swung her around. 'What's you and your mum been up to today?' he asked.

Georgie threw her hands around his neck and began to cry. 'I was naughty.'

Jed looked at Frankie. 'What's she done?'

'She picked Harry up and dropped him, so I sent her to her room, that's all.'

Jed laughed. 'She's as strong as an ox. You'll never get bullied at school, will ya, Georgie girl?' he said proudly.

'I thought we was getting a takeaway tonight with Sammy and Kerry. I went out and got us some wine and beers earlier.'

Putting his daughter down, Jed gave Frankie a tight squeeze. 'Something came up, babe. You know me and Sammy can't afford to turn work down. 'Ere, take that,' Jed said, handing Frankie some rolled-up notes.

'What's that for?' Frankie asked.

'Your takeaway. Just 'cause me and Sammy have to graft, it don't mean you and Kerry can't enjoy yourselves. There's a oner there, go and buy yourself something to wear tomorrow with whatever you don't spend.'

Georgie cheekily held her hand out. 'Can I have sweetie money?'

Jed threw a fiver at his daughter. 'That's my girl, loves a bit of wonga, she do,' he said, laughing at Frankie.

'Daddy,' Harry said as he toddled out of his bedroom.

Jed picked his son up, kissed him on the forehead, and immediately handed him to Frankie. 'I'm running late. I've gotta have a shower, babe, I stink,' he said.

Sitting Harry on the floor, Frankie went to make the kids some dinner. Jed really annoyed her sometimes. He had all the time in the world for Georgie, but paid Harry very little attention whatsoever. Frankie opened a tin and slopped the contents into the saucepan. As she stirred the beans and sausages, suspicions began to arise in her mind over Jed's recent behaviour.

When they first moved to Wickford, Frankie had banned Jed from working nights and also going out without her. Jed had agreed to her new rules and for the first year or so had been as good as gold. During the past eighteen months, however, he had begun to come and go as he pleased again. He often stayed out all night, blaming it on work, and Frankie let him do so because she knew that Sammy was working alongside him.

Frankie forgot her worries as she saw her best friend's car pull up outside. Kerry was Sammy's girlfriend and Frankie had hit it off with her from the word go. Their trailers were side by side, and they spent many hours in each other's company when the boys were out grafting.

Sammy and Jed worked together all the time now. They were both wheeler-dealers, but earned very decent money. From the phone calls that she and Kerry overheard, both girls knew that the lads paid people to steal cars, caravans and lorries for them, which they then doctored and sold on. Kerry and Frankie never questioned their men on what they actually did. Both girls were looked after well financially, so they cared for their children, went shopping regularly, and generally minded their own business.

If it wasn't for Kerry's advice, Frankie wasn't sure if her and Jed's relationship would have ever got back on track. Things had been so strained when they had first moved to Wickford that Frankie couldn't bear Jed being anywhere near her. In the end, Kerry had given her a talking to.

'If you don't start having sex with Jed, he will end up going somewhere else for it, Frankie. I know it's difficult, mate, but once you get back in the swing of it, you'll be OK.'

'But I can't bear him touching me. Every time he tries to, I can picture him with that Sally girl.'

'Just have a bottle of wine, shut your eyes and think of England. If you don't, you'll end up losing Jed in the end. He's a good-looking bloke, he's got money and someone will snap him up if you don't start putting out, Frankie.'

Frankie had got paralytic the first time they'd had sex again, but after that, things had improved each time. Jed had been tender and loving towards her and Frankie had sort of responded in her own way. Occasionally, she would get a flash of him groping that Sally tart, but she would immediately try and banish the thought from her mind. She had to make herself forget; it was the only way to move on.

As her mobile rang, Frankie took the call outside. The kids were kicking up a din, and she couldn't hear, let alone make herself be heard.

'Frankie, it's Nan. I've decided to do a surprise party for your grandad on Sunday for his birthday. He thinks I'm just having a few people over for a barbecue, but it's really in his honour. I've told Jock on the quiet and he's coming over early to take him to look at a pigeon, then he'll take him up the pub. While your grandad's out I can get everything organised.'

'Can Jed come with me, Nan? Seeing as it's a party,' Frankie asked.

'No, love. Raymond'll be here and Joey and Dominic, so I'd rather you just came with the kids.'

'OK, what time?'

'Get here by two-ish.'

Frankie said goodbye and went back inside the trailer. It was such a shame that her family still refused to accept Jed. Apart from Joey, none of them knew that he had cheated on her that time, but even after all these years they still refused to allow him into their lives.

Pouring the kid's sausages and beans onto two plastic plates, Frankie smiled as her boyfriend reappeared.

'You all right, babe?'

'Yeah, fine. I've gotta pop over to my nan's on Sunday; it's my grandad's birthday. Have you gotta get off right now?' Frankie asked.

Jed didn't want to push his luck. 'I'll tell you what, why don't me and Sammy have that takeaway with you and Kerry first and then we'll get off? The only thing is, we've got two lorries to cut and shut, so we might not be back till tomorrow lunchtime.'

Frankie smiled as Jed pulled her towards him and started getting fruity. 'Stop it, Kerry'll be walking in in a minute,' she said, as Jed shoved his hand inside her tracksuit bottoms. He ignored her and expertly inserted his finger inside her.

'What you doing, Daddy?' Georgie asked, bemused.

'Just showing your mum how much I love her,' Jed said laughing.

Frankie pushed him away. Good job the kids were too young to understand what Jed was really doing.

An hour and a half later, Jed and Sammy both kissed their girlfriends and children goodbye.

'Yous two ain't ate that much,' Frankie said, as she let go of Jed and happily munched on another prawn ball.

'We can't work properly on a full stomach. We'll get some beers on the way to ease the boredom,' Jed explained.

'What time did you say you'll be back?' Kerry asked Sammy.

'Dunno, it's hard to say. I reckon about eight or nine in the morning, but it could be later. What do you reckon, Jed?'

'We'll be back by twelve at the latest,' Jed replied.

As soon as the trailer door slammed shut, Kerry topped up their wine glasses to the brim. She smiled at Frankie. 'While the cats are away the girlies must play,' she said, giggling.

*   *   *

258

Sammy and Jed laughed as they stopped the motor, changed out of their work clothes, put on their best togs, then headed off towards Rush Green. Leading a double life was hard work sometimes, but both lads thrived on the excitement and the lies.

'Yous two ain't ate that much,' Sammy said, mimicking Frankie's voice.

'Little does she know I've got roast chicken with all the trimmings later. I know I compare 'em a lot, Sam, but Sally do knock spots off of Frankie in both the kitchen and the bedroom, you know.'

Sammy laughed. 'Same 'ere, mate. That Julie sucks me cory like no girl's ever sucked it before. And she cooks a mean chicken korma.'

Chuckling, Jed turned up the stereo. Sammy was a big fan of Billie Jo Spears and 'Blanket on the Ground' was his favourite song. As Sammy sang along with Billie Jo, Jed sat deep in thought. When Sally had turned up at his door all those years ago with Luke in her arms, he would have never envisaged himself falling for her and being so happy. He still fucked about with other birds, but nowhere near as much as he used to. Their romance had only started up again because of the maintenance payments. He didn't want her brute of a father on his case, so he'd started being nice to her again.

They'd met up a few times, just so he could give her some wonga, but it was when she had got her council flat in Rush Green Gardens that he'd really begun to see her in a different light.

Luke had had a big part to play in their love affair. At first, Jed had flatly refused to see the boy, but once he'd agreed to, he'd adored him on sight. Dark, feisty and brazen, Luke was like his little double. He was three now, would soon be four, and even at that tender age, the little sod had the gift of the gab. Lukey boy was everything that Jed had ever wanted in a son. Alice and Jimmy loved him as well, and he often stayed over at their house. He loved the tractor, the horses and the dogs. The kid was an out-and-out travelling boy.

259

Harry, on the other hand was not. He was a timid child, in his own little world, and, as much as Jed tried, he couldn't love him anywhere near as much as he had grown to love Lukey boy. He cared about Harry, obviously, but only because he was his son. It was Luke who tugged at his heartstrings and filled his stomach with pride. His parents felt the same way, especially his dad, who was totally besotted with Luke.

His mother was full of suspicion. She had never been Frankie's biggest fan. 'You sure Harry's yours? Blond hair, blue eyes – he looks and acts sod all like any of us. I always said she was an old whore, that Frankie. I bet that kid belongs to some gorjer mush.'

Thinking of his number-one son again, Jed smiled. Lukey boy and Georgie were so alike, it was uncanny at times. They had never met, for obvious reasons. Jed would love to introduce them, but he couldn't risk Georgie saying something to Frankie.

Jed's affair with Sally had started again just over two years ago. He'd been popping round hers to see Luke and at the same time Sally had just kind of won him over. He could honestly say that he loved her now, probably more than he did Frankie, but leaving Frankie was never going to be an option, as he could never be parted from Georgie girl.

Sally was extremely tolerant. She understood his predicament and was more than happy to share him. The only thing he hadn't told her was that Frankie was pregnant again. He had told Sally that he and Frankie no longer slept together, but other than that, he was reasonably honest about his life at home. Frankie, on the other hand, knew nothing of his involvement with Sally or Luke. He had never mentioned seeing the boy, paying maintenance or anything.

Not one to be outdone by his cousin's romance, Sammy had rekindled his affair with Sally's pal, Julie. She also had a flat on Rush Green Gardens and Julie and Sammy had recently had a son together called Tom.

'You're quiet. What's up?' Sammy said, turning the stereo down.

'Just thinking about stuff.'

'Like what?' Sammy asked.

Jed smiled. 'Can you imagine what the girls would do if they found out what me and you were really up to?'

'Kerry would no doubt chop my bollocks off, and I reckon your Frankie would probably do the same to you,' Sammy said, chuckling.

Jed playfully punched his cousin. 'Moving the girls on that bit of land in Wickford was the best move we ever made. They'll never find out about our other lives while they're stuck in the middle of nowhere, will they?'

Sammy shrugged. 'I fucking hope not.'

Arriving at their destination, Jed laughed as he bumped the Shogun onto the kerb. 'Just remember Harry Mitchell, Sammy boy. If me and you can get away with what we did to him, we can get away with anything, mush.'

CHAPTER TWENTY-EIGHT

Eddie Mitchell grinned as he studied the photocopied details of the six properties. Two of them weren't his cup of tea, three were possibilities, but it was the cottage in Rettendon that really caught his eye.

'What do you think of this one?' he asked Stuart.

Stuart stared at the piece of paper and nodded. 'It looks nice, but where is Rettendon? I've never heard of it.'

Eddie laughed. Stuart was from Hackney and had rarely set foot outside London. In fact, Stu was the only person Ed knew, apart from his Auntie Joan, who spoke about Essex as though it was as remote as Timbuktu.

Itching for visiting time, Eddie decided to do some press-ups to take the edge off his impatience. At fifty press-ups, Eddie stopped for a breather. Four weeks, four measly weeks and he would be out of this shit-hole for good.

Thinking over his stretch, Eddie knew that the only thing he would miss about Wandsworth Prison was Stuart. Once Stu had been convicted, they'd both been moved off the remand wing, but thankfully, they'd still been allowed to share a cell. Ed had been offered the chance to spend his last six months at an open prison, but had opted not to, as he hadn't wanted to be parted from his young cellmate. Usually, inmates wouldn't have much say on the matter, but since a new guvnor had taken over and that evil screw, Carter, had left, Eddie had the whole of the prison system sussed.

Eddie felt desperately sorry for Stuart. Three weeks ago, his young pal had opened a letter that had broken his heart. His girlfriend, Carly, had met someone else and was pregnant by him. 'I've done all this bird for her, thinking we had a future together and she don't even want me, Ed. What am I gonna do with my life now? I can't go back to Hackney 'cause of Jonesey's mates. He was part of a gang and I'll get lynched if I go back there.'

Stuart had become like a son to Eddie over the years. 'Fuck Carly. She ain't worth a toss, mate. If she can't wait for ya after what you did for her, then she ain't worth knowing. As for Hackney, fuck that shit-hole as well. I promise you, Stu, on the day you get released from here, I'll be waiting outside them gates for ya, boy. You'll have a flat, a job and a bird waiting, you got that?'

Stuart had cheered up over the past week or so. He was still bitter about Carly at times, but was now looking forward to his future. 'You won't regret helping me out and taking me on, Ed. I'll be the best worker you ever had and I won't let you down, I promise,' he repeatedly told Eddie.

As Eddie finished his exercise routine, Stuart smiled. 'I take it Gina's coming to visit?'

Eddie nodded. Frankie, Gary, Ricky and Raymond visited him occasionally, but since his conviction he was no longer allowed three visits a week, so he saved most of his allowance for the woman who had stolen his heart. God only knows what spell Gina had cast on him, but she had something about her that sent tingles down his spine. She had awoken something inside him that he had only ever felt with Jessica in the past.

He wasn't stupid. They'd never eaten together, slept together or even shopped together, so there was always a chance that he would come out of nick, move in with Gina, then things would go dreadfully wrong. He couldn't see that happening, though. They clicked, were besotted with one another and, most importantly, they both wanted the same things out of life.

Eddie nodded politely at the guard as he unlocked the cell.

Being in love was the best feeling in the world and, considering the circumstances, he felt blessed to have been given a second chance.

Bored with waiting for Jed to return home, Frankie got herself showered and dressed, then knocked at Kerry's. 'I'm gonna pop over to Lakeside and have a mooch round. You coming with me?'

Kerry shook her head. Sammy had promised to take her out for lunch and she was determined to get herself dolled up to look her best for him. 'Sammy'll be back soon and we're going out later. What you going to Lakeside for? You gotta get anything special?'

'My nan's having a barbecue for my grandad's birthday on Sunday, so I've gotta get my grandad a present. I might buy myself a new outfit as well. Why not, eh? Jed's always telling me to treat myself out the money he gives me and I rarely do. I always spend it on the kids.'

Kerry smiled. 'I'll do a deal with ya. I'll look after Georgie and Harry while you go to Lakeside, then when you get back, you look after my two while me and Sammy go out for a boozy late lunch.'

Frankie immediately agreed. It was hard work dragging Georgie and Harry around the shops and she could browse much better on her own. 'I'll get going now, then. When Jed gets home, tell him I'll be back by two.'

Not knowing what on earth to buy for her grandad, Frankie's first stop was Debenhams. She wanted to get him something practical, so after a lot of umming and aahing, she chose a waterproof jacket that he could wear while messing about with his pigeons.

While Frankie was standing in the queue waiting to pay, she felt a tap on her shoulder and turned around. It was her old schoolfriend, Stacey.

'Stacey! You look fantastic. It's so lovely to see you,' Frankie gushed.

264

Frankie had knocked about with Stacey for years, but they'd lost contact when she'd settled down with Jed.

As Stacey hugged her, Frankie felt ever so dowdy standing beside her old friend. Stacey was incredibly slim and much more attractive than Frankie remembered her being.

'Let's go for a coffee so we can have a proper catch-up, shall we?' Stacey suggested.

Ten minutes later they were sitting at a table opposite one another, both nursing a cappuccino.

'So, how are the kids? I heard you'd had a little boy as well.'

Frankie grinned. 'They're great, thanks. Georgie's four now, she starts school in September, thank God. She drives me mad – she's four going on fourteen. Harry's nearly three. He's a little darling, he is no trouble whatsoever, bless him. What about you? Do you still see Demi and Paige?'

'We're all still in touch, but I don't see them as much as I used to. I'm engaged now,' Stacey said proudly, showing Frankie her rock.

Frankie admired the beautiful ring. It had a massive diamond and Frankie wondered if it was real or fake.

'Wow, that must have cost a fortune. Who's the lucky man? Do I know him?'

Stacey shook her head. 'Oh, he's gorgeous, Frankie. His name's Ashley and I met him in Hollywoods in Romford. He's really fit – he's a professional footballer.'

'Really!' Frankie said impressed. 'Who does he play for?'

'Millwall. He's not in the first team yet, but he reckons next season he will be. He's a brilliant player, Frankie. I go to all the games to cheer him on. Ashley's amazing, he really is.'

'He sounds wonderful, Stacey. When are you getting married?'

About to answer, Stacey stopped herself and squeezed Frankie's hand. 'Hark at me going on about myself. Tell me about your life. I'm sorry it didn't work out with Jed.'

'What do you mean?' Frankie asked, puzzled.

'I've seen him with Sally Baldwin. I don't know her, but my

265

sister used to go majorettes with her. She's got a son with him, hasn't she? I saw them shopping together in Romford last week, acting all lovey-dovey. So, when did you actually split up? Who are you with now?'

Frankie felt herself go all hot, then felt the colour drain from her cheeks.

'Are you OK, Frankie?' Stacey asked, concerned.

Desperate to find out some more information, Frankie sipped her cappuccino and tried to ignore her shaking hands. 'I'm fine. Being pregnant makes me come over all funny sometimes. Now, where was we?'

'We were talking about you and Jed splitting up.'

Frankie forced a smile. If she told Stacey she was still with Jed, Stacey would probably clam up. As hard as it was, she had to lie to find out the gossip. 'We split up a few months back. It's Jed's kid I'm pregnant with, but I'm happy on my own for now.'

'You did know that he was with Sally, didn't you?' Stacey asked.

Frankie nodded. 'Yes, of course. Jed had a son called Luke with her. I'll be honest, I didn't know they were back together, but I suppose he's hardly gonna tell his ex, is he?'

Stacey moved nearer to her friend. 'You've always been far too good for Jed, anyway. I used to see him down the Berwick with that cousin of his and they were always with different girls. Jed's a player, Frankie, and you're so pretty, you could get anyone. That Sally's welcome to him, if you want my honest opinion.'

Desperately trying to stem the tears threatening to pour down her face, Frankie stood up. 'I have to go now, Stacey. My neighbour's looking after the kids for me and I said I wouldn't be long. Have you still got my mobile number?'

Stacey nodded. 'Yeah, if you've still got the same number, it's in my old address book,' she lied. Although she felt sorry for Frankie, Stacey had no intention of getting involved with her again.

About to walk away, Frankie turned around. 'You don't happen to know where that Sally lives, do you, Stacey?' she asked, her voice trembling.

Unable to believe the change in her once feisty, glamorous best friend, Stacey led Frankie outside the coffee shop. Pulling a tissue from her handbag, she handed it to her and sat her down on a nearby bench. 'I'm so sorry if I've upset you, Frankie. I really didn't mean to.'

'I'm fine, honest I am,' Frankie wept.

Stacey felt sad. There was a time when Frankie was the dog's bollocks, could pick any lad she wanted, but not any more. She had changed beyond belief. 'I've got to go now, Frankie. Ashley is taking me up the West End tonight. I don't know Sally's actual address, but I do know that she lives in Rush Green Gardens. Good to see you, and look after yourself, mate.'

As Stacey walked away from her, Frankie held her head in her hands and sobbed.

Back in Wandsworth, Eddie and Gina were busy discussing where they were going to live. With Eddie due for release in the next few weeks, he had asked Gina to find them somewhere nice and cosy to rent for now. Then, if all went well, they could look at possibly buying a place of their own next year.

'I thought that cottage in Rettendon was perfect. How long was the lease on it?'

Stroking Eddie's massive hands, Gina smiled. It had been a long wait and she could barely believe that this time next month she and Eddie would be sharing a house and waking up next to one another every morning.

'It's a six-month lease with an option for another six months. The estate agent said it's owned by a wealthy couple in their early sixties who have just retired and are going to live in Australia with their daughter for a year. It's a lovely place, Ed, and I know we can afford it, but it's ever so expensive compared to the others, don't you think?'

Eddie laughed and leaned forward for a kiss. 'Money's never been an object with me – you, of all people, should know that. I've got dough stashed all over the place, and me father left me a fortune. Anyway, I want us to live somewhere nice. Fuck me, we deserve it, we've waited long enough. Between you and me, sweetheart, I could buy ten cottages just like that one you wanna rent tomorrow for cash if I wanted to.'

Gina grinned. She couldn't wait to hold Eddie in her arms without the prison officers and the inmates watching them. 'I've decided that when you get out, I'm going to take at least a couple of months off work. That way we can spend some real quality time together. We can chill out, go shopping, visit nice restaurants. We can even go away on holiday if you like.'

Eddie laughed. 'Forget the shopping, all I wanna do is make love to you morning, noon and night.'

Gina shuddered as Eddie stared intently into her eyes. She had bought herself one of those vibrators recently and it had kept her company at night while she lay in bed imagining Eddie doing all sorts of naughty things to her. Feeling herself pulsating down below, Gina quickly changed the subject.

'So, have you had a chance to speak to your sons or Raymond about us living together yet?'

Eddie shook his head. Gary and Ricky knew that he had a woman visiting him regularly, but he hadn't told them how serious things were. As for Raymond, Eddie was dreading telling him. He was Jessica's brother and the conversation was bound to prove difficult.

'I'll tell you what we'll do. When I get out I'm gonna organise a big family get-together. You come to it with me. I can introduce you and at the same time we'll tell everyone we're living together.'

'I can cook a meal or something, if you want, and you can invite your family round to the cottage,' Gina offered.

Eddie squeezed Gina's hand. 'I'll book a restaurant. Indoors is just for us, babe. I don't want anyone knowing where we're living, because I just want our new home to be about me and you. People are fucking nuisances, Gina. You tell 'em where you live and they're forever knocking on the bastard door. That's why that Rettendon place is perfect for us. It's rural, out of my manor and secluded. Tomorrow, I want you to go to that estate agent and sign the contract. I'll settle up with you when I get out. If the nosy gits ask, just tell 'em I'm working away or something.'

Gina smiled seductively at Eddie. The cottage in Rettendon would become their first love nest and the thought of having Eddie all to herself literally made her feel like the luckiest woman alive.

In Wickford, the atmosphere wasn't quite as lovey-dovey as it currently was in Wandsworth. Frankie had barely said a word since she came back from Lakeside and Jed was becoming pissed off by her silence.

'Cat got your tongue or summink? For fuck's sake Frankie, if I've done something wrong, just spit it out like you usually do, will ya?'

On the journey back from Lakeside, Frankie had barely been able to see the road markings along the A13. She had been crying so much that she had very nearly caused a fatal accident. A lorry driver had tooted and cursed at her as she'd swerved into his path. Frightened, Frankie had immediately pulled over into a pub car park. She knew Jed would probably be there when she got home and she needed to think fast about what she was going to say to him.

Knowing how clever Jed could be, Frankie decided that the only way to catch him out was to try to act normal. If her boyfriend had any inkling that she knew he'd been spotted with Sally, he would move heaven and earth to cover his tracks. Positive that this was the best way to play things, Frankie dried her eyes, put on a false smile and drove towards home.

The trouble with that was, with Jed now standing only a few feet away, spouting his usual cocksure rubbish, Frankie wanted to smash his smarmy face in. Unable to control her emotions any longer, she lunged towards him, lashing out with her fists.

'I know you've been seeing that slag Sally again, you fucking bastard.'

As Frankie caught her philandering boyfriend on the chin with a right hook, Jed managed to grab both of her arms.

'I can explain. Calm down, you're frightening the kids.'

Realising that both of her children were screaming, Frankie put her head in her hands and slumped onto the sofa.

Desperate to buy himself some time to create a story, Jed made a big issue of comforting the children. 'Sammy ain't gone out yet, so I'm gonna take 'em next door. We can talk properly then, just the two of us,' he said solemnly.

Annoyed with herself for blurting out her findings, Frankie began to cry. She was still crying when Jed returned five minutes later.

'It's not what you think,' he said as he sat down opposite her.

'Well, what is it, then? You were seen out shopping with the old slapper in Romford, playing happy families. You were all over one another, apparently. How you gonna explain that, Jed?'

'I promise you it ain't what you think, Frankie. Look, I didn't tell you because I knew you'd react like this. I have seen Sally and I have been paying maintenance for Luke. I had to. At the end of the day, he's my kid and I didn't wanna end up in court. I swear there is nothing between me and Sally. She's with another geezer now, right loved-up she is, and as for someone telling you we were all over one another, that's bollocks. Sally's fat and ugly now – I wouldn't give her one if she was the last woman in Essex.'

'Well, why ain't her own boyfriend taking her fucking shopping, then?' Frankie screamed.

'Once I took her shopping Frankie, once. And the only reason I did that was because it was Luke's birthday. She asked me to buy him this plastic car and it was massive, too heavy to carry, so I took her there to get it.'

'But why didn't you tell me?' Frankie said.

Jed shrugged and at least had the gall to look sheepish. 'It's awkward, ain't it? I'm frightened to speak to you about it, but Luke will always be my son. This is all my fault, I know that, I'm the one that made mistakes, but I have to acknowledge the boy. What type of bloke would I be if I didn't, eh?'

Frankie had stopped crying, but was still fuming. 'I don't want you seeing that slut or that kid any more unless I'm with ya. I mean it, Jed. If you're spotted out with 'em again and I find out, I'm leaving you and taking the kids with me.'

'OK, but out of interest, who told you they saw me?'

'It doesn't matter who told me. All that matters is you don't go behind my back no more. I ain't some mug, Jed, and I won't be treated like one.'

Breathing a sigh of relief that his lies had been believed, Jed smiled. 'How about we go out for something to eat? It'll be nice. Just me, you and the kids.'

'You go with the kids. I've got a really bad headache. I could do with a lie-down.'

Frankie flinched as Jed went to cuddle her. 'Do you want me to bring you back a takeaway?' he asked.

'No, I had something to eat earlier,' Frankie lied.

As Jed shut the trailer door, Frankie stared at him through the net curtain. The bastard was lying, she was sure of that. All she had to do now was prove it.

CHAPTER TWENTY-NINE

Over the next few days, Jed behaved like the perfect boyfriend. He cooked, cleaned, looked after the kids and barely left Frankie's side. Frankie was extremely suspicious. In her book, him sucking up to her just proved his guilt even more.

On the Sunday morning, Frankie got woken up by Jed kissing the back of her neck and thrusting his erect penis up against her buttocks. She immediately jumped out of bed. 'Sorry Jed, I ain't got time this morning. I've gotta get the kids ready for me grandad's birthday party, ain't I?'

Jed sighed as Frankie rushed out of the bedroom. Putting his hands behind his head, he lay back on the pillow and glanced at his erect cock. He hadn't really wanted to fuck Frankie anyway, he'd only tried it on with her out of pity. Thinking of Sally, Jed grinned. He was seeing her later, so he would save all his stamina for her.

Frankie smiled as Kerry poked her head around the trailer door. 'What time we got to leave?' Kerry asked.

'About one. I think my nan said the party starts at two, but it don't matter if we're a bit early.'

Frankie was looking forward to the day ahead. Getting away from Jed was a bonus on its own and Frankie couldn't wait to introduce Kerry to her family. It had been Jed's idea that she take Kerry to the party with her.

'Look, I know I ain't welcome, so why don't you take Kerry with ya? She can help you keep an eye on the kids, and if she

272

takes the boys with her, it'll give Georgie and Harry someone to play with.'

Thrilled by the prospect of her best friend accompanying her to her old house, Frankie had asked Kerry immediately and had been delighted when she had said yes. What neither girl realised was that it had all been Sammy's idea. He had cooked it up so he could spend the day with Julie.

Frankie put her outfit on and glanced in the mirror. 'What you up to today?' she asked Jed.

'Sammy and I have got a lorry to chop up. I dunno what time we'll finish, but you and Kerry'll probably be back well before we will.'

Frankie nodded and picked up her phone and handbag. 'Kids, come on, we're going now.'

'Enjoy yourself, babe,' Jed said, opening the door for her.

'Don't work too hard,' Frankie replied sarcastically.

Over in Rainham, Joyce was in full peacock mode. Extremely proud of her beautiful house, there was nothing Joyce liked more than showing off her wealth to all her friends.

Rita and Hilda glanced at one another as Joyce began to boast about how much Eddie had paid for the swimming pool. Joyce had begged them to come over early to give her a hand with the food, but even though they had only been here an hour, she had already driven them up the bloody wall.

Desperate to give her ears a rest, Hilda decided to make a start on taking the cutlery outside. 'Give us a hand, Rita. You take the plates.'

Out of earshot, Rita turned to Hilda. 'She's brain damage, ain't she? I wouldn't mind, she only got this house 'cause Eddie felt guilty and gave her the bastard thing.'

Hilda agreed. 'It's as though she's forgotten that she used to live in a council house opposite us, ain't it? I dunno about you, mate, but I'm gonna pour meself a large gin and tonic in a minute.'

Rita laughed. 'Pour me one, too. I might be able to suffer her more if I get a bit tiddly.'

Unaware that her friends were taking the piss out of her, Joyce went upstairs to get changed into her new frock. Joyce had spent ages searching for the appropriate number and she had finally found the dress of her dreams in a little boutique near the Cherry Tree in Rainham. Long, sleeveless and satin, with a leopard-skin design, it had cost her a small fortune. Susan, who owned the boutique, had said she looked absolutely stunning in it and, as Joyce admired herself in the mirror, she couldn't help but smile. I really do look a million dollars – that Susan was right, she thought smugly.

Hearing the doorbell, Joyce secured her diamanté earrings and floated down the stairs. She had arranged her husband's sixty-fifth birthday party with precision. Jock had taken Stanley out for her and she had ordered him not to bring her husband back until at least three o'clock. She had told the other guests to arrive at two, so that everybody was there by the time her husband returned home.

'Joey! Dominic!' Joyce exclaimed, kissing both boys lightly on each cheek.

Hearing a little yap, Joyce nigh on jumped out of her skin. She looked down and pointed at the little dog sporting a red bow around its neck. 'What's that? Who does it belong to?'

Laughing, Joey picked the Chihuahua up. 'Nan, meet Madonna. She's mine and Dom's, we bought her last week. Gorgeous, isn't she?'

Joyce politely patted Madonna on the head. She had a cute little face and was certainly more practical than those big, cumbersome Rottweilers she'd given away to Pat Murphy.

'Madonna's panting. I think she's thirsty, Joey,' Dominic said.

Telling the boys to get the dog some water, Joyce went to answer the door again. 'And don't use one of my good dishes. There's an old saucer on the windowsill with a plant standing on it. Rinse it out and use that,' she shouted.

By half-past two all of the guests had arrived. Joyce had been choosy who to invite and had kept the numbers to a lucky select fifty. Family-wise, Joyce had invited Raymond and Polly,

274

Joey, Dominic and Frankie, who was bringing her friend Kerry and, reluctantly, she had invited two of Stanley's cousins and their miserable wives. The rest of the numbers were made up by neighbours and friends. Joyce had asked Jock to invite a few of Stanley's pals from the pigeon club and also the bus depot where Stanley used to work.

At five to three, Joyce insisted that everybody gather in the lounge to await Stanley's arrival. As it was mid-August, the weather was hot and clammy and by the time everybody squeezed into the room, it was like a sauna.

Frankie stood next to Kerry with Harry in her arms. Georgie had taken an unhealthy interest in Madonna and wouldn't leave the poor dog alone.

'What do you think of my family, then?' Frankie whispered.

Kerry giggled. 'I think your uncle's well hot.'

'Raymond's married. His wife's over there. Behave yourself or I shall tell Sammy you've been acting like a floozy,' Frankie joked.

'He's here. Everybody be quiet,' Joyce shouted, in a false posh voice.

Joyce waited until she heard the front door click shut. 'Stanley, help me lift this,' she yelled.

As Stanley opened the lounge door he was gobsmacked.

'Surprise!' everyone shouted.

He turned to Jock. 'I take it you were in on this as well.'

Jock patted him on the back. 'Happy birthday, Stanley. You might be sixty-five, but you don't look a day over fifty, mate. It must be because you took that early retirement, you lazy bastard.'

'He looks young because I look after him so bloody well,' Joyce shouted cockily.

Raymond had offered to be in charge of the barbecue for the day as a favour to his mum. He turned the steaks over and glanced around to see where his miserable wife had got to. Raymond and Polly had tied the knot two years ago. Before they had married, their relationship had been fantastic, but since they'd wed it had gone drastically downhill.

Just lately, things had got even worse. Polly never seemed to stop moaning and her constant disapproval of their lifestyle drove Raymond up the wall. He was currently running Ed's salvage yard for him. The jewellery business had done his head in, so he'd resigned and gone back to a job he knew inside out. The money wasn't fantastic and if Polly wasn't whinging about their lack of finances, she was kicking off about their inability to conceive a child.

Spotting Polly standing next to Vicki with a face as black as thunder, Raymond sighed. They had only been trying for a child for the past eighteen months and Polly was already insisting that if she hadn't fallen pregnant by Christmas, they must look into adoption. Raymond had no intention of adopting. He wanted his own kids, not some other bastard's. He and Polly had recently been to see a quack who had sent them for tests, which confirmed there was sod all wrong with either of them.

'Some couples just take longer to conceive than others. You need to be a bit more patient,' the doctor had told them.

Unfortunately, Polly didn't know what the word patient meant. Whether it be wealth, children or a new designer handbag, she wanted everything the moment she set her mind to it. In other words, she wanted everything yesterday.

Glancing around the garden, Raymond smirked as he saw his mother trying to get his dad to dance with her. They might argue like cat and dog, but at least their marriage had lasted the duration, he thought.

Seeing Dougie walk past him, Raymond waved. Dougie was Eddie's pal, and Vicki, his wife, had been Jessica's best mate. Vicki had even called her little girl Jessica in honour of his sister.

Prodding a fork into the sausages to test if they were cooked, Raymond thought about Eddie. His brother-in-law had looked as fit as a fiddle the last time Raymond had seen him, and was due for release very soon. Raymond put the sausages onto a large plate. If Ed was going back into loan-sharking and wanted him to be his right-hand man once again, he would jump at the chance. He missed the excitement and riches of his past career and if Polly didn't like his decision, she could go and fuck herself.

Jed told Sally to duck down as he neared his parents' gaff. With Frankie's grandparents throwing a party just down the road, the last thing he needed was to be spotted with a bird in the motor.

'Slow down a bit, Jed,' Sally said, as her head made contact with the glove compartment.

'You can sit up now, and remember what I told ya: don't put your foot in it about me and you, as I don't want me mum sticking her oar in.'

Jed leaped out of the Shogun and unclipped Luke from the child-seat in the back. He took his son to visit his parents regularly, but they'd never been properly introduced to Sally before. They'd only met her once, and that was when her father had turned up shouting and screaming at their house.

'It ain't bloody right. Me and your father love little Lukey boy with all our heart and we deserve to know what his mother's like. You're on good terms with her now, ain't you, Jed? So bring the bloody girl round for dinner,' Alice kept insisting.

With his mother on his case, Jed felt he'd put the imminent introduction off as long as he possibly could. His dad knew that he was in a relationship with Sally, but because Frankie was up the duff again, he was reluctant to admit the truth to his mum.

'Please don't mention that Frankie's pregnant in front of Sally. Things are awkward enough as they are and Sal will be upset if she finds out Lukey boy's gonna have yet another brother or sister that he can't have no contact with. And don't you ever put your foot in it with Frankie, either. She'll chop my fucking nuts off if she ever finds out that Sally came round yours for dinner.'

Unaware that her son had been playing both girls, Alice promised to keep schtum.

Alice beamed as she opened the front door. 'Hello, Sally, I've been dying to meet you properly, love. Why don't you and Lukey boy come and sit in the kitchen with me while Jed and his father talk business.'

'Me and Dad ain't got no business to discuss,' Jed snapped.

Alice linked arms with Sally and glared at her son. 'Sit in the front room and have a beer, then. Me and Sally want to get to know one another, and we ain't gonna be able to do that with you and your father butting in.'

Knowing when he was beaten, Jed winked at Sally and followed his father into the lounge.

Unaware that Jed was currently playing happy families less than a mile down the road, Frankie was busy keeping tabs on her daughter.

'Where is she now? She's already had three hot dogs. She ain't gone up to that barbecue again, has she, Kerry?'

Kerry craned her neck. 'I can't see her, mate, but don't worry, she won't have gone far.'

Frankie sipped her drink and said nothing. Whenever she took Georgie out, she had a habit of skipping off and getting lost.

'There she is. Oh, you'd better go and get her, Frankie. Look what she's doing.'

Seeing her daughter pick up a sausage that Joey's dog had been nibbling, Frankie ran over and grabbed her by the hand before she could eat it.

'Chuck that sausage on the floor. It's not yours, it's the dog's and it's all dirty.'

Georgie started to cry. 'I don't feel well, Mummy.'

'I ain't bloody surprised with the amount you've eaten. You've only got a little tummy, Georgie, why do you have to be so greedy, eh?'

Kerry laughed at the annoyance on Frankie's face. 'Is she OK?'

'No, she's a bloody pest. She doesn't feel well now, the greedy little cow.'

Feeling as sick as a dog, Georgie sat on the grass and seconds later was violently sick all over her new party frock. 'I'm sorry, Mummy,' she wailed.

Frankie found some wipes in her handbag and tried to clean her daughter up. Not having much joy, she turned to Kerry. 'She's smothered in it. I think I'll take her over to Alice and Jimmy's. They've got spare clothes there, and Alice can give her a bath. We can pick her up on the way home. Look after Harry for me. I'll be ten minutes,' she said, as she dragged her troublesome daughter from the garden by the hand.

Joyce was highly embarrassed by the commotion. 'Kids, eh? Makes you wonder how we coped, doesn't it? Now let me get you both another drink.'

Rita waited for Joyce to walk away, then turned to Hilda. 'What a greedy little horror that child is. I reckon it's the pikey in it, don't you?'

Hilda nodded. 'She looks like a gypsy kid as well, don't she? And as for Joycie's dress, what a fucking eyesore that is.'

Rita burst out laughing. 'I thought that. She looks like Bet Lynch, don't she? And it looks a size too small on her.'

A few feet away from Rita and Hilda, Stanley was having a fabulous time. He was standing with his mates Jock, Brian and Derek from the pigeon club, Ralph and Sid, who he'd worked with on the buses and his two cousins, who he hadn't seen for years.

Bored with the conversation revolving solely around pigeons, Ralph decided a change of subject was imperative. 'So, tell me, Stanley, however did you end up in a house as fantastic as this one? You didn't win the football pools after you took an early retirement from the bus depot, did you?'

Remembering how he and Joycie had obtained the house, Stanley's mood darkened. 'It's a long story. I'll tell you another time, but not today.'

Ralph playfully goaded his old colleague. 'Come on, tell us now. We ain't seen you for years, Stanley, and we want to know your secret. Last time I saw you, you were a meagre bus driver living in that council house in Upney. You must have had a change of fortune somewhere down the line, so what was it? I mean you don't buy houses like this on a bus driver's pension, do you?'

Stanley glared at his old pal. He'd been having a thoroughly good time until they had brought up the topic of how he'd acquired the house. With the brandy affecting his diplomacy, Stanley decided to be extremely blunt. 'I thought you knew what I had been through – it was plastered all over the news and the papers. My daughter, Jessica, was murdered by her villainous bastard of a husband, who then gave me and Joycie this house out of guilt. Now, can we change the fucking subject?'

Alice and Sally were getting along like a house on fire. Unlike Frankie, Sally was passionate about cooking, was terrific company and would make a boy like her Jed a wonderful wife.

'Have you ever met Frankie?' Alice asked her.

'No. The only time I've ever seen her is when me and my dad came to your house that Christmas.'

Alice laughed. 'Shame Frankie never left Jed when she found out about you. Knows when she's on to a good thing, that's why. Never liked her, I ain't. Lazy little cow she is, she can't even cook. My Jed should be with a decent girl like you, Sally. You'd be a good little wife for him, you would.'

Sally beamed. Her own mum had died when she was a child. She had never got on with her stepmum, but she'd taken to Alice on sight.

'Answer that,' Alice shouted as the doorbell rang.

Seconds later an ashen-faced Jed ran into the kitchen, followed by Jimmy. 'Answer it, Mum. It's Frankie. What am I gonna do? I told her I was working.'

Alice took charge. 'Leave it with me, I'll get rid of her. Shut this door or go out the back. I'll tell her you've gone to Cambridge.'

'But me motor's outside,' Jed said.

'Stop panicking. I'll soon get shot of her. I'll tell her you've gone with your brother Billy and he drove, for a change.'

Jed grabbed Sally's hand. 'Let's take Lukey out the back, babe. I ain't worried about Frankie – I couldn't give a fuck about her – but I don't want her kicking off in front of our son,' he lied.

Alice opened the front door.

'Why's Jed's motor here? He told me he was working,' Frankie asked suspiciously.

'He is working. Him and Jimmy went off in Billy's motor to Cambridge. Is that what you've come round for, to spy on him?'

Frankie felt her cheeks redden. 'No, of course not. I've been at my nan's, she's having a party for my grandad's birthday. Georgie's not well. She's eaten too much and been sick all over her dress. I was wondering if you'd clean her up and look after her for me until later.'

Alice smiled as she took her granddaughter by the hand. 'You go back to the party and enjoy yourself. Georgie can stay here tonight with us. I'll let her have a kip, then bath her and make her all better. You can get Jed to pick her up tomorrow.'

Smelling a rat, Frankie insisted on picking Georgie up herself after the party had ended, thanked Alice and walked away.

Kerry apologised as she bumped straight into Stanley. 'I'm so sorry,' she said, as she edged over to where Frankie was standing with Joey.

Kerry handed Frankie her drink. Frankie had been quiet all day, even more so since she had dropped Georgie off. She grabbed her friend's arm.

'Look, tell me to mind my own business if you want, but I know something's wrong. Is it Jed? Have yous two been rowing again?'

Desperate to spill the beans to someone, Frankie picked up Harry and urged Kerry to follow her over to the big tree. Joey and Dom were standing nearby and Frankie didn't want them to hear what she had to say.

'I think Jed's seeing that Sally again. He told me he was working today, yet his Shogun's at his mum's. I bet he's took Luke over there, then he's going back round that slag's flat,' she said bluntly.

'What! No, never, Frankie.'

Frankie explained to Kerry about bumping into Stacey in Lakeside. 'I've had all this once before and I know all the signs. I mean, how many times has Jed said he's working nights in the past year or so? The bastard's round at that old tart's place, I know he is. When he comes in from a night's work, he ain't even sweaty or dirty, Kerry. He goes out and comes home in his old work clothes, but knowing how devious Jed is, he's probably got a change of clothes in his Shogun.'

Kerry stared open-mouthed at her friend. 'Well, if what you're saying is true, where is Sammy when all this is going on? Him and Jed go to work together and come home together, don't they? It can't be true, Frankie. Jed can't be seeing that girl, not if my Sammy's with him.'

Frankie shrugged. 'Alice never mentioned Sammy. She told me Jed was out with his dad and brother. Listen, I know roughly where that Sally lives and it ain't far from here. Why don't we take a detour on the way home and see if Jed's or Sammy's motor's outside there?'

Kerry shook her head. 'We don't need to spy on 'em, Frankie. Jed and Sammy are both out working to earn money for us and our kids, so let's drop the subject, shall we?'

Joyce had opted not to book a band or a disco. She had made Raymond drag the stereo system and speakers into the garden for her and, in her opinion, the music she'd chosen to play was just right for the mixture of guests. As Joyce took off Bobby Darin and put on the Everly Brothers, she received her first complaint.

'Nan, can't we have something a bit more modern on?' Joey asked her.

Joyce shook her head vehemently. She was tipsy now, the

party had been a great success and everybody was thoroughly enjoying her choice in music.

Breaking into a verse of 'Wake Up Little Susie', Joyce linked arms with Joey and led him towards Stanley's cousins. 'Go and get Dominic and Madonna,' she ordered him.

Joyce had never liked either of Stanley's cousins or their sour-faced wives, but today, having been on the brandy and Baileys for the past few hours, she sort of liked everybody.

'You remember my grandson, Joey, don't you?' she said as Joey, Dominic and the dog walked towards her.

'I remember you, Joey. My, haven't you grown. The last time I saw you, you were knee high,' said Elaine, Stanley's cousin's wife.

Joey shook hands with everyone. 'This is Dominic and this is Lady Madonna,' he said, stroking the head of the Chihuahua.

Elaine made a fuss of Madonna and smiled. 'So what are you up to these days, Joey? Are you working, love?'

Joyce smiled proudly as she entered into the conversation. 'He's gay.'

Elaine looked at her quizzically. 'I beg your pardon?'

'Our Joey's a gay man, aren't you, love? Dominic's his homo-sexual boyfriend and they've bought themselves a dog because they obviously can't have kids.'

Reasonably intoxicated herself, Elaine started to laugh. Joyce was having a wind-up with her, surely? 'You are funny, Joycie, you always was,' she giggled.

Joyce was furious. How dare this old bat laugh at her gay grandson? 'Just because my Joey likes a bit of cock, doesn't mean you can say what you like and hurt his feelings,' she yelled.

Dominic looked at Joey in embarrassment and horror. 'Madonna's tired. Shall we take her home now?'

Red-faced, Joey grabbed his boyfriend's arm. 'Yes, let's get out of here,' he shouted.

Not ten feet away from Joycie, Polly and Raymond were in the middle of a vicious argument. Raymond had been chatting

283

to Dougie for the past hour and had returned to find his wife steaming drunk and in a stroppy state of mind.

'If you want to go home, then go. I'm staying here,' Polly told him adamantly.

Raymond was furious. Polly's mother was an alcoholic, who'd made a complete show of herself at their wedding by pissing herself in the middle of the dancefloor, and he was beginning to wonder if it ran in the genes. Seeing his dad look over, Raymond grabbed Polly by the arm. 'We're going home right now and that's final,' he shouted.

As Raymond dragged Polly past them, Kerry turned to Frankie. She had thought about what her friend had been telling her earlier, and bits of the story were starting to ring true.

Clocking her friend's puzzled expression, Frankie smiled. 'What's the matter?'

Kerry shrugged. 'I dunno, just thinking about what you said. You're right about a couple of things.'

'Like what?'

'Like Sammy never comes home dirty, either. His clothes are dirty, but he always smells sweet. Surely if he was chopping lorries and vans up, he'd stink of sweat?'

'Why don't we drive down to Rush Green Gardens where that Sally lives? Jed and Sammy both said they were working tonight, so let's see if they're telling us the truth, shall we?' Frankie suggested.

'What about the kids?' Kerry asked.

Frankie looked around. Kerry's two boys and Harry were all fast asleep on a blanket on the grass. 'I tell you what, I'll ring Jimmy and Alice and tell 'em Jed'll pick Georgie up tomorrow. She's far too cute for her age and she would be the one to say something to Jed. The boys'll be fine – they're knackered; they won't even know if we take a detour. Anyway, we're only gonna drive there to see if we can spot a familiar-looking motor, ain't we?'

Kerry chewed her fingernails. Decisions, decisions, decisions, she thought. She smiled at Frankie.

'OK, let's do it.'

CHAPTER THIRTY

Luke was sitting on Jed's lap when Georgie woke up and ran into the kitchen. Desperate for his sordid secret not to come to light, Jed chucked his son over to Sally as though he was playing pass the parcel. He was annoyed with his mum for allowing Georgie to see him. How was he meant to explain that to Frankie?

'Don't mention no names,' he hissed at both Sally and his mum.

With her sickness having now subsided, Georgie sidled over to Luke. 'What's your name?' she asked shyly.

Before Luke could open his mouth, Jed made a grab for his daughter and handed her to Alice.

'His name is John and his mum's a friend of Auntie Shannon. You need a bath, Georgie girl. You smell like a fucking hospital ward,' he said, kissing her on the nose. 'And don't tell Mummy you saw me here, will ya? You'll get Daddy into trouble because he's meant to be working.'

'I won't tell her, Daddy, I promise,' Georgie said sincerely.

When Alice took Georgie upstairs, Jed stood up and urged Sally to do the same. 'Come on, let's get going.'

'I can't believe how alike they are, Jed. Can't we stay for a little bit longer? I won't mention Luke's name, I promise.'

Jed put his arms around Sally and rubbed his groin against her. 'I wanna get you home so I can fuck ya, you horny bitch.'

Sally giggled, then, as Jimmy walked into the room, pushed Jed away.

'We can't go until I've said goodbye to your mum and thanked her for the lovely day.'

Determined to leave before Georgie reappeared, Jed picked up Luke and grabbed Sally by the hand. 'You'll see me mum again. I'll take the pair of yous out for lunch. Now, move your arse. You've got me that hard, me cory feels like it's gonna burst.'

Frankie thought she knew how to get to Rush Green, but somehow she managed to get lost. When she finally found it, she wasn't sure where Rush Green Gardens was, and drove round and round in circles.

'Look, there's a garage there, by them traffic lights. Pull in there and we can ask someone,' Kerry suggested.

Frankie pulled into the forecourt and wound her window down. 'Excuse me. Could you tell me where Rush Green Gardens is, please?'

The man filling his car up nodded. 'Go out that entrance, do a right, go straight on at the traffic lights and Rush Green Gardens is a couple of hundred yards down on your right.'

Frankie thanked him and glanced at Kerry. The boys were fast asleep in the back, but both girls still felt nervous.

'Look out for the sign for me,' Frankie said.

Kerry nodded. Her guts were churning and she didn't feel much like talking.

Frankie slowed down as she went through the lights. A boy racer in a kitted-out Cabriolet tooted behind her and she stuck two fingers up. 'Fuck off, you prick,' she yelled.

'I think this is it. Go right here,' Kerry urged her.

Frankie turned into the entrance. It was definitely a council estate and was made up of small blocks of flats. The road went round in a horseshoe and Frankie's heart was beating like mad as she drove around it.

'There's Jed's motor,' Kerry screamed.

Frankie bumped the car up onto a kerb and turned off the ignition. 'Fucking cheating bastard! What am I gonna do, Kerry?

286

Should I find out where Sally lives and knock on her door?'

Kerry said nothing. If Jed was at it with Sally, then what the hell was Sammy up to? She squeezed Frankie's hand. 'If we knock on the door and create havoc, it ain't gonna do us no favours. For all we know, Sammy might be in a pub while Jed has popped round to see Luke.'

Frankie shook her head. 'They're both up to no good, I bet ya.'

As a man walked past with a pit bull and looked inside the car, Kerry felt a shiver go down her spine. 'Look, let's go home before anybody sees us. We'll put the kids to bed and then we can discuss our next move,' she said.

Frankie restarted the ignition and, with tears in her eyes, drove off the estate.

Unaware that a spying mission had just taken place, Jed was in the middle of getting his end away.

'I'm ready to come, but I want you to come first,' he said generously, as he slid his tongue inside Sally's vagina.

Hearing Sally groan and then feeling her shudder, Jed released his tongue and urged Sally to put her mouth around his rock-hard penis. Smiling, Jed sat up so he could watch Sally work her magic on him. Unlike Frankie, who always spat out his sperm, Sally liked to swallow, and observing her do so only added to the intensity and thrill of his orgasm.

He came, grinned and hugged her. 'You OK, babe?'

Sally lay her head on his chest. She had grown to love Jed so much, it had begun to tear her to pieces every time he went back home. She circled her finger around his belly button.

'I wish it could be like this all the time.'

'Whaddya mean?' Jed asked her, knowing full well what she meant.

Sally smiled at him. She had to tread carefully. If she started putting pressure on him, it could go against her. 'Sorry, I'm being soppy again, aren't I? We've had such a nice day today. I loved spending time with your mum and dad, and I just wish it could be like this all the time. You know, we could be a proper family.'

Jed kissed her on the forehead. 'We will be one day, babe, I promise. Just bear with me, eh?'

Jed glanced slyly at his watch. 'I'm gonna have to go and pick Sammy up in a minute, babe. We've gotta pick some wonga up from a geezer in Barking.'

Sally nodded understandingly. 'When will me and Luke see you again?'

Jed smiled as he stared at his sleeping son. 'Me and Sammy are gonna tell Kerry and Frankie that we're working away next weekend.'

He threw fifty quid at her. 'Treat yourself to summink to wear, and sort out a babysitter for Friday night, so we can go out for a nice meal or something.'

Sally threw her arms around Jed's neck. She loved the thought of having him all to herself for the weekend.

Jed gently released her arms from around his neck. He stood up and strolled over to the front door. 'Bye, babe. I love you.'

With all three boys snuggled up in bed together, Kerry handed Frankie a glass of wine. 'So, what happens now?'

Frankie nervously chewed on her lip. 'We're gonna have to spy on 'em again, see if we can catch 'em red-handed.'

Kerry shrugged. Frankie might be adamant that Jed was cheating on her, but Kerry trusted Sammy with her life. He had always been a wonderful boyfriend and father and she had never had any reason to distrust him.

'I still think you've got it all wrong, Frankie. I don't think either Jed or Sammy would cheat on us.'

'Well, how do you explain Jed's Shogun being there, then? Remember, Stacey told me she saw him and that slag in Romford looking all loved-up.'

Seeing Frankie's eyes well up, Kerry hugged her. 'I really don't know, mate.'

* * *

288

Jed was well prepared as he walked into Sammy's trailer. He knew Frankie would have her suspicions about his motor being outside his parents' house.

'All right, girls? How was the party?'

'It was good. The kids loved it, didn't they, Frankie?' Kerry said nudging her pal.

Frankie sipped her drink and glared at Jed. 'Georgie wasn't well, so I took her to your mum and dad's house. I told 'em you'd pick her up tomorrow. Anyway, enough about our day, let's talk about yours. Been working hard, the pair of yous, have ya?'

Jed had always prided himself on being clued up. Frankie was on to him, he sensed it. 'So, what was a matter with Georgie?' he asked brightly.

'She ate like a pig and then was sick everywhere. You ain't answered my question yet. I said, have you been working hard?'

Jed glanced at Sammy. He needed to come up with a story, and he needed to think of one fast. He smiled at Frankie. She had seen his motor at Sally's; it was the only thing he could think of. He cleared his throat.

'Actually, we knocked off work early. Billy was driving, so we came back to Rainham and had a few beers. Look, Frankie, I don't wanna lie to you, so I'm gonna tell you the truth. Sally rang me earlier. Luke was ill and she was really worried about him. I dropped Sammy off at the pub on the way home and shot round there. I didn't stay long, but I had to pop round there to check he was OK. You do understand, don't you?'

Kerry breathed a huge sigh of relief. 'Of course she understands. Don't you, Frankie?'

Frankie nodded dumbly. Jed was a convincing liar, she knew that from past experience, and even though she wanted to believe his story, when she saw him smirk at Sammy, she knew she couldn't trust him.

Over the next few days, Jed was torn between the devil and the deep blue sea. Frankie definitely had his card marked, there were no two ways about that.

As Sammy sat beside him on the cart, Jed made a clicking noise with his mouth. 'Trot on,' he shouted, as he clumped his horse's arse with the reins.

'What am I gonna do?' he asked Sammy. 'I can't let Sally down this weekend – she'll be heart-broken, yet I can't chance Frankie snooping around there, can I? If she catches me red-handed, she'll leave me and take the kids with her, I know she will.'

'We'll just have to be careful from now on. If Frankie did see your motor the other night, then you can't park it outside Sally's any more,' Sammy said.

'I think I'm gonna buy a cheap truck or car that Frankie don't know about, 'cause even if I park the Shogun in a road opposite Sally's, chances are she'll fuckin' spot it,' Jed replied.

'You don't even know for sure if Frankie saw your motor or that she knows where Sally lives. She might have had the hump over something else you'd said or done. Georgie ain't grassed you up, has she?'

Jed shook his head. 'Georgie ain't said sod-all. Frankie saw my Shogun at Sally's, I'm sure of it. I saw the look of relief on her face when I admitted I'd been there. She must have done some detective work and some cunt's told her where Sally lives. I can't take no chances, Sammy, so do us a favour and ring that car-dealer mate of yours. See if he's got a cheap old van of some kind. I don't want nothing decent, 'cause I'm gonna leave it parked up on me dad's land over in Tilbury.'

Sammy smirked. He liked to think of himself as a cunning character, but Jed always seemed to beat him hands down. 'Has anyone ever told you that you are one slippery bastard, Jed O'Hara?'

Whipping his horse on the arse once more, Jed laughed. 'You ain't exactly Snow White yourself, you cheeky fucker.'

On the following Friday, Jed put on his work clothes, kissed the kids goodbye and gave Frankie a cuddle. 'I really don't wanna go to work. I wish I could stay 'ere with you and the chavvies,' he lied.

Frankie smiled politely. She didn't believe for a moment that Jed was going to work, but she had to play it cool, otherwise she would never find out the truth. 'What time will you be back on Sunday?' she asked.

'About lunchtime. I thought we could take Georgie and Harry out to a carvery. Sammy and Kerry'll probably come as well.'

'That'll be nice,' Frankie said, forcing a smile.

As soon as the boys drove off, Frankie dragged the kids into Kerry's trailer. 'I'm gonna go for a little drive and I want you to look after my babies for me. I can't take Georgie with me, she's too clued-up,' Frankie whispered.

Georgie's ears pricked up. 'You going out, Mummy?'

'I've just got to pop over Nanny Joycie's to pick something up. You're staying here with Harry. I need you to look after him for me.'

Georgie jumped up and down. 'Can I come too?'

'No, you can't. Nanny Joyce isn't very well today. I won't be long and if you behave yourself for Kerry, I'll bring you and Harry back a Happy Meal.'

'Can I have a Big Mac and nuggets?' Georgie asked innocently.

'No, you bloody well can't!' Feeling anxious, Frankie picked up her keys and slammed the trailer door.

Jed O'Hara was on edge as he stared out of Sally's living-room window. His sixth sense had convinced him that Frankie was on the prowl and he didn't want to leave Sally's flat in case he bumped into her.

'Daddy,' Luke giggled, clinging to his leg.

Jed moved away from the window. He lay down on the floor and lifted his son up in the air above him. There was no way Frankie would find his motor, as he'd left it in Tilbury. Sammy's pal had got him an old Datsun truck for two-hundred quid and he'd driven to Sally's in that.

Sitting up, Jed lay his head against Sally's bare legs. 'Who's meant to be babysitting?' he asked.

'Me mate, Lisa. She's coming round at eight.'

Jed looked at Sally with pleading eyes. Instinct told him it would be unwise to go out tonight. 'I don't fancy going out for a meal, babe. Let's get a takeaway, cancel the babysitter and have a drink indoors. I wanna spend some quality time with you and Lukey boy, and later I'm gonna rip them knickers off and give you a right good seeing to.'

Sally nodded happily. As long as she was with Jed, she didn't care what they did.

Frankie felt incredibly nervous as she drove her car around Rush Green Gardens – it was only 7.30 and still light. Jed's Shogun was nowhere to be seen and she didn't know whether to laugh or cry. Knowing how crafty her boyfriend could be, Frankie pulled out of the estate and drove up and down the roads nearby. If Jed had any inkling that she was on to him, the first thing he would do was hide the motor elsewhere.

About to make her way home, Frankie decided to have one last look around Rush Green Gardens. She drove onto the estate, and gasped in disbelief as she spotted Sammy walking along with a pretty blonde girl. The bird was holding his arm and they had a kid with them in a pushchair.

Blinded by panic that her car would be spotted, Frankie quickly reversed out onto the main road. Seconds later her mobile rang. Praying she hadn't been caught, Frankie shook as she held the phone to her ear.

'It's only me, Frankie. Pick up some more wine on the way home. Well, is Jed's motor there?'

Unable to break her friend's heart over the phone, Frankie quickly ended the call. 'I won't be long. I'll get some wine, and we'll talk when I get back,' she said.

As soon as Frankie walked into her trailer, Kerry knew that something was amiss.

'Where's the kids?' Frankie whispered.

'In bed. What's the matter?'

Frankie's eyes filled up with tears. 'I didn't see Jed or the

Shogun, but I did see something. I'm so sorry to have to tell you this, Kerry, but I saw Sammy walking along with a bird and a kid. The bird was holding his arm, and the kid must be young 'cause it was in a pushchair.'

Kerry looked at her incredulously. 'No, you must have got it wrong. Where did you see him? Are you sure it was Sammy?'

'I saw him in Rush Green Gardens and I'm a hundred per cent sure it was him. I quickly reversed out the turning. I didn't want him to recognise me car.'

Kerry's heart started to quicken. 'If it's true, I'll kill him, Frankie. Where do ya reckon he could have been going?'

Frankie shrugged. 'Either back to the bird's place or what about that little social club we saw on the estate? In fact, he was walking towards that.'

Leaping off the sofa, Kerry rushed towards the bedroom.

'What you doing?' Frankie asked her.

'Waking the kids up. We're going to find the bastard, Frankie.'

Unaware that his girlfriend was on the warpath, Sammy was sitting with one arm around Julie and the other holding his son on his lap.

The Rush Green Community Centre was cheap and cheerful and, considering it was just a minute's walk away from Julie's flat and kids were welcome, it was a handy little number. Tonight there was a disco on, and as the DJ put on the Robin S dance-floor hit, 'Show Me Love', Sammy began singing the words in Julie's ear.

Pulling up in the car park, Frankie grabbed Kerry's arm and opened the car door. Kerry had drunk a whole bottle of wine on the journey and there was no way Frankie could allow her to go into the club alone.

'Hang on, the kids are all asleep. I'll lock the doors – I'm coming in with ya.'

Sammy was so busy serenading his bit on the side that he didn't notice Kerry and Frankie walk into the club.

'There he is, the cunt,' Kerry screamed as she stormed over to the table with the empty wine bottle in her hand.

'You can't come in here with that, love,' a man said, grabbing her arm.

Pushing the man away, Kerry broke into a run and lunged towards Sammy. 'You fucking bastard. I'm gonna kill you, you cunt,' she screamed, as she lifted the bottle and smashed it as hard as she could over Sammy's head.

Julie screamed as the glass shattered over both her and Tom. She grabbed her son and ran over to the bar. 'Help me! Call the police!' she screamed.

With blood pouring down his face, a dazed Sammy fell to the floor, holding his head. 'Stop it, Kerry. I can explain. It ain't what you think,' he mumbled.

Seeing Kerry was about to cut Sammy to pieces with the jagged edge of the bottle, Frankie snatched it out of her hand. 'You'll get nicked. He ain't worth it,' she urged her friend.

Sobbing with temper, Kerry aimed her right foot into the side of Sammy's face. 'Your kid, is it? You cheating, no-good bastard. I want you out of my life, for good, do you hear me?'

Frankie did her best to pull Kerry off him. 'Come on, let's go. We can't leave the kids in the car.'

'Let's go? I ain't fucking going nowhere. Right, where's that old slag gone?'

Petrified for the safety of Julie and her baby, the barman had hidden both of them behind the bar.

'Leave her alone,' Frankie shouted, as two men grabbed hold of Kerry's arms and tackled her to the floor.

'I'll kill that wanker and her. I'm gonna kill the fucking pair of 'em,' Kerry sobbed.

Desperately trying to free Kerry so they could both get away, Frankie had no choice but to kick and punch the two men holding her friend. Seconds later she was also restrained, but unfortunately not by more punters. As two police officers handcuffed her and Kerry, Frankie started to cry.

'You can't nick us. Our kids are outside in the car,' she sobbed.

The policewoman shoved her towards the exit. 'Tough shit. You're both nicked.'

CHAPTER THIRTY-ONE

Frankie and Kerry were released at 10 a.m. the following morning. They had both spent a sleepless night in a cell at Romford police station. One phone call each was all they'd been entitled to. Kerry had rung her sister to come and collect Sammy Junior and Freddy, and Frankie had contacted Joey and Dominic to pick up Georgie and Harry.

'Let's walk into Romford and get a coffee and some breakfast,' Frankie suggested. Kerry was in a really bad way and Frankie was worried about her.

'I'm not hungry. What the hell am I gonna do, Frankie? It's as though my whole life with Sammy was just one big fucking lie.'

Frankie linked arms with her best friend. 'Let's get a hot drink down us and we can discuss what we should do next.'

With tears in her eyes, Kerry looked at Frankie. 'I can never forgive him for what he's done to me, Frankie. I can't go back to that trailer. You're gonna have to pick up mine and the kids' stuff for me. Me and Sammy are history. I hate him, and I hope he dies of terminal cancer.'

Over in South Woodham, Joey and Dominic were having problems of their own. Ever since they had picked the kids up last night, Georgie had not eaten or slept.

Seeing his niece was about to chase Madonna once more, Joey picked up the dog, put her out in the garden and locked the back door. He turned to Dominic. They had planned to go to a friend's house for lunch, but there was no way they could take the kids with them.

'You'll have to ring Rob and tell him we can't make it today,' Joey said.

'Can't you ring Jed, see if he can pick the kids up?' Dominic replied.

Joey shook his head. 'Frankie said he's working away this weekend and she made me promise not to call him. Let's just find a pub with a kids' play area or something. I don't know exactly what trouble Frankie's in, but they have to release her soon, surely?'

Dominic picked up Harry. 'Do you want to go out to play?'

As Harry giggled and hugged Dominic, Joey went into the kitchen and knelt down to speak to Georgie.

'If I take you out to play, will you promise me you'll eat some lunch at the pub?'

Georgie was bored with being stuck indoors. 'I promise I'll eat all my lunch, Uncle Joey,' she lied.

Frankie thanked the waitress as she brought over her jumbo sausage in a roll and two mugs of steaming coffee. Unlike Kerry, Frankie was ravenous.

'So what exactly did they charge you with?' Frankie asked her friend.

'ABH. They said Sammy had needed twelve stitches in his head or something.'

'What did you tell them? Did you admit to it?'

'I said it was a shame the bastard didn't need twelve-hundred stitches. To be honest, Frankie, that woman who nicked us was quite nice to me once she heard the full story. She said she's gonna speak to Sammy and if he agrees not to prosecute, the charges will probably be dropped.'

Frankie nodded. 'They just gave me a caution for affray. I think them men that grabbed hold of you told the Old Bill I was kicking and punching 'em. I ain't gotta go back or nothing.'

As Frankie munched on her roll, Kerry drank her coffee in silence.

'So, what you gonna do now? I ain't gonna be able to handle living in Wickford without ya. Where you gonna go?' said Frankie.

'Somewhere where Sammy can't find me. My sister's just moved to Pitsea. I've only been to her new house once and Sammy ain't got the address, so I might stop there for a bit. There's no point me going to me mum's, as he knows where she lives and I don't wanna cause her no grief. If I give you my key, I need you to grab my clothes, the kids' clothes and some of their toys for me. I can meet you somewhere or you can bring 'em to my sister's house if you want, but be careful you ain't followed.'

Frankie nodded as Kerry handed her the key to her trailer. Living on that remote piece of land without Kerry was going to be lonely and boring, especially when Jed was at work, but she couldn't burden Joey and Dom, and apart from her grand-parents, she had nowhere else to go.

'I wonder if Jed was round at Sally's and if that bird Sammy was with is one of her friends. I mean, Jed had to be involved somehow, it's too much of a coincidence that both old slappers live on the same estate.'

Kerry nodded. 'I'd like to know where they parked the motor. Surely Jed never dropped Sammy off then went to work on his own. After what's happened lately, I hate both of 'em, Frankie. My family warned me not to get involved with a travelling boy, they said they were bad news, and they were so bloody right.'

'My family said the same and I wished I'd have listened to them now. What am I gonna say to Jed? Sammy's bound to have told him what happened. I wish I had proof that Jed was at it as well – I could leave him then. This is such a mess, Kerry, and I know this is a horrible thing to say, but I really wish I wasn't pregnant again.'

Kerry squeezed Frankie's hand. 'Can I borrow your phone to ring my sister?'

'I haven't got it on me. It's under the seat in the car and the battery'll be well dead by now. Let's walk down to that cab firm in the high street. We can get a taxi, go pick the car up, find a phone box, and then I'll drop you at your sister's.'

Kerry gave a weak smile. 'Thanks, Frankie, and I want you to know, whatever happens in the future, you are and always will be the best friend I've ever had.'

Unaware of the heartache his sister was currently going through, Joey sipped his beer and smiled as Dominic pushed an excited Harry on the swing. Georgie was on the roundabout with three other little kids and seemed very hyper, considering she hadn't yet eaten or slept.

'Come and sit down at the table now, Georgie. I've ordered you and Harry burger and chips,' he shouted.

The sun was blazing and, enjoying the heat, Joey tilted his head so his face was facing its rays. He shut his eyes and as Madonna, who was perched on his lap, adoringly kissed his chin, he smiled.

'Where's Georgie?' he heard Dominic shout, a minute or so later.

Joey opened his eyes and looked at the roundabout. His niece was nowhere to be seen. 'She was on there,' he said, pointing to the apparatus. He immediately stood up and ran over to the other kids still sitting on there.

'The little girl that was on here with you, where did she go?'

'Don't know,' one kid mumbled. The other two looked at him blankly.

As Dominic ran towards him with Harry in his arms, Joey felt a sense a panic. Surely no one could have snatched her. He'd only looked away for a minute or two, at the most.

'You check inside the pub while I search out here. Check the toilets in case she's gone in there, Dom.'

The pub that they'd chosen to take the kids to had woodland nearby, so Joey ran towards it. 'Georgie, Georgie!' he shouted at the top of his voice. After a fruitless five minutes of peering behind trees, he ran back towards the pub.

'Any joy?' he asked Dominic hopefully.

Dominic shook his head. 'I've just been talking to the guvnor. He and the barmaids have looked everywhere. She's not inside the pub, Joey.'

Ashen-faced, Joey started to cry. 'What are we gonna do? What am I gonna tell Frankie?'

Dominic was also scared. Only last week there was an awful story in the paper about a young girl being snatched by a paedophile. 'There's only one thing we can do, Joey. We have to call the police.'

Over in Rush Green, Frankie had just picked up her car and stopped at a phone box so Kerry could ring her sister.

'Aren't you going to ring Joey?' Kerry asked her.

'No. I'm gonna pop home first, see if Jed's there.'

Kerry and Frankie were both quiet on the journey to Pitsea. Kerry felt as if the bottom had fallen out of her world and Frankie was dreading going home, as she guessed that Jed would be there waiting for her.

As Frankie pulled up outside Kerry's sister's house, she leaned over and hugged her best friend. 'Keep your chin up and I'll get your stuff and ring you as soon as possible. I've put your sister's phone number in my purse.'

Kerry opened the car door. 'Thanks for everything, Frankie, and good luck with Jed. I've a feeling you're gonna need it, mate.'

Frankie felt sick as she approached Wickford. Sammy was bound to have contacted Jed and she wasn't in the mood to listen to him or his bullshit.

As she pulled up on the land, the first thing she saw was Jed's Shogun. Seconds later he came out of Sammy's trailer and walked towards her. 'You all right, babe? I've been so worried about you, been ringing your phone all day, I have.'

Picking up her bag and phone, Frankie pushed him away as he tried to hug her. 'Me battery's dead. I need to charge it.'

Jed followed her inside the trailer. 'Sammy told me what happened. Where are Georgie and Harry?'

300

Frankie plugged her phone into the charger. 'They're with Joey.'

Seconds later, Sammy burst into the trailer. 'Where's Kerry?' he yelled.

Frankie glared at him. 'Get out of my trailer.'

'Tell me where she is, Frankie. I've every right to know where my boys are.'

Frankie stood with her hands on her hips. 'You lost all your rights last night, you dirty, cheating scumbag. I've no idea where Kerry has gone and even if I did know, I wouldn't tell you.'

'I'm sorry. It ain't what you think, Frankie. If I can see Kerry, talk to her, I can explain. I've been to the gavvers and got her charges dropped. I told 'em it was all my fault.'

'Well, that's fucking big of you! Both of yous are born liars. All these weekends you've supposedly been working away and I bet the pair of you have been out whoring.'

Frankie pointed at her unusually quiet boyfriend. 'Him with that slag Sally and you with that old dog you was with last night. And I bet the kid that was with you is your fucking kid. Animals you are, the pair of ya.'

Realising that Sammy's presence was riling Frankie to the point of no return, Jed ushered him outside. 'Let me speak to her, smooth things over. I'll find out where Kerry is for ya, don't worry,' he whispered.

Jed walked back inside with his hands in a surrender pose above his head. 'Whatever Sammy has done has nothing to do with me, Frankie. I was working last night. Ring me dad if you don't believe me, he was working alongside me.'

'You've probably already spoken to your dad and clued him up as to what to say. Don't treat me like I'm some fucking idiot, Jed, 'cause I ain't. You were with that Sally last night, I know you was, so just be a man and admit it.'

Jed sank to his knees in front of her. 'I swear I weren't, Frankie. On my life, I wasn't and I can prove it. Me and me old man had a drink in a little boozer in Norfolk last night. We were in there a good couple of hours and we were chatting to the old mush that runs it. Get in the motor now and I'll drive you up there. You can ask the man for yourself if I was in there.'

Frankie shook her head. Norfolk was miles away and she couldn't be arsed. Deciding Jed could, for once, be telling the truth, she flopped onto the sofa. 'You must have dropped Sammy round that bird's before you went to work. Don't insult my intelligence by pretending you know nothing about what he's been up to, Jed.'

Jed ran his fingers through his hair. Frankie believed he had been to Norfolk, so he decided not to push his luck. 'Yeah, I did know about the bird and yeah, I did drop him round there. He met her in a boozer one night, her name's Julie. I've told him he's fucking mad and I've begged him to end it. "You've got too much to lose, Sammy. You'll never find a girl as decent as Kerry," I've told him.'

'How long's he been seeing her? Is the kid she's got his?'

Jed shook his head. 'Nah, it ain't his kid. I think he's been seeing her about six months – well, that's what he told me. I wasn't there when he met her, he was out with his brothers. To be honest, Frankie, he don't tell me much 'cause he knows I don't agree with what he's doing. I know I had a fling with Sally that time, but I could never have carried on seeing her behind your back. I couldn't live with the guilt. Sammy's a dinlo, I've told him that.'

Frankie looked Jed in the eyes. His face was a picture of innocence and if he was lying, the bastard was a world-beater at it.

'Where is Kerry? Is she OK?' Jed asked in a concerned voice.

'She's fine. She's gone to visit her cousin up north,' Frankie lied.

'Up north! Whereabouts does her cousin live, then?'

'I dunno. She did say, but it was a place I'd never heard of.'

'Where you going?' Jed asked as Frankie stood up.

'I'm gonna ring Joey and go and pick the kids up.'

Frankie switched on her phone and punched in Joey's number. Her brother answered immediately, his voice full of panic. 'What? I can't understand what you're saying, Joey. Talk slower, will you?'

'What's up?' Jed asked, concerned.

Frankie let out a piercing scream. 'Georgie's gone missing,' she sobbed.

Unaware of the chaos she had created, Georgie O'Hara had managed to climb up a big tree. It was the mention of burger and chips that had made her run away. Some days she felt incredibly hungry and would eat all day long, but there were other times when the mention of food made her feel tearful and agitated. Today was one of those days, hence her little adventure into the woods.

About to climb further up the tree, Georgie stopped in her tracks as she heard the distinct tone of her father's voice.

'Georgie! Georgie girl!' he shouted. His voice sounded upset and frantic.

Georgie scrambled down and ran out of the woods as fast as her little legs would carry her. 'Daddy! I'm here, Daddy,' she screamed.

CHAPTER THIRTY-TWO

Eddie Mitchell opened his eyes, remembered what day it was and smiled. Five years he'd done, five long, poxy years and today was the day that he was finally set free.

Ed stared at the ceiling as he reminisced over the time he'd spent in Wandsworth. He'd been a broken man on his arrival, his fatal mistake had cost him not only his freedom, but also his mind. Picturing Jessica's pretty face, Eddie wondered if she could see him from heaven and, if that was the case, he hoped that she approved of Gina and was pleased that he'd found happiness again.

Wiping a solitary tear from his eye, Eddie sat up. It was time to start concentrating on his future instead of dwelling on the past. Gina was coming to pick him up today and he couldn't wait to spend some time alone with her.

It was only last week that Eddie had admitted the romance to his two oldest sons.

'We'll be waiting outside the gates for you, Dad. We've decorated the spare room and we want you to move in with us until you buy your own place,' Gary said.

Ed hesitated, then told them the truth. 'Look, there's some-thing you need to know, lads, but you can't tell a soul – not yet, anyway. You know that private detective, the one that stood up for me in court?'

'What, that Gina bird?' Ricky asked.

'Yeah, Gina. Well me and her have become really close. She's the one that's been visiting me and stuff and we've decided to move in together.'

Gary looked at his father as though he had lost his marbles. 'You're having us on, right? You can't be serious – you barely know the fucking woman.'

Eddie glared at his eldest boy. 'What I do with my life is my choice, got that? Gina is a wonderful woman and if it all goes tits-up between us, which it won't, it's my problem, nobody else's.'

'Where you gonna live? You moving into her place?' Ricky asked, shell-shocked.

'We've rented a place in the countryside. It's a new beginning for both of us and I thought yous two would be pleased for me. Yous boys are both still young, you're happy playing the field and so you should be. I'm knocking on a bit now and I just wanna be settled and part of a couple again. You understand where I'm coming from, don't ya?'

'Of course we do,' Ricky said, nudging his brother.

Ed turned to Gary. 'What about you, son?'

'I want you to be happy, so I hope it works out for ya, Dad,' Gary replied grudgingly.

Stuart waking up snapped Eddie back to reality. He could barely believe that the longed-for day had finally arrived.

'You awake, big man?' Stu asked.

'Sure am. You OK, boy?'

Stuart jumped off his bunk and smiled at Eddie. He was going to miss his pal terribly, but at the same time he was pleased that Ed's sentence was over.

'I don't wanna sound like some soppy cunt, but I ain't 'arf gonna miss ya.'

Overcome by emotion, Eddie stood up and hugged the lad he'd grown so attached to. 'I'll write and visit and, before you know it, you'll be out of this dump and working alongside me. Without you, Stu, I don't think I could have got through this bit of bird, and I want you to know that I will be indebted to you for ever for that. When you get out, your life will change, son, I guarantee it.'

*   *   *

Gina was nervous as hell as she drove towards Wandsworth. Visiting Eddie in prison was one thing, but being alone with him on the outside was different gravy. She'd had butterflies in her stomach for the last few days now, but all of a sudden they felt more like bats flapping about. Eating was also out of the question. Her appetite had gone AWOL recently and she hadn't been able to eat a morsel since breakfast yesterday morning.

Gina pulled up outside the prison and checked her make-up in the mirror. She was sweating a lot more than usual and she was sure this was to do with her nerves rather than the hot weather. From the first time Gina had met Eddie Mitchell she had dreamed of him throwing her onto a bed and making mad, passionate love to her. Hopefully, by the end of the day, her dreams would finally have come true.

Oblivious to the fact that her father was currently strolling through the prison gates and into the arms of his new girlfriend, Frankie was having the day from hell. Alice and Jimmy had invited themselves over, and Alice's obsession with Georgie was really beginning to grate on her. She nudged Jed and gesticulated to him to follow her into the bedroom.

'What's up?' Jed asked.

'Your mum, that's what. She's spent all morning playing with and fussing over Georgie, yet she's barely glanced or spoken to poor Harry. I know she was always desperate for a girl in the family, but it ain't right, favouring one grandchild over the other.'

Jed sat next to Frankie on the bed, and desperate to keep the peace, put an arm around her shoulder. 'She don't mean it. Me mum loves Harry, I know she does. Anyway, me dad's been playing with Harry, so he don't feel left out.'

As Alice's raucous laughter echoed around the trailer once more, Frankie sighed. 'I've got a really bad headache, Jed. Do you mind if I lay down for a bit? If I take some tablets and shut my eyes I should be able to get rid of it. Wake me up when we're gonna have lunch.'

'I'll wake you in about half-hour. You can't be rude, Frankie, my parents don't come over here that often.'

Frankie closed her eyes and was relieved when Jed slammed the door. She wasn't tired and had lied about the headache just to get away from Alice. Wondering if Jed was slagging her off to his parents, Frankie tiptoed over to the crack in the door and put her ear to it.

'Tell your nan and grandad what your dad told you to say to your teacher when she told you off, Georgie,' Jed said proudly.

Georgie stood up, put her hands on her hips and grinned at Alice and Jimmy. 'Daddy told me to say, "Fuck off, you dinlo."'

Alice started to laugh so much she very nearly wet herself. 'You're a proper little O'Hara, Georgie girl, ain't ya? Come 'ere and give your nanna a cuddle.'

Absolutely seething, Frankie stormed out of the bedroom. 'Don't you dare encourage our daughter to swear,' she yelled at Jed.

'Where's your sense of humour? I was only mucking about. Right, who's hungry? Shall I go and get the fish and chips now?' Jed replied, desperate to change the subject.

'I want sausage, chips and a pie,' Georgie shouted.

'Get your mother a decent size bit of cod and I'll have rock eel,' Jimmy told his son.

Jed glanced at Frankie. She had a right cob on, he knew that. 'I'll get Harry the same as Georgie, and what do you fancy, babe?'

'I dunno. I think I'll come with you.'

'You can't leave the kids,' Jed said immediately. He didn't fancy an earful and he'd promised to ring Sally.

'I'm sure your mum and dad are capable of looking after them for ten minutes, Jed,' Frankie said sarcastically.

Angry that his preplanned phone call had now gone up the Swannee, Jed glared at her. 'Move your arse, then, I'm fucking starving,' he spat.

Frankie put her trainers on, ran out to the Shogun and slammed the passenger door. 'Don't speak to me like shit in front of your parents and don't keep laughing and encouraging Georgie to swear. It ain't funny, Jed. If she repeats what you say, you ain't the one who's gotta stand up that school wishing that the ground would open up and swallow you. I'm sure, because of the trouble they've had trying to get Georgie in from the playground, that her form teacher, Mrs Lawson, thinks we're bad parents as it is.'

Jed started the engine. 'Bollocks to Mrs Lawson. If she don't like my family, tell her to go fuck her grandmother!'

Eddie Mitchell grinned as Gina ran towards him and threw herself into his arms. He kissed her passionately and immediately felt an erection.

'I want you so badly. Let's go home,' he said, his voice gruff with passion.

Gina's hands shook as she restarted the ignition. She had felt his erection rubbing against her and the thought of seeing it in the flesh sent shivers down her spine.

'What do you think of my new car?' she asked.

Eddie laughed. The sporty BMW definitely suited her image. 'How you gonna tail people in this? You'll stand out like a sore thumb,' he joked.

Gina laughed. He knew full well that this car was for pleasure. She owned two other insignificant-looking motors that she used for business purposes. 'I was up at the crack of dawn. I went to Tesco's and I've prepared us a lovely salad for when we get home. You're going to love the cottage, Ed, it really is adorable.'

Unable to stop himself, Eddie put his hand on her leg and teasingly moved it up to her crotch. As her breathing deepened, he smiled.

'Fuck the salad. The only thing I want to eat is you.'

Frankie waited in the Shogun while Jed queued up in the chip shop. Remembering that her dad was due to be released today, she rang her brother, Gary.

'Is Dad out yet, Gal? Have you heard from him?'

'No, I ain't heard a word,' Gary said, glancing at Ricky.

'Is he gonna be staying at yours? I did ask him, but he said he weren't sure.'

Unable to tell Frankie the truth, Gary said as little as possible. 'He said he's gonna stay at some mate's house. I think he wants time to clear his head.'

'Where does his mate live, then?'

'I ain't sure, Frankie, but don't forget Saturday night. You're still coming, ain't ya?'

'Yeah, Jed's got to work, so his mum and dad are having the kids for the night. What restaurant are we going to? You will pick me up, won't ya?'

'I'll pick you up at half-six. We've booked the steak house in Canning Town – the guvnor is an old pal of grandad's. We're going back to the Flag after. Ronny and Paulie have organised a bit of a welcome-home do in there. Trouble is, Dad didn't want any fuss and I dunno if he's gonna like it.'

Frankie laughed. 'Well, I could certainly do with a good night out and I'm sure once Dad gets a few drinks down his neck, he'll have a great time. Don't tell him I'm coming, Gal. Tell him I can't make it, so I can surprise him.'

'I've already told him you ain't coming. Listen, I've gotta go now, Frankie. Me and Ricky have just spotted some geezer that owes us some money. I'll see you on Saturday at half-six, and make sure you're ready.'

Ending the call, Frankie glanced inside the chip shop. There were still a couple of people in front of Jed in the queue, which gave her just enough time to ring Kerry.

'All right, mate? How are you?'

'Yeah, not bad. What did Sammy say when he realised the rest of my stuff was gone? Did you tell him what we planned?'

'Yep. I told him I went out for the afternoon, so you must have come back and took it while I wasn't there. He was well pissed-off, but I think he believed me. He keeps asking if I've heard from you and stuff and I keep telling him I ain't heard a word. I dunno if he believes you've moved up north, though. I heard him telling Jed that he thinks that's a load of bullshit.'

'He went round my mum's again yesterday and she told him to politely fuck off. Where are you now?'

'Sitting outside a chip shop waiting for Jed to get served. The bastard's on his phone in there. I bet he's talking to that slag, Sally.'

'Probably. How did you get on with Georgie's teacher?'

'Oh, it was awful. The woman looked at me like a piece of shit and warned me about her future obedience. Georgie ain't gone in today. She had belly ache this morning, so I kept her off. Alice and Jimmy dashed over when Jed told 'em, so I'm stuck with them for the day as well. Jed told Georgie to swear at the teacher and they were laughing about it as though it was great. Scum of the earth, they are. I hate 'em, Kerry. Listen, Jed has just been served, so I'll ring you again tomorrow.'

Jed smiled as he handed Frankie the big bag of food. 'Who you been on the phone to?' he asked.

'Me brother. I wanted to know if me dad was out yet. What about you? I saw you on the phone in the chip shop. Ringing Sally on the quiet, was ya?'

Jed's smile turned into a scowl as he did a U-turn and very nearly killed a cyclist. 'You're doing my head in lately, Frankie. I'm getting sick of you accusing me of stuff, so why don't you shut the fuck up before I properly lose me temper.'

Eddie Mitchell grinned as Gina pulled up outside the cottage. Her description of it was spot-on – it was romantic, secluded and beautiful. As Gina unlocked the front door, Eddie grabbed her by the hand.

'I wanna carry you over the threshold,' he said.

Gina giggled as he picked her up. 'We're not bloody newly-weds, Eddie.'

'Where's the bedroom?' he asked.

'Put me down and I'll show you.'

Eddie followed her, threw himself on the bed and urged her

to lie down next to him. He sat up and took off his shirt and trousers. He was already as hard as a rock and gagging for it after five years in clink.

Gina was nervous, he could sense that, so he tried to ease her fears. 'Relax, it'll be fine. Let me undress you.'

He lifted her T-shirt over her head and unclipped her bra. Her breasts were firm and buxom.

'Stand up, let me look at ya,' Eddie whispered, as he urged her to step out of her jeans and knickers.

Eddie stared at her in awe. He'd known Gina was fit, but naked, she had the body of a model. She reminded him of that Page Three bird, Linda Lusardi – she was just as bloody gorgeous. Desperate for his years of celibacy to come to an end, Eddie ripped off his pants, grabbed hold of Gina and threw her onto the bed.

Gina gasped as Eddie's tongue sidled down her body and made contact with her clitoris. 'Oh, my God. I want you so much,' she panted.

As she screamed out his name, Eddie grinned and moved his way up the bed. 'I am gonna fuck you better than you've ever been fucked before,' he whispered.

Unaware that her dad was currently bouncing up and down on top of his new girlfriend, Frankie's day was going from bad to worse.

Jed, Jimmy and Sammy had all gone off to the local pub hours ago and had just returned home very drunk. Alice had done Frankie's head in all afternoon, talking a load of old crap, and Georgie had been hyper all day.

Frankie smiled at Harry who was fast asleep on her lap. Sometimes her kids were the only thing that made her life worth living. 'I'm just going to put Harry to bed and then it's bath and bed for you, Georgie girl.'

'Not tired,' Georgie said, clambering off her nan's lap and onto her dad's.

Frankie tucked Harry in, kissed him on the forehead and

311

then walked over to Georgie. 'Come on, you've gotta get up for school tomorrow.'

'Don't wanna go a bed, Mummy.'

Jed opened another can of lager. He was drunk now, really drunk. Tickling Georgie, they both giggled. 'She ain't tired. Let her stay up for a bit. She can go to bed when me mum and dad go home,' he slurred.

Sick of being overruled, Frankie stood her ground. 'It's gone eight o'clock, Jed. How is she meant to concentrate at school if she's had a late night?'

Alice burst out laughing. 'If that Mrs Lawson tells you off again Georgie, you tell her that your nan'll come up the school and give her a right-hander.'

As Jimmy, Jed and Sammy all burst out laughing, Frankie looked at her so-called family in horror.

'What is wrong with you mob? Do you want to see her get expelled, or what? Now, I'm telling you Georgie, get off Daddy's lap and let's get you bathed.'

Georgie screamed blue murder as Frankie made a grab for her.

Jed clasped his hand around Frankie's wrist. 'You wallop her and I'll wallop you.'

Aware that Jed was drunk and trying to look big in front of his parents, Frankie pushed his arm away, picked up her sobbing child, and calmly walked into the bedroom.

Eddie and Gina lay knackered and naked in one another's arms. They'd been at it hammer and tongs for hours, and the sex had been absolutely mind-blowing.

'I dunno about you, but I'm absolutely starving,' Ed said, kissing Gina on the forehead.

Still drenched in sweat, Gina smiled. 'I must have a shower before we eat.'

The bathroom was en suite and Eddie smiled as he listened to her singing. Being out of nick was an amazing feeling, but being with Gina was even better. He had thought he would feel guilty the first time they slept together because of Jessica, but he hadn't even thought of his deceased wife.

As Gina came out of the shower with a towel wrapped around her, Ed stood up and kissed her passionately.

'Where's the clothes and the phone you bought me, babe?'

'All your clothes are in the wardrobe and your phone's on charge downstairs.'

'I'll have to ring me kids after dinner. They'll think I've been fucking abducted.'

Gina put on her dressing gown. 'Right, my lord, I'm gonna go and cook us some dinner. You've worn me out and I'm gasping for a glass of wine.'

Eddie stared at her. Gina was beautiful, he was a man of impulse and that was a fatal mixture. 'Marry me,' he said bluntly.

'You're such a wind-up merchant,' Gina said, laughing.

Still stark-bollock naked, Eddie dropped to one knee and grabbed Gina by the hand. 'I'm not winding you up. I love you, Gina Mulcahy, so would you do me the honour of becoming my wife?'

With tears in her eyes, Gina knelt down next to him. 'Yes, Eddie, I would.'

CHAPTER THIRTY-THREE

After two days of continuous eating, drinking and making love, Eddie felt that it was time to get his arse in gear again.

Being with Gina was everything he had hoped for and more, but there were a lot of things he needed to do and he couldn't stay hidden in his love nest for ever.

Eddie sat at the kitchen table opposite Gina. 'Listen, I'm gonna have to pop out for a bit today, babe. I wanna check on the business and go over a few things with Gary and Ricky. I've got an appointment with the probation officer, then I must go and see me Auntie Joan. I also need to have a proper chat with Raymond. If he's coming to that meal on Saturday, I'm gonna have to tell him about me and you beforehand, ain't I?'

Gina nodded. 'If you're going to be out all day, I might hit the shops and get myself a new outfit for the weekend.'

Finishing the last of his bacon sandwich, Eddie stood up and held his fiancée in his arms. 'We'll pop up Hatton Garden at some point next week to buy you a massive rock. Can't have other geezers thinking you're not taken, can we now?'

Gina grinned. 'There aren't many geezers about that could compare to you, Eddie Mitchell.'

Feeling himself getting hard again, Eddie pressed his manhood against his wife-to-be. 'You're right, babe, there ain't.'

*   *   *

Frankie and Kerry were sitting opposite one another in a café in Pitsea Market. 'So, what's been happening? How are things with Jed? Are you still arguing?'

Frankie nodded. 'He reckons he's working away again this weekend, but I don't believe him. I might drive to Rush Green, see if I can catch him out. If I pick you up, will you come with me, Kerry?'

Kerry took a gulp from her can of Coke. 'I think you're wasting your time driving round Rush Green. You don't honestly think after what happened with me and Sammy that he's gonna leave his motor nearby, do ya? Jed's devious, Frankie, it'll take more than sitting outside Sally's flat to catch him at it.'

'Well, what else can I do, then? I need to find out the truth somehow. Even Georgie blurted out that slag Sally's name the other day. She'd heard Jed on the phone to her and told me that Daddy had a girlfriend, so I've got to do something.'

Kerry shrugged. 'Why don't you have a word with your dad or your brothers? Perhaps they can get someone to follow Jed for ya.'

Frankie automatically shook her head. She felt far too embarrassed to involve her nearest and dearest. 'I can't tell anyone in my family about this. Remember, they all hated Jed from the word go and I couldn't stand hearing the "I told you sos".'

'Has Sammy said anything else to you? He went round my mum's again yesterday. Shouting and screaming about taking me to court so he can get access to see the kids, he was. I don't even think he's bothered about me. What am I gonna do, Frankie? I can't keep 'em away from school for ever. My sister reckons I should let him see the boys. She said the courts will make me if I don't and she said I'll get in trouble for not enrolling 'em into a new school.'

As Kerry's eyes filled with tears, Frankie felt her own do the same. They were in shit street and the future for both them and their kids looked very bleak indeed.

*   *   *

315

Over in Whitechapel, Auntie Joan was delighted to see her favourite nephew. 'Ere you go, boy,' she said handing him a big chunk of her homemade bread pudding. She had tried to take him a bread pudding at the prison once, but the screws wouldn't let her in with it.

'What about when I threw your pudding at that miserable git in Wandsworth? His face was a picture, the unfeeling bastard. What was his name again?'

Eddie laughed. Joanie throwing the bread pudding at Carter had gone down a treat with his fellow inmates. She'd been the talk of the wing for days. She'd also attacked Carter once for grabbing her arm and ordering her to leave. That had also gone down in Wandsworth folklore.

'Carter, his name was. How's Reg? You seen much of him lately?'

'Yeah, Reg popped round 'ere last week. He reckons Paulie and Ronny's number's up in the old sharking game. They kept getting turned over, apparently, and now word's got about, people have started to knock 'em, left right and centre.'

Eddie shook his head in disbelief. 'I told Paulie he should have stuck with me. Ronny's been a laughing stock for years and there ain't many borrowers that are gonna take the threats of an alcoholic cripple seriously. Shame Paulie never listened, Gary and Ricky have been raking it in while I've been away and he could have been part of all that, the silly bastard.'

Joan nodded. 'Reg has got a feeling that Paulie might come to you cap in hand for a job now you're out. Would you take him back on, Ed?'

Eddie shrugged. 'No way! There's too much water under the bridge, if you know what I mean. Maybe I can lend him some dough or something if he's going through a sticky patch. Cut us another slice of bread pudding, will ya, Auntie? Fucking handsome that was.'

Joan studied Eddie carefully as she watched him devour his second slice of pudding. He looked ever so well, considering he'd only just come out of clink, and she had a feeling she knew why. 'Come on then, spill the beans. You've met a woman, ain't ya?'

Eddie grinned. Joanie was a wily old fucker and there were no flies on her. 'You remember that private detective that spoke up for me in court?'

'Was she the pretty girl with dark hair?'

Ed nodded. 'That's her. Gina, her name is, and we're sort of giving it a go.'

Joan was made up. Eddie had been in a terrible state over Jessica and she was thrilled he had managed to move on from such an awful tragedy.

'Well that Gina's certainly doing something right, boy. Got a right glow about you, you have. I've never seen you look so bleedin' well.'

'You are coming out for the family meal on Saturday, ain't ya? Gina's coming with me and you can meet her properly. I might sit her next to you, with me on the other side.'

'Yep, I'll be there. Is it common knowledge you're with her? Or should I let you tell Reg and Vi?'

Eddie shrugged. 'Gary and Ricky are the only ones I've told so far and I'm gonna tell Raymond when I leave here. It's a bit awkward, ain't it? I'm not good at telling people that type of stuff. I dunno what to say, so I thought I'd just bring Gina to the meal and introduce her as a friend at first. I don't want people thinking badly of me, Auntie. I'll never forget Jessica, and Gina ain't some kind of replacement for her, you know.'

'I understand, boy, and I should imagine all your family will be happy for ya. The only ones who might find it difficult to digest is the twins, I suppose.'

Eddie agreed. 'Frankie ain't coming on Saturday, so I'm gonna take her out for lunch next week and speak to her. I don't see Joey at all now, and I should imagine you know why that is.'

Joan nodded. 'I heard the rumours and I couldn't believe it at first. Funny old world, ain't it?'

'It sure is. I can forgive most of the things my kids do, but I can't stomach that. I've disowned him; he disgusts me.'

Feeling embarrassed and also agitated, Eddie stood up. 'I'd best go now. I've got a thousand-and-one things to do today.'

Joanie hugged Eddie tightly. He didn't realise that she'd seen the tears in his eyes when he'd spoken about Joey, but she had. 'You've been a good father. Always remember that, won't ya?'

Eddie smiled sadly. 'Thanks, Auntie, I will.'

Back in Pitsea, Frankie and Kerry were having a browse around the local market. Georgie was at school, Kerry's sister had her boys, so they only had Harry with them today.

'Is Harry OK? I ain't heard a peep out of him for hours,' Kerry asked.

'He's still asleep, bless him,' Frankie said, looking inside her son's pushchair.

Spotting the record stall, Kerry stopped dead and grabbed her friend's arm. 'That's it. I've got it.'

'What you on about?' Frankie asked, bemused.

Kerry smiled and pointed to the record stall. 'Cassettes. That's what you can do, Frankie, tape 'em.'

Frankie didn't have a clue what her friend was on about. 'What you talking about? Tape who?'

'That man over there sells cassettes and it's just given me an idea. Why don't you hide a tape recorder in Jed's Shogun and record his and Sammy's conversations? That's the way to find out the truth about everything. Sally, that slag Julie – we can even find out if her kid belongs to Sammy.'

Frankie was unsure. The idea sounded extremely risky. 'Where am I meant to hide a tape recorder? And even worse, say Jed finds it?'

'I'll get you a small one and you can hide it in the back of the Shogun somewhere. You can put a blank tape in and press the record button just before Jed goes out. It's got to be worth a try, Frankie. How else you gonna catch him?'

'I don't know if I like the sound of it, Kerry. How am I meant to run out there and press "record"?'

'Do it on a night when they're supposedly working away. You can run out and do it while Jed's having a shower, or you can pretend that Georgie or Harry has left one of their toys in the motor. Go on, Frankie. Can you imagine all the juicy conversation we'll hear?'

'Say they've got the music on? Jed always listens to music when he's driving. We ain't gonna be able to hear anything then, are we?'

Kerry shook her head. 'They won't be listening to music if they're going over to them two old tarts, will they? Oh, go on, Frankie, please say you'll do it. I need to know if that Julie's kid belongs to Sammy. I mean, my boys might have sisters and brothers dotted about all over the place, for all I know.'

Frankie pondered before reluctantly agreeing. 'You're gonna have to find the smallest tape recorder ever invented, and don't buy a cheap one, because we won't hear sod-all.'

Kerry grinned. 'I'll tell my mum what we're gonna do. She'll pay for it, I know she will. Now let's go and ask that man what are the longest cassettes we can buy.'

As Kerry dragged her towards the record stall, Frankie shook her head in disbelief. She must be mad to even consider Kerry's idea. Jed would go mental if he found the tape recorder, and what Frankie had to do now was decide whether, if their plan went wrong, it was worth getting a good hiding for.

Stuck in the salvage yard in Dagenham, Raymond was chuffed to bits to see Eddie. 'Where you been? I thought you'd fucking emigrated,' he said, as he gave him a bear hug.

'It's a long story. Lock up and let's go for lunch. There's stuff we need to discuss.'

Raymond didn't need telling twice. Just lately, working in the scrap game had been boring him to tears and now that Ed was out he was hoping to work alongside him once more.

There were no decent food-based boozers in Dagenham, so Eddie drove into the lanes in Rainham and pulled up outside the White Hart.

'If there's no one we know in here, we'll eat here. If we get recognised we'll have a drink, fuck off and find somewhere else,' Eddie said.

As luck would have it, there were only a handful of people in the pub and neither Eddie nor Raymond knew any of them. Ed ordered a couple of beers and handed Raymond a menu.

'Order me the scampi. I'm just going for a slash,' he told him.

Raymond ordered the food and sat down at a table at the far end of the pub. 'Over 'ere, Ed,' he shouted, as his pal reappeared.

Eddie sat down, took a sip from his bottle of Bud and grinned. 'It feels weird when you first come out of nick, Raymondo. It's just so bleedin' wonderful to be able to pop into a boozer for a bit of lunch and a couple of beers. I never used to appreciate shit like this before.'

Raymond nodded understandingly. 'So, what you been up to since Monday? I rang the boys and they said they hadn't seen you yet. You're popping over to see 'em later today, ain't ya?'

Eddie nodded. 'I just wanted to get me head together, to be honest with ya. It's strange when you first come out. It takes a while to get used to living in the real world again.'

'So, who you been stopping with? I thought you'd have gone to stay with Gary and Ricky.'

Eddie shook his head. It was now or never, and even though he dreaded telling Raymond, he knew he couldn't avoid it any longer. 'There's something I need to tell you, something that you might not like. I can't lie to you, Ray, so I'm gonna come clean with ya. Do you remember that Gina from my trial? You must remember, you dropped some dough off to her a couple of times for me.'

'The private detective bird?'

Eddie nodded. 'Well, after my case, I wrote to her and thanked her for her help and she came up to visit me. We just sort of clicked. I was stuck in nick and lonely, and even though I still miss Jessica like mad and think about her every single day, I had to try and move on with my life.'

Raymond felt his stomach turn over. 'What are you trying to tell me, Ed?'

'I've decided to give it a go with her, Ray. Gina rented a cottage out in the sticks and I've moved in with her.'

Raymond stood up and pushed his chair away with force. He couldn't quite believe what he was hearing. 'You don't hang about, do ya? Two days you've been out, two cunting days and you've bagged another bird already. You're unbelievable, Ed, fucking unbelievable.'

As Raymond bolted out of the pub, Eddie chased after him and grabbed his arm. 'Don't be like this, Ray. I loved Jess, you know I did, and I wouldn't hurt you for the world. Hear me out for fuck's sake, will ya?'

Unable to stop himself, Raymond broke down. 'Jess was my sister, Ed. I loved her so much. How do you expect me to feel?' he wept.

Eddie felt awkward as he hugged his strapping pal. 'I'm really sorry I've upset you, mate. Go on, let it all out.'

Feeling like a complete idiot, Raymond quickly pulled himself together. 'I'm sorry as well. I don't begrudge you being happy again, I really don't and I feel like a right prick for making a scene, but I'm going through a shit time of it myself at the moment. Me and Polly ain't getting on – all we do is argue. The salvage yard does me head in; I miss the excitement and the life that the old loan-sharking brought with it.'

Eddie put an arm around Ray and led him back towards the pub. 'That's the other thing I wanted to talk to you about. Gary and Ricky have done wonders while I've been away, but there's only so much the two of them can do. I think me and you need to get back into the fold, don't you? Let's eat our lunch, then we can talk about it properly, eh?'

Frankie's mind was all over the place as she picked Georgie up from school. She hadn't made her mind up yet whether to go through with Kerry's wacky idea and the indecision was making her feel ill. She had told Kerry that she'd do it, but had since had second thoughts about her ability to pull it off.

Georgie clambered into the back of the Shogun and slapped her brother on the head to wake him up. 'What's for tea, Mum? I'm hungry.'

'You can have hot dogs or chicken nuggets.'

'I don't want them. Can't I have burgers?' Georgie whinged.

'Yes, there's some in the freezer, Georgie.'

'Don't like your burgers. Can't I have McDonald's burgers, Mum?'

'No, you can't. Now shut up, because I'm trying to drive.'

As Georgie began rambling on about not wanting any dinner, Frankie ignored her for once. She was far too worried about her own problems today to worry about her daughter's fussy eating.

Frankie sighed. She desperately needed advice and the only person she could think of to turn to in her hour of need was Joey.

Raymond was buoyant as Eddie outlined their plans for the future. 'So, what we'll do is have a meeting with the boys on Sunday. I'll arrange everything. If you can just hold the fort at the salvage yard until after the weekend, I can sort someone to come in and take over from ya from Monday onwards.'

Raymond nodded. 'I'll tell Polly tonight. I'm gonna be straight with her and if she don't like it, she knows what she can do. I do love her, Ed, but she's doing my head in over this baby thing. The doctor told her to relax and it'll happen naturally, but she's like a woman possessed.'

Eddie laughed. He hadn't told Raymond that he'd proposed

to Gina and had no intention of doing so until the time was right. 'I need to ask you something. I'd like to meet with your parents and speak to them in person. I know I can never make things right for what I did, Ray, but I'd like to try. Can you organise a meet with them for me?'

Raymond held his hands up. 'I dunno about that, Ed. Me dad's still very bitter about the whole thing. I can have a word with me mum, if you like. She asked after you only last week, funny enough.'

'What did she do with all me clobber out of the house, do you know?'

'Gary's got it all. Put it in storage, he did. I thought he told you when you first went in nick.'

'He probably did. I was on a different planet when I first got banged up, weren't I?'

Raymond smiled. 'Me dad goes to his pigeon club tomorrow night. Shall I ring Mum while he's out, see if I can get her to meet up with you?'

Eddie nodded. 'I will truly understand if she don't wanna see me, but I desperately need to apologise in person. It's what Jessica would have wanted, I know it is.'

CHAPTER THIRTY-FOUR

On Saturday morning, Frankie dropped Georgie over at Alice and Jimmy's house.

'Ain't you leaving Harry 'ere as well?' Alice asked abruptly.

'No. Joey and Dom want Harry to stay at theirs. They're taking him out for the day tomorrow.'

Alice was pleased. Jimmy had gone off to some horse fair and if Harry wasn't stopping over, it meant she had Georgie to herself for the day.

Frankie said goodbye to her daughter and headed towards South Woodham Ferrers. She was glad that her brother had offered to look after Harry, as she knew Joey and Dom would take proper care of him.

Alice and Jimmy had always favoured Georgie and for that reason alone Frankie didn't like leaving her son with them.

Driving along the A13, Frankie heard her mobile ringing.

'All right? It's me. Are you alone?'

Frankie smiled when she heard Kerry's dulcet tones. 'Yeah. I've just dropped Georgie off at the scumbags' and I'm on me way over to Joey's. Him and Dom are gonna babysit Harry for me tonight. Are you OK?'

'I'm fine. I've got it.'

'Got what?' Frankie asked.

'The tape recorder. Me mum's mate's boyfriend got it for us. Someone chored it for him. It's perfect, Frankie, it's only little,

324

but it's like one of them small ones what the police use when they're undercover.'

Frankie was still undecided whether she could go through with their plan. 'I had a look around in the Shogun when Jed was in the shower yesterday and I don't think there's anywhere to put it, Kerry.'

'You can't back out now. Please, Frankie, do it for me. I need to know if Sammy's got a kid with that slag before I let him have access to the boys. If Jed finds it, just blame it on me. Say I did it or forced you to do it or something. You'll find somewhere to hide it. Why don't you stick it under the driver's seat or you can always hide it in the back of the motor somewhere.'

Frankie had a better idea. 'Why don't we go back to Rush Green and hunt down that Julie? We can threaten her or something, and we'll make her tell us if it's Sammy's kid.'

'No. She ain't worth getting nicked again for. Anyway what about Jed? He's got to be at it as well. You can't just shove your problems under the carpet, Frankie, you need to confront 'em head-on, otherwise you'll end up living a lie like I did.'

Frankie knew what Kerry was saying made sense, but she was keen to speak to Joey about what she should do first. 'Look, I'm nearly at my brother's now. I'm gonna ask his opinion and then I'll ring you when I leave.'

Kerry was a bit annoyed. She had gone to a lot of trouble to put their plan into action and had even borrowed fifty quid from her mum to pay the bloke who had nicked it. 'I'll tell you something, Frankie. If you bottle out of doing this, I shall come over to Wickford and plant the thing my bastard self. Sammy and Jed are utter scumbags and I, for one, won't rest until I know every detail of their sordid fucking lives.'

Unaware that his youngest son was currently living only a few miles away from him, Eddie groaned as he shot his load inside Gina. They had discussed using contraception, but had decided not to bother. What was the point when they'd both agreed to having kids?

'You all right, babe?'

Gina smiled. Eddie was an unselfish lover, an expert in the sack, and he always made sure that she was satisfied. She laid her head on his chest.

'I love living here. It's so peaceful, isn't it?'

Eddie twiddled with her long dark hair. 'Funny enough, I've been thinking about that. Why don't we contact the estate agent and put in an offer that the old couple can't refuse?'

'They might not want to sell. They've only gone to Australia for a year, I think.'

'They'll sell if I offer 'em silly money for it. I ain't a man that ever takes no for an answer, Gina. You should know that more than anyone.'

Gina's eyes shone as she sat up in bed. 'Shall I ring the estate agent on Monday to set the ball rolling? Oh, Ed, wouldn't it be wonderful if we bought the place. We could decorate it to our own taste and we could . . .'

Eddie put his finger over her lips. 'There's no ifs about it, darling. If you want us to purchase this place, then I will make sure we fucking well get it.'

Joey listened intently while Frankie told him the story. He had guessed she'd had something important on her mind and Dom, being Dom, had thoughtfully offered to take both Harry and Madonna out for a walk, so they could have some privacy.

'So, what do you think I should do, Joey? What would you do if it was Dom? Would you plant the tape recorder or would you just confront him?'

Unable to stop himself, Joey gave a sarcastic laugh. 'Don't be speaking about Jed and Dominic in the same breath, Frankie. Dom's a beautiful man inside and out. As for Jed, well you know my opinion of him. I think he's an uncouth, pikey piece of shit. You must never forget that our mum would still be alive if it wasn't for you meeting him.'

Annoyed that her brother wasn't being his usual supportive self, Frankie felt her hackles rise. 'I came here to ask for your advice, not for a fucking lecture, Joey. I know what you're saying about Mum but, say I hadn't got with Jed, say I'd met another boy and Dad didn't like him? It was Dad that nearly chopped Dominic's cock off, remember? And you can't blame Jed for that.'

Realising that he'd been a bit unfeeling, Joey immediately apologised. 'I'm sorry. You're right: Dad is to blame for Mum's death, nobody else. As for Jed – you've got to find out the truth, Frankie. I know it's gonna be hard for you with two kids and one on the way, but if Jed is leading a double life, it's best you find out now, rather than later.'

'Do you think hiding the tape recorder in his motor and pressing "record" will work? I mean, say he finds it?'

Joey shrugged. 'If he finds it, he finds it. That's the chance you're gonna have to take. Whether you'll find out what you wanna find out, I don't know, but I suppose it's worth a try. I've never trusted Jed from day one. He's a con man and a liar, I'm sure he is.'

Frankie nodded. 'I can't let Kerry down now, so sod it, I'm gonna go for it. Apart from Jed going ballistic if he finds it, what have I got to lose? I'm not that happy with him now, anyway. We were so in love when we first got together, but everything seems to have changed recently.'

'What do you mean? He doesn't hit you, does he?'

'No, he doesn't hit me. Jed's really good in some ways, like with money. He's very generous to me and the kids, but I just sense he don't love me like he used to. We only have sex about once or twice a month now, whereas a few years back we were at it all the time. He works away a lot and when he is at home he rarely tries it on with me any more. I tried it on with him recently, but he pushed me away, and said he was tired. Do you think he don't fancy me when I'm pregnant? Or is it because I've put on weight?'

Joey hated seeing his sister upset. He moved next to her and hugged her. 'I don't know what Jed's problem is, Frankie, but chances are if you and him aren't sleeping together that often, he's probably getting it somewhere else. There's nothing wrong with you. You're still so pretty and you haven't put on that much weight.'

Joey's kindness was too much for Frankie and she burst into tears. 'I'm so unhappy. What am I gonna do, Joey?' she sobbed.

Joey didn't really know what to say or do. The Frankie of old had been such a fiery, strong character. He hated seeing her like this; it was as though Jed had sapped every bit of life out of her.

Frankie dried her eyes with a tissue. She felt silly for blubbing and was keen to change the subject. 'I'm going for a meal with the family tonight. They've arranged it for Dad.'

Joey looked at her in horror. 'Whaddya mean? Is he out, then?'

Frankie felt awful. She'd had so much on her mind that she'd forgotten to tell her brother that their dad had been released. 'I'm so sorry, Joey, I forgot to tell you. Dad got out earlier this week. Gary and Ricky rang me and invited me to the meal. They've booked a restaurant in Canning Town.'

Joey was fuming. How could Frankie ask him to babysit, then go out celebrating with their dad? Their beautiful mum was dead and it was their father who had bloody well killed her. He stood up and walked over to the window. 'Can you leave now, Frankie? I feel ill and I need to lie down before I spew my guts up. You make me sick sometimes, you really do.'

Joyce watched Stanley walk down to the pigeon shed, then bolted into the living room. She picked up the phone and then quickly put it down again. Should she or shouldn't she? She couldn't make her mind up.

Joyce poured herself a small sherry and stared at the phone. Raymond had rung her the other day and informed her that Eddie had been released.

'He wants to meet up with you, Mum. I think he wants to apologise to you in person. He said it's what Jessica would have wanted him to do.'

Joyce's first reaction was to say no. Stanley would be so against it and he'd have a bloody fit if she met up with Eddie behind his back and he found out. Twenty-four hours later, Joyce had changed her mind and had called Raymond back. Her son had given her Eddie's mobile number and had urged her to call him in secret.

'Don't breathe a word to anyone, because you don't want Dad finding out,' he'd said.

Joyce took the piece of paper out of her purse. Unlike Stanley, she had always been fond of Eddie and even though she could never forgive him for what he had done, she felt that she should at least hear what the man had to say. He had given her the beautiful home she now lived in, after all.

She dialled his number. 'Eddie, it's Joycie,' she said, her voice shaking.

'Hello, Joycie, love. I'm so pleased that you called. How are you?'

'I'm OK. Listen, I can't stay on long, as Stanley's in the garden and I don't want him to know I've been in contact with you. Raymond said you wanted to meet me for a chat. What about next Friday? I've got to pop to Romford to pick up some curtains. Can you meet me there?'

'What time? And where?'

'Is twelve o'clock OK? I can meet you in the Bull pub. I often pop in there for a crafty tipple when I'm out shopping on a market day.'

'That sounds fine, Joycie. We can also have a bite to eat, if you like. Thanks for calling, I truly appreciate it.'

Hearing the back door open and close, Joyce quickly put the phone down. Meeting up with Eddie might prove to be a big mistake, but she had to see him again, even if it was only to discuss a certain subject that had been playing on her mind.

Frankie left Joey's house and immediately rang Kerry. 'I'll do a deal with ya,' she said.

'What?' Kerry replied.

'I'll hide the tape recorder in Jed's Shogun if you come to that restaurant with me tonight.'

Kerry didn't feel much like going out. She was still too wound up over Sammy to enjoy herself. 'Oh, do I have to, Frankie? I've got no money and I feel like shit.'

'Please, come with me. You don't need no money, my brothers are paying for everything. I really don't wanna go on my own, Kerry. I don't see much of my dad's family and for all I know they might blame me for him getting locked up. Raymond's gonna be there, you know, my uncle who you fancied at the barbecue round my nan's.'

'OK, you've twisted me arm. How did you get on with Joey? What did he say about our plan?'

'He said we should go for it. He then threw me out because I'm going out with my dad tonight.'

'What! He threw you out of his house?'

'Sort of. I'll tell you all about it later. Get to mine for six. Gary and Ricky are picking us up at half past.'

Frankie ended the call and drove towards home deep in thought. She couldn't wait to catch up with her dad properly, but was dreading the big family meal. She wasn't overly keen on her dad's family, especially his brothers, Ronny and Paulie. Ronny was always drunk and had glared at her in court, and Paulie had always ignored her since she was a child.

Thinking of Kerry, Frankie smiled. They were like the terrible twosome when they socialised together and they were bound to have a laugh tonight, whoever was there.

Gina studied herself in the mirror. She had treated herself to a sleeveless, long, red pencil dress, but was now worried that it was a bit over the top for the occasion. 'Eddie, come here a minute,' she shouted.

Eddie walked into the room in a dark grey suit, crisp white shirt and tan leather shoes. 'Wow, you look amazing,' he said.

Gina smiled at him. 'It's not too much, is it? I don't want to feel like a fish out of water.'

Guessing that Gina was nervous, Eddie took her hands in his. 'You look sensational, honest you do. Don't worry about tonight, everything will be fine. Jessica never had much to do with my family, so there'll be no animosity. I don't want to make you feel awkward, so I'll just introduce you as a friend, if you like. Gary, Ricky, Raymondo and me Auntie Joan all know the score and we'll just leave the rest to wonder, eh?'

Gina put her arms around Eddie's neck. 'You're such a gentleman. I can't wait to become your wife.'

Laughing, Eddie grabbed the cheeks of her arse and thrust himself towards her. 'I'm having ungentlemanly thoughts. Get that dress off and let's have a quickie before we leave, eh?'

Unable to resist the man she had fallen head over heels for, Gina stripped naked within seconds.

Frankie and Kerry giggled as Gary handed them both a cocktail.

'I know I shouldn't really be drinking, but after all the shit I've had to put up with this month, I think I deserve a few, don't you?' said Frankie.

Kerry nodded. 'I had a drink through both of my pregnancies. As long as you don't go too mad, it's fine.'

'So, do you still fancy Raymond?' Frankie sniggered.

'Not really. He is gorgeous, but he's far too old for me. So, who's who then? Who's that loud bloke in the wheelchair?'

Frankie raised her eyes. 'That's my uncle Ronny. He's an alcoholic, so if he gets lairy, it's because he's pissed. The bloke next to him on the left is my dad's other brother Paulie, and the one on the right is my dad's uncle Reg.'

'Who's that over there, talking to your brother?'

'That's my dad's uncle Albert and the three women are his aunt Joan, aunt Vi and Sylvie. Sylvie used to go out with my grandad, Harry. He was the one I told you about, the one that got murdered.'

'Yeah, that was awful. Have they still not caught the people that did it?'

331

Frankie shook her head. 'I don't think so. My dad will catch 'em one day, though. He won't let it rest, he's not the type.'

Kerry smiled. She had heard so much about Frankie's dad and was looking forward to meeting him. 'What time's your dad getting here?'

About to answer, Frankie was tapped on the shoulder by Auntie Vi.

'Hello, darling. How are you?'

Frankie stood up and gave the old lady a kiss. 'I'm fine, thanks. How are you?'

Vi looked her up and down. As Joan approached, she nudged her and smiled at Frankie.

'You getting fat or you pregnant again?'

'Pregnant,' Frankie said embarrassed. She wasn't even that far gone and obviously looked enormous already.

'How many's that now?' Joan asked.

'This will be my third,' Frankie replied.

'You still with that pikey lad?' Vi asked.

'Yeah, I'm still with Jed.'

Joan and Vi both laughed. 'They know how to knock 'em out, them pikeys, don't they, Joanie?' Vi quipped.

Joan agreed. 'They're the same as the blacks and the Indians, ain't they? Bang 'em out one after the other – none of 'em know when to bleedin' well stop.'

As the two old women wandered off, Frankie sat down, red-faced. 'Nosy, racist old cows,' she whispered to Kerry.

John, the ex-guvnor of the Flag in Canning Town had been invited and was standing by the window waiting for Eddie to arrive.

'This is him. Oh, sorry, no it ain't,' he shouted.

Kerry laughed. 'Is the restaurant open to the public tonight or is it just us?' she asked Frankie.

'I think it's just us. The owner, that man over there in the black suit, was a friend of my grandad's. He's known my dad since he was a little boy, so he offered to shut it so we could have some privacy. My uncles have organised a bit of a party back at the Flag later. Gary reckons my dad won't wanna go, but we can go if you like.'

'Yeah, why not. My sister's looking after the boys, so I can stay at yours. What time do you reckon Jed and Sammy will be back tomorrow?'

'About lunchtime, I suppose. Don't worry, you'll be long gone by the time Sammy comes back.'

'Eddie's here and he's got a woman with him,' John shouted.

Gary and Ricky looked at one another. Neither had thought to ask their dad if he was bringing Gina. Because it was a family do, they'd sort of surmised that he wasn't.

'Shit, what we gonna do about Frankie? Dad don't know she's here, does he?' Gary whispered.

Ricky shrugged his shoulders. 'It's a bit late to worry about that now, ain't it?'

Frankie sat with bated breath, waiting for the door to open. John must have been seeing things. Her dad had only been out of prison for a matter of days, so there was no way he could have met a woman.

'Are you OK?' Kerry asked.

'Yeah. Don't take no notice of John, my dad still loves my mum, he's probably got a female relation with him or something.'

As the door flung open and her dad strolled in with his arm around an attractive, dark-haired woman, Frankie felt the bile rise at the back of her throat. She turned to Ricky.

'Who the fucking hell is that?'

'I dunno. Dad's friend, I think.'

Fuming, Frankie stood up and marched over to her father. 'Who's she?' she shouted.

Eddie felt the colour drain from his face. He would never have brought Gina with him if he had known Frankie was going to be here.

'Hello, darling. This is Gina, she's a friend of mine. Gina, this is my daughter, Frankie.'

Gina held her hand out, but Frankie pushed it away. She turned to her father. 'How could you, Dad? You've only been out five poxy days and you're shagging some old tart already. You make me sick, you're a fucking disgrace.'

Eddie hated being spoken down to in public by anyone. 'Watch your mouth, Frankie. What kind of talk is that, eh? You ain't mixing with the pikeys now, love, so show some bloody respect. Gina's a friend of mine and I want you to apologise to her this minute.'

The restaurant fell silent apart from Vi, Joanie and Ronny's voices.

'Attractive, ain't she, Joanie? He didn't hang about, did he?' Vi said.

'Good luck to him. Can't bring the other one back to life, can he? He's a good boy, is Eddie, he deserves a bit of happiness,' Joan replied.

'Maybe I should do my fucking Sharon in. It'll be worth it if I end up with a bit of crumpet like that,' Ronny joked.

Eddie's eyes were blazing as Frankie spat at his feet and walked away. 'I told you to apologise to Gina,' he shouted.

Frankie picked up her handbag and grabbed Kerry by the arm. She stormed over to the door.

'Where do you think you're going, young lady?' Eddie asked her.

'Home. I ain't sitting 'ere watching you fawning over that old slapper all night. I bet poor mum's turning in her grave right this minute. Don't you ever contact me again, Dad. You're now dead as far as I'm concerned.'

And on that parting note, Frankie flung open the door and slammed it so hard that it could be heard in nearby Bow.

CHAPTER THIRTY-FIVE

Eddie woke up the next morning with a splitting headache. The previous evening had been a disaster from start to finish.

After Frankie had stormed out of the restaurant, Eddie had had a proper scream up at Gary and Ricky.

'You stupid pair of pricks! Why didn't you tell me Frankie was coming? I wouldn't have brought Gina with me if I'd have known.'

'You never said you were bringing Gina with you. Frankie wanted it to be a surprise for you,' Gary said, glancing at Ricky for support.

'Oh, it was a fucking surprise all right. I told you I'd moved in with Gina, so surely it was obvious that she would be coming with me. If yous two had a brain, you'd be fucking dangerous.'

'It ain't our fault, Dad. We only did what Frankie asked us to,' Ricky said abruptly.

'I don't want yous two anywhere near me tonight. Just keep out of my way,' Eddie shouted.

The evening had then gone from bad to worse. Ronny had got paralytic and kept talking about Jessica's murder and then, at half-past nine, he fell head-first out of his wheelchair, cut his head open and had to be taken to hospital in an ambulance.

Paulie wasn't much better. He also had far too many drinks and spent the evening chewing Eddie's ears off about working alongside him once again. In the end, Eddie had no choice but to give it to him straight.

'It ain't gonna work, Paulie, me and you grafting together. Listen, if you've hit a rough patch and you need a few quid to tide you over, just ask me. You ain't gotta pay me back, it's a gift.'

Paulie had thrown Eddie's kind offer straight back in his face. 'I don't want your fucking charity. You've always thought you were something special, ain't ya? We were partners once and all I wanted was for us to be that again. I bet Dad's turning in his grave as we speak. You know, our wonderful dad that cut me and Ronny out of the will and gave you all his fucking money.'

Embarrassed that Paulie had kicked off in front of Gina, Eddie had dragged him out to the bogs. 'Don't you dare bring Dad into this. You walked, remember? You was the one who wanted to go it alone with Ironside. Well, it ain't my fault if things have gone tits-up for ya. You made your choice, Paulie, so it's up to you to fucking well live with it.'

Paulie had left shortly after and gone to the Flag. Ed was appalled to learn that his brothers had planned a party there for him.

'I didn't go inside for robbing a bank or emigrating with a load of gold bullion. I went in there for killing me own wife, who I happened to have loved dearly. It's hardly cause for a coming-out celebration, is it, Reg? My brothers must be the thickest pair of cunts I know,' he'd said to his uncle.

'You OK, Ed?'

Eddie rolled over and smiled at Gina. On the journey home, she'd insisted that she had enjoyed herself. 'I got on famously with both of your aunts and Sylvie,' she'd said brightly, not mentioning any of the other shit that had happened.

Eddie kissed her. 'I'm all right. I was just thinking about Frankie. I'll have to go and see her at some point, won't I?'

Gina smiled. 'She'll come round. She's only a young girl and, having lost her mum, it must be hard for her to see her dad with another woman.'

'Let's hope you're right. She's a stubborn little fucker, is Frankie. Takes after me, she does.'

336

'She's a very pretty girl and she looks like you. She's got your eyes and mouth.'

Eddie laughed. 'She's got my temper as well, unfortunately.'

Gina sat up. 'I think I've got a bit of a hangover. Shall we go out for lunch today? I can't be bothered to cook.'

Eddie rolled on top of her and pinned her down to the bed. 'Your wish is my command, my angel.'

Frankie studied the tape recorder. 'It is small, ain't it? I didn't think you could buy 'em this tiny.'

Kerry pressed the record button. 'Let's talk for a minute and we'll play it back. It's really clear, Frankie, you can hear everything. My mum's mate said they're ever so expensive to buy in a shop.'

Frankie had cheered up somewhat since the previous evening. She was still furious with her father, but after stomping out of the restaurant, she and Kerry had gone to a local pub and had a right good laugh. It had done her the world of good and they had even got chatted up by a couple of blokes.

'Say something, then,' Kerry urged her.

Giggling, Frankie started to sing Whitney Houston's 'I Will Always Love You'. She stopped at the end of the chorus. 'Jed's got the country and western version of this. Dolly Parton sings it, I think.'

Kerry stopped the tape and rewound. 'I bet Dolly Parton sounds a bit better than you do, and she's got bigger knockers,' she said as she pressed the play button.

Frankie was surprised by the quality of their recording. 'Cor, it's really clear,' she said, as Kerry turned the volume up.

Kerry grinned. 'Brilliant, ain't it? We can find out everything them bastards are up to with this little beauty.'

Frankie agreed. 'Let's hope they say they're working away again soon.'

'I can't wait until then. If Jed and Sammy go to work tomorrow, put it in the motor then. They're bound to talk about what they've been up to this weekend when they're alone.'

'OK. If I can, I'll do it tomorrow.'

Kerry stood up. 'I'd best be going now before Sammy gets back. Hide that somewhere safe, Frankie. Whatever you do, don't let the kids get hold of it or, worse still, let Jed find it.'

'I'll hide it in the top of my wardrobe.'

Kerry hugged her friend. 'Good luck. Once we find out what the shitbags are really up to, we can both move on, can't we?'

Over in South Woodham, Harry had had a restless night's sleep and Joey was worried about him. 'I don't think we should take him out today. I'm sure he's got a temperature, and he's really not himself. Do us a favour Dom, ring Frankie, and if she's in, take him home for me.'

'Aren't you coming with us?'

'No. I can't believe she went out last night celebrating with my dad. I don't want to see her at the moment, she winds me up. I'll tell you what, if you take Harry home for me, I'll buy you lunch. Deal?'

Dominic smiled. Joey could be very over-dramatic at times, but he loved him dearly. 'OK. Deal.'

After making love to Gina, Eddie showered, got dressed, then rang Gary.

'I'm sorry for shouting at you last night. Apologise to Ricky for me as well. It weren't yours or his fault, it was just one of them things.'

Gary was very understanding. 'Don't worry, Dad, it's forgotten. You still up for tomorrow? What time are you and Raymond meeting us?'

'We'll meet at yours. I'm picking Raymondo up at nine. You'll have to fill me in on everything that's been going on, then you can take me round and show me any new clients. I think the best thing to do, Gal, is halve the work and we'll work in pairs. That way we can expand a bit and get stuff done a lot quicker. You stick with Ricky and me and Raymond'll pair up. It'll be like old times, won't it, boy?'

Gary laughed. 'The East End'll be shaking in its boots, Dad.'

'Now, what shall I do about Frankie? There's no point me ringing her today, she'll only put the phone down on me. I think I should pay her a little visit, but I don't wanna turn up and bump into that pikey cunt. When ain't he about? And what's her actual address?'

Gary gave him directions. 'It's just like a field, Dad. I think Jed works away a lot of weekends, so you're probably best turning up then. What I'll do is ring her next Friday and find out if he's away. If he is, I'll let you know and you can turn up there unexpected.'

'Cheers. I can't leave things as they are. Me and Frankie were getting along so well and I'm dying to see the grandkids.'

Eddie smiled as he ended the phone call. Gina had just walked into the room in faded tight jeans, a black fitted T-shirt that enhanced her ample breasts, and tan, knee-high leather boots.

'Wow, you look hot. Where we going, sexy?'

'Wherever. I haven't been in any of the local pubs around here. Shall we go for a drive and see where the car takes us?'

'Sounds good to me, babe.'

Joey hugged Dominic as he opened the front door.

'Thanks for doing that for me. How was Frankie? Did she say anything about me?'

'No. She thanked us both for looking after Harry and said she'll keep an eye on him. She didn't seem too worried when I said we thought he had a temperature. She said he had a bit of a cough and cold last week, so it was probably something to do with that.'

Joey nodded and then changed the subject. 'I'm starving. Where shall we go for lunch?'

'Shall we try Rettendon for a change? There's a pub there called the Bell that's meant to do a mean Sunday roast.'

'Sounds great. Don't drive though, Dom. Let's both have a drink today and let our hair down. Call a cab; it's my treat.'

Dominic pecked his boyfriend on the lips. 'Do you think the driver will let us take Madonna with us? I don't want to leave her home alone.'

Joey laughed. Both he and Dominic were so besotted with their new addition to the family that they paid the woman next door fifty pounds a week to babysit Madonna while they went to work.

'Of course they'll take Madonna, and if they dare say no, I'll get her to bite the evil driver.'

Over in Rainham, Frankie plastered on a false smile as Jed walked in. The tape recorder was hidden in her jacket pocket and the jacket had been carefully folded up at the top of the wardrobe.

'You all right, babe?' Jed asked, handing her a cheap bunch of flowers.

'I'm fine. And you? How was work?'

'Knackering. Get us a beer, will ya?' Jed ordered, as he picked up Georgie and flopped on the sofa.

'Say hello to Harry, then,' Frankie urged him.

'Hello, Harry. Come to Daddy,' Jed said in a sarcastic tone.

Aware that Jed was being facetious, Frankie stormed into the bedroom. She was determined not to lose her temper with him, as she didn't want to give him an inkling that she was on to him.

'What's up?' he shouted out.

'Nothing. I'm just gonna change the beds,' she said in the calmest voice that she could.

Opening the wardrobe door, Frankie put her hand on her jacket and fingered the tape recorder. Jed was a bastard to their son and the quicker she could find an excuse to leave him, the better.

Eddie took a sip of his beer and stood up. 'Just going to the toilet. Won't be a minute, babe.'

Gina smiled and studied the menu. She'd had quite a lot to

340

drink last night, which must be the reason she was hungrier today than usual.

'I think I'll have the hunter's chicken,' she said, as Eddie sat back down.

Eddie shook his head. 'We ain't staying 'ere. The bogs are fucking rotten.'

'What's that got to do with us having some lunch?' Gina asked, laughing.

'Me Auntie Joan. Whenever I was a kid and she took me anywhere, the first thing she did was check the khazi. "If the khazi is rotten, imagine the state of the kitchen," she'd say, and then she'd drag me out.'

'You're having me on,' Gina said, laughing.

Eddie downed the rest of his beer and stood up. 'I ain't, babe. Come on, drink up and we'll find somewhere else to eat.'

Joey ordered the food at the bar and thanked the guvnor again for allowing Madonna inside the pub.

'As long as it doesn't bark or run about, you're OK,' the pleasant landlord had told him.

Joey walked back to the table, sat down and grinned. 'Nice pub, isn't it? The customers are a bit old, but they all seem friendly and the food smells amazing.'

Dominic agreed. 'I think Rettendon is an area where a lot of people choose to live after they've retired. I don't know about you, but after spending the week in the City with all its bedlam, I'm happy to while away my weekends in a pub like this.'

Joey burst out laughing. 'We're like an old married couple, me and you. And Lady Madonna is our baby!'

Eddie and Gina pulled up outside the Bell.

'This looks a bit more like it. You can always tell if the food's up to scratch by the amount of cars in the car park at lunchtime.'

Gina giggled. 'You're very fussy for a man that's been eating prison food for years. And I thought you said you could tell if the food was good by the toilets.'

'Shut up and move your carcass,' Eddie said affectionately.

Dominic dropped his knife and fork and crouched down.

Seeing his boyfriend clutching his chest, Joey began to panic. 'Help, I think he's ill,' he said to the people sitting at the next table.

Dominic, who was deathly white and also shaking, immediately waved the people away. 'I'm fine. I choked on the beef,' he mumbled.

With Madonna clutched to his chest, Joey crouched down next to him. 'You sure you're not having a heart attack or something? Whatever's wrong? Please don't die on me, Dom.'

Remembering the awful experience he'd once had at the hands of Joey's father, Dominic put one hand protectively over his private parts and pointed towards the left-hand side of the pub with his other. 'Joey, your dad is in here. He's standing at the bar with a dark-haired woman.'

Joey shook his head in disbelief. 'It can't be. Are you sure?'

'Of course I'm bloody well sure.'

Petrified for his partner's safety, Joey moved towards the people on the next table and urged Dom to do the same.

'You don't mind if we sit here with you for a minute, do you? We need to sit with our backs to the bar.'

Seeing the fright in the two young men's eyes, the greyhaired lady made room for them. Then, being nosy by nature, she turned to Joey, 'Who are you hiding from, dear?'

'My dad. I'm gay and he can't accept it. He's already attacked my boyfriend once and cut him with a knife. He's a real nutter; he's just come out of prison for murdering my mum.'

Dominic kicked Joey under the table to shut him up. He could see the look of astonishment on the woman's face. Her husband looked like he'd just seen a ghost, and the other lady was totally dumbstruck.

The woman stared open-mouthed at her husband and sister.

342

For thirty years they'd all lived in Rettendon and they'd thought it was such a safe, quiet little village. Now there was a mass-murderer on the loose and he was standing at the bar in their local pub.

'Shall I call the police?' the lady asked Joey.

'No,' Dominic said, turning around to see if Eddie was still there. He turned to Joey. 'Your dad's got his back to us, he's facing the bar. I suggest we get out of here while we can.'

'Thanks for your help,' Joey said, as he gingerly stood up.

'Don't worry, we'll watch you and make sure he doesn't follow you,' the woman replied.

Gina was the first to spot Joey and Dominic. As a private detective she had to have eyes like a hawk and it had been her that Eddie had hired to tail the boys when they'd first got together. Eddie had called himself Mr Smith and had told her that Joey was the son of a friend, but Gina had always known the score. Grabbing Eddie's arm, she pointed out of the window.

'I don't really know how to say this, but Joey has just run out the door with a Chihuahua in his arms.'

Eddie looked at her as though she had lost the plot. 'What? Don't be silly. What the fuck you on about?'

Gina dragged him over to the window. 'Look, sprinting across the road. It's definitely Joey and I think that's Dominic with him.'

On impulse, Eddie ran outside the pub. 'Joey!' he yelled.

Hearing Eddie's voice, Joey and Dominic picked up speed.

'Oi! You leave that boy alone. He's told me all about you and if you chase after him, I'm calling the police,' shouted a voice behind him.

Eddie turned around and came face to face with an elderly woman with grey hair who seemed to be chasing after him. 'I'm his dad. I only wanna speak to him.'

'We don't want the likes of you around here; this is a decent area with decent people,' the woman said bravely.

Realising that Joey had blabbed to the old biddy, Eddie ignored her and ran across the road. 'Joey!' he yelled again.

As his son, his lover and the dog disappeared down a remote country lane, Eddie gave up the chase, and ran back to the pub. If that old cow called the Old Bill, he'd have some explaining to do to his probation officer, and he couldn't chance being banged up again.

Gina was standing outside the boozer and, as Eddie approached, he could see the grey-haired woman, the guvnor and all of the other customers staring at him through the windows. Embarrassed beyond belief, he marched straight over to the motor.

'Where you going, Ed? I've ordered our lunch,' Gina shouted.

Eddie's eyes clouded over and, unable to stop himself, he repeatedly booted the door of Gina's new BMW.

'Fuck lunch. I ain't hungry any more. Get in this car and cunting well drive it, Gina. Now.'

CHAPTER THIRTY-SIX

Frankie shut the Shogun door and ran back inside the trailer. She was pleased with the hiding place she had found. Jed had never looked after his motors very well and there was a loose bit of plastic interior in the back that she had managed to fit the tape recorder behind.

'You off, then?' she asked as Jed came out of the bedroom.

'I might have another couple of slices of toast. You trying to get rid of me or something?'

'Don't be silly. I just want to get some housework done before I take Georgie to school. I might have a mooch around the shops later and I don't want to have to clear up when I get back.'

'All right, I get the hint. I can get something to eat in the café. Me and Sammy have got to go to Newmarket today to look at a couple of trotting mares. I'll probably be back around teatime or something.'

As Jed started the engine, Frankie glanced at the clock. The cassette was an hour long; surely that would be enough time for Jed and Sammy to hang themselves.

Frankie sat the kids at the breakfast table and handed them each a bowl of Rice Krispies. She then picked up her mobile and went into the bedroom.

'Kerry, it's me. I've done it.'

Within days of being back in the fold, Eddie Mitchell had found out exactly where Albie Clark was living.

Gary and Ricky had done a fine job of running the firm while Ed was inside. They were his sons, extremely well respected, and no one dared knock 'em, apart from one silly man called Albie Clark.

Eddie had known Clarky, as he was better known, for many years. An arrogant piece of shit, Clarky had owned a builders' yard in Bromley-by-Bow, but had recently gone skint.

If Eddie had known that Clarky had come to them cap in hand, he'd have warned the boys not to lend him a penny. Gary and Ricky hadn't known who he was, had lent him twenty grand and the bastard had done a runner with it.

'It was a one off, Dad. Everything else has gone smoothly. We would have told you before, but we didn't want to upset you while you were in nick,' Gary explained.

It had taken Eddie only two days to find out where Clarky had done a runner to. He'd sold up, moved to Gloucestershire and had bought a cottage and a garden centre.

Ed took the bit of paper out of his pocket. 'Slow down, Ray, I think it's along 'ere somewhere. This is it, Bluebell Cottage. Don't pull in, hide the motor around the corner.'

Eddie grinned as Clarky's wife Martha answered the front door. Years ago, Martha Riley, as she was then known, had been the local bike in Canning Town. Eddie had shagged her when he was only fourteen years old. She had been thirty when she seduced him and he thought he'd died and gone to heaven. Soon afterwards, both Ronny and Paulie had shafted her too, and Ed immediately lost interest in her. Even as a teenager, he didn't want his brothers' sloppy seconds.

'Hello, Martha. Long time no see.'

'Eddie! What do we owe this pleasure?' Martha squealed in delight.

'I was just passing through the area. I'd heard you'd moved 'ere, so I thought I'd pop in and say hello. Your Albie about, is he?'

Martha gave a naughty giggle. 'He's just called. He'll be

back in ten minutes. Come in, boys. I'll make you a nice cup of tea.'

Eddie sat down at the kitchen table and glanced around. The place was certainly worth a few quid and wasn't the mark of a man on his uppers. 'Cheeky cunt, he ain't short of a few bob,' he whispered to Raymond.

Martha handed them both a mug of tea and smiled as she heard the front door close. 'This is Albie now. He'll be so surprised to see ya, Ed.'

'Hello, Clarky. Nice place you've got here, mate,' Eddie said chirpily, when Albie opened the kitchen door.

Albie Clark's face immediately drained of colour. 'Eddie, I heard you were out. In fact, I was gonna come and see you next week,' he said shakily.

Eddie sipped his tea and grinned. 'What a coincidence! No need now, is there? I've come to see you, me old cocker.'

Gina ended the phone call and jumped up and down with glee. 'I've been in contact with the owner of your property,' the estate agent informed her. 'And he said that he is willing to sell if you up the offer by ten thousand pounds.'

Gina had no doubt that Eddie would stump up the extra cash. He had some grovelling to do, especially after smashing up her new car the other day.

Thinking of their wonderful relationship, Gina grinned. Eddie was everything she had expected him to be and much, much more. Gina hadn't been frightened by Eddie's behaviour the other day. She had known what he was all about from the beginning. The only thing that did frighten her was the strength of her feelings for him. She loved him more than she had ever loved anyone and no matter how bad his temper became, she knew she would always forgive him. Eddie Mitchell was like a class-A drug to her and, whatever happened in the future, she knew she was hooked on him for life.

*   *   *

347

Back in Gloucestershire, Eddie Mitchell stood over Albie Clark with a kettle of boiling water in his hands. Clarky was kneeling on the kitchen floor and quickly covered his face with his arms as he realised what Eddie intended to do.

'Please, Eddie, don't hurt me. I'll pay you back every penny, I promise. I've got five grand upstairs and I can get you the rest by the end of next week.'

Eddie laughed sarcastically. Raymond had taken Martha upstairs, so he and Clarky could talk in private.

'No one mugs me or my sons off. You took a fucking liberty and now you're gonna pay, you cunt.'

Clarky screamed as Eddie poured a couple of splashes of boiling water over his right leg. 'Stop squealing like a school-girl, get your fat arse upstairs and get me that five grand. Don't even think of doing a runner, Clarky, 'cause if you do, I'll kill ya stone dead.'

Jed O'Hara was not in the best of moods. Driving up to Newmarket had been a complete waste of time. He could trot faster himself than the two horses he'd just seen.

'Why didn't you knock the geezer down on the price, Jed?' Sammy asked him. 'If you'd have offered him a grand apiece, we could have took 'em to Southall and flogged 'em for twelve, thirteen-hundred each.'

Jed disagreed. 'Dog's meat, mate. That's all them two nags were fit for, to be chopped up and put in cans of Chum.'

'There's a boozer over there. Let's stop and have a beer,' Sammy suggested.

Jed shook his head. Usually he was up for a beer whatever the time of day, but today he was in a rush to get back.

'What's a matter with you? You've been a miserable bastard all day,' Sammy said.

Jed shrugged. 'I just wanna get home.'

Sammy laughed sarcastically. 'What, to Frankie? You usually can't wait to get away from her.'

Jed stopped at the red traffic light and turned to his cousin.

'I'm clued up, ain't I, Sammy boy. Frankie's been acting really strange recently. She's up to something, I know she is, and I won't rest until I find out what.'

Albie Clark lay on the floor, writhing in agony. He had just given Eddie the five grand and, instead of being grateful, Eddie had chosen to pour the kettle of boiling water over his head.

'I think I'm dying. Call an ambulance,' Albie mumbled. His skin was on fire and he could already feel the blisters forming on his face.

Eddie crouched down next to him. He could see that Albie was on the verge of losing consciousness. 'I'll be back next week for the rest of the dosh. Fifteen grand you owe me, plus an extra five for causing me so much inconvenience. If you don't pay me on time, Clarky, I will douse you in petrol, set you alight and watch you burn. Do you understand me?'

'I promise, I'll pay,' Albie whispered. He could barely speak through pain.

Martha screamed when she ran into the kitchen and saw the state of her husband. His face was red raw and his shirt was stuck to his body.

'Help me, Martha,' Albie croaked.

Raymond came flying down the stairs with his hands over his groin. 'Sorry, Ed, she kicked me in the bollocks and got away.'

Martha picked up a frying pan and lunged towards Eddie. 'What have you done to him, you bastard? Look at his face! You're an animal, Mitchell.'

'I'm sorry, Martha. He knocked me for money, so he had to be taught a lesson,' Eddie said, grabbing the frying pan out of her hands.

'Whether he owes you money or not, he don't deserve to be disfigured for life, does he? Get out of my house,' Martha yelled.

'I'll be back next week for the rest of my dough,' Eddie said, pushing Raymond towards the front door.

'Give us that frying pan,' Martha said, chasing after Eddie.

Eddie handed it to the distraught woman and laughed. 'I suppose there's little chance of a bunk-up for old time's sake, is there, sweetheart?'

Frankie's heart turned over when she returned home from picking Georgie up from school. Jed had told her he wouldn't be back until teatime, so something must be wrong.

Petrified in case he had found the tape recorder, Frankie walked nervously into the trailer. 'I didn't expect you back yet. How did you get on in Newmarket? Sorry about the state of the place, I'm gonna do the housework in a minute,' she gabbled.

Jed sat on the sofa with a can of lager in his hand and a smirk on his face. He could sense Frankie's nervousness. His premonition was right; she was definitely up to no good, the bitch. 'I thought you were doing the housework this morning. That's why you wanted me out of the way early, wasn't it?' he asked sarcastically.

'I didn't get time in the end. Georgie wouldn't eat any breakfast and by the time I got some down her and got Harry dressed, it was time to drive to the school.'

Jed stood up and ordered Georgie to take her brother into the bedroom. 'Go and play with your toys while I talk to your mum, there's a good girl.'

Frankie felt incredibly apprehensive as Jed kicked the bedroom door shut and walked towards her. 'What are you doing? What am I meant to have done?' she asked, as he pushed her up against the fridge.

Jed stood an inch away from her. His breath was hot and it stank of cigarettes and beer. 'You're up to something and I wanna know what it is,' he snarled.

Frankie could feel her legs shaking. 'I don't know what you're talking about, Jed, I swear I don't.'

Enjoying her fear, Jed grabbed her around the neck. He smirked and gently squeezed her windpipe. 'If I ever find out you've been out with another bloke, I will take the kids away from you and you will never see 'em again.'

'I swear I've never even looked at another bloke since I've been with you,' Frankie said honestly.

Frankie breathed a gentle sigh of relief as Jed released his grip on her and walked away. He was barking up the wrong tree, and as long as he hadn't found the tape recorder, nothing else mattered.

Over in rural Essex, Gina ran to the front door and threw her arms around Eddie's neck. 'The estate agent called today. I tried to ring you, but your phone was switched off. The owner wants to sell, but he wants ten thousand more. Can we still buy it, Eddie? Please say yes.'

Eddie picked Gina up and carried her into the living room. Usually there was nothing more Ed liked than bartering over a deal, but on this occasion he couldn't be arsed. If Gina was desperate for him to buy this property, then he wasn't going to balls it up by refusing the old couple's asking price. Ed put her down on the sofa and gently manoeuvred himself on top of her.

'I've had a rethink, I don't really wanna buy it now,' he lied.

'Why? What's changed your mind?'

'Them people in the local pub that were calling me a murderer. How dare they be so callous? We're gonna have to move further out than here,' Eddie said, laughing.

Gina playfully punched him. Ed could be such a joker at times. 'So, it's a yes, then? Can I ring the estate agent back in the morning?'

'Of course it's a yes. And my pal's coming to take your car tomorrow to fix it,' Eddie replied.

Gina hugged him and stroked his short dark hair.

'What's for dinner? I'm starving,' Eddie said, leaping up.

'Salmon steaks and salad. Shall I prepare it now?' Gina offered.

Eddie nodded and followed her out into the kitchen.

'So, how was your day?' Gina asked.

Opening a bottle of red wine, Eddie poured two glasses and

handed one to Gina. When he had been with Jessica he had rarely talked about his business, but with Gina, he felt he could open up to her a little bit more. Jessica had been quite naive, whereas Gina was much more clued up about what went on in his world.

'I went to see that geezer down in Gloucestershire, you know the one that owed me money.'

'Oh, that's right, yeah. He owed you quite a bit, didn't he? Did he pay you all right?'

Thinking of the mess he'd left Albie Clark's face in, Eddie sniggered. 'Oh, he paid all right. In more ways than one.'

CHAPTER THIRTY-SEVEN

Frankie sat on the sofa and stared aimlessly at the TV. Concentrating on the actual programme was an impossibility – she had far too much on her mind.

Jed had just popped next door to Sammy's and had taken the kids in there with him. He had barely spoken to her at all this morning and, as Frankie mulled over her fucked-up life, she suddenly realised that she no longer loved him. As she thought back over their relationship, she finally admitted to herself that things hadn't been right for years. Jed's affair with Sally, the beatings she'd received at his hands, his recent deception, which she was yet to find out the truth about: everything had now taken its toll and this time there was no going back.

Frankie stared at her handbag. She had retrieved the tape recorder from the Shogun last night and couldn't wait to listen to it. As soon as Jed and Sammy went off to work, she would take Georgie to school, then drive straight over to Kerry's so they could hear the evidence together. It didn't matter that Harry would also be there. He had only just turned three and was far too young to understand what was going on, or what a bastard his father was.

Leaving Jed was not going to be easy. He'd threatened on numerous occasions that he'd never let her take the kids away from him. 'Them chavvies belong to me and don't you ever forget that. If you ever took 'em away from me, I'll snatch 'em back and make sure you never set eyes on 'em again,' he'd warned.

Spotting Jed coming out of Sammy's trailer, Frankie sighed. Proof was what she needed, proof of his indiscretions and, surely, once she had that in her hands, he would have to set her free.

Over in Rainham, Stanley was distraught. Ernie and Ethel were his two favourite pigeons; he'd had them since they were squabs. This morning, Stanley had gone down to the shed at the usual time and found Ernie lying at the bottom of his coop. Stone cold, he was. He'd obviously croaked it in the night.

Ethel had a forlorn look about her and, as Stanley picked her up to stroke her, he could have sworn he saw tears in her eyes. Ernie had been her mate and Stanley was worried that without him, Ethel would pine and probably die too.

'What am I gonna do, Joycie? Ethel looks ill. I think I'm gonna have to bring her indoors so I can keep me eye on her.'

Joyce didn't need one of Stanley's dramas this morning. She was due to meet Eddie at lunchtime and had enough on her plate without worrying about some poxy pigeon. She turned to her husband. 'I ain't having them dirty bastard birds in here. Stick Ethel in with one of the others. Put her in with Willie.'

Stanley shook his head furiously. 'Ethel and Ernie were two of a kind, Joycie. She loved him like I did. She hates Willie. She tried to tear his feathers out once.'

'Well, she'll have to tear 'em out again, 'cause she ain't bleedin' coming in 'ere, shitting and stinking.'

Stanley flung open the kitchen door, turned around and glared at his wife. 'You are one nasty, cold-hearted woman at times, do you know that, Joycie? Anyone else would be sympathetic, but not you. You've got a heart of fucking stone.'

Joyce winced as he slammed the door behind him. If Stanley was annoyed by the lack of sympathy she had shown to his dead pigeon, good job he didn't know who she was meeting today.

Feeling on edge, Joyce took the bottle of brandy out of the cupboard and poured a small shot. Whatever the outcome of today, Stanley must never find out that she'd met up with Eddie. If he did, there'd be murders.

Frankie gave a half-smile as she handed the tape recorder to Kerry. Kerry's sister had gone shopping in Basildon and had taken the boys with her, so it was just the two of them, along with Harry, who was busy playing with his teddy bear.

Kerry stared at the play button. 'I dunno about you, Frankie, but I need a glass of wine first. Do you want one?'

Feeling her stomach churning, Frankie nodded. Both girls sipped their drinks in silence.

'So what are you gonna do if you find out that Sammy is the father of Julie's baby? I had a chat on the quiet to my brother Gary the other day about your predicament. He reckons that if Sammy goes to court, you're gonna have to give him access to the boys, whether he's got a secret family or not,' Frankie said, breaking the ice.

Kerry nodded. 'I know that, but I still need to know the truth. The thing is, Frankie, I have a lot on Sammy. I know loads about his dodgy dealings and stuff. If I find out that that kid ain't his, then I'll probably let him see the boys once a week. But if that kid is his, then he ain't seeing 'em and if I have to, I'll resort to blackmail.'

'What exactly you got on him, then?'

Not wanting Harry to hear what she was about to say, Kerry turned up the volume on the TV and moved closer to Frankie.

'Sammy and Jed ain't what you think they are, Frankie. They rob people, mainly old people.'

Frankie looked at her in horror. 'What do you mean, they rob old people?'

Kerry shrugged. 'I've overheard 'em talking. I confronted Sammy once and he sort of admitted it. All I know is they target old people who live alone and then they con them out of their life savings. They call it grunting and I think, apart from selling the odd horse or ringing the odd motor, that's how they earn all their money now.'

Frankie was appalled. 'I can't believe it. How could anyone be so callous?'

Kerry put an arm around her friend. 'Surely you must have had your suspicions? I know I did. I mean, Sammy and Jed have always got plenty of dough, and all these weekends they say they're working away, you can bet your bottom dollar they're out partying and shagging. Apart from conning people, I don't think they work at all now, Frankie. They used to, but I think the gavvers started sniffing around that yard they were renting and Jed's dad urged 'em to lay low for a while.'

Thinking of her own grandparents, Frankie shuddered. What sort of bloke was she living with? 'So, how do they rob 'em? They don't burgle them or beat 'em up and stuff, do they?'

Kerry shook her head. 'I think they tend to target people who ain't got no close family. They befriend 'em and do odd jobs for 'em and stuff. Sammy admitted to me that one old boy signed his house over to him and Jed recently. There was another one that died last year and left them all of his money. I think they'd made him write a will.'

'Mummy, I'm thirsty.'

Frankie was in shock as she picked up her son. 'Let's get you a drink and you can play in the garden,' she whispered.

Frankie left the back door open and returned to the living room. 'Why didn't you tell me all this before?'

Kerry held her arms out in protest. 'I'm sorry, Frankie. You were so happy with Jed and I was happy with Sammy; there seemed no point in telling you. I also thought that you probably knew but, like me, you never said anything out of loyalty. Things are different now, though, aren't they? It's me and you against the world.'

Desperate to find out exactly what sort of animal Jed really was, Frankie picked up the tape recorder and pressed play.

*   *   *

Joyce sat nervously in the Bull in Romford. Part of her now wished that she had never arranged to meet up with Eddie, as all she could think about was Jessica.

Jessica had once been Joycie's reason for living. Desperate for her daughter to lead a life of luxury and not end up in a council house like she had, Joyce had been overjoyed when Jessica first brought Eddie home.

Eddie was everything that Stanley wasn't. Tall, handsome, rich and exciting, from the first moment Jessica had met him, Joyce had binned all her Mills & Boon books and had lived her daughter's romance with her. Everything had been perfect until that tragedy of all tragedies and now, sitting alone in the pub, her daughter's murder was all she could think about. Overcome by sad memories, Joyce didn't notice Eddie stroll towards her.

'Hello, Joycie. What would you like to drink?'

As Joyce came face to face with Eddie for the first time in years, she found she could barely breathe. Prison hadn't altered him. He was dressed stylishly, was as handsome as ever and the only sign of his life behind bars was the odd grey fleck in his short, dark hair.

Joyce's voice shook as she answered him. 'I'll have a glass of white wine, please,' she whispered.

Eddie got the drinks, returned to the table and gave her an awkward peck on the cheek. 'You look ever so well, Joycie. How's Stanley these days?' he asked politely.

Joyce took a very large gulp of wine to help her find her voice. She could see that Eddie also felt apprehensive and she wanted to put him at ease.

'Brain damage he is. Done my bleeding head in this morning, he did. Do you remember that pigeon you bought him? He called it Ernie.'

Eddie nodded. 'I bought him two and he called the other one Ethel, didn't he?'

Joyce nodded. 'Well, Ernie croaked it last night. Anyone would think it was me that had popped me clogs, the way Stanley's behaving this morning.'

Eddie laughed. He had also been nervous about seeing Joyce again and was pleased she had broken the ice. 'Are you hungry? Shall I get us a menu?'

Joyce shook her head. 'I'm not hungry, but I wouldn't say no to another glass of wine. Then we'll have a chat, there's stuff we need to talk about.'

Frankie and Kerry stared at one another. Both their faces were filled with frustration as neither could believe that their wonderful plan had failed.

'What a waste of fucking time that was. Where did you hide it, Frankie?'

'In the back, behind the plastic interior on the door.'

Kerry let out a deep sigh. They had just listened to ten minutes of silence, half an hour of muffled voices, of which they couldn't understand a word and then twenty minutes of Tammy Wynette. The only clear thing they had heard was Tammy singing 'Stand By Your Man', which seemed kind of ironic, considering the circumstances.

Agitated, Kerry poured herself another glass of wine. 'You're gonna have to do it again, but this time you need to put it in the front of the motor.'

'I can't do that. Jed's bound to find it in the front. He tried to strangle me the other night, Kerry. Can you imagine what he'd do if he knows I've set him up?'

'It's a chance you're gonna have to take. We're never gonna find out the truth if it's hidden behind the bloody interior. It's too far away to get a clear recording, Frankie.'

Frankie shrugged. 'The only place I can think of in the front is the glove compartment, and I can't put it in there, as Jed is always opening it.'

Kerry's eyes shone as she picked up Harry's teddy bear and waved it at Frankie. 'Take out some of the stuffing, put it in here and then shove it under the passenger seat. Jed will just think Harry's left one of his toys in the car; he won't clock on, I know he won't.'

Frankie felt uncomfortable. 'How am I gonna fit it in there?'

Kerry ran out to the kitchen and returned with some scissors and a needle and cotton. 'Give us it here. I'll do it and I'll leave a small gap so you can put your hand in to press "record".'

Frankie said nothing as her friend cut open Harry's teddy bear. Once Kerry got a bee in her bonnet there was just no stopping her.

Eddie Mitchell felt emotional and uncomfortable as he apologised to Joycie. He couldn't not mention Jessica's murder, he had to say something.

'I am so sorry, Joycie. I loved Jessica just as much as you did, you know that much is true.'

Seeing the sad expression in Eddie's eyes, Joyce squeezed his hand. 'It's OK. I know it was an accident. Let's not talk about it, eh?'

Relieved to be able to change the subject, Eddie asked Joyce about Frankie. 'Have you seen her or spoken to her lately?' he enquired.

Joyce shook her head. 'I haven't heard from her for a few weeks. Between me and you, Eddie, I don't think she's happy with that Jed. She won't admit it, but I can tell and, as for the kids, have you seen Georgie since you've been out?'

'No. Why?'

'I'm sure there's something wrong with her, Ed. She hates being indoors, gorges on food and then doesn't eat for days, and whenever she stays with me and Stanley, she never sleeps of a night. Last time she stopped over, I never slept a wink. I'm sure she's got issues, or maybe it's just the bloody gypsy in her.'

Eddie was bemused. Gary and Ricky had also mentioned Georgie's unusual behaviour recently, but he hadn't taken too much notice of their comments. When Georgie was a baby, Frankie had brought her up to visit him in prison, but towards the end of his sentence, she had only come alone or brought Harry with her.

359

'How's little Harry doing?'

'He's a lovely little boy. He's got such a sweet nature and with his blond hair and blue eyes, he reminds me so much of Jess and Joey when they were his age. Haven't you seen Frankie since you got out, Ed? Why haven't you visited the kids? Is it because of Jed?' Joyce asked.

'Frankie ain't talking to me, Joycie. I was gonna pop round there this weekend to try and sort things out with her, but Jed's there, apparently. If I come face to face with him, I dunno what I might do and I don't wanna end up back in nick, do I?'

Joyce took a sip of her wine. The sadness she'd felt earlier had now faded and she was rather enjoying Eddie's company. It was good to be able to discuss her grandchildren with somebody other than Stanley. Her husband was often more interested in his poxy pigeons than he was in his family.

'So, why have you fallen out with Frankie? Last time I saw her she said that you and her were getting on well.'

Eddie shifted uncomfortably in his chair. He was dreading telling Joycie about Gina, but he knew it would be better coming from him than Frankie or somebody else.

'Last weekend, Gary and Ricky organised a meal for me up in Canning Town. It was no celebration, just a family get-together for me old aunts, brothers and uncles. Anyway, I took a woman with me. It's not what you think, Joycie. Gina her name is, she stood up for me in court and she's been a really good friend to me since. Well, to cut a long story short, Gary and Ricky never told me that Frankie was coming. If I'd have known she was gonna be there, I wouldn't have taken Gina in the first place. Course, Frankie's walked in and kicked off good and proper. You know what a temper she's got on her, don't you? Fucking embarrassing it was. She called my friend Gina an old tart and all sorts. Actually, the night was a disaster from start to finish. Paulie kicked off, Ronny got pissed and fell out of his wheelchair. A usual Mitchell night out, if you know what I mean.'

Joyce gave a half-smile. The mention of Gina had thrown

her a bit, but she had agreed to meet Eddie because there was something important she wanted to discuss with him.

'Do you know the main reason why I came here to meet you, Eddie?'

Eddie clicked his fingers at the barmaid. 'Can you bring us over another bottle of wine, sweetheart?' he asked.

He had a feeling that he wasn't going to like what Joyce had to say. He turned to face her. 'What's on your mind?'

Joyce held his stare. 'After everything that's happened, I want you to do something for me.'

'What?'

'I want you to make things up with Joey.'

Eddie looked at Joyce as though she was mad. 'No way. I've disowned him. That boy is no son of mine. The thought of what he is makes me wanna puke every time I think of it. I can't stomach it. I'm sorry, but I can't handle it, Joycie.'

Joycie had pre-planned her speech in bed last night and as she leaned towards Eddie, she didn't hold back. 'If I can forgive you for murdering my only daughter, why can't you forgive Joey for being gay? He is a wonderful boy, Eddie, a real credit to you. His boyfriend Dominic is a lovely lad and also has a heart of gold. They are always round at ours and, without their support, I don't think I would have ever got over Jessica's death. Being gay isn't a crime. Them two boys love one another and if you won't do it for my sake, I want you to do it for Jessica's memory. Jess loved that boy and she would be so upset by your behaviour, Ed, she really would.'

Eddie looked down at his feet. He would do anything to please Joyce, anything but this. 'I saw Joey last week. I was in a pub in Rettendon and he was in there with that Dominic. He ran off and I chased him and called him, but he just bolted, Joycie.'

'Well, can you blame him? I know what you did to that poor Dominic, Eddie, and you were bang out of order. Joey never told me, Frankie did. How could you do that, eh? How could you terrorise that poor lad?'

Eddie couldn't look Joyce in the eye. She was staring at him like his headmaster used to and he had no answers for her.

'I don't know why I did it. I just can't handle Joey being a poof, I suppose. I can't believe a son of mine has turned out that way – it's unbelievable.'

Joyce smiled at the barmaid as she brought the wine over, then turned accusingly back to Eddie. 'I am willing to forgive you, Eddie, for all that you've done, but if you don't make things right with that boy, I swear I will never speak to you again. If you loved my Jessica as much as you say you did, then you will swallow your pride and do it for her.'

'I don't even know where he lives and I ain't got no phone number for him,' Eddie mumbled.

Fishing through her handbag, Joyce waved a piece of paper in front of him. 'Joey and Dominic are living in South Woodham Ferrers. That's their address and don't you dare let me down.'

Unusually for him, Eddie was suddenly overcome with remorse. Joycie's words had hit a nerve and he felt pure guilt flowing through his veins. Joycie was right, Jessica would be disgusted over the way he had treated Joey. Aware that his eyes were welling up with tears, Eddie grabbed the piece of paper off Joycie and stood up.

'I'd better be going now. Do you want me to give you a lift home?' he asked, trying to keep the emotion out of his voice.

Joyce shook her head. Her speech had hit him like a ton of bricks, she knew that, and she was thrilled for her Jessica's sake. As Eddie bent down to kiss her goodbye, Joyce grabbed his hand.

'Another thing, please don't treat me like some silly old fool, Eddie. I know you have feelings for this Gina woman, I saw it in your eyes. Just do what I've asked you to do and you have my blessing to move on with your life, OK?'

Eddie paused before answering. 'OK, I'll sort it.'

CHAPTER THIRTY-EIGHT

Frankie lifted the net curtain and watched with interest as Jed got into the passenger's side of Sammy's truck. Jed usually drove everywhere, but had said something about going to check on the horses. Frankie smiled. With Jed and Sammy out of the way, she had the perfect opportunity to put the plan into action.

Georgie had already gone to school, and Frankie felt incredibly guilty, as Harry kept asking after his favourite teddy bear, which had been operated on and was now hidden in the boot of her car.

'You must have left it over Kerry's, darling. Mummy will go and get it for you next week,' she lied. Harry was an angel. She had told him not to tell his dad that they regularly went to visit Kerry and he never had. It was as though he knew the score in his own little way.

Frankie checked on her son and was pleased to see him playing happily on his bedroom floor with some plastic building blocks. She ran out to the car, opened the boot and took the teddy out of the plastic bag. Something didn't feel right about this. Kerry had done her best, but the tape recorder showed clearly through the bear.

Frankie went inside the trailer and chewed on her fingernails. If she hid it under the passenger seat in the Shogun and Jed or Sammy picked it up, they would definitely notice the bulge in the bear and all hell would break loose. Desperate not to get herself caught, Frankie racked her brain for an answer.

'Got ya,' she mumbled, as she caught sight of Harry's Postman Pat lunchbox on the table.

Kerry was no expert with a needle and cotton and Frankie easily unpicked the loose stitching with her hands. She took out the tape recorder, placed it inside the lunchbox, then covered it with one of Harry's T-shirts.

Frankie pressed the record button, shut the lid and turned up the TV. The box was plastic and there was a small gap where it closed, so hopefully it could still pick up the sound.

Keeping an eye out in case Jed returned, Frankie sewed the teddy bear up, stopped the tape and played it back. The recording was crap. She couldn't hear anything clearly – it was muffled.

Desperate for an answer, Frankie opened the kitchen cupboard. Spotting Jed's masking tape, she grabbed it and took a pair of scissors out of the drawer.

Feeling pleased with herself, Frankie ran out to the Shogun. Jed never locked his motor; there was no need to where they lived. She opened the door, put the tape recorder under the passenger seat and secured it with masking tape. All she had to do now was press 'record' when Jed was going out next and pray that he played into her hands.

Over in Rettendon, Gina was worried about Eddie. Today, he wasn't his usual vibrant self and had barely said a word to her since breakfast this morning. Concerned that he was having second thoughts about their relationship, Gina made her way into the lounge and sat down opposite him.

'What's the matter, Ed? I know you've got something on your mind. It's not something I've done, is it?'

Eddie held out his arms. 'Of course it ain't nothing you've done. Come and give us a cuddle and I'll tell you all about it.'

Relieved that whatever was on his mind was nothing to do with her, Gina snuggled up next to him. Eddie kissed her lovingly on the forehead.

'I went to see Joycie, Jessica's mum, yesterday. I had to see her, I wanted to apologise face to face. Anyway, she was OK with me, but she gave me a right bollocking over Joey. She reckons I'm bang out of order for the way I've treated him and she made me promise to sort things out for the sake of Jessica's memory.'

'And what are you going to do?' Gina asked softly. She knew that finding out that his son was gay had been awfully diffi-cult for Eddie to deal with. In her job, she had heard of similar situations in the past, and men like Eddie could never accept homosexuality in their families.

Eddie shook his head. 'I dunno. Joycie knows me and you are together, I think. I mentioned you a couple of times and she sort of clocked on. She said as long as I make up with Joey, she's OK about us. She also said if she can forgive me for murdering Jessica, then I can forgive Joey for being gay.'

Gina squeezed his hand. 'Joyce sounds like a lovely woman and she has got a point, Ed. Being homosexual isn't a crime, especially in this day and age. I have a couple of male gay friends and they are the nicest people you could ever meet. Why don't you find out where Joey's living and go and see him? I'd offer to come with you, but under the circumstances, it would probably be a bad move.'

'I've got his address, Joycie gave it to me. No wonder he was in that boozer the other day, he's only living in South Woodham Ferrers.'

Gina smiled. 'Why don't you go there now? There's no guar-antee he'll be indoors, but it's worth a try. He doesn't work on a Saturday, does he?'

Eddie shrugged. 'I don't think so. To be honest, I don't know much about him any more. I think he's got an office job up town or something, but I ain't sure what he does now. Last I heard he was in the post room or something.'

Gina stood up and handed Eddie his car keys. 'Come on. Go now and while you're gone, I'll prepare us a nice seafood pasta.'

Eddie reluctantly stood up. 'I shouldn't be long. Wish me luck, I think I'm gonna need it.'

*   *   *

365

Frankie smiled as Harry clambered onto her lap with his patched-up teddy bear in his hand.

'Love you, Mummy,' he told her.

Georgie moved away from her father and threw her arms around Frankie's neck. 'I love you too, Mummy.'

'You wouldn't if you had to put up with what I put up with,' Jed muttered.

Frankie ignored Jed's nasty comment.

'Aren't you going out again?' she asked him.

'Yeah, in a bit. Me and Sammy are going for a beer with me dad and me brothers.'

'What time are you leaving? Are you driving or is Sammy?'

Jed laughed. 'What are you, a fucking gavver? I'm driving and I'll leave when I'm good and ready.'

Minutes later, Jed stood up and cockily sauntered towards the shower. Frankie stared at his back. She was still recovering from the shock of finding out that he conned old people out of their life savings. If only she could get that on tape as well, she could blackmail the bastard when she left him. If she threatened to go to the police with her evidence, he would surely have to leave her and the kids alone.

Frankie waited until she heard him turn the water on and sneaked outside. It was time to press the record button.

Terry Baldwin smiled as his daughter handed him a mug of coffee. He often popped round to visit Sally and his grandson and even though he didn't understand the unusual relationship she had with Jed, he accepted it for her sake.

'So, have you told Jed yet?' he asked her.

Sally shook her head. 'I'm seeing him tomorrow. He's coming round for dinner so I'll tell him then.'

As Sally rambled on about baby names, Terry studied his daughter carefully. Sally was happy at the moment, Terry knew that. In the past she had suffered from terrible depression, but ever since Jed had come back into her life, she had been fine.

'Why don't you get Jed to move in here with you? It will

be difficult bringing up two kids on your own,' Terry urged her.

Sally had never told her father that Jed still lived with Frankie. He wouldn't agree with the set-up, it wasn't his style. 'We're happy as we are, Dad. Jed likes living in his trailer and I like living here. He's very set in his ways and so am I, but we're happy. Surely that's all that matters, ain't it?'

Terry nodded. Sally was right, and as long as she was happy, then so was he.

Over in South Woodham, Joey and Dominic were sitting in the garden, enjoying the last of the summer.

'Isn't it hot, considering it's October?' Dominic said.

Joey nodded and smiled. 'I love living out here, it's so bloody peaceful.'

Dominic leaned across and kissed Joey gently on the lips. 'Shall I get us another beer?'

'Yeah, go on,' Joey replied, as Madonna began yapping like mad.

Dominic stood up. 'I think I heard the doorbell.'

Joey nodded. 'It's probably Anne from next door. I saw her this morning and she said that she was baking us another cake.'

Dominic whistled as he followed Madonna into the hallway. She looked so cute when she barked and, if she wasn't wearing her pink bow, she might have even looked vicious.

'Stop barking,' Dominic said as he picked her up. He opened the door and dropped the dog in shock. 'Go away. Leave us alone,' he shouted, as he tried to shut the door.

Eddie jammed his foot into the door. 'Please, listen to me. I haven't come here to cause any trouble. I just need to speak to Joey, it's important.'

Dominic felt his legs begin to buckle and grabbed hold of the staircase to support himself.

Eddie felt awkward as the snarling Chihuahua flew at him. 'Get off me, will you?' he said, as it clung to his trouser leg. Feeling it nip his right ankle, he picked it up and held its head so it couldn't bite him again. He then handed it back to the quivering Dominic.

'I ain't gonna hurt you, I promise. Now, where's Joey?'

'In the garden,' Dom stammered.

Eddie walked through to the kitchen. He could see Joey lying on a sun lounger through the window and he felt incredibly nervous as he walked towards him.

'Hello, son.'

Joey jumped out of his chair. 'Who told you where I lived? What have you done to Dominic?'

As Joey backed away from him, Eddie was upset by the fear in his son's eyes. For years, Eddie had enjoyed the impact he had on people that had wronged him, but not his own son.

'I just want to talk to you, Joey. I haven't touched Dominic, I swear I haven't.'

'Where is he, then?' Joey asked accusingly.

Dominic, who had been on the verge of passing out, had now managed to pull himself together and was watching the reunion from the window. Hearing Joey call his name, he ran outside, clutching Madonna in his arms.

'It's OK, Joey. Your dad hasn't touched me. He just wants to talk to you.'

'I've got nothing to say to him,' Joey said coldly.

'Joey, he's your dad. Just listen to what he's got to say,' Dom replied sternly.

Eddie glanced at Dominic gratefully. 'Actually, I want to talk to both of you. I need to apologise for my behaviour in the past. Let's go inside. I could murder a beer, if you've got any spare.'

'That's not all you could murder. You murdered my mum,' Joey screamed.

As Joey's eyes welled up, Dominic took charge of the situation. 'There's beers in the fridge. Go and sit in the lounge while I speak to him,' Dominic told Eddie.

Annoyed by his own tactless turn of phrase, Eddie cracked open a can of lager and sat on the sofa. Joey hated him, he could see it in his eyes. Even the dog despised him and had tried to fucking bite him.

Dominic put Madonna on the grass and held Joey tenderly in his arms.

'I don't want him here. He killed my mum,' Joey said tearfully.

'Sssh, it's OK. Listen, you have to pull yourself together and talk to him, Joey. He's your dad, he knows where we live and if you don't speak to him today, he'll come back another time. Just hear him out, see what he has to say for himself.'

Joey shook his head. 'I can't. I hate him.'

Dominic decided to try the firm approach. 'Look, I know what your dad did was awful, but I also know that it was an accident. I read the newspapers, Joey, and every article said how much he had loved your mum. Being bitter is not going to help you move on in the long run. Nothing can bring your mum back and I'm sure if she is looking down, she would want you to speak to your dad and, if possible, forgive him.'

'Do you really think that? But what about what he did to you?'

Dominic shrugged. 'OK, I was frightened at the time, but he only really threatened me, Joey. I know he made a little cut on my you-know-what, but I don't think he would have taken things any further. Let's both go inside and have a sensible conversation with him, eh? I'm willing to forget about the past and, even though it's more difficult for you, because of your mum, you have to try to let go of it as well.'

Joey nodded and stood up. 'OK, but if he starts or says anything abusive about me or you, I will never speak to him again.'

Apart from waiting for the jury to deliver their verdict, Eddie Mitchell could never remember feeling more on edge in his life as when Joey walked into the lounge. 'You've got a nice place here. Is it rented?' he asked awkwardly.

Dominic brought in a case of beers. 'We've bought it, actually. Shall I leave yous two to speak in private?'

369

'No,' Joey said immediately.

Eddie smiled at Dominic. 'Sit down. You're Joey's partner, so you should also listen to what I have to say.'

'What do you want to say, then?' Joey asked, stroking Madonna's head. She didn't like his dad; she was obviously a good judge of character and kept snarling.

Eddie cleared his throat. He shouldn't really tell Joey that he'd met up with Joyce in case he told Stanley, but knowing how close Joyce had always been to her grandson, he knew he wouldn't get his nan into trouble.

'I've come here today because I want to try and make things right between us again. I saw your nan yesterday, we met and spoke for ages. Please don't tell your grandad, as you'll get her into trouble. She thinks the world of both you and Dominic and she kind of made me see sense. I want to apologise for the way I've treated you in the past. You seem very happy together and although I can't even pretend to understand your preferences, I really do wish you all the happiness in the world.'

Joey nodded. 'What about Mum?'

Eddie stared at his son. The hurt in his eyes was clear to see and, unusually for Eddie, he broke down. 'I'm so sorry, Joey. I loved her so much, I really did. Your mum was my life and when she died a part of me died as well.'

Joey had rarely seen his father cry before; he hadn't even believed Eddie was capable of showing such emotion.

'If only you hadn't tried to kill Jed. I hate that Jed – this is all his fault. If Frankie hadn't got with him none of this would have happened.'

With all the emotion in the room affecting her, Madonna decided to join in with a howl.

Eddie laughed at the dog's antics and wiped his eyes. He felt stupid, really stupid. How could a big macho geezer like himself sit here blubbing in front of two gay lads and a dog with a pink bow around its neck?

'What's the dog's name?' he asked politely.

370

Dominic smiled. 'She's called Madonna, after the singer. Joey chose it, he likes her music.'

'Have you seen Frankie? She said she was going out for a meal with you, but I wasn't happy about it, so we haven't spoken since,' Joey asked his dad.

Eddie thought about lying, but quickly decided against it. Joey and Frankie were bound to speak at some point soon, so it would be better to mention Gina now if he wanted to start with a clean slate.

'The meal was awkward, Joey. I didn't know that Frankie was coming and I took a woman with me; she's a friend. Frankie got the wrong end of the stick, which I don't blame her for. She walked out and we haven't spoken since.'

'Is that the woman you was in the pub with?' Joey asked.

Eddie nodded. Best he didn't mention that Gina was a private detective and was the one he had hired out of the Yellow Pages to follow Joey and Dominic to confirm their relationship.

'She stood up for me in court. Her name's Gina and she's a very nice lady, Joey. No one will ever replace your mum, but it's nice to have a bit of female companionship, if nothing else.'

Seeing his dad in a slightly different light, Joey nodded. 'I won't be annoyed if you like Gina. Mum's been dead for ages now and you should try and move on with your life if you can.'

Eddie was shocked by his son's sensible attitude. 'Thank you, Joey. That means a lot to me.'

Dominic cracked open some more beers and handed them out. 'So, are you living locally, Eddie? We saw you in the Bell, didn't we?'

Eddie nodded. It was too soon to tell Joey he was living with Gina. 'I'm renting a pal's place in Rettendon. What about yous two? What made you move out here?'

Dominic smiled. 'We got sick of living in London. We both work up town and it's nice to have a bit of peace and quiet for a change.'

Eddie sipped his beer. Joycie was right, Dominic was a nice

lad and very sensible. He turned to Joey. 'Are you still working in the post room?'

Joey laughed. 'I'm in the Stock Exchange now, I'm only a junior, but I love it. Dom got me the job and I'm doing really well at it.'

Eddie was impressed. Joey working in the Stock Exchange was something he would never have predicted.

'And what about Frankie? I was shocked to find out she was pregnant again. She's so young to be a mother of three. Is she happy, Joey? Does Jed treat her OK?'

Joey shrugged. 'I hate him, Dad, I always have done. I've always sort of blamed him more than you for mum's death and even before that I never liked him. He's flash, loud, uncouth and I don't think Frankie's been happy with him for ages. She even sort of admitted it to me once.'

Dominic stood up. 'I do a mean stir-fry, Eddie. Are you hungry?'

Eddie shook his head. Gina was cooking and he didn't want to outstay his welcome. 'I'd better be going soon. Gina is cooking me dinner tonight.'

'Is she staying at yours?' Joey asked, as Dominic left the room.

'Will you be upset with me if I say she is?' Eddie replied.

Joey shook his head. 'No, but I'd want and expect you to be honest with me.'

Eddie smiled. 'OK, I'll tell you the truth. When I was inside, Gina was a friend and started to visit me after my court hearing. As the years passed, I began to have feelings for her. They wasn't feelings like I had for your mum – I will never feel that way about any woman again – but I do like Gina very much. I'm not good on my own, Joey, so Gina rented the cottage in Rettendon for us to live after my release.'

Joey was surprised by not only the intensity of the conversation he was having with his father, but also his sudden willingness to forgive him.

'I'm pleased for you if you've found some happiness, Dad.

I was broken-hearted that time when Dom and I split up. I felt so lonely without him.'

Eddie ran his hands through his hair. It had been his fault that Joey and Dominic had split up that time and he was now full of remorse.

'I'm so sorry for reacting the way I did over your sexuality. I was naive, immature and stupid. Dominic is a really nice guy, I like him very much and I'm pleased that he makes you so happy. I never thought that I'd say this, Joey, but I am so proud of you for how you've turned out. You've got a good job, a lovely home, a sensible partner and I'm proud to call you my son.'

With tears in his eyes, Joey stood up and hugged his father. 'Thank you. Your acceptance of the way I am was all I ever wanted. You always seemed closer to Frankie and I was closer to Mum. I thought you wanted me to act and be like Gary and Ricky, but I could only ever be me, Dad.'

Eddie held his son tightly. They hadn't ever spoken like this and it felt so bloody good to do so.

'I'm sorry I made you feel that way, boy, but I always loved you as much as the others, I swear I did. I had this macho thing going on, and I suppose, in that thick head of mine, I wanted you to turn out like me. I can honestly say now, after everything that's happened, I'm glad that you didn't.'

Dominic grinned as he walked back in the room with Madonna in his arms. He was no longer scared of Joey's father – in fact, he rather liked him.

Joey held his arm out to Dom. 'Come on, group hug,' he said.

Eddie laughed, as the dog gave him a lick on the side of his face. If Stuart and the other inmates could see him now, they'd have a field day, he thought. Eddie pulled away from the group hug. 'Listen, I'd better be getting back now. What are yous two doing tomorrow?'

'We've got nothing special planned. We usually just go to a pub for Sunday lunch,' Joey said.

'Why don't you come over to mine for dinner? I'd really like you to meet Gina and you can bring Madonna with you.'

Joey glanced at Dominic who immediately nodded. 'OK, we'd love to.'

CHAPTER THIRTY-NINE

Frankie emptied the can of spaghetti hoops into the saucepan and put them on a low gas. The kids were still outside playing, so it was an ideal opportunity for her to ring Kerry without Georgie earwigging.

Kerry answered immediately. 'Well, did you do it?'

Frankie explained that she had been worried about the bulge in the teddy bear, so had instead secured the tape recorder under the passenger seat with masking tape.

'Jed didn't get back 'til after midnight and he was up and out again early this morning. The tape recorder's still in there, but when he gets back tonight, no matter what time it is, I'll sneak outside and get it.'

'Will you come straight over to me after you've taken Georgie to school tomorrow?' Kerry asked.

'You bet I fucking will.'

Eddie Mitchell was in a rather buoyant mood. His visit to Joey yesterday had gone much better than expected and he could barely believe that in less than an hour his son would be coming over for lunch.

Gina was absolutely thrilled for Eddie. He'd been full of the reunion when he'd arrived home yesterday and she'd enjoyed listening to every single detail. Gina had been busy preparing the lunch all morning and was desperate to make a good impression.

'Pass me the coriander, Ed. It's in the cupboard next to you, on the left-hand side.'

Eddie handed it to her. 'That was Stuart on the phone. He's got his release date through, he gets out the week before Christmas.'

Even though Gina had only ever seen Stuart when she had visited Eddie in prison, she felt as if she knew him personally. 'I am so pleased for him, Ed. I know it's a couple of months away yet, but you'll have to be there to meet him when he comes out.'

'Oh, I will do. Can I ask you a big favour, Gina?'

'Yeah, go on.'

'Is it all right if Stuart stays here in one of the spare rooms for a couple of weeks until he finds his feet? He can't go back to Hackney where his family and friends are because of that rapist he killed, and I can't see him spending Christmas alone.'

Gina wiped her hands on the tea towel, walked over to Eddie and draped her arms around his neck. 'Has anyone ever told you that under that tough exterior of yours, you really are a pussy cat, Mr Mitchell?'

'No, not lately,' Eddie said laughing.

'Well, I'm telling you that you are. And as for Stuart, he is welcome to stay here for as long he wants.'

Eddie held her close and pushed his groin against her. 'I don't 'arf love you. You're one in a million yourself, sweetheart.'

Jed smirked at Sammy as old Mr Franks opened the back door.

'We've done all the jobs you asked us to do. Anything else you need doing?'

Mr Franks shook his head. He had been extremely lonely since the death of his wife, Vera, and he liked having Jed and Sammy around. It was a bit of company for him and they were such lovely boys.

'You got time for a cup of tea and a chat, lads?'

'Yeah, go on. We've got a spare half an hour or so,' Jed replied.

Sammy grinned as Mr Franks stood in the kitchen talking about the war.

'Senile old cunt,' he whispered to Jed, as the old man turned his back.

Jed who had pretended to be riveted by the conversation, gulped down his tea and looked at his watch. 'Can you sort us our money out now? We've got another job to do this afternoon,' he said.

Mr Franks smiled. He had a habit of rambling on, his Vera had always told him that. 'How much do I owe you this time?'

'Five-hundred pound,' Jed replied boldly.

Mr Franks scratched his head. He was sure they only usually charged him a hundred, but he did get things muddled up sometimes. He counted the money out of his savings tin and handed it to Jed.

'Are you coming back again next Sunday?'

'Yep, same time. Same price.'

As Mr Franks stood at the door waving them off, Jed and Sammy got in the Shogun and roared with laughter.

'I only swept the path. What did you do?' Sammy asked his cousin.

'Painted one door,' Jed replied.

'Shall we up the price to a grand next week?' Sammy suggested.

'No. We don't wanna frighten him off. I was chatting to him today while I was painting. He's got a niece who lives in Australia and a nephew that he ain't seen for years that lives in Leeds. Let's keep him sweet and in a couple of weeks we'll get him to make a will, eh?'

Sammy rubbed his hands together. 'Do you think he'll fall for it?'

Jed chuckled. 'With my charm and gentle persuasion, of course he will.'

*   *   *

377

Gina smiled as Eddie formally introduced her to Joey and Dominic. She had taken off the expensive engagement ring Eddie had bought her and replaced it with some costume jewellery.

'It's a pleasure to meet you both, and who is this little darling?' she said, stroking Madonna.

Dominic laughed. 'This is Lady Madonna. Joey and I obviously aren't going to have any kids, so we decided to buy ourselves our very own little baby.'

Eddie led the boys into the lounge and told Gina to pour them some drinks.

'Dinner smells nice. What are we having?' Joey asked.

Eddie laughed. 'Don't ask me, Gina has prepared about five different dishes. There's prawn curry, chicken tikka and Christ knows what else she's cooked.'

Dominic admired the property first and then Gina. 'She seems extremely nice and she's very pretty,' he said.

Eddie looked at Joey and gently squeezed his arm. 'Gina is lovely but, as I said yesterday, no one will ever replace your mum in my eyes.'

Joey put his hand on top of his father's. 'I know that, Dad. I understand, honest I do.'

In another part of Essex, Jed had just been told he was about to become a father yet again.

'Well, say something. You are pleased, aren't you?'

Jed nodded. In a way he was pleased for Luke, as it meant he would have a brother or sister to play with. Looking at it from a different angle, Jed wasn't so chuffed. Sally had no idea that Frankie was also pregnant and he daren't ever let Frankie find out that Sally was up the spout again. Frankie would be bound to blame him, even if he had told her that Sally had a boyfriend.

'Do you want another beer?' Sally asked. She was a bit disappointed by Jed's reaction – he wasn't exactly ecstatic. She handed him a can of Foster's and sat down next to him. 'Are you sure you're OK about it, Jed? I don't want our relationship to suffer because of this. I have been taking the pill, honest I have.'

Jed put his arm around Sally. He guessed that she had stopped taking her contraception on purpose, but wasn't about to say so. 'I'm fine. It's just awkward, you know, having two with you. I wanna leave Frankie, you know I do, but I can't walk away from Georgie and Harry. One day they'll be old enough to make their own choices, then I can leave and they can live with us.'

Sally laid her head on his shoulder. 'I told my dad. He was OK about it.'

Remembering his beating at the hands of Sally's father, Jed pushed her head away and stood up. If Terry Baldwin knew that Sally was pregnant with his child and also found out that Frankie was, he would probably skin him alive.

'What's up? You look ever so white,' Sally said.

'I'm gonna get off, babe. I think I'm coming down with something and I don't want you and Lukey boy to catch it.'

'What about your dinner? I've cooked you a roast chicken.'

Jed bent down and gave her a kiss. 'I'll try and pop round tomorrow and eat it cold if I can. I've gotta go, Sal, I feel as sick as a dog.'

Jed ruffled Lukey boy on the head, opened the door and bolted down the stairs. He was still hiding the Shogun in Tilbury, so he clambered into his old pick-up truck and rang Sammy.

'What's a matter?' Sammy asked.

'I need a drink, a good fucking drink. Tell Julie your aunt's just died and meet me downstairs.'

Sammy smirked. 'OK, give us five minutes.'

Back in Rettendon, the atmosphere was jolly and the drinks were flowing freely.

'That was my funniest Christmas ever, Joey, the one when your nan got pissed and came on to your grandad.'

Joey squealed like a pig and spat his mouthful of drink back into his glass. 'No, she never did! How long ago was that?'

Eddie could barely explain for laughing. 'It was only about five years back. You and Frankie had been out and had already gone to bed, I think. Anyway, Joycie was pissed – slaughtered she was – and her and Stanley went upstairs. Next thing me and your mum heard was a commotion on the landing and then I saw poor Stanley run out the bedroom in his Y-fronts.'

Joey was by now laughing hysterically. 'What did he say? Tell me what he said,' he insisted, slapping his hands on his knees.

'"Don't you ever touch me in that way again, Joycie. If you do, I'm going to sleep downstairs on the sofa,"' Eddie said, imitating Joyce's voice.

Gina had tears streaming down her face. Joey and Dominic were wonderful company: so much so that she had felt terribly guilty earlier, remembering how she had taken money from Eddie years ago to follow them and report back to him. As for Eddie, he was on top form today. If his work ever dried up, he could certainly earn a good living as a stand-up comic.

Joey nudged Dominic. 'Tell Dad and Gina about Nan embarrassing us. You know, about us being gay.'

Dominic shook his head. He liked both Joey's father and Gina very much, but seeing as Eddie had once put a knife to his penis and threatened to chop it off, he didn't think talking about their sexuality was a particularly good move.

Eddie sensed the lad's reluctance to tell the story. 'Tell us, Dominic, it's fine. I'm cool about things now.'

As Ed smiled warmly at him, Dominic laughed. 'OK, then. Well, we was round Joey's nan's. She had invited us to a dinner party. Anyway, there was all these people there; I didn't even know half of them. All of a sudden, someone gets up to do a speech and then another speech follows and then Joey's nan stands up. I can't remember her exact words, but she said something to the tune of, "My grandson is a gay man and this is his boyfriend, Dominic." She then made us both stand up and admit to everybody at the table that we were a couple. Joey and I were so embarrassed when she broke into song and starting singing "Congratulations".'

Knowing Joyce as well as he did, Eddie laughed. He nudged Gina. 'She's a one-off, our Joycie. You're gonna have to meet her one day. She's a fucking scream, honest.'

Joey wiped his eyes with his cuff. 'And what about the "gay and proud" T-shirt with the pink lettering? Nan bought it for me for Christmas and when I said I wouldn't wear it, she handed it to grandad and told him he could wear it when he cleans out the pigeon shed.'

Eddie stood up holding his privates. 'I've gotta go a toilet, else I'm gonna piss meself laughing. Gina, bring in a couple of bottles of that vintage champagne,' he chuckled.

As Gina and his father left the room, Joey leaned across and kissed Dom on the lips. 'I'm having such a good day. I really like Gina. What do you think?'

Dominic smiled. He hadn't seen Joey enjoy himself so much for ages. 'I think she's lovely and I also like your dad. Once you get to know him, he's a sound type of bloke.'

'Do you really think so?' Joey asked proudly. He had never really thought of his dad in that way before.

Gina walked back into the room and handed the boys a champagne flute each.

'Where's Madonna?' Joey asked.

Gina smiled. Madonna had just eaten a plate of fillet steak and was currently lying in the garden with her legs in the air basking in the sun.

'She's fine. She's in the garden sleeping off her dinner.'

Eddie walked in, picked up a champagne bottle and popped the cork. He poured everybody a glass and held his up.

'To us and new beginnings,' he said.

Joey, Dominic and Gina all raised their glasses. 'To us and new beginnings.'

381

CHAPTER FORTY

Frankie stood in the shower and stared at her stomach as she sponged herself down. She was nearly four months gone now, and even though this pregnancy had been the easiest out of the three, she felt more unattractive than she ever had before. Usually Frankie was in and out of the shower in minutes, but this morning she felt much dirtier than she'd in a long time. The reason was that she'd had to have sex with Jed.

Jed had come in late last night and had not only been drunk, but also amorous. Frankie had told him that she had a headache, but he hadn't listened and had pinned her to the bed. 'We ain't had a bunk-up for ages. Don't you love me any more?' Jed had slurred.

All Frankie could think about was getting her hands on that tape recorder, so she hatched a plan. 'Go and have a shower and I'll be ready and waiting for you,' she said in the most seductive voice she could muster.

'I ain't dirty,' Jed replied.

'You've been out working all day. Jump in the shower, it won't take you a minute.'

Cursing under his breath, Jed did as she asked, which gave Frankie the perfect opportunity to creep outside, get the tape recorder and hide it in the wardrobe.

The sex had been all over in minutes. When Jed was drunk, he was only concerned about receiving pleasure rather than

382

giving it. Frankie wasn't bothered by his selfishness. The boyfriend she'd once lusted after now made her skin crawl.

'Hurry up, Frankie. What the fuck you doing in there?' Jed shouted.

Frankie turned the shower off. 'Sorry, I won't be a sec.'

Putting the king-size towel around her, Frankie shuddered as she stared at her drab reflection in the mirror. In less than a couple of hours, she would have listened to the cassette and its contents would be sure to map out her future.

Stanley sat at the table with his head in his hands. Distraught didn't begin to cover the way he'd felt this morning when he had walked into the pigeon shed and found Ethel had followed Ernie to the pearly gates of heaven.

Not knowing what to do to lift Stanley's depression, Joycie made him a cup of tea and cut him a slice of homemade apple pie. ''Ere you go, love, eat this – it will make you feel better.'

Stanley lifted his head and ungratefully pushed the plate away. 'How is a slice of apple pie going to make me feel better? Ethel's just died – don't you understand how upset I am? I told you she was heartbroken over Ernie. If only you'd have let her live indoors for a bit, she'd have probably got over her loss.'

Feeling herself losing patience, Joyce picked up the dish-cloth and furiously wiped the sink. 'You're gonna have to pull yourself together, Stanley. I know you're upset, but it's a fucking bird that's snuffed it, not me or your grandkids. Can't you pop down to the pet shop and buy yourself another one?'

Stanley looked at his wife in disgust. Joyce really didn't have a clue. He stood up. 'You are one callous, self-centred old crow. Buy another one, buy another one! What do you think my Ethel was? A fucking chicken you pick up in Sainsbury's? I loved Ernie and Ethel, Joycie, loved them with all my heart I did, but you wouldn't understand that, would you? And I'll tell you why, shall I? Because you're an evil old witch!'

As the front door slammed, Joyce ran to the window and was surprised to see Stanley drive away. 'Where's he going?

The silly, bald-headed old tosspot,' she mumbled to herself.

Ten minutes later the phone rang and Joyce ran into the hallway. Perhaps Stanley was ringing to apologise for the awful names he had called her.

As she pressed the receiver to her ear, Joyce was greeted by silence. 'Is that you, Stanley?' she shouted angrily.

'Nan, it's me. Can you talk?'

'Oh, hello Joey. Yes, your grandad's just stormed off in one of his little tempers. I'm here on me own. Aren't you at work, love?'

'Yeah, but I had to ring you. Guess who I had dinner with yesterday?'

Joycie was still smarting from Stanley's comments and wasn't really in the mood for guessing games. 'Frankie?'

'No, my dad. He came round on Saturday, Nan, he said that he had spoken to you. He invited me and Dom around to his house yesterday for dinner and we had such a good time. We really have cleared the air and we got on better than we have done ever. He was really nice to Dominic and he even invited Madonna over and gave her a plate of fillet steak.'

Joyce grinned. She knew the speech she had given Eddie had hit home, but she hadn't expected a reconciliation to happen this quickly.

'Joey, I'm so, so pleased. I know what happened to your mum was awful for all of us, but your dad's a good man deep down – he always was. Have you made any plans to see him again?'

'Yeah. The four of us are going to a pub on Friday night.'

Joyce paused. 'What do you mean the four of you? Who else is going? Frankie?'

Annoyed with himself for putting his foot in it, Joey bit his lip. His dad had said that his nan was aware of Gina, so he may as well tell her the truth.

'Actually, Nan, Dad's friend Gina is coming. She was there yesterday, she cooked the meal for us. She's a really nice lady and I'm sure that you'd approve of her.'

384

Joyce felt her eyes well up. She knew that Eddie had to move on with his life, but the thought of him being with another woman still cut like a knife. 'I've got to go now, Joey, your grandad's just come back,' she lied.

Joyce replaced the receiver, walked over to Jessica's framed photo and picked it up. 'Well, I think Eddie's finally moved on now, my darling, and I hope you're OK about that. More importantly, he's made things right with our Joey and I hope if you can see that from heaven, my angel, you can finally rest in peace.'

Frankie was filled with adrenalin as she handed the tape recorder to Kerry. The boys were playing in the garden, Kerry's sister was round at her mate's, so it was just the two of them and a bottle of wine. Kerry poured two drinks and handed one to Frankie.

'You ready?' she asked.

Frankie held her breath as Kerry pressed the play button. Unlike their last failed attempt, Jed and Sammy's voices could be heard quite clearly this time.

'And how was the wonderful Frankie today?' Sammy asked sarcastically.

'As miserable as fucking usual.'

Sammy laughed. 'Where we going now, then?'

'Let's go and see them pair of Dorises over in Barking, eh?'

'Who's Doris?' Frankie whispered to Kerry.

'They're talking about two old tarts. That's what Sammy calls 'em, the dirty pair of bastards,' Kerry replied.

'You ever shagged a blackie before?' Sammy asked.

'Nah, but I can't wait to stick my cory into that Angela's tight pussy. I wanna just see what it's like. What about you? You ain't shafted a black bird, have ya?' Jed replied.

'Nah. But let me know if it's any good and I might shove my cock up Angela's tight black pussy an' all,' Sammy joked.

Kerry and Frankie looked at one another in disgust.

'I hate him. I have to leave him now,' Frankie cried.

Kerry grabbed Frankie's arm. 'Sssh. They're talking about that Julie.'

'She keeps banging on about having a brother or sister for Tommy boy. I've been stalling her, but I might agree to it soon. I mean, it don't look like Kerry's coming back, does it? I miss me boys, but a minge is a minge at the end of the day and seeing as Julie's a better fuck than Kerry, I might as well lay me hat at hers or, better still, get her to move in with me.'

Kerry dropped her wine glass on the floor in shock. She stood up and pressed the pause button. 'The fucking no-good bastard! He will never see my boys again, Frankie, I'll kill him if I have to. How could he say stuff like that about me? I gave him the best years of my life.'

As Kerry burst into tears, Frankie put her arms around her and squeezed her tightly. 'It's OK. Let it all out, mate. It's not you, Kerry, it's Sammy – the man's an animal and so is Jed. They are both fucking arseholes and how we fell for their sweet talk and charm in the first place, I will never know. We're better than them, worth far more, and we'll get over this, I know we will.'

Stanley was sitting at a table in the Orsett Cock public house. He had never frequented this particular boozer before, but a few of his pals from the pigeon club used it regularly and were rather fond of the place.

As his mate Brian handed him a pint of beer, Stanley noticed the blonde lady staring at him again. He had seen her clocking him earlier – she wasn't one of their usual crowd. Seeing her smile at him, Stanley gave a nervous wave and turned to Brian.

'Who's that woman with the blonde hair? Is she with one of the men? Only I've never seen her before.'

'I can't remember her name, I've only met her once before myself, but she's a new member of the club. Derek was telling me that she has the most incredible insight and knowledge of

386

pigeons. She's new to the area apparently, recently widowed, I think, and Derek said she's moved here from the East End to be closer to her daughter and grandchildren.'

Stanley was impressed. A woman who knew and could talk pigeons: that was a first. He glanced at her again and as the woman caught his eye, she boldly walked towards him.

As Brian stood up, Stanley panicked. 'Where you going? Don't leave me on me own with a woman I don't know.'

Brian laughed. 'Just nipping to the gents. I won't be long.'

Apart from Joycie and his beautiful deceased daughter, Stanley had never felt all that comfortable in women's company. As the blonde lady sat down next to him, the first thing he noticed was her massive cleavage. She had a low cut white top on and, in Stanley's opinion, her breasts looked like a couple of rugby balls. Not knowing what to say or do, Stanley began to shuffle his feet. He then began choking and a sudden coughing fit came over him, as it always did when he was nervous.

'Are you OK?' the woman asked, concerned.

'Been eating peanuts. One went down the wrong hole,' Stanley replied, gasping for breath.

The woman waited until his coughing fit had subsided, and smiled. She held her hand out. 'Pleased to meet ya. I'm Patricia, but everyone calls me Pat the Pigeon.'

Stanley's hand shook with nerves as he returned the gesture. As a young boy, he had been obsessed by women's breasts, but Joycie's were like a pair of fried eggs compared with the pair confronting him now. Not knowing where to look, he stared into Pat the Pigeon's eyes. They were beautiful, as blue as the sea and full of honesty.

'Pleased to meet you. My name is Stanley,' he stammered.

Frankie and Kerry looked at one another in utter disbelief. They had just listened to half an hour of vulgar conversation and had felt the need to pause the tape again. It was Kerry who finally ended the silence.

'What a pair of cunts! I can't believe it,' she said bluntly.

Frankie said nothing. She was still in shock from what they had learned and it was now blatantly obvious that all the weekends Jed and Sammy were supposedly working away, they were actually spending around Sally's and Julie's. And, if that wasn't bad enough, they had also spoken about other girls they had on the go. They had even bragged about what they had done to two prostitutes the previous month.

'I feel sick. He made me sleep with him last night – say I've caught something?' Frankie wept.

Kerry hugged her friend. 'It's all over now. Once you leave him, he can't hurt you any more. I dunno about you, but I need another drink. I'll open another bottle of wine before we listen to the rest.'

'I don't wanna hear no more. My stomach can't take it,' Frankie replied tearfully.

'We have to, Frankie. We don't want them dirty bastards getting their hands on our kids, do we? All we've got so far is evidence of their philandering and we need evidence of their dodgy dealings to be able to get our own back. If we can prove that they are robbing old people, we can threaten to go to the police to stop them seeing the kids. And if they don't agree to our rules, we can take the tape to the fucking police.'

Frankie watched her friend go into the kitchen, then gratefully accepted another drink. She shuddered as Kerry pressed the play button again. The contents of the tape had been far worse than she had envisaged. Jed obviously hated her with a passion and the way he had spoken of his sexual encounters with other women made her feel sick to the stomach.

Kerry nudged her. 'Who's Harry Mitchell? Do you know him?'

Frankie stared at her blankly. 'Of course I do. He was my grandad, the one I told you about. Why you asking?'

'I'm sure Sammy just mentioned him. Shall I rewind it?'

Frankie nodded. Kerry must be wrong, Jed hadn't even known her grandfather. As Kerry pressed 'play' again, Frankie listened intently.

'Do you know who that old grunter Mr Franks reminds me of?' Sammy said.

'Surprise me. Come on, who? It certainly ain't Arthur Daley,' Jed replied jokingly.

'Harry Mitchell. Don't you think that Franks looks like him?'

Shocked by the mention of her grandfather's name, Frankie got down on her knees and crawled towards the tape recorder. The voices were still clear, but there was now music in the background. Putting her ear right next to the speaker, all Frankie could hear was Jed's laughter. Then she heard his voice.

'I don't remember what Harry Mitchell's face looked like when he was alive. The only vision I've got of that rotten old shitcunt is the face we left him with on his deathbed. Do you remember him begging me to stop beating him, Sammy boy? "Please don't kill me," the silly old cunt was saying. Best night of my life, that was. Getting revenge for my own grandad, God rest his soul, beats fucking any bird I've ever shagged.'

Frankie stopped the tape, turned white and collapsed on the carpet. Kerry crouched down next to her. She couldn't understand the recording properly because Patsy Cline was singing in the background.

'What is it, Frankie? What did they say?'

Without warning, Frankie clutched her stomach and started to heave. Kerry was frightened now, really frightened.

'Are you OK? Is it the baby?'

Frankie shook her head. 'They killed my ...' she whispered. She couldn't finish the sentence, the words just wouldn't come.

Kerry sat Frankie up and propped her against the sofa. She looked incredibly ill and scared.

'I think I should call an ambulance. You really don't look well, Frankie.'

As Kerry stood up, Frankie gripped her arm as though she would never let it go. 'No, please don't.'

Kerry crouched down again and cradled Frankie's ashen face in her hands. She was crying herself now. She was frightened, really frightened.

'What is it, Frankie? Please tell me.'

Frankie met her gaze with a haunted look in her eyes. Her voice was wobbly and sounded nothing like her own.

'Jed and Sammy, it was them that murdered my grandad,' she croaked.

CHAPTER FORTY-ONE

Kerry looked at Frankie in bewilderment. This couldn't be happening, it couldn't be true. Jed and Sammy might be womanising con men, but surely they weren't capable of murder?

'Are you sure that it's your grandad they're talking about? I mean, Mitchell is quite a common name, ain't it? Say they're talking about a different Harry Mitchell?'

Thinking of her grandfather's awful death, Frankie retched. 'I'm sorry,' she said, as a mouthful of vomit flew over the carpet.

Kerry ran into the kitchen and returned with a cloth and a plastic bucket.

'It's definitely my grandad, I just know it is. The thing is, what do I do now? I can't tell my dad, because he will kill Jed and get himself locked up for life,' Frankie wept.

Kerry kneeled down next to her. 'You have to tell someone. What about Gary and Ricky? They'll know what to do, won't they?'

Frankie shook her head. 'I can't tell them, in case they tell my dad. I know me and my dad aren't speaking at the moment, but I do love him and I can't see him go to prison again. He will kill Jed, Kerry, he won't be able to stop himself. I so wish my mum was alive; she would know what to do.'

'Well, in that case I think we should go to the police. We can hand them the tape and get them to listen to it in front of us. They will have to lock Jed and Sammy up then and when they do, I hope they throw away the fucking key.'

Frankie could feel her legs wobbling as she stood up and sat on the sofa. She could hear Harry laughing in the back garden and her heart was filled with pain. One day she would probably have to explain to her children that their daddy was a cold-blooded murderer.

Kerry sat down next to Frankie and hugged her. She looked frightfully ill and Kerry was really worried.

'I know this isn't easy, Frankie, but you need to start making plans immediately. You're not going to stay at the trailer tonight, are you?'

'Of course not. I never want to see Jed again. I need some stuff, though: my clothes, the kids' clothes, I'll have to pop back there to collect some belongings.'

'We'll both go. I ain't letting you go on your own. We can load up the motor before Jed gets back. Just grab what you can, then we can go straight to the police station with the tape,' Kerry suggested.

Frankie felt a shiver go down her spine. Jed was a dangerous, violent psychopath, and she had to get the kids away from him fast.

'Alice and Jimmy are meant to be picking Georgie up from school today; they're taking her home to have tea with them and Jed was gonna pick her up later. I'm gonna have to get her out of school early and then we'll go and get my stuff. I'll tell her teacher that there's been a family tragedy or something. We can take the kids to the police station with us: I don't want Jed or his family near them ever again.'

Kerry stood up and held out her hand. 'Come on, let's get our skates on.'

Over in Orsett, Stanley was thoroughly enjoying the company of Pat the Pigeon. He had got over his initial nervousness and was now totally captivated by this unusual woman with the raucous, hearty laugh.

Pat squeezed Stanley's hand. She hadn't left his side since she'd introduced herself earlier, and unlike Joyce, had shown great compassion for the deaths of his beloved pigeons, Ethel and Ernie.

'I've got just the tonic for you, Stanley. George and Mildred, my finest, have produced some striking squabs. Why don't you come round, have a look and take your pick? I've had loads of people trying to buy 'em off me. I was gonna keep 'em all for myself, but seeing as you're suffering such an awful bereavement, I'd like you to have one. It's a gift – I don't want paying for it.'

Stanley was overwhelmed by Pat's kindness. She had a wonderful knowledge of breeding and racing pigeons and obviously had a heart of gold to go with it. He stood up and smiled at her.

'That's very kind of you. Let me get you another drink, my dear. G and T again, is it? Would you like a double this time?'

Pat the Pigeon laughed. 'Oh, you are naughty, Stanley. Go on, then, I'll have a double.'

Stanley walked up to the bar with a spring in his step. He could see the envious glances from some of the other men and it made him feel a million dollars that Pat had made a beeline for him.

'How's it going, Stanley? That Pat's been all over you like a rash. That's why me and Brian stayed up the bar – we didn't want to intrude. What's she been saying to you?' Derek asked him.

'She's going to give me one of her squabs,' Stanley said proudly.

Derek laughed. 'And the rest.'

'What do you mean?'

'I can see the way she's looking at you, Stanley. She wants to give you more than a squab, mate.'

Stanley felt his heart start to pound in his chest. In all the years he had been with Joycie, no woman had ever come on to him and, even before he had met Joycie, he hadn't exactly had the luck of Errol Flynn with the female sex. His hand shook as he handed the barmaid the money.

'Pat's just being friendly. I'm sure you've got it all wrong,' he told Derek.

Derek chuckled. 'No, I ain't. Pat has a vulture look about her and by the looks of it, you're her prey, mate.'

Stanley picked up the drinks and returned to the table. His legs were trembling and he had no idea how to stop them from doing so.

'Are you OK, Stanley?' Pat asked, concerned.

Stanley looked into her kind blue eyes and smiled. 'I'm fine, Pat, honest I am.'

Georgie O'Hara's teacher looked startled when Frankie barged into the classroom and nigh on dragged her daughter outside.

'I need to take Georgie home, something terrible has happened,' she gabbled.

Mrs Lawson stared at Frankie. 'Are you OK? Would you like me to get you a glass of water?'

Frankie shook her head. Since leaving Kerry's sister's house, she had felt full of absolute panic and she couldn't stop herself from shaking.

'I'm fine. I just need to take Georgie home with me now,' she insisted.

Mrs Lawson was exceptionally concerned. She could smell the wine fumes on Frankie's breath, and it was obvious that Frankie was in no fit state, physically or mentally, to take her daughter anywhere. She ushered Frankie along the corridor. The headmistress would know how to handle this.

'I need to speak to the headmistress first, she will need you to sign a form for her. Wait here, I'll be back in a minute.'

Frankie waited for the teacher to disappear out of sight, then ran back to the classroom. She spotted Georgie immediately. She was sitting at the far end of the classroom.

'Quick, we've gotta go,' she said, grabbing her daughter's arm.

Frankie had ordered Kerry to park outside the main door and stay in the car with the boys. Georgie was unable to run very fast, so Frankie had to carry her, and by the time she reached the car, she was knackered.

Kerry leaped out of the driver's seat and opened the back door.

Frankie told Harry to get in the front. Georgie had opened the door while they were driving along once before and she needed to sit next to her to keep an eye on her.

'Just drive, quick,' she urged Kerry. She was frightened the teacher or headmistress would try and stop them from leaving the premises.

As Kerry sped out of the school gates, Frankie breathed a huge sigh of relief. Part one of the plan was accomplished and, once they'd completed two and three, Jed would hopefully be out of her life for ever.

Alice O'Hara was fuming as she hung up the phone. She had given the school her phone number in case Georgie ever had an accident or was ill and they'd just called her. She dialled Jed's number.

'You'd better sort out that fucking stinking old whore of yours, boy. Her headmistress has just rang me and said Frankie's been up the school and taken Georgie girl out of her class in the middle of her lesson. They were worried, said they thought Frankie had been drinking and looked unstable. What's all that about, eh, Jed? Has she taken her just to spite us? She knew me and your dad were picking her up today, the dirty, no-good shitcunt.'

Jed's heart immediately started to beat wildly. Whatever his old girl thought of Frankie, he knew the mother of his kids well enough to know that she would never turn up pissed at the school and drag Georgie out of her class without a bloody good reason.

'Leave it with me, Mum, I'll sort it, don't worry,' he said. He ended the call and immediately tried to ring Frankie. There was no answer.

'What's up?' Sammy asked him. They were on their way to deliver a mare to a geezer in Southend.

'It's Frankie. Something bad's happened. She must have found out about me and Sally. We need to turn back, now!'

'Can't you sort it later?' Sammy asked annoyed. It had been hard for him to sell this poxy horse and he didn't want to mess up the deal.

Extremely pissed off, Jed grabbed Sammy's arm.

'What you doing? You nearly made me kill us just then,' Sammy complained.

Jed stared at him. 'I said, we need to go home. Do as I say and turn this fucking horse-box around now!'

Sammy glanced at him. 'I can't turn it around on a main road like this.'

Fuming, Jed made Sammy pull over so he could swap seats with him. He then grabbed the steering wheel and, not giving a shit about the other motorists, shot across the central reservation.

'Mind the fucking horse, you've probably just killed it,' Sammy shouted.

'Fuck the horse and fuck you,' Jed snarled.

Over in Orsett, Stanley was beginning to feel extremely light-headed. He had been so upset this morning over Ethel passing over to pigeon heaven that he hadn't eaten any breakfast.

'So, have you buried Ethel yet? What did you do with Ernie?' Pat asked him.

'I've buried them both in the garden. I'm gonna make a nice little cross and get a plaque made for 'em. At least they're together again. Inseparable in life and death, eh?'

Pat leaned over and pecked him on the cheek. 'That's a lovely burial, Stanley. And you are such a lovely man.'

Seeing Brian look his way with a big grin on his face, Stanley stood up. 'I suppose I'd best be getting home, Pat. I feel a bit tiddly, to be honest, I'm not used to drinking early in the day any more.'

Pat grabbed his arm and forced him to sit back down. 'Why don't you come back to my house first and have a look at my squabs? I'll do you a nice bit of lunch and you can have a couple of coffees to sober yourself up a bit.'

'Oh, I don't know. I really should be getting back,' Stanley replied nervously.

Pat smiled. She had a very pretty smile that lit up the whole of her face. 'There's no need to be afraid of me, Stanley. I think you're a charming man and I want us to be good friends, that's all.'

Stanley immediately relaxed. 'OK, then, let's go back to yours.'

In Wickford, Frankie and Kerry were busy filling up black bin bags with the kids' toys.

'Where's your teddy, Harry?' Frankie asked her son.

Harry ran into his bedroom and came out clutching the bear in his arms. 'Put it in that bag, there's a good boy,' Frankie urged him.

'Can I take my dollies with me?' Georgie asked.

Frankie stroked her daughter's hair. 'Of course you can. Be a good girl and put them in one of these bags for Mummy.'

Kerry had spoken to her sister on the way and she had kindly offered Frankie a place to stay for a few days. After that, Frankie had no idea where she was going to live or what she was going to do, but she didn't have time to worry about that now. Getting away from Jed was all that mattered.

'Where's the tape? Have you still got it?' Kerry asked, grabbing her arm.

Frankie pointed to her handbag. 'Don't worry, I won't lose it, it's zipped up.'

'Did you name him after your grandad, Frankie?' Kerry asked pointing at Harry.

Frankie went cold and dropped the bag she was holding. She had been so stunned earlier by the contents of the tape that she hadn't given a thought to her son's name or who had chosen it for him.

'Are you OK, Frankie? What's the matter?'

Frankie shook her head. 'Jed named Harry after my grandad. How evil is that? I wanted to call him something else, but he insisted we call him Harry and now I know why.'

Kerry shuddered. 'He's an animal, Frankie. He's one sick bastard and you should tell the police about that as well. Now, hurry up, we need to get going. It's giving me the creeps being back here.'

Frankie opened her wardrobe door. She wouldn't be able to take all her clothes – all she needed was enough to get her by.

'Put the other bags in the car while I pack my stuff,' she shouted out to Kerry.

Kerry ran in and out to the car with the bin liners. 'Go and get in the car and don't touch the handbrake,' she ordered the kids.

The Fiesta was small, so was the boot, and with the kids inside, there was very little room for so many bags.

'Frankie, you're gonna have to leave some of this stuff here, I can't fit it all in,' Kerry yelled.

Frankie ran out of the trailer and began taking certain bags out of the boot. 'As long as I've got the kids' stuff, I ain't so worried about mine,' she said.

About to run back inside, Frankie heard the distinct noise of a diesel engine approaching. 'I think Jed and Sammy are back,' she cried.

Kerry ran over to her and pushed her inside the trailer. 'It might not be them. It could be someone else.'

'No one else comes here, you know they don't,' Frankie wept.

Huddled together for support, the girls shook like leaves on a windy day as they stared through the net curtains. Their fears were confirmed as the horse-box pulled into sight with both Jed and Sammy inside. Petrified for their own safety and that of their children, both Frankie and Kerry let out piercing screams.

CHAPTER FORTY-TWO

'Daddy, Daddy!' Sammy's boys screamed as soon as they spotted their father.

Frightened that Sammy would kidnap his sons, Kerry flew out of the trailer and ran towards them. 'Get back in the car now,' she yelled, as she came face to face with Sammy for the first time since she had found out about Julie.

Frankie felt physically sick when Jed walked inside the trailer. He spotted the black bags immediately, glanced inside, then turned to her. 'Going somewhere nice, are we?' he said, his eyes sparkling with danger.

Frankie didn't know what to do or say. She didn't want Jed to kick off in front of the children, but she could hardly deny she was leaving him.

'I'm going away for a while. I'm not happy with you any more and I need to get my head together.'

As Georgie ran inside and clung to her father's legs, Jed lifted her into his arms. In the last few days he had got his head around the news of Sally's pregnancy, and if Frankie wanted to leave, he would move Sally in.

'Go on, then, fuck off, but don't think you're taking my kids with ya.'

Frankie could hear Kerry and Sammy shouting at one another outside. She heard Kerry scream and ran to the door. Kerry was lying on the ground holding the side of her face.

'Get away from her, you bastard,' Frankie screamed, as she

pushed Sammy out of the way and stood guarding her friend.

'Get in the horse-box, kids. All of ya, now,' Jed yelled.

When Frankie grabbed hold of Harry, Kerry stood up and picked up Sammy Junior. They ran back inside the trailer and ordered the kids to stay in the bedroom.

'Where's Georgie and Freddy?' Frankie cried.

Georgie and Freddy were already inside the horse-box and as Jed and Sammy ran back towards the trailer, Frankie and Kerry tried desperately to shut and lock the door.

'What are we gonna do?' Kerry wept, as Jed and Sammy began kicking it. Knowing that the door would be caved in within seconds, Frankie unlocked it. She was petrified and could hear the boys crying in the bedroom.

Kerry was beside herself. Sammy had turned on her, had punched her hard, but there was no way she was allowing him to take her kids away. Kerry was more aware of the travelling way of life than Frankie was and she knew that if Jed and Sammy drove off with their kids, there was every chance that they'd disappear into thin air with them. Gypsies were very loyal to their own, they never grassed and Jed and Sammy could easily find a place to hide on a remote site miles away, where they would never be traced.

As Frankie and Jed started to argue again, Kerry noticed Sammy go into the bedroom. She spotted Frankie's iron on the side and immediately picked it up. She had to stop him.

Sammy was stunned by the whack over the back of his head. He turned and tried to grab the iron, but when Kerry hit him again, he fell to the ground clutching his head. Unable to stop herself, Kerry went on hitting him.

Sammy Junior screamed when he spotted his father covered in blood. 'Stop it, Mummy! Stop hitting Daddy,' he cried.

Hearing the commotion, Jed ran over to the bedroom. 'You evil fucking bitch! You've fucking killed him, ain't ya?' he yelled, knocking the iron out of Kerry's hand.

Frankie pushed Kerry out of the bedroom. 'Get out of here and take the kids with you,' she whispered.

As Jed bent over Sammy and tried to wake him up, Kerry clung to Frankie. 'I can't leave you here. Say Jed really hurts you?'

'Don't worry about me, just take the kids with you. Do it for me, I beg you. I'll get rid of Jed and meet you at your sister's. As soon as you get away, ring the police and tell 'em Jed's gone off his head. Send 'em here, but don't say nothing about the tape yet.'

Jed was too concerned over his cousin's well-being to notice that Kerry had crept outside with the children. She put them in Frankie's car and ran over to the horse-box. 'Quick, get in the Fiesta,' she yelled at Georgie and Freddy.

Her youngest immediately obeyed her orders, but Georgie was paralysed by fear at what she'd seen.

'This is important, Georgie. You have to come with me,' Kerry said, grabbing the child's arm.

Hearing Georgie screaming blue murder, Jed left Sammy's side and bolted outside the trailer. Seeing Kerry manhandling his hysterical daughter, he lunged at her, fists flying.

'You fucking whore, leave her alone,' he screamed, as he whacked Kerry in the side of the head.

Frankie followed Jed outside and screamed as he grabbed hold of Georgie. She picked up a brick and ran towards him.

'Let her go. Kerry, quick, grab her,' she shouted, as she hit him over the head with the brick.

As quick as lightning, Kerry picked Georgie up and shoved her inside Frankie's motor. She jumped in the driver's seat and, as she turned on the ignition, she saw Jed running towards her, clutching his head. Petrified for her friend's safety, Kerry froze.

'Drive, just fucking drive,' Frankie screamed.

Totally traumatised by what they had witnessed, the kids were all screaming.

As Jed yanked open the driver's door, Kerry put the Fiesta in gear and rammed her foot on the accelerator. Jed clung onto the door for what seemed like ages, but in reality was only seconds.

'Daddy, Daddy,' Georgie wept, her tearful face pressed against the window.

'I'm gonna kill you, you fucking slag,' Jed screamed, finally losing his grip on the metal doorframe.

As her boyfriend hit the ground with a thud, Frankie dashed back inside the trailer. Sammy was still out cold and she had no idea whether he was alive or dead.

Frankie knew that for her own safety she had to get away. The problem was, she had no idea where she had put her handbag and it still had the tape inside. Wishing that she'd given the bag to Kerry, she searched frantically for it. Where she was going to run to, she had no idea, but all she had to do was find the bag, get away and call the police.

Jed was feeling extremely battered and bruised. The Fiesta had been travelling about fifteen miles an hour when he'd lost his grip and hit the ground. His shoulder was killing him – it felt as if it was dislocated – and his head didn't feel much better. Frankie had hit him three times with a brick and he had blood pouring down his face to prove it. Dishevelled, he staggered back towards the trailer.

'Come back 'ere, you stupid bitch,' he screamed, when he saw Frankie run off in the opposite direction.

Holding his shoulder, Jed immediately forgot about his pain and broke into a sprint. Frankie was dicing with death. Once he caught her, he might just kill her for the amount of grief she'd caused him.

Stanley was sitting in Pat the Pigeon's conservatory sipping a steaming cup of coffee. Her house was small, smart, clean and homely and Stanley had just chosen a squab, which he'd arranged to collect the following week.

'She's a real beauty, ain't she, Pat? I've already got a small cock to keep her company,' Stanley said seriously.

Pat the Pigeon burst out laughing and when Stanley realised the error of his wording, his face turned the colour of beetroot. Noticing this, Pat diplomatically changed the subject.

402

'So what you gonna call her then, Stanley?'

Stanley smiled. He was bowled over by Pat's kindness.

'She has a pretty face, just like the lady that bred her, so, if you don't mind, I thought I'd call her Patricia, after you.'

Pat felt herself come over all sentimental. She had been very lonely ever since her husband, Vic, had died. She had known as soon as she looked at Stanley that he had that very rare, special something about him.

'Tell me about Joyce, your wife. Is your marriage a happy one?'

Stanley sighed. He didn't like speaking badly of Joyce to people he barely knew, but he felt as though he had known Pat for years.

'Joycie's a difficult woman to understand at times. She's always been very materialistic, whereas I'm not and we don't have a great deal in common, to be honest. Our daughter Jessica's death brought us closer together for a short time, but over the past couple of years we've drifted apart again. Joycie is very set in her ways and she's always made me feel that I'm not good enough for her.'

'Oh, my God! That's awful, Stanley. I didn't know you'd lost your daughter. What happened to her?'

Stanley's eyes welled up. 'It's a long story, but to cut it short, she got murdered by her villainous bastard of a husband. It was Joyce that encouraged our Jessica to marry him in the first place; I was totally against their relationship all along. And do you know the thing that Joycie did that hurt me the most, Pat?'

'Go on, you can talk to me about anything, Stanley.'

'She accepted the house that we now live in from the bastard that murdered her. It was obviously compensation for our daughter's death. Blood money, I call it, and I'll never forgive my Joycie for that.'

Pat moved across the room, sat next to Stanley and hugged him tenderly. 'If you ever need a friend or a shoulder to cry on, you know where to come,' she told him.

Stanley smiled at her and as their lips brushed, he quickly

snapped back to reality. He immediately stood up. In all the years he had been married to Joycie, he had never so much as looked at another woman and he was too old to start all that philandering malarkey now. He hadn't tried his bits and bobs out for years and he probably wouldn't be able to stand to attention, anyway.

'I'd best be going now, Pat. Thanks for the chat and the coffee. I'll pop back and pick up the squab next Saturday, if that's OK?'

Pat nodded and stood up to see Stanley out. 'Look after yourself and remember, if you ever need to talk, just knock on my door.'

Stanley smiled gratefully. 'Thank you, Pat. I truly appreciate your kindness and it's been a pleasure meeting you, my love.'

Back in Wickford, Jed had just caught up with Frankie. He'd clumped her and was now marching her back to the trailer with his hand clasped around her neck.

'What you gonna do to me? Can't we just sort this out like adults?' Frankie pleaded.

'Shut it, you dinlo,' Jed said, as he roughly shoved her inside their once happy home.

Sammy was awake now, but was still concussed and confused. 'What happened? I can't remember anything,' he said weakly.

Jed ordered Frankie to sit on the sofa. He helped his cousin up and sat him on the bed. 'Stay 'ere while I deal with Frankie,' he told him.

Fearing for her life, Frankie crept over to the kitchen drawer. She took out the bread knife, crept back to the sofa and hid it between two of the cushions. Jed had already punched her hard and had also hurt her neck, but she wouldn't allow herself to think of the pain. Her children were all that mattered now.

Jed left Sammy lying on the bed and sauntered towards Frankie. He had no real intention of killing her – all he wanted was custody of the kids – but if she didn't agree, he would have to consider his options. He had once loved Frankie, but if she fucked him about, she would get her just desserts. He sat down next to her and spoke to her in a deceptively calm voice.

'I can't believe that you were gonna do a runner with my kids. Now, if you wanna leave me, fine, but I want custody, Frankie. So what's your decision?'

Frankie looked at him with hatred. She could barely believe that Jed was responsible for the murder of her grandfather, but she knew it was true, she had the proof inside her handbag.

'You will never have custody of them kids. You're evil and I know all your fucking secrets,' she spat.

Jed laughed. It was a nasty sadistic laugh. He grabbed her by the shoulders, pushed her onto the sofa and straddled her.

'So what do you know, then? Come on, spit it out, clever clogs.'

'I know all about you and that Sally and I know plenty of other stuff.'

'One of your dinlo mates been telling tales on me again, have they?' Jed hissed.

Frankie flinched as he tried to kiss her. 'Get off me, you bastard!' she screamed.

Jed chuckled. The silly bitch obviously thought he was going to rape her, but he had no intention of doing so. Compared to Sally, she was a shit fuck anyway.

'So, where's your slag of a friend took my chavvies?' he asked her.

'Somewhere where you won't find 'em.'

Getting annoyed by Frankie's lack of co-operation, Jed put his hands around her throat and gently squeezed her windpipe with his thumbs.

'Tell me where the kids are, or you're fucking dead meat.'

Frankie felt a fire in her belly that she hadn't felt for years. Unable to stop herself, she gobbed in his face. 'I would rather be killed than you get your hands on them kids,' she croaked.

Jed wiped the spit off his face with his T-shirt. He stood up

405

and paced up and down the trailer. The stupid fucking bitch was making life extremely difficult for herself, but he wasn't sure that he could personally kill her. He stormed into the bedroom and shook Sammy to wake him up a bit.

'I might need you to do away with Frankie for me. I can't do it,' he whispered.

Sammy clutched his sore head. He felt too ill to do away with a wasp, let alone Frankie. 'I can't do it, Jed, not today I can't.'

Frankie put her hand between the two cushions, picked up the knife and her handbag. She had to get out of here and it was now or never. She crept towards the trailer door and opened it. As Jed ran out of the bedroom, she clutched the knife in both hands and pointed it towards his stomach.

'Touch me and I'll kill you,' she said boldly.

Jed laughed. 'Put the knife down, Frankie, you dinlo.'

Frankie shook her head. Suddenly, she had no fear, just a desire for revenge.

'I know what you did to my grandad and I'm gonna tell the police everything,' she said, edging towards him.

Jed was stunned. How could she know about Harry Mitchell? Apart from him and Sammy, no one knew.

'You're talking rubbish. Now, just drop the knife, Frankie.'

Shaking her head, Frankie held the knife firmly in her grasp. She had a demonic look on her face, a look that worried Jed immensely.

Sensing Jed's fear as he backed away from her, Frankie started to laugh. 'The boot's on the other foot now, ain't it, Jed? Did you do this to my poor old grandad, did ya? Did you terrorise him before you killed him?'

'I dunno what you're talking about. You're mental,' Jed said in denial.

Frankie sneered at him. 'Tell me the truth, else I'm gonna fucking kill ya.'

'I didn't touch your grandad, honest I didn't.'

Frankie took a deep breath. She knew she was ready to stab

the bastard and before he died, she wanted him to know how clever she was.

'I recorded you and Sammy talking in the motor, you mug. I've got all the evidence on tape and I'm going to the police with it. Always thought you was the genius, didn't you, Jed? But you ain't now, 'cause I've beat you hands down.'

Jed stared at Frankie's handbag. Chances were, if she was telling the truth, which was probable, the evidence that could put him away for life was inside that poxy bag of hers. Determined not to let Frankie get one over on him, Jed darted to his right and made a grab for her handbag.

'I hate you, you cunt, I fucking despise you,' Frankie screamed, as she pulled back the knife and plunged it deep into his guts.

Having had no luck with her earlier phone call, Kerry was now inside the police station. She had rung the Old Bill as soon as she'd got to her sister's house, but they hadn't believed the seriousness of her allegations.

'We'll get someone over to Wickford as soon as possible. We're very busy at the moment; there has been a multiple pile-up along the A127,' the policewoman said. Kerry was furious. The stupid woman obviously thought it was just another domestic.

As the person in front of her came out of the reception area, Kerry rushed into the small room. There had been four people in front of her and waiting her turn patiently hadn't been easy.

'Please help me. My friend's life is in danger and I know that her boyfriend is a lunatic.'

The copper looked at the distraught young girl and instantly believed her.

'What's the address? I'll send someone over there immediately,' he said.

Sammy was now as alert as he could be. He did not know that Frankie had actually stabbed Jed, but was aware that she knew he and Jed had killed Harry Mitchell.

407

As Jed lay on the floor, looking like death warmed up, Frankie stared at him with a vicious look on her face. The colour had drained from his skin, he looked as white as a ghost, but she knew he wasn't dead yet. Determined to finish the job off, she pulled the knife out of his stomach and plunged it in again.

'Die, you bastard. Fucking die!' she yelled.

Sammy crept over to the bedroom door. He had heard Jed mention the tape and the handbag and he knew he had to get his hands on it.

Frankie didn't hear Sammy open the bedroom door. In her frenzied frame of mind, she had sort of forgotten he was even there. As Frankie stood over Jed, Sammy crept up behind her and grabbed her in a headlock. He gasped when he saw the blood on Jed's T-shirt and his deathly white face.

'What have you done to him, you stupid bitch?' he whispered.

'I've stabbed the bastard and I hope he dies a painful death,' Frankie replied calmly.

In a weird sort of trance, Frankie allowed Sammy to take the knife out of her hand. Her job was done; Jed would very soon be dead.

'The police will be here soon,' she said in an expressionless voice.

Sammy bent down and took the horse-box keys out of the pocket of Jed's jeans. He stood up and pointed the knife at Frankie.

'Give me your handbag,' he demanded.

Frankie clung on to her bag for dear life. 'Get away from me!' she screamed, moving backwards.

Jed looked as if he was dying, but Sammy couldn't call an ambulance before he got rid of that tape. Using all the strength he had left, he punched Frankie as hard as he could in the face. She fell backwards, hit the ground and, as she did so, Sammy grabbed the bag and ran.

Frankie held on to the sofa for support and hauled herself up. Without the tape there was no evidence and she couldn't understand why she hadn't given her bag to Kerry earlier. She staggered outside the trailer.

'Give me my bag back,' she screamed, as she tried to stop Sammy from driving away. She stood in front of the horse-box waving her arms. 'Please just give me my handbag,' she wept. She was distraught now, totally inconsolable.

Aware of sirens in the distance, Sammy reversed back and drove away. He avoided running over Frankie, but only by a few inches.

Frankie laid on the ground and sobbed her heart out. Visions of when she and Jed had first met flooded through her muddled mind. She remembered their first kiss, their first date in Cambridgeshire and the day she had lost her virginity to him. She even remembered the time when he had proposed to her in the car park of a pub.

'You bastard. You fucking traitor,' she screamed hysterically.

Overcome by grief, Frankie knelt on all fours and pummelled the grass with her fists. She could hear a police car approaching and she knew she was in serious trouble. Without the tape there was no evidence and she would probably be sent to prison, but as long as Jed was dead and couldn't get custody of the kids, she didn't really care.

Kerry sat nervously in the back of the police car. Because Frankie lived in a field in the middle of nowhere, the police didn't have a clue how to find the place, so Kerry had agreed to accompany them. She hadn't told the Old Bill that she'd been at the trailer earlier. If she was carted off for questioning, there would be nobody to look after the children and keep them safe.

The kids had still been hysterical when she had left them at her sister Joanne's house. Her mum was on her way over to help calm them down.

'Slow down, it's just down the road here on the right,' Kerry said nervously. She was dreading what she might find when they got there. Say Sammy was dead. She might get life and never see her boys again.

As the copper turned right, Kerry immediately spotted Frankie kneeling on the grass. She leaped out of the police car and ran over to her.

'Are you OK? Where's Jed? What's happened? Is Sammy still alive?'

Frankie looked at her with an unusual, vacant expression. 'Sammy's OK, he drove off, but I think Jed's dead.'

As Frankie began rocking to and fro, Kerry took her shivering body into her arms.

'What do you mean, Frankie? What happened to Jed?'

Frankie began to snigger, then her snigger turned into a manic laugh.

'I stabbed him. I think I killed him. He's evil, and I had to get him away from my kids. I've no regrets, Jed deserved to die, but say nothing to the Old Bill, Kerry, and I mean nothing. There's no point now, Sammy took the tape with him.'

CHAPTER FORTY-THREE

Unaware that his daughter had just been carted off to an Essex police station, Eddie Mitchell was on top form in a West End restaurant. He clicked his fingers at the short, dark-haired foreign waiter with the moustache.

'Oi, Manuel, bring us another bottle of champagne over, mate.'

Gina giggled and playfully punched Eddie. The waiter really did look like the one out of *Fawlty Towers*, but instead of sharing the joke between themselves, Eddie had to go that extra mile.

'You'll get us bloody barred in a minute,' she scolded him.

Ed held his hands up. 'I know nothing,' he said in a mock foreign accent.

Raymond and Polly both burst out laughing. They were like love's young dream at the moment because Polly had just received confirmation that she was eight weeks pregnant – hence today's celebration.

Eddie winked at Raymond as 'Manuel' topped up their glasses.

'So, have you told Joycie and Stanley the good news yet?'

Raymond squeezed Polly's hand. 'No. We haven't even told Polly's mum and dad. We're desperate not to tempt fate after waiting so long, so we're gonna get the twelve-week scan out the way before we make any big announcements.'

Eddie tutted with annoyance as his phone started ringing again. He'd told Gary and Ricky that he was busy today and they were making a fucking nuisance of themselves as per usual.

'Answer it, Ed, it might be urgent,' Raymond advised him.

Eddie snatched the phone off the table. 'This had better be important, Gal. What the fuck do you want?'

Gary was not in the best of moods. Stevens, the bent cop they had on their payroll, had contacted him earlier with some disturbing news and he was pissed off that his father had been ignoring his phone calls.

'Why ain't you been answering your poxy phone? It *is* bastard well important! Our Frankie's been arrested. From what I can gather, she's stuck a knife through Jed.'

DI Blyth was shocked as she walked into the interview room and came face to face with Frankie. Gone was the pretty girl she remembered from her father's court case and in its place was a bedraggled, pregnant woman with a vacant expression on her face. She had been furious with Frankie for making her a laughing stock at Eddie Mitchell's trial, but one look at the state of the girl now told her to let bygones be bygones.

'Hello, Frankie. I'm DI Blyth, do you remember me?'

Frankie stared at her and nodded.

'That's good. Now I've just been speaking to DC Burkinshaw, who tells me that you have refused legal advice and want to start the interview now. I'd rather you didn't do that, Frankie, because in the long run, it could prove beneficial to you to have a solicitor present. You are allowed one phone call. Have you used that privilege yet?'

'Yes, my friend Kerry is the only person I want to speak to. She isn't at home right now, so can I call her again later?'

DI Blyth nodded. 'What about the legal advice, Frankie? We have a duty solicitor who is happy to represent you.'

Frankie smiled and shook her head. 'No thank you, I really don't need one. I've already told everybody the truth. It was me that stabbed Jed and I hope the bastard dies a slow, painful death.'

*   *   *

412

Joyce sat opposite her husband with a look of suspicion plastered across her face. She knew her Stanley like the back of her hand and since he'd arrived home earlier, he hadn't once mentioned their row, was acting oddly and his face was full of guilt.

'I think I'll have a glass of sherry. Do you want a beer, Stanley?'

Stanley nodded dumbly. He had been a bit wild today, by his standards. He'd gone to another woman's house, had unholy thoughts, divulged his marital problems, and if Joycie ever found out what he'd been up to, she would bastard well kill him.

Joyce smiled as she handed Stanley a can of bitter. He had been up to no good – it was written all over his ugly clock.

'So, where did you go earlier? Anywhere nice?'

Stanley felt his face redden. 'No, dear. I popped to the pub,' he mumbled.

Joyce glared at him. She had smelt a strong whiff of women's perfume on his jumper and even though she was positive that most women in the world would find her Stanley repulsive, there was always the one old bag that was desperate. Joyce exercised her fingers and then, with a vicious look on her face, grabbed his meat and two veg and squeezed them.

'What you doing?' Stanley squealed in agony.

'If I ever find out you've been unfaithful to me, Stanley Smith, I will personally castrate you and feed your bollocks to them pigeons of yours. Do you understand me?'

'I ain't done nothing, Joycie, I swear I ain't,' Stanley pleaded with a pained expression.

Hearing a car pull up outside, Joyce let go of Stanley's private parts and ran over to the window. 'It's Frankie's car. Go and answer the door, Stanley. Chop-chop.'

Still holding his groin, Stanley did as he was told. He recognised the caller immediately.

'Hello. You're Frankie's friend, aren't you? Where is she? Is she with you?'

Kerry burst into tears. 'No. Frankie's been arrested. She tried to kill Jed.'

Alice O'Hara was sitting in the Optimist with Jimmy, drinking a pint of Guinness.

Jimmy rarely took Alice anywhere with him, but today was her birthday and she deserved the occasional treat.

'Nice pub this, ain't it, Jimmy? Can you bring me 'ere again for lunch one day?'

Jimmy shook his head. 'I've told you before, Alice, pubs are for the men to talk business and relax, a woman's place is the home. You know that, love.'

As Alice took a sip of her pint, she was suddenly overcome by a feeling of dread.

'What's up?' Jimmy asked, as he noticed the colour drain from her cheeks.

Alice took her psychic powers extremely seriously. Her nan had read tea leaves and her mum was a dab hand with a crystal ball. She stood up and urged Jimmy to do the same.

'We've gotta go home. Something terrible's happened, I know it has.'

Jimmy didn't know whether to laugh or cry. Alice was usually right when she had one of her funny turns, but he still had a full pint left.

'Can't we finish our drinks first? Another five minutes ain't gonna matter, is it?'

Alice grabbed his arm. 'There's no time to waste, we need to go now, Jimmy.'

Over in Basildon, Sammy had just pulled up outside Kerry's mum's house. Twice Kerry had attacked him now, and it was time for the bitch to receive her comeuppance. Sammy Junior and Freddy boy were his kids, just as much as they were hers, and now Julie had agreed to move in with him, she could look after them for him.

When Kerry's mother, Val, answered the door, Sammy pushed her into the hallway.

'Get out of my house, else I'll call the police,' Val screamed.

Having now recovered from his earlier concussion, Sammy pulled back his right fist and smashed Val viciously on the jaw. 'Where are my fucking chavvies?' he yelled.

Val sank to the floor, cupping her chin in her hands. 'I don't know, honest I don't,' she wept.

Sammy pulled back his right leg and booted Val full in the stomach. As she screamed, he bent down, grabbed her by the hair and forced her to stand up.

'Me and you are going for a little ride,' he told her.

'Where are you taking me?' Val sobbed.

'You're gonna show me where my boys are, and if you refuse, I'm gonna fucking burn you alive.'

Alice screamed as Jimmy turned into the drive and she spotted the police car. 'Dordie, Jimmy, dordie, the gavvers are here, the gavvers!' she cried.

Knowing his wife's fear of the police, Jimmy opened the driver's door. 'You wait 'ere if you like. I reckon our Jed's been nicked.'

Desperate to put herself out of her misery, Alice ignored Jimmy's advice and followed him towards the police car. Two officers got out and walked towards them.

'Are you Mr and Mrs O'Hara, the occupants of this property?'

Deathly white, Jimmy clenched Alice's hand and nodded.

The older officer continued. 'You need to come with us. There has been a serious incident and your son is at Basildon Hospital. We've been ordered to accompany you there.'

'What son? I've got three,' Jimmy said in a shocked whisper.

'It's Jed. Jed O'Hara. He's fairly poorly by all accounts, so the quicker we get you there, the better.'

Jed was her youngest son and, even though as a mother you shouldn't have favourites, he had always been the apple of Alice's eye. She let out a wail and felt her legs go from under her.

'Not my chavvie, not my beautiful Jed,' she sobbed.

* * *

Up in the City, Joey had just returned from his lunchbreak and sat back down at his desk.

'Your nan rang. She sounded a bit upset and asked if you could call her back. She said it was urgent,' his colleague informed him.

Praying that his grandfather hadn't fallen ill, Joey nervously dialled her number.

'What's up, Nan? Is Grandad OK?' he asked, fearing the worst.

'Oh, Joey, thank God you've rung me back. Me and your grandad are in a right old state. Frankie's friend has just been round here and she reckons Frankie has stabbed Jed and been arrested for it. She said he might even be dead.'

Joey couldn't believe what he was hearing. It couldn't be true – there must be some mistake. 'Christ Almighty! Just stay there with Grandad, I'm on my way over now.'

Eddie, Gary, Ricky and Raymond marched into Chelmsford police station like characters out of the movie *Reservoir Dogs*.

Eddie was determined to be at the front of the queue. 'Sorry, but I'm gonna have to go in first, this is really important,' he said to the other two people waiting.

'Well, that's tough shit. I've been waiting 'ere for half an hour and I've gotta sign on soon,' said a junkie-looking creature.

Ricky glared at the creature and as he stood up, pushed him back down on his seat. 'My sister's locked up in here, so we're first. Got it?'

Seeing Gary also glare at him, the junkie nodded. He didn't fancy an argument with these geezers, and the woman sitting next to him was too busy staring at her newspaper to argue the point.

Eddie repeatedly pressed the buzzer in reception. As soon as he'd found out that Frankie had been carted off to Chelmsford nick for questioning, he rang his solicitor, Larry, and told him to meet him there ASAP.

'Come on you cunts, open up,' Eddie cursed.

The bloke behind the desk had disappeared out of sight and Eddie was becoming more impatient by the minute. He turned to Raymond.

'I tell you something, if Frankie did try to kill that pikey piece of shit, he must have done something pretty bad to make her flip and when I find out what it is, I will personally destroy the little fucker.'

Over in Basildon Hospital, Alice was screaming blue murder. Not only had a doctor just told her that Jed was in a critical condition and being operated on, but she had learned that Frankie had been arrested for causing her son's injuries. Aware that the staff were getting annoyed with Alice for causing a scene, Jimmy tried his best to calm her down.

'Let's go and get some fresh air, eh? If you keep shouting and screaming, you're gonna make yourself ill, love.'

Alice flew at him and pummelled his chest with her fists. 'Fresh air! I don't want no fucking fresh air, I wanna get my hands on that no-good whore, and beat the fucking granny out of her. And I tell you something else I want, I wanna know where them chavvies are. Georgie should be 'ere with us. She'll make her daddy better, I know she will.'

As Alice began crying hysterically, Jimmy wrapped his arms around her and held her tightly to his chest. If Jed died or ended up with some kind of disability, as a proud travelling man, he would be expected to get revenge for his boy. Reigniting his feud with Eddie Mitchell was something that Jimmy didn't relish, but blood was thicker than water and if Jed did not recover, he would have no choice but to kill for his memory.

Kerry's mum, Val, was all of a quiver as Sammy sped towards her eldest daughter's house. She'd had no choice but to tell him where the kids were staying, as if she hadn't, she was positive Sammy would have kept to his word and killed her.

Val held her throbbing jaw and pointed. 'Next left, then first right,' she mumbled.

Sammy was stony-faced as he followed Val's directions. He had no idea if Jed had pulled through, but he was determined to get his kids for him, find out what hospital he had been taken to, and take them up there. Even if Jed had died, the kids had every right to say goodbye to their wonderful father.

'Where now?' Sammy shouted, as he pulled into a cul-de-sac.

'Park here. It's that house over there, number four.'

Sammy turned to Val. 'Right, you go up to the door and knock and I'll be right behind you.'

Neither Frankie's Fiesta nor Kerry's car were anywhere to be seen and Sammy just hoped that if she was out, the kids weren't with her.

As Sammy put his hood up, Val walked unsteadily up the path.

'Who is it?' her daughter Joanne shouted.

Val flinched. She had been hoping the kids weren't there, but she could hear their little voices. 'It's me, love.'

As Joanne opened the door, Sammy knocked Val out of the way, swung out an arm and pushed Joanne backwards into the hallway.

Sammy Junior was the first to appear. 'Daddy, don't hurt Auntie Joanne!' he screamed.

Freddy just burst out crying.

'Boys, go and get in the truck now,' Sammy ordered them.

As Joanne stood up and tried to hit him, Sammy kicked her in the crotch.

'Uncle Sammy, stop it,' Georgie said, hugging his legs.

'Where's your brother?'

'He's asleep on the sofa.'

'Go and wake him, Georgie, and take him out to the truck. Your daddy's not well and we're going to see him.'

Petrified by her uncle's behaviour, Georgie obediently led Harry outside the house. Sammy pushed the door to, and smiled at the fright on Val and Joanne's faces.

418

'So, where is the slag?' he asked Joanne.

Joanne shrugged. 'I don't know, honest I don't.'

Sammy edged closer to the two terrified women and waved his finger in both their faces. 'Don't even think of calling the gavvers, will ya? 'Cause if you do, I swear I will come back and mutilate the pair of ya.'

Laughing at the looks on their faces, Sammy winked and walked away.

Eddie sat down in an interview room opposite DI Blyth. After a lot of screaming and shouting, she had finally agreed to give him five minutes of her time.

'Thanks for seeing me. Frankie's my only daughter and I can't help her if I don't know exactly what's happened. I recognise you – didn't you have something to do with my trial?'

Blyth nodded. 'Yes, I was the one that ferried Frankie to court. For personal reasons, I was transferred over to Chelmsford two years ago.'

'So, is Jed alive?' Eddie asked nervously.

'Jed is currently being operated on in Basildon Hospital. He was stabbed twice with a bread knife and his injuries have been described as life-threatening.'

Eddie ran his fingers through his hair and leaned back on his chair. 'Listen, I dunno if you've got kids yourself, but I know what my Frankie's all about. My daughter wouldn't hurt a fly and she wouldn't even know how to stab a steak, let alone her boyfriend. She ain't violent, it's not in her nature.'

DI Blyth shrugged. 'Frankie has already admitted to attempting to murder Jed and I just hope for her sake that he doesn't die.'

Eddie stood up and paced up and down the room. 'Is she here? I need to speak to her.'

'She was here, but she isn't now. She was in shock and didn't feel too well, so she has been escorted to Broomfield Hospital for the sake of her baby.'

Feeling both anxious and incompetent, Eddie slammed his

fist against the wall. 'My solicitor will be here in a minute. He's gonna represent Frankie, sit in with her while she does her interview.'

As Eddie Mitchell looked at her, DI Blyth felt a slight twinge of guilt. She had insisted that Frankie wasn't in a fit state of mind to be interviewed, but she had been overruled by her not-so-sympathetic DS.

'I am so sorry, Mr Mitchell, but the interview has already been concluded. I advised Frankie not to speak without a legal representative, but she was very insistent that she didn't need to be represented.'

Eddie crouched down and held his head in his hands. 'Frankie, what the fuck have you done?' he whispered.

Back in Rainham, Joey was doing his best to console his drunken grandmother.

'Cursed this family is and it's all my bloody fault,' Joyce ranted, as she topped her glass up with yet another sherry.

Stanley raised his eyebrows at Joey and put his forefinger to the side of his head to insinuate Joyce wasn't the full shilling.

Joey sighed. He had phoned his father but there was no answer, and he had also rung Basildon police station, which he believed was the nearest one to Wickford. They informed him that his sister wasn't there. He was at a loss as to what else to do for now and he had no number for Frankie's friend, Kerry. The only thing he could do was wait for Dominic to arrive. His boyfriend had just left work, was always good in a crisis and he would know exactly how to handle matters.

Joyce took a gulp of her sherry. 'If only I hadn't opened the door that day, my Jessica would still be alive and Frankie wouldn't have murdered Jed.'

Stanley had had a gutful of his wife spouting rubbish. He almost wished he was still round Pat the Pigeon's house.

'Whatever you going on about? You silly old bat.'

'The gypsy. The one that cursed me on the doorstep years

ago when I refused to buy her lucky heather. Gone downhill ever since, my life has, that and the day I married you, you bald-headed old bastard.'

'Don't have a go at Grandad, Nan. None of this is his fault,' Joey said, annoyed.

Joyce snorted. 'Don't be sticking up for him. He's got some old tart on the firm. Coming home here smelling of some old whore's perfume. I ain't putting up with it, I deserve better.'

Joey looked at his nan in amazement. 'Don't be silly. Who would want Grandad?'

'That's what I thought,' Joyce said, bursting into tears.

Stanley stood up and stomped out of the room. He would rather spend the night in his pigeon shed than have to hear one more word from Joycie's argumentative mouth.

DI Blyth insisted on picking Frankie up from the hospital herself. The girl had been fully checked over and both she and the baby had been declared fit and well.

As DC Burkinshaw followed her along the corridor, Blyth turned to him. 'I'm going to drive Frankie back to the station alone; you go with one of the other officers. We need to chat, woman to woman.'

About to argue that driving a potential murderer back alone wasn't in the rule book, Burkinshaw quickly shut his mouth. DI Blyth had that 'don't mess with me' look on her face.

Once inside the car, Blyth explained to Frankie that her father had been to the police station and had spoken to her.

'What did he say when you told him that I'd stabbed Jed?' Frankie asked.

Blyth glanced at Frankie. She was fiddling frantically with her hands and rocking slightly in her seat and Blyth couldn't believe that the doctors had passed her as fully fit.

'He was shocked, and very upset that you hadn't taken my advice and had a solicitor present for your interview. I don't think you are very well, Frankie. If I turn this car around now and drive back to the hospital, you can tell the doctors that you feel strange and muddled and we might be able to scrap that interview you did and do a new one when you feel a bit better.'

Frankie shook her head. 'I'm fine, honest. Can I ask you something?'

Blyth nodded.

'Is Jed dead yet?'

Blyth looked at her. 'No. Why? Do you want him to be?'

Frankie shrugged. 'I just want my children to be safe and they will never be safe while Jed's alive.'

Knowing she was now getting somewhere, Blyth bumped the car onto a kerb. 'And why is that, Frankie? What has Jed done to your children?'

Frankie gnawed at her already bitten fingernails. 'Can I ring my friend when I get back to the police station? You did promise me.'

Blyth handed Frankie her mobile phone. She was desperate to understand what had turned a sweet, innocent girl into a violent lunatic.

'You can use this, but you mustn't tell anyone back at the station. I'm not allowed to let you use it and if you tell on me, you'll get me into all kinds of trouble.'

'I promise I won't tell,' Frankie said, snatching the phone off her.

It was Joanne who answered.

'Don't tell her Sammy's took the kids,' Kerry whispered, frantically waving her arms. Frankie had enough on her plate and she wanted to break the news that the children had been snatched as gently as she possibly could.

Kerry grabbed the phone. 'Frankie, I've been worried sick about you. Where are you now?'

'I'm still with the police, but don't worry, I'm fine. Jed's not dead yet, which is a shame. Where are the kids? Are they OK?'

Frankie sounded strange, very unlike her normal self, and instinct told Kerry not to say she had no idea where the kids were.

'The kids are fine. Listen Frankie, you have to tell the police about the tape, you've got to tell them everything.'

'No, I can't. And you must promise me, Kerry, that you never mention it to anybody.'

Kerry was bemused. Frankie sounded as though she was high on drugs or something. 'You must tell them, Frankie. If you don't, they won't understand what you did and why you did it.'

'I'm not going to tell 'em, I can't, and one day I will tell you why, but I can't really talk properly now. You won't say anything about it, will you? Promise me, Kerry, that you won't.'

'I promise that I won't say anything unless you want me to,' Kerry replied sadly.

Frankie smiled. 'Put the kids on, I want to talk to them.'

Kerry looked at Joanne. They had rung the police, told them that Sammy had taken the children and they were waiting for someone to come round. The police hadn't seemed particularly concerned when they had heard that Sammy was the father of two of the kids and the uncle of the other two. Kerry and Joanne didn't mention that Sammy had been violent earlier. They were too frightened of any repercussions.

'The kids are out,' Kerry said.

'Where? Who with?'

'Me mum. She's took 'em to McDonald's,' Kerry lied.

Frankie was bitterly disappointed. She had been so looking forward to speaking to her children; she needed to tell them how much she loved them. Her eyes filled up with tears.

'I need you to look after them for me until everything's sorted, Kerry. Can you do that for me? I will give you my dad's number, he will give you some money and help you out.'

Kerry started to cry. 'Of course I can. Can I come and see you, Frankie? When are the police letting you go?'

Frankie ended the call without giving an answer or saying goodbye. She tearfully handed the phone back to Blyth.

'What do you not want your friend to say anything about, Frankie? Please tell me, I want to help you.'

423

Frankie stared out of the window. Blyth seemed trustable, but what was the point of telling her about the tape when Sammy had run off with it? Without any evidence it was her word against Jed's and, unless the bastard died, he would easily convince everyone that she was lying.

Frankie put her head in her hands. Telling her dad about the tape was not even on her radar. He would definitely believe her, but Jed was dangerous and she couldn't risk her dad doing life in prison or, worse still, ending up dead like her mother had.

'Talk to me, Frankie. Please tell me what's bothering you,' Blyth said kindly.

Frankie shook her head. 'The only thing I can tell you is that Jed is a traitor. The rest is a secret and for my dad's and my children's sake, that's the way it will have to stay.'

CHAPTER FORTY-FOUR

Aware that Harry was crying again, Alice lifted him up and sat him on her lap. Since Jed had returned from the operating theatre none of the family had left his side, and understandably the kids were getting bored.'You're a big boy now and big boys don't cry,' Alice said, wiping Harry's nose with a tissue.

'Will we be going home to Mummy tonight?' Georgie asked innocently.

Alice's top lip took up a snarling position. 'You won't be living with your mother any more. She's evil and she'll be going to live in prison.'

Seeing the distressed look on Georgie's face, Alice softened and urged the child to sit on the chair next to her. 'Don't get all upset now. You and Harry can live with me and your grandad, and when your dad gets out of hospital, he can live with us too.'

'You're gonna have to toughen them up a bit, especially him,' Shannon said, pointing at Harry.

'Oh, I will do. Now the doctors have said that Jed's gonna be all right, he's bound to get custody of the kids, which means I can have 'em whenever I want. I'll knock little Harry boy into a travelling mush in no time, you just wait and see.'

Jimmy stood up. 'Where the hell has Marky bloody well got to? The café's only ten minutes away and he's been gone well over an hour now.'

Alice shrugged. 'I hope he's on his way back. I'm that hungry,

425

I could eat a scabby horse. Try his mobile again, Jimmy.'

'I've been ringing him. He ain't poxy answering. If he's gone home to get his head down without telling us, I'll have his guts for garters.'

Alice, Jimmy, Shannon, Marky, Billy, Sammy and the kids had all spent the night at the hospital. Since finding out that Jed was out of the woods, their mood had turned from morose to jovial, and Mark had offered to get them some much-needed breakfast from a nearby café.

Alice leaped out of her seat as a nurse poked her head around the door. 'For fuck's sake, can't you just let us have some family time? As soon as my Jed wakes up, you'll be the first to know.'

When the nurse made a quick exit, Shannon laughed and tickled Georgie. 'If you ever see that old whore of a mother of yours again, I want you to tell her that Auntie Shannon's gonna beat the granny out of her.'

'Just shut it, Shannon,' Jimmy said angrily.

The kids were distressed enough as it was without his trappy daughter-in-law sticking her oar in.

As Harry started crying again, Alice handed him to her husband. 'Can you take him for a walk or something? He's doing my head in with his whining.'

Sammy and Billy followed Jimmy out of the room. Minutes later, Alice grabbed Shannon's arm. 'He's waking up. Dordie, thank you God. He's gonna be OK. Jed, it's Mum, can you hear me?'

'Where am I?' Jed whispered.

Alice moved her chair and squeezed his hand. 'You're in Basildon Hospital, boy. The old whore stabbed ya, didn't she? Don't you worry, the police have locked her up now. She's in a cell, where she belongs.'

'I'm so thirsty,' Jed croaked.

Alice had tears in her eyes as she held a cup of water to his lips. 'You had to have an operation. Internal bleeding you had and a punctured bowel. Laparotomy or something, the doctor called it.'

Shannon stood up. 'I'm gonna see if I can find the boys, tell 'em Jed's awake.'

'Don't tell them nurses yet. I wanna spend some time with my boy before they start poking their trunks in,' Alice said.

'What exactly did the quacks say, Mum? That bitch ain't done me no permanent damage, has she?'

'They told us you'll make a full recovery, boy. No thanks to that evil whore, though. What type of woman tries to murder the father of her chavvies, eh? I hope they give her fucking life.'

'Daddy, talk to me, Daddy,' Georgie shouted.

Alice lifted her granddaughter up and sat her on her lap. 'Now you mustn't touch Daddy 'cause he still ain't very well.'

Jed smiled. 'Hello, Georgie girl,' he said, stroking her arm.

Georgie was too young to understand exactly what had happened, but she knew that her mum had done something bad to her dad. 'Where is Mummy?' she asked.

'Where's Dad? Is Harry here as well?' Jed whispered, swerving Georgie's question.

Alice nodded. 'Billy, Sammy and your dad have been up here all night. Harry kept whinging, so they've taken him out to get some fresh air. Marky was here as well, he went to get some grub and then disappeared into thin air. I wanted to contact Sally, Jed, but none of us have got her number. I'm sure her and Lukey boy would want to be here.'

'I don't know her number off by heart, Mum. Sammy will sort it, I'll get him to contact her. Has Frankie been charged yet? Has anyone told you anything?'

'Your father asked earlier and one of the gavvers said she'll be up in court later today, but will probably get bail. She ain't coming near them chavvies, Jed. I'll fucking kill her if she comes within two hundred yards of 'em, on my Georgie girl's life, I will.'

'You'll have to look after Georgie and Harry for me until I get meself sorted, is that OK?'

Alice smiled. 'That's no problem, boy.'

Georgie had picked up snippets of the conversation and was now more confused than ever. She tugged on Alice's skirt. 'Can I see Mummy tomorrow, Nan?'

Shannon and Sammy returning saved Alice from having to answer the awkward question.

'It's mayhem out there. Someone said there's been a bad road accident. I found Sammy on me way back. Jimmy and Billy have taken Harry to the café with 'em. They've given up on Marky, they're getting our food themselves.'

'Can I have five minutes alone with Sammy?' Jed croaked. He was tired again now and needed to speak to his cousin before he drifted back off into the land of nod.

Alice lifted up Georgie. 'I wanna stay here with Daddy,' she pleaded.

'Daddy's tired. Come with Nanna and she'll buy you a chocolate bar.'

As the door closed behind his family, Jed turned to Sammy. 'Where's the tape?'

'In me pocket. Do you wanna see it?' Sammy teased.

Jed was fuming. That tape contained enough information to put them inside for donkey's years. What was Sammy trying to do, kill him off?

'Get rid of it, you dinlo. The hospital's probably swarming with Old Bill as we speak. I can't believe your brains, Sammy boy, ain't ya got none?'

Sammy laughed. He was absolutely thrilled that his cousin was out of the woods, but still couldn't resist winding him up. He pulled out a see-through plastic bag from his pocket that contained nothing but ashes and a charred piece of plastic.

'There's the clever Frankie's fucking tape,' he said cockily.

As ill as Jed felt, he couldn't help but try to laugh. Wincing, he urged his cousin to give him a hug.

'Well done, Sammy boy. We're in the clear, mush.'

*   *   *

Outside the magistrates' court, Ricky flicked his fag butt into a bush and nudged Gary. 'What are them fucking two doing 'ere?'

Furious that his half-brother had brought his boyfriend to the court with him, Gary marched over to Joey.

'Whaddya think you're doing, bringing him 'ere with ya? You ain't at the fucking gay parade now, you know.'

Clocking what was occuring, Eddie walked over to Gary. 'Leave them alone,' he ordered.

Gary glared at his father. 'You've changed your fucking tune, ain't ya?'

Eddie put a protective arm around Joey's shoulder. 'I had a lot of time to sit and think while I was in prison and I came to the conclusion that life's too short to be bitter and twisted. Joey and Dominic might be gay, but they're good lads and what they do in their own time is entirely up to them, not us.'

As Gary and Ricky stormed off, Joey hugged his father. 'Cheers, Dad.'

Dominic smiled. 'Thank you, Mr Mitchell.'

Eddie shook Dominic's hand. 'And no more, Mr Mitchell. You call me Eddie from now on, OK?'

Raymond had wanted to come alone to the court, but his mother had had other ideas.

'Look, you don't wanna upset yourself. Stay at home with Dad and I'll ring you as soon as we know Frankie's got bail,' he'd pleaded with her the day before.

Unfortunately for Raymond, Joyce loved a drama and had no intention of missing out on this particular one.

'Frankie's our grandchild and me and your dad want to be there to support her. It's what Jessica would have wanted,' she insisted.

As Eddie acknowledged him, Raymond put an arm around his father's shoulder.

'Please don't start an argument with Eddie, will you Dad? Today's about Frankie and none of us need any extra grief.'

Stanley tutted and pointed at Joyce. He was still in the dark that his wife had already met up with Eddie and had all but forgiven the man who had murdered their daughter.

'Best you tell Mouth Almighty that, not me,' he mumbled.

Joyce had ears like a bat. 'What did you just say?' she asked.

'Nothing, dear,' Stanley replied sarcastically.

Desperate not to get into an altercation with Stanley, Eddie walked over to Larry, his solicitor.

'What's up?' he asked as Larry ended his phone call. He had a glum expression on his usually cheerful face.

Larry sighed. 'There's been a bit of a hitch, I'm afraid.'

Eddie glared at him. Larry had been positive that Frankie would get bail when he had spoken to him yesterday.

'Hitch! What fucking hitch?' he exclaimed angrily.

'The main magistrate today is none other than Rupert Dickens.'

Eddie scratched his head. 'Who the hell is Rupert Dickens? I've never fucking heard of him.'

'Rupert Dickens is George Dickens' brother. You know, the same George Dickens that we blackmailed at your trial, who passed away shortly afterwards due to a heart attack, which the doctors said was caused by stress.'

'Fuck! Can't you get him thrown off the case? I don't care what it costs,' Eddie spat.

Larry shook his head. 'I've just tried to wangle it, but I'm afraid there is little I can do. I'm sorry, Eddie, but we just have to hope for the best.'

'Excuse me?'

Eddie swung around and came face to face with two youngish girls. One looked familiar, but he couldn't quite place her.

'You're Frankie's dad, aren't you?' the familiar one asked.

'Who wants to know?' Eddie replied cautiously.

'You probably don't remember me, but I'm Frankie's friend, Kerry. I was with her at the restaurant that night when you and her had a row.'

Eddie nodded. 'I'm sorry about that night. Things were a

bit awkward, if you know what I mean. Listen, thanks for looking after the kids for Frankie. How are they? Are they here with you?'

Joanne prodded her sister in the stomach. 'Tell him, then,' she hissed.

'We really need your help, Mr Mitchell. Sammy, Jed's cousin, came to my house yesterday and snatched my boys – he's their father. He also took Georgie and Harry with him as well,' Kerry stammered.

Eddie looked at Kerry in horror. He had asked the Old Bill where his grandchildren were and had been told they were with Frankie's friend, Kerry, and were safe and well.

'Have you rung the Old Bill? What time did he take 'em?'

'Yesterday afternoon. We told the police, but because he's the dad of my two and uncle to Frankie's, they didn't seem that bothered. I'm frightened for their safety. I haven't told Frankie yet: I didn't want to worry her until she got bail.'

Eddie turned to Larry. 'You're gonna have to help me get the kids back. Knowing them pikey shitbags they could be anywhere by now. Go through the official channels so everything's kosher.'

Larry nodded. 'Come on, we need to go inside now. I'll sort it, don't worry.'

Stanley glared at Eddie as he took his seat in the gallery. 'Murderer,' he mumbled under his breath.

'Shut up,' Joyce spat, punching him on the leg.

'Unlike you and our Raymond, I'm loyal to our Jessica,' Stanley spat back.

Eddie glanced at Joey as Frankie stood up. She looked frail and ill and Ed was shocked by the change in her appearance since he'd seen her that night in the restaurant.

DI Blyth smiled at Frankie as she nervously confirmed her name. She was sure Frankie would get bail and was also sure that she could help her, if only she would tell her the truth about what had really happened.

Larry stood up and addressed Dickens.

431

'I am not only here representing Miss Mitchell today, I am also a family friend that has known the defendant for many years.'

Spotting Kerry, Frankie smiled and waved. 'Where are the kids?' she mouthed.

Dickens immediately turned on her. 'For goodness' sake, Miss Mitchell. Control yourself and show some respect. This is a courtroom, not a fairground.'

'Bastard. He ain't gonna give her bail,' Eddie whispered to Raymond.

Larry continued. 'Miss Mitchell is a doting mother of two young children. She is currently pregnant with her third child and, apart from one caution, has never been in trouble with the police before. I therefore plead with you to show some compassion and grant Miss Mitchell bail.'

As the magistrates whispered between themselves, Eddie feared the worst.

'Frankie looks ill, Dad. I'm so worried about her,' Joey whispered.

Eddie squeezed his son's shoulder. 'Frankie's a tough cookie, she'll be OK,' he lied.

Dickens cleared his throat. Revenge was a sweet thing and if he refused Frankie bail today then she would be taken to Chelmsford Crown Court for a second hearing next week. Dickens knew that his brother's influential friends over at Chelmsford blamed Mitchell for George's death, so young Frankie's chances of bail were looking fairly bleak.

'We have weighed up both sides of this application, and we are seriously concerned that if Miss Mitchell is allowed bail, she will not turn up for her trial.'

Glancing at Eddie, Dickens smirked. 'Application for bail rejected.'

Eddie jumped up. 'You fucking cunt! I'll have you for this,' he screamed at Dickens.

'You evil bastard,' Gary and Ricky shouted, as they grabbed hold of their father to stop him from throttling the heartless magistrate.

Frankie turned to her family and friends with tears streaming down her face.

'Look after Georgie and Harry for me. Tell 'em how much I love 'em and tell 'em what their mummy did, she did for them.'

Alice and Shannon were furious when they clocked Jimmy and Billy walking towards them, minus their breakfast.

'Where you been? Jed's wide awake. Sammy said you were going to the bloody café. Absolutely starving we are, Jimmy.'

'Take the kids and Shannon for a walk while I speak to your mother,' Jimmy ordered Billy.

Noticing that both her husband and son were ashen-faced, Alice felt a shiver go down her spine. 'What's a matter? Don't tell me, they've let that old whore out and given her custody of the chavvies.'

Jimmy had tears in his eyes as he wrapped his wife in his arms. 'It's our Marky. He's dead, Alice.'

Alice pushed Jimmy away. 'Dead! What are you talking about? He only went to get some breakfast. He was probably tired and went home to get some kip, you dinlo.'

Jimmy shook his head. 'Marky's been involved in a fatal road accident. There were no witnesses, but the gavvers reckon that he probably fell asleep at the wheel of my motor. He hit an old couple driving on the opposite side of the road. The other man's dead and the woman's critical. Marky died at the crash scene, there was nothing anybody could do.'

Alice screamed and pummelled her fists against Jimmy's chest. 'It can't be my Marky – they must have got it wrong. I'm psychic, Jimmy, I would have known. I always know when something's wrong, you know I do,' she sobbed.

Jimmy grabbed his wife and stroked her long dark hair. 'They're not wrong, darling. Me and Billy saw my Land Cruiser smashed up on the way to the café. We stopped, but it was too late – he was already dead.'

Alice sank to her knees and grasped Jimmy's ankles. 'It must be a similar motor. It ain't my Marky, I know it ain't.'

Jimmy crouched down and tilted his wife's chin towards him. 'Alice, it was definitely Marky. It was me that identified him.'

CHAPTER FORTY-FIVE

'When I say strip, I mean strip, Mitchell. You need to take your knickers off as well.'

Frankie looked at the two prison officers in horror. One was tall, fat and she looked and spoke like a man, and the other was short with a skinhead haircut.

'Why have I got to take my knickers off?' Frankie asked in a nervous whisper. She could sense the two prison officers were enjoying her embarrassment and discomfort.

'I need to check that you're not carrying any drugs on you. Listen, Mitchell, don't mess with me, 'cause if you do, I'll insist that the prison doctor comes in here to give you a full internal, and you won't enjoy that, trust me.'

Tears streamed down Frankie's face as she stepped out of her knickers.

'Now, turn around and bend over,' the shaven-headed screw ordered.

Unable to stop her legs from shaking, Frankie did as she was told.

'She's clean,' the fat screw said.

'Can I please get dressed again now?' Frankie asked, as she was told to turn around.

The smaller screw nodded and as Frankie hurriedly started to put her clothes back on, she felt sick and degraded.

Urging Frankie to get a move on, the two screws accompanied her towards the hospital wing.

435

'You've got to be five months pregnant to be able to stay on this wing, and you're not. You'll probably stay in here overnight, and you'll be moved to the remand wing tomorrow. I know for a fact there was no room in the hospital wing yesterday, so you might be taken to a cell straight after you've had a check-up.'

Frankie was ravenous; she hadn't had anything to eat or drink for hours. 'Can I have some dinner?' she asked as she was escorted through a corridor.

'Hark at her,' the bigger screw said to the other.

'This ain't a holiday camp, love,' the shaven-headed one sniggered.

As Frankie reached the hospital wing and heard the screams and voices of the other inmates, her hunger rapidly disappeared.

'It's another white slag,' shouted an African-sounding voice.

'Oi, pretty girl, you're mine,' a woman yelled.

'Lick my pussy, bitch,' somebody shouted.

'Take no notice of them junkie cunts,' she heard another girl scream.

Too frightened to look to her left or her right, Frankie kept her head bowed and stared at her feet. As she heard somebody chanting monkey noises at her, she started to weep.

'Move, Mitchell, we ain't got all day,' said the big screw.

'You're gonna need to toughen up in here. Any sign of weakness, you'll be like a lamb to the slaughter,' said the other.

Frankie breathed a sigh of relief as she was ushered into a little room. Surely the rest of the prison couldn't be as bad as the hospital wing and, if that was the case, her walk of terror was finally over.

Eddie Mitchell was beside himself as he paced up and down his living room with a large glass of Scotch in his hand. He picked up his phone and tried Larry's number again. 'Why the fuck ain't you been answering? What's going on?'

'Ed, I'm on my way over to you now. I'll be with you in

436

about ten minutes. I'll explain everything when I get there,' Larry replied.

Eddie threw his phone across the room in temper. He'd felt sick to the stomach when Frankie had been banged up earlier, and not knowing where his grandchildren were was giving him a double fucking headache. He turned to Gary and Ricky.

'If Lal's driving all the way over 'ere then it's bad news, I'm telling ya. He'd tell me over the fucking phone if he had anything good to say. Frankie's gonna be upset enough as it is. How the fuck am I meant to tell her that we don't know where her kids are?'

'Don't tell her, Dad. If the law ain't on our side, we'll sort it ourselves. We can easily get the kids back, trust me,' Gary said.

Eddie smashed his fist against the wall. 'We can't just fucking kidnap 'em, we'll all get nicked.'

Realising that Eddie was in a foul mood, Gina decided to make herself scarce. 'I bet yous boys haven't eaten all day. I'll go and rustle you something up.'

'Food's the last thing on our fucking minds. Have you forgotten that my daughter's just been banged up and my grand-kids could be anywhere in the bastard country?'

Ricky was quite taken with his dad's new girlfriend and immediately stood up for her. 'Calm down, Dad. Don't take it out on Gina, she's only trying to help. Me and Gal are both hungry, we ain't eaten since this morning. Starving ourselves ain't gonna get Frankie out of nick or help us find the kids, is it?'

Eddie ran his hands through his hair. Realising the error of his ways, he followed Gina into the kitchen. 'I'm really sorry, babe. I'm so fucking stressed, I don't mean to take it out on you.'

Gina hugged him. 'I understand, but you must try and calm yourself down, Ed. For all you know the kids could be with Alice and Jimmy. I shouldn't think for one minute that Sammy's run off to the other end of the country with them, and even if he has, you've got a clever fiancée who happens to be a private detective.'

Eddie held Gina's face in his hands and kissed her on the forehead.

'Dad, Larry's just pulled up outside,' Gary shouted.

Ed dashed to the door and as soon as he clocked Larry's expression, knew his premonition of bad news had been spot-on.

Larry walked into the lounge and gratefully accepted the glass of Scotch that Ricky poured for him. He sat down in an armchair. 'Right, the good news is the kids are safe and well and are being looked after by Alice and Jimmy. The bad news is, until Frankie is released from prison, we don't have a cat in hell's chance of getting them back. And the unexpected news is that Jimmy and Alice's eldest son, Mark, got killed in a car crash this morning. He was in Jimmy's motor and had just left Basildon Hospital, by all accounts.'

Eddie smirked. 'How tragic! And if you want my honest opinion, it couldn't have happened to a nicer fucking family.'

Gary grinned. 'What goes around comes around, eh, Dad?'

Eddie stood up and began wearing out the carpet once more. 'There must be some way we can get custody of the kids. Gina and I are willing to look after 'em. Surely the authorities must realise they're better off living with us than a load of fucking tinkers, and if they won't allow it because of my record, I'm sure Joycie will have 'em live with her. All Georgie and Harry need is a base, then we can all muck in. Joey and Dominic said they'd help out at weekends.'

Larry held his hands in the air and shook his head. 'Eddie, I have spent all afternoon going over every legality possible. I have spoken to a policeman friend of mine and also a social worker who I've had dealings with in the past. We can apply for a temporary custody order, but I've been told in no uncertain terms that you will most certainly be wasting your time. In the eyes of the law, Jed is the innocent party in all of this. He's also Georgie and Harry's father, therefore will automatically get custody of them.'

438

'This is bollocks! I ain't having some fucking jobsworth telling me what's best for my grandkids. I will fight this all the way, Lal, however much it costs. As for that shitbag Jed, how is he meant to look after 'em if he's fighting for his life in fucking hospital?'

'I've checked that out, and disappointingly, Jed is already on the road to a full recovery. In a strange way, Eddie, it's a shame that Frankie didn't achieve what she obviously intended. If Jed had died, we would have had a much stronger chance of getting custody of the children. However, as it stands, all we can do now is concentrate on getting Frankie out on bail. If we succeed, there is a very good chance that the children will be handed straight back to her. If we fail, I really don't know what the answer is.'

Eddie slammed his now empty glass on the coffee table. 'And what about if I sort things my way?'

Larry shrugged. 'False passports and a life abroad with the children would be your only option. I can help you organise it, but it's really not a wise move, Eddie, trust me on this one. Listen, I have to dash now, my wife has organised one of her infamous dinner parties and I'm extremely late as it is. I'll call you tomorrow, we'll talk more then.'

Gary and Ricky looked at one another as their father left the room. 'You know, don't ya?' Gary said.

'Definitely,' Ricky replied.

Eddie saw Larry out and slammed the front door. Fuck the legal system, it was time to sort things out the Mitchell way.

Back in Holloway, Frankie had now been checked over by medical staff and, due to shortage of space, told she was well enough to be taken straight to a cell on the remand wing, D3.

After another walk through many corridors, the fat screw grabbed Frankie's arm, and smiled at her. 'This is your new home, Mitchell, in you go,' she said callously.

As Frankie was shoved inside the cell, she came face to face with three other girls. One was tall, black, with short afro hair, one was mixed race, and the other was a thin-faced white girl.

Desperate to make friends with somebody, Frankie forced a smile. 'Hello. My name's Frankie. What's yours?' she whispered.

'You got any gear?' the white girl asked her.

'What do you mean?' Frankie asked, perplexed.

'Drugs! Are you divvy or what?' the girl replied.

Frankie shook her head. 'No, I'm afraid I haven't,' she said apologetically.

'What 'bout fags or baccy? You must have some shit on you,' the black girl asked.

'I'm sorry, I ain't got nothing. I'm pregnant, so I don't really smoke any more,' Frankie replied honestly.

The black girl made a kissing noise with her teeth and glared at Frankie. 'Don't lie to us, whore, 'cause when we find out you been telling us porkies, I gonna cut that scrawny white throat of yours.'

Petrified by the manic expression on the girl's face, Frankie felt her legs start to wobble, then fell to her knees. 'I'm not lying. I haven't got anything, I swear I haven't,' she cried.

The black girl sniggered. Ever since she'd been abused as a child by her parents, then shoved into care, she'd always got off on terrorising other people. It was her sadistic acts of violence that had granted her so much respect in the notorious south London posse she now belonged to. She crouched down next to Frankie. 'Take your tracksuit bottoms off, white girl,' she ordered.

'Don't touch me. I beg you, please leave me alone,' Frankie wept.

While the other two girls egged her on, the black girl smirked, pinned Frankie down with one hand and put her other hand inside Frankie's tracksuit bottoms.

'No! Please, no,' Frankie screamed, as the girl inserted two fingers inside her vagina.

The girl ignored Frankie's obvious distress. 'Turn on your front,' she ordered.

As Frankie did as she was told, she felt the girl's fingers enter her anus, and bit her lip. Part of her wanted to die, but as images of Georgie and Harry flashed through her mind, she knew, whatever happened inside this prison, she had to keep it together for the sake of her children.

Suddenly the black girl released her fingers, stood up and laughed. 'So, you ain't no liar. You say you got no drugs and you ain't got no drugs.'

Frankie scrambled to her feet. She had to be strong. She was her father's daughter after all. 'If you ever touch me again, I swear I will kill you,' she said boldly.

The black girl smiled, then held out her right hand. 'I like you – you got spunk, Frankie. My name's Marion, but everyone know me by my street name, Killer. Welcome to Holloway, sister.'

CHAPTER FORTY-SIX

Eddie arranged a 1 p.m. meeting at Auntie Joan's the following day. Years ago, when Ed's father Harry was alive, they'd always held their most important meetings upstairs in Joanie's house. They didn't so much now, but Joan had always left the decor of the room the same, in case the boys ever needed to use it.

After a lot of thought, Ed had taken the decision not to include Raymond on this particular jaunt. Ray had only just come back into the firm, and after what had happened with Jessica, Ed felt that it was inappropriate to involve him in another bloodbath. Deep down, Eddie felt that Ray would approve of his plan, but he wasn't going to mention it to him. The fewer people who knew about this one, the better.

Gary and Ricky were already at Joanie's when Ed arrived.

'You boys go on upstairs and I'll make you a pot of tea and a couple of plates of sandwiches. I've got some rock cakes in the oven and I've made you a nice bread pudding for you to take home with you, Ed.'

Eddie hugged his aunt. Joanie understood his and his brothers' lifestyles like the old-timer that she was. Ed told Gary and Ricky to go upstairs. He needed a quiet word alone with his aunt. 'I'm gonna need a favour, Auntie, an alibi for the boys. Will you do it for us?'

'Of course I bloody will.'

Eddie held his aunt's head in his hands and kissed her on the forehead. 'I love you, Joanie, you're a diamond.'

442

'I know I am, now don't go all sentimental on me. Get your arse upstairs, before I burn your bastard rock cakes.'

Over in Rainham, Joey and Dominic were having lunch with Joyce and Stanley in the Albion. Joey had been so upset over his sister's imprisonment that he had taken the rest of the week off work. Worried about Joey, Dom had followed suit.

Joyce ate her last piece of scampi and put her knife and fork down. 'I still can't believe they put her in a women's prison. In my eyes, Frankie's still a kid. How will she cope? She'll be mixing with murderers, druggies and all sorts in there.'

Seeing the distressed look on his grandson's face, Stanley kicked his wife under the table to urge her to shut up.

Joyce glanced at Stanley, kicked him back twice as hard, then carried on talking. 'So, have you spoken to her yet, Joey?'

Joey's eyes welled up. 'She rang last night to speak to the kids. She'd rung Kerry first and Kerry had told Frankie that the kids were staying at ours. I didn't know what to say, so I pretended that Dom had taken them to McDonald's. What am I gonna do if she rings again later and asks to speak to them? If I say Dom's taken 'em out again, she's bound to get suspicious that I'm lying.'

'I think Frankie should know the truth. She's every right to know that the gyppos have snatched her poor babies,' Stanley said bluntly.

Joey shook his head. 'Dad said Frankie won't cope in there if she thinks the O'Haras have got the kids. He's told us to lie for the sake of her sanity.'

Stanley slammed his pint down on the table. 'That sounds about right, coming from your father. He's a born fucking liar who lied his way out of murdering your poor mother. He should have got life, the bastard.'

Aware that Joey was about to cry, Joyce punched Stanley on the arm. 'If you ain't got anything constructive to say, then don't say nothing, you evil old goat!'

443

'I'll get us all another drink. Same again, Joycie?' Dominic asked, as Stanley stomped off to the toilets.

Joyce nodded, and when Dominic walked away, patted Joey's arm. 'Don't worry yourself, love. I bet this time next week Frankie's got bail and is round at mine and your grandad's with the kids.'

Joey sighed. 'Let's pray to God you're right, Nan, 'cause if the crown court refuses her bail, Frankie and them poor kids' lives will be ripped apart for ever.'

Unaware that her family were currently discussing her welfare, Frankie was lying on her bunk, staring blankly at the ceiling. Since their initial humiliation of her, Marion, Liz and Jackie, her three cellmates, had been nothing but friendly towards her, but Frankie couldn't be arsed making small talk with them. Not only had they put her through one of the worst experiences of her life, but in six days' time she would be out of this shit-hole and, hopefully, would never have to see them again.

Her dad had paid for his own solicitor, Larry, to represent her and Larry had come to see her this morning. 'You must be strong. Keep your chin up and I promise I'll get you out of here next week, Frankie. Your kids are fine – missing you, of course – but they're being well looked after by Kerry and Joey,' Larry said, repeating the speech Eddie had insisted on.

Picturing Georgie and Harry's innocent little faces, Frankie smiled. She couldn't wait to see them again; being without them felt like her heart had been ripped out.

'What you smiling at, sister?' Marion asked, walking towards her.

'Mind your own business,' Frankie replied bravely.

Kissing her teeth, Marion shook her head and turned to Jackie and Liz. 'I getting sick of this shit. We try to be nice to our sister, Frankie, but she keep showing us lack of respect. I think we need to teach her some. What do you think?'

Jackie and Liz both felt sorry for Frankie. The poor girl was over four months pregnant, but they were too frightened of

444

Marion to stick up for their new cellmate. Marion – or Killer as she preferred to be called – had a reputation for being one of the best fighters in Holloway and no one dared disagree with her in case she turned on them.

'Yeah, teach her some,' Jackie said solemnly.

'It's what she deserves,' Liz unwillingly chipped in.

Yesterday, when Marion had attacked her, Frankie had felt fearless afterwards. The embarrassment of her ordeal had given her courage and she had gone as far as threatening to kill her cellmates if they ever touched her again. Now, as Marion flashed her an evil grin that showed off two gold teeth, Frankie was suddenly petrified. She didn't belong in prison – these women were animals.

'Please don't hurt me. I'm sorry if I haven't felt like talking much, but it's only because I'm missing my children.'

Getting off on Frankie's fear, Marion grabbed her long, dark hair and yanked her off the bed. 'For showing Killer lack of respect, I want you to kiss my feet and beg my forgiveness.'

Remembering Larry's promise to get her bail, Frankie decided she might as well make her short stay in Holloway as easy as possible.

Marion laughed as Frankie knelt down, bowed her head and made contact with her Adidas trainers. 'Now, say the words, "I sorry for being a bitch. I beg you to forgive me, Killer."'

With tears in her eyes, Frankie bit her lip and repeated her tormentor's order.

Jed O'Hara winced as he propped himself up in his hospital bed. The painkillers the nurse had given him were fantastic and he was in much less agony than the previous day.

'How's Mum? Is she with you?' Jed asked, as his father walked in with Georgie and Harry in tow.

Jimmy shook his head. Marky's death had sucked the life out of all of them, none more so than Alice, who was in a terrible state. 'Your mother's inconsolable, boy. I left her indoors with Billy and Shannon. She ain't in no fit state to look after the chavvies – that's why I brought 'em with me. What about you, are you still in pain? Did the doctor come and see you this morning?'

Unusually, Jed wasn't in the mood to talk about himself. He was more worried about his mum and Marky's wife and sons. 'The doc said I'll be fine, and the painkillers they've given me are shit-hot. Don't worry about me – what about Tina and the boys? Have you been to see her yet?'

Jimmy shook his head. Tina was Marky's wife of eleven years and it had been Jimmy who had broken the news to her on the phone yesterday. The poor girl's screams of anguish would live with him for ever.

'Her and the boys have gone down to Suffolk to stay with her mother. Her father picked her up last night. I rang her again this morning, but she didn't really wanna speak to me. The only thing she did say was that she wanted me to sort out all the funeral arrangements. She said she ain't up to it.'

Jed remembered his grandfather's funeral as though it were yesterday. He'd only been young at the time and it had upset him immensely to watch Butch's trailer go up in smoke with him inside it. 'Will Marky be burnt in his trailer like me grandad was?'

'No, that's an old tradition. Your grandfather always insisted he wanted that kind of send-off, so I chose to grant him his final wish. Marky will have a proper funeral. I spoke to your mother about it this morning and she wants him to be laid to rest in Upminster, so she can visit him every day.'

Aware that his children had barely said a word since they'd walked in, Jed smiled at them. 'How about giving your dad a cuddle?'

Georgie clasped her brother's hand and led him over to the bed.

'Have you missed me?' Jed asked.

Georgie nodded. 'Dad, can we see Mummy today? Me and Harry have missed her, too.'

About to gently explain that Mummy was on a long vacation at Her Majesty's pleasure, Jed was stopped from doing so by the door opening.

'Surprise!' Sammy shouted, as Lukey boy ran into the side ward, followed by Sally.

'Daddy,' Luke screamed as he spotted Jed, then lunged at him.

Georgie and Harry stared at the intruder, glanced at each other and burst out crying.

Back in Whitechapel, Ed, Gary and Ricky were polishing off the rest of Auntie Joan's rock cakes. The plan had already been discussed and all of them were happy that it would work.

Feeling bloated, Gary pushed his plate away. 'I had Ronny on the phone late last night, Dad. He was pissed out of his head and calling you every cunt under the sun. I was in bed with some little bird at the time, so I pretended I had a bad reception and cut him off.'

Eddie laughed. 'I know why he rang you. I had Paulie on the phone again the other day, begging me to let him and Ronny come back to the firm. They're both skint, I know they are, but they won't admit it. I told Paulie I'd give 'em money if they needed it. I also told him in no uncertain terms that I'd never work with him or Ronny again. We don't even need anyone at the moment and Stuart's joining up with us when he gets out of nick at Christmas.'

'How is Stu?' Ricky asked.

'He's good. He seems to have got over that old slapper of a bird of his, and he's doing buttons to join the firm. He's gonna fit in well with us – he'll be a big asset,' Ed replied.

'How's Gina?' Gary asked.

Eddie grinned. 'Yeah, good. We're gonna get married next year, all being well. I had a little chat with her last night about giving up her job. It's too dangerous for a woman to be doing what she does for a living.'

Knowing how chauvinist his father could be when it came to women and work, Ricky smirked. 'What did she say when you told her to retire?'

'She was all right about it. She ain't exactly agreed yet, but she will do. If she don't, I'll have to give her an ultimatum – it's me or the job,' Ed said, chuckling.

'Have you heard from Frankie, Dad?' Ricky asked.

'No, but Joey's spoken to her and so has her mate, that Kerry bird. They said she sounds OK in there. She's sharing a cell with three other girls, by all accounts. Joey said she was desperate to speak to the kids, but him and Kerry did a good job of lying, like I told 'em to.'

'My heart goes out to Georgie and Harry. They must miss Frankie something chronic and I bet they're getting pushed from pillar to post with them pikey cunts,' Gary said.

Ed's expression darkened. 'Right, enough chitchat let's go over this plan again. Gal, you repeat it back to me.'

'We're all at the restaurant celebrating Joanie's birthday. She's had too much to drink and takes a tumble. Me and Gal pick her up and insist on taking her home. When we get back here, we make a right old racket, including Joanie, who's gonna have a little singalong up the path. If her neighbours show their faces, all well and good. If they don't, both me and Rick make a point of knocking on a few doors and making 'em laugh about Joan's antics. Once inside the house, I get changed, jump over the back fence into the alleyway, leap on the motorbike and head off to Upminster to do the deed. Approximately three-quarters of an hour later, Ricky changes into my outfit, puts my checked cap on and makes sure he's seen outside in the street. Once clocked, he comes back inside, changes into his own clobber and knocks at Irene's next door. He tells Irene that Joanie's fine, we've put her to bed, but asks if she can keep an eye on her when we have to leave in a couple of hours. In the meantime, I've interrupted Marky's funeral and disposed of Jed. Then, I leave the bike leathers and helmet at the salvage yard, pick up the van, then drive back to Joanie's, leaving the van in the same spot where I picked the bike up. That's it, I think. Job done.'

Eddie smiled proudly. Gary hadn't left out one single detail, probably because he'd been taught by the best.

'I'll tell you something what we haven't accounted for,' Ricky said.

Gary and Eddie turned to him. 'Go on,' Ed urged.

'There's a good chance that Georgie and Harry will be at the funeral with Jed. Surely we can't shoot their father in front of 'em.'

Eddie shrugged. 'I'd already thought of that and yes, it would be unfortunate if that were the case. It can't be helped, though. Frankie's trial is the following day, we've the perfect alibi, and it's our only hope of getting her the kids back. Georgie and Harry are only nippers – they'll soon get over their father's death, especially once they're back with Frankie.'

Gary glanced at his brother. Killing Jed was one thing, but doing it in front of Georgie and Harry was another.

Clocking his son's apprehension, Eddie stood up and slammed his fist on the table. 'I am head of this family, I make the rules and what I say fucking goes. Now, do we understand one another?'

Gary and Ricky looked at each other, turned back to their father, smiled and spoke in unison. 'Yes, Dad.'

CHAPTER FORTY-SEVEN

Alice O'Hara washed her hands and took off her apron. Jimmy had wanted to get the caterers in to do the food for Marky's funeral, but Alice had been insistent on preparing it herself.

'Sally's offered to help me and I need to keep meself busy. Marky loved my cooking and he'd want me to do the food, I know he would.'

Pleased that his wife seemed to be functioning again, Jimmy had left her to it.

Alice glanced at the clock. Marky's funeral service wasn't until three o'clock, but all the family were coming over this morning. 'Jed, Sally, it's gone seven. Start getting yourselves ready, 'cause Billy and Shannon'll be here soon,' she shouted.

Sally got up and helped Jed out of bed. Against the doctors' advice, Jed had discharged himself from hospital a couple of days ago.

'Thanks for all you've done, but I have to go home, my mum needs me,' Jed explained.

'I understand that you've been through a traumatic time, but you must remember to exercise every day and use the wheel-chair if you go out,' the doc had insisted.

Jed had left the wheelchair in reception. 'If you think I'm being pushed about in one of them like some old grunter, you can think again,' he'd told Sally.

As Luke woke up and hugged his father, Sally smiled. 'Will Georgie and Harry play with me today, Daddy?'

450

Jed gingerly lifted his son onto his lap. Georgie and Harry had both blanked Luke for the past two days – in fact, they'd barely said a word to anybody. He turned to Sally. 'I'm gonna tell the kids the truth today. I'll sit 'em down and explain everything gently.'

'Has Georgie or Harry asked why Luke keeps calling you, "Dad"?' Sally asked.

Jed nodded. 'Georgie has. I told her that Luke doesn't have a dad of his own, so he's borrowing hers. I also think today would be a good time to tell Mum you're pregnant again. Saying farewell to Marky's gonna destroy her, and it might help her get through it if she knows she has another grandchild on the way.'

'That's a great idea, but if I was you, I'd tell both your mum and the kids after the funeral. Today should just be about your brother, not us.'

Jed shrugged. 'OK, I'll tell 'em this evening.'

Out in rural Essex, Gina and Eddie were eating their breakfast.

'Why are we having your aunt's birthday lunch today if she's not seventy until Saturday? Wouldn't it have been more sensible to organise something at the weekend for her?' Gina asked.

Ed shook his head. 'This was the only day all the family could make it. Anyway, Joanie's got something arranged at the weekend with all her old pals from the bingo hall,' he lied.

As Ed began munching on another bacon sandwich, Gina eyed him with suspicion. Before she'd become a private detective, she'd taken a psychology course and instinct told her that something was amiss. Guessing it must be to do with Frankie, Gina decided to probe. 'Have you spoken to Frankie at all this week?'

Eddie threw his sandwich on the plate and gave a sarcastic chuckle. 'I ain't spoken to her since that night she found out

451

about me and you. Frankie can be a stubborn fucker; she gets it from me. I know she's OK, though. She's spoken to Joey and Larry's been up to visit her a couple of times.'

'Ed, promise me something.'

'What?'

'If by any chance Frankie doesn't get bail, and the kids have to stay with Jed, promise me you won't do anything stupid.'

Eddie smiled, held Gina's hands and stared sincerely into her eyes. 'I promise I won't do nothing stupid. You have my word, babe.'

Alice broke down as soon as the flowers, family and friends started to arrive. Jimmy felt like crying himself but, as a man, it was his duty to be strong.

Due to the few glasses of alcohol he'd already consumed, Jed was unable to be around his mother's heartbreak. Feeling emotional, he hobbled out the back and sat on a chair. He smiled as he watched all the kids running around. Spotting Georgie and Harry sitting alone on the grass, he called them over. His mum had vented her concerns earlier. She had told him that neither child was eating properly, especially Georgie, who had barely swallowed a morsel for the past three days.

Holding Harry's hand, Georgie led him over to their father.

'Why don't Daddy get you both a sandwich? Your nan said you didn't eat breakfast this morning.'

About to agree, just to please her dad, Georgie changed her mind as Luke ran over and clung to her father's legs. 'Not hungry,' she said sulkily.

Luke sidled over to Georgie and smiled. He tried to hug her, but Georgie pushed him away roughly and he fell backwards onto the grass.

Slightly inebriated and sick of all the deception, Jed grabbed both Georgie and Harry roughly by the arm. 'Kids, I'm burying me brother and I don't need this shit today. This is Luke and best you start being nice to him, 'cause he's your fucking brother.'

In a Canning Town restaurant, Auntie Joan was playing her part in the plan to the full. All the Mitchell clan were well aware of how partial Joan had been to a glass of snowball over the years, so Ed had made her up a big jug of the stuff, and had lied to everyone that it was full of alcohol.

Eddie locked eyes with Gary and smirked. So far, the pretence was working like a dream. Ed counted the heads at the table. Himself, Gina, Raymond, Polly, Gary, Ricky, Aunt Vi, Reg and Albert were all there. The only ones he was waiting on now were Joey and Dom.

When the restaurant door opened and his son and Dominic walked in, Eddie winked at Joanie. It was time to put stage two into motion.

Jimmy O'Hara put a protective arm around his wife. 'We have to go now, Alice, the undertakers are waiting.'

Alice threw her arms around his neck. 'I can't face it, Jimmy, I really can't. I've got one of me bad feelings. It was seeing that fucking magpie that started me off.'

Seeing Jed poke his head around the door, Jimmy gesticulated for him to have a word with his mother. Jed nodded and urged his father to leave him to it.

'Mum, you have to come to the funeral. I need you, Dad needs you, so does Billy and Tina and the kids.'

Alice shook her head. 'I can't, I've got a bad feeling, Jed, a really bad one. If I go to Marky's funeral, something is gonna go wrong, I know it is.'

Jed hugged her. 'Nothing is gonna go wrong, Mum. Look, I was gonna tell you this later, but I might as well tell you now. Sally's pregnant again, she's just over three months gone. You are gonna be a grandma again, sweetheart.'

Through her tears, Alice managed a smile. 'That's wonderful news. If it's a boy, will you call it Marky for me?'

'Of course I will, but only if you come to the funeral.'

Alice held her son in her arms. Jed was her youngest, had always been her favourite and, staring at Marky's flowers earlier, she'd been consumed by guilt for favouring Jed.

'Well?' Jed asked.

Alice nodded. 'Come on then, let's go.'

Aunt Vi looked at Eddie in horror. Joanie had just toppled off her chair and landed on her arse. 'You silly bastard – she's pissed. Whatever did you put in that fucking snowball you gave her?'

Excusing himself from Gina, Eddie walked around the other side of the table. He bent down. 'Are you OK, Auntie?' he asked.

'Yeah, but I've had enough now. When you get to my age, you can't keep up with the pace any more,' Joan lied.

Eddie picked his aunt up and sat her back on her chair. 'Do you want to go home, Auntie?'

Joanie nodded. 'I've had a wonderful time, but I need me bed now,' she slurred.

Vi stood up. She was absolutely furious with Eddie for getting Joanie so drunk. 'She could have really hurt herself just then!' Vi turned to her nephew, 'We're no spring chickens, ya know. A man of your intelligence should have known better. We've got brittle bones at our age, you could have bastard well killed her.'

Eddie smiled. 'Joanie's fine, Vi. She's had a fantastic birthday lunch, one she'll never forget.'

Vi picked up her handbag. 'I'm coming home with you, Joanie. I'll stay there with you tonight. I keep reading these stories in the *Sun* where people who have had too much to drink are dying in their sleep. Apparently, you can choke on your own vomit.'

Eddie glanced at Ricky and Gary. Vi being involved was not part of their plan. Gary leaped out of his seat and grabbed Joanie's arm. 'Me and Rick will take Auntie home, Dad.'

454

Vi picked up her handbag. 'I'm coming with you, Joanie.'

Joanie turned to her. 'No, you bloody well ain't. Last time you stayed round mine, you drove me up the bleedin' wall. I'm fine now, honest Vi, I just need a little lie down. The boys can take me home and I'll see you tomorrow at the bingo. I'll ring you later this evening.'

Each holding one of Joanie's arms, Ricky and Gary led their aunt from the restaurant. Once safely inside their motor, Joanie started to laugh. 'Well, that was a fucking close shave, eh boys?'

Jed sat alongside his family in the first funeral car. Tina, Marky's wife, had been beside herself leaving the house and had chosen to sit in the car behind with her own parents and Marky's sons. Billy, Shannon and little Mush had opted to travel with them. The horrendous journey was made easier for Jed by Georgie's fascination with Luke. Ever since he had told her that Lukey boy was her brother, she wouldn't leave him alone. Even Harry seemed taken with him now, which was surprising, because Harry was rarely taken by anything or anyone.

'Daddy, I'm hungry. Can me, Harry and Luke have McDonald's?' Georgie asked.

Jed ruffled her hair. He hoped that Georgie would be just as excited when he explained later that Sally was her new mummy. 'Yes, darling, but first we've got to go to Uncle Marky's funeral. I'll get you a McDonald's later.'

As Alice started sobbing again, Jimmy put his arm around her. 'Something awful's gonna happen, I know it is. I wanna go back home. I think we should all go home!' Alice screamed.

Jed saw Sally's look of horror. He put a comforting arm around his girlfriend's shoulder. 'It's OK, Mum's just upset. She thinks she's psychic, but I'm sure she ain't really,' he whispered.

As Gary turned into her road, Joanie spotted old Bobby Smith walking along. 'Toot your fucking horn and stop 'ere, quick,' Joan ordered.

'Bob, 'ere a minute,' Gary shouted as he opened the driver's side window. He and Ricky didn't know Bobby Smith from Adam, but he wanted the man to take a good look at their faces.

Clocking Bob's startled expression, Joanie opened the back door of the Range Rover. 'Bob, it's me, Joanie.'

Bob grinned and walked towards her. 'Hello, Joanie. What you doing in a posh motor like this?'

'I'm pissed, believe it or not. You know my Eddie, don't ya?'

Bob nodded.

'This is Gary and Ricky, his eldest sons. It's my seventieth at the weekend and me family took me out to lunch today to celebrate. I was necking them old snowballs, Bob, like there was no tomorrow. I feel ill now, I do.'

Ricky nudged Gary and they both jumped out of the motor and shook Bob's hand.

'Pleased to meet you, mate. I'm Gary and this is my brother Ricky,' Gary said loudly.

'Hello Bob, Auntie Joanie often speaks highly of you,' Ricky lied.

Pleased as punch by the compliment, Bob grinned from ear to ear. He'd always had a crush on Joan, but she'd never shown any interest in him until now. 'Make sure you take care of her, boys. Do you want me to check on her later, make sure she's OK?'

'There's no need, mate. We're staying with her for a good couple of hours. We certainly won't leave her until she's sobered up.'

'Pleasure to meet you, lads,' Bob said, as Gary and Ricky got back inside the motor.

On the short distance to Joanie's house, Ricky turned to his aunt. 'Well, he got a fantastic look at us and we said our names a couple of times. He seemed a nice old boy an' all.'

Joanie coughed. 'Can't stand him – fucking old lech, he is. Now, pull up 'ere and you can knock at Irene's, Gary.'

Gary glanced at his watch. Time was getting on and he needed to be quick. The crash helmet and leathers were already upstairs at Joan's. All he had to do was make sure he was seen by Irene, then it was time to get changed and make tracks.

Eddie sat in the restaurant laughing and joking with Raymond as though he didn't have a care in the world. He did – his insides were doing somersaults – but he daren't let anyone clock it, especially Gina, who was as bright as a button.

Gina was thoroughly enjoying herself. She was sat with Polly, Joey and Dominic and having a right old laugh. Out of all of Eddie's family, Gina had taken a shine to Joey the most. He was an intelligent lad, with the most wonderful sense of humour, and Gina adored both him and Dominic.

Having had a go at Eddie earlier for getting her sister drunk, Vi was now pissed herself, and chewing Reg and Albert's ears off. Vi had never known anyone gay in her life before. When she was young, gay meant happy, and she couldn't understand or believe that Eddie had accepted Joey and Dominic's relationship.

'I mean it ain't fucking right, is it? I think it's bastard well disgusting, and if he was a son of mine, I'd have him shot, I swear I would.'

Aware that Vi's voice was getting louder by the second, Reg stood up and urged her and Albert to do the same. If Eddie heard what Vi was saying, there'd be hell to pay. 'Me, Albert and Vi are gonna make a move now. Thanks for inviting us, Ed, we've really enjoyed it.'

Eddie shook Reg and Albert's hands, kissed Vi on the cheek, then nervously checked his watch. The service for Marky's funeral was at three o'clock and Ed had given Gary strict instructions not to arrive at the cemetery until at least quarter-past. Gary knew where to hide – Ed had taken him over there a couple of days earlier and shown him the perfect spot. They'd gone armed with a couple of bouquets. Jessica was buried nearby and they'd lain them at her graveside.

Noticing that Eddie kept checking his watch, Gina smiled at him. 'Are you waiting to make a move?'

457

Ed leaned towards her and kissed her. 'Don't be silly, I ain't had me fucking dessert yet.'

Gary felt sick with nerves as he headed towards Upminster on the Yamaha. He was a dab hand with a gun and so was Ricky – their father had taught them how to use one at a very young age. While his dad was inside, Gary had been forced to shoot four men. He'd killed one and purposely just injured the other three. This, however, was different; he'd never had to kill a man at a graveside burial in front of so many people before.

Hitting a pothole along the A13, Gary felt bile rise in his throat. He quickly pulled over, took his helmet off and chucked his guts up. Wiping his mouth with his hand, Gary took deep breaths. Desperate to straighten himself out, he thought of Jessica, his beautiful stepmum. He then thought about his father's prison sentence, Frankie being stuck in Holloway and poor little Georgie and Harry being motherless.

Feeling anger surge through his veins, Gary restarted the bike's engine. Jed O'Hara had ripped his family to shreds, and it was high time for the evil, pikey cunt to pay the price.

CHAPTER FORTY-EIGHT

Ricky Mitchell put on his brother's bomber jacket and checked cap and studied himself in the mirror. He was slightly taller than Gary and not quite as broad-shouldered but, other than that they looked very similar. Both of them had short, dark hair and walked with a swagger, so, providing nobody stood a foot away from him, Ricky could easily pass as Gary.

Auntie Joan was in her rocking chair, knitting a baby coat for her friend Lil's great grandson. She fleetingly thought of Gary and said a silent prayer that he would be OK. Joanie had helped Eddie out a few times over the years by providing alibis. She never asked any questions, as if she knew the implications beforehand, she'd probably worry herself to death. As Ricky walked into the room dressed in Gary's outfit, Joan put her knitting down.

'Well, do you think I'll pass as him?'

Joanie smiled. 'Course you will. Two peas in a pod, you are.'

Ricky pulled the net curtain to one side and looked out of the window. He needed to be seen by at least two people. 'Who's that over there washing their car, Auntie?'

'That's Norma's son, Backward Brian. Washes that car every day he does. I wouldn't mind, but the bastard thing don't even work. It ain't got an engine.'

'Right, I'm gonna pop out now and make sure Backward Brian has a butcher's. I'll wave and shout out something to him. Be a good idea to ask him if he knows the time. Backward

459

or not, he might remember that if the Old Bill come sniffing round asking questions.'

Joanie stood by the window and watched Ricky saunter outside. Whatever Ed and the boys had planned today was obviously a biggie and, not for the first time, when she watched the news in the next couple of days, Joan would probably guess what it was.

Eddie Mitchell savoured the last of his apple pie and put down his spoon. He glanced at his watch. It was twenty-past three and Gary should be in position by now. For obvious reasons, Eddie had told Gary and Ricky not to contact him on his mobile. The Old Bill were too cute for their own good these days; they could trace all sorts. The suspense of the wait would probably kill him, but Ed had told the boys that he would ring Joanie's at six o'clock and ask if she had sobered up. 'Yes' would mean that everything had gone to plan, and 'no' would mean that something had gone terribly wrong.

Joey waved his hand in front of his father's face to catch his attention. 'Can me and Dom jump in with you and Gina on the way home, Dad? We've had too much to drink to bother with trains.'

'Course you can. Me and Gina came by cab today, and the same driver's gonna pick us up again later.'

Joey was taken aback. His father detested using public transport of any kind, and that included taxis. He usually drove everywhere, whether he was drinking or not. 'I've never known you use a cab in your life, Dad. Is there something wrong with your motor?'

Eddie shook his head. 'Them Essex police are fucking murder for drink driving. Two pals of mine have just lost their licences out there. I wanted to have a good drink today and, seeing as I'm still on probation, decided to be sensible for once.'

Gina squeezed Eddie's hand and winked at Joey and Dominic. 'Wonders will never cease! Your father's a changed man, Joey.'

'I'm really proud of you, Dad,' Joey said sincerely.

As Dom, Joey and Gina all praised him, Eddie glanced at his watch again. The only reason he'd chosen to come by taxi was so the driver could be a witness if need be. Eddie looked up and, aware of his family all grinning at him, grinned back. That old saying was right: ignorance was most certainly fucking bliss.

Alice O'Hara breathed a sigh of relief as she walked outside the church. The service had been sad, but beautiful and, considering she'd seen a lone magpie on her windowsill this morning, she was thankful it had gone without a hitch.

Jimmy led Alice back to the funeral car. They had chosen a church a mile away from the cemetery, so had to travel a short distance for the burial.

'Are you OK, love?' Jimmy asked.

Alice dabbed her eyes with his hankerchief. 'I'm as OK as I can be. I'm pleased the service went well and the sun's come out for him, Jimmy. It would have been awful burying him in the rain.'

Jimmy agreed. Considering it was nearly November, the weather had been extremely kind to them. 'There ain't arf some people 'ere, Alice. The Smiths have come all the way from Cardiff, and I saw Sonny Tyler and his family, they live on that site up in Glasgow.'

Pleased that her son had got such a wonderful turn-out, Alice gave a weak smile, then burst into tears again.

'What's a matter, Alice?'

'I'm dreading seeing my Marky be put in that ground. Go and find Jed: I just wanna get the burial over with, then I'll be OK. I've still got a bad feeling, you know, it won't go away. Say they drop his coffin and he falls out of it or something? That magpie was pecking at the window, trying to get in the kitchen. You know my phobia of them poxy birds – one for sorrow, two for joy.'

Jimmy kissed Alice on the forehead. 'You've gotta calm down, love, or you'll make yourself ill. Nothing is gonna go wrong with Marky's burial, I promise you that faithfully.'

*　　*　　*

461

Dressed in biker leathers, Gary Mitchell was crouching down by a big headstone at the back end of the cemetery. His father had chosen a spot where the graves were old, covered in moss and the names of the deceased unreadable.

'No one's visited these poor fuckers for years, so you ain't gonna bump into no visitors. This will do just nicely and it'll only take you two minutes to get from here over the wall,' were Eddie's exact words.

Gary stared through the scope of the rifle. His dad had brought the untraceable gun here late last night and had hidden it in some undergrowth. He'd also put some paint on either side of the wall, so Gary knew exactly where to climb over and also where to find the gun. Gary felt his heart-rate quicken as he spotted a hearse pulling into the main gates. This was them – he could see Jimmy O'Hara's ugly mug in the car behind.

Aware that he was sweating profusely, Gary put down the rifle, took the binoculars out of his pocket and glanced around the rest of the cemetery to ensure he couldn't be seen. He could see a couple of old dears standing by graves, but they were probably half-blind and also a good couple of hundred yards away from him.

Gary picked up the rifle again and turned his attention back to the O'Haras. He gasped as Jed got out of the car holding Georgie and Harry's hands. He had prayed the kids wouldn't be here, but he still had to go through with it whether they witnessed their father's death or not.

Relieved as Georgie and Harry left Jed's side and skipped along in front with another little boy, Gary focused solely on Jed. It was nearly time now. Ten more minutes and Jed would be out of his family's life for ever.

Back at the restaurant, Eddie and Joey were discussing Frankie. 'I'm sure she knows that Jed's got the kids, Dad. She screamed at me last night and called me a liar, and Kerry said she did the same to her. She told me that someone had told her that the kids were with Jed. I didn't admit it, in case she was trying to get me to own up, but she ain't stupid, you know.'

Eddie put a comforting arm around his youngest son's shoulders. 'You've done great, boy, and stop worrying, 'cause Frankie will be out tomorrow, and she'll have her kids back in no time.'

'How can you be so sure? And even if she does get bail, it doesn't alter the fact that she still tried to kill Jed. I mean, she's bound to be sent back to prison again when her trial comes up, ain't she?'

Eddie shook his head. 'Once we get Frankie out, we'll get her to open up, tell us what really happened. Jed must have done something pretty bad to make Frankie flip like that, and I'm determined to find out what it is. I'm paying for the same QC who represented me. You must remember him – posh, cocky, clever bastard called James Fitzgerald Smythe.'

Joey nodded. Dominic and Gina were both still deep in conversation and it was good to have five minutes alone with his dad to talk about Frankie. 'Go on.'

'Well, Larry took me to see Smythe earlier this week. He reckons, worst ways, we can go down the old self-defence route. Obviously, Frankie will have to tell the court that Jed used to beat her up on a regular basis, and Kerry will also have to stand up and testify the same. I know for a fact Smthye will get Frankie off. Charging me an absolute fortune he is, but from experience we know he's worth every penny.'

Joey lifted up his glass. 'To Frankie coming home.'

Eddie glanced at his watch. Jed should be taking his last breath any time now and that moment definitely needed celebrating. He clicked his fingers. 'Waiter, bring us over a bottle of your finest champagne, mate.'

Gary put down his rifle and looked through the binoculars once more. The O'Haras seemed to be taking for ever to move; they weren't even anywhere near the graveside yet. Glancing around the rest of the cemetery, Gary's bowels loosened as he saw a man heading his way with flowers in his hand. As the man suddenly turned to his left, Gary breathed a sigh of relief. He couldn't wait to get the job done and get out of this bastard place.

Hand in hand with Sally, Jed followed his parents and Marky's wife and sons on the sombre walk towards his brother's graveside. The burial had been slightly delayed due to the number of people who still hadn't arrived back from the church. Travellers' funerals were always big affairs, and Marky's was no exception.

Billy and Shannon walked alongside Jed and Sally. Sammy had come alone, and had turned up late.

'There's no fucking room anywhere. The car park's chocka and so are all the roads outside. Half the mushes, including most of Dad's family, ain't even back from the service yet,' Billy moaned.

Jed ignored his brother and turned to Sammy. 'Where was you this morning? I thought you were coming to the house.'

Not wanting everybody knowing his business, Sammy pulled Jed to one side. 'The gavvers turned up at Julie's with some bitch jobsworth of a social worker. They threatened to arrest me unless I gave the boys back to Kerry. They took 'em there and then. I'm fucking gutted, Jed. How can they hand 'em over to that slut when they know she's a violent psycho?'

About to offer Sammy some words of comfort, Jed was interrupted by his own kids tugging at his trouser leg. 'Luke fell over and cut his knee, Daddy,' Georgie said.

Jed bent down to examine Luke's knee, and at that precise second, the distinct sound of gunshots filled the warm autumn air. Mayhem quickly ensued. Frightened for their lives, the pallbearers dropped Marky's coffin and ran for cover. Women, children and men were screaming. Even the vicar dived behind a gravestone while chanting extracts from the Bible.

Sally was hysterical. Jed was covered in blood, lying on his back, cuddling Luke. 'Call an ambulance. Jed's been shot,' she screamed.

464

When the shots had been fired, Jimmy had automatically thrown himself on top of Alice to protect her.

'Why us? I knew it. I knew something bad would happen today. Where's Jed and Billy? Where's Georgie girl? Why didn't you listen to me?' Alice sobbed.

Jimmy stood up and ran to where a crowd had gathered. He spotted Billy and Sammy standing nearby. 'Where's Jed?' he yelled. Billy pointed towards the crowd. Filled with dread, Jimmy pushed his way through. Jed was covered in claret, but was sitting up, cradling Lukey boy in his arms.

'Are you OK, boy? Where you been shot?' asked Jimmy.

Tears were streaming down Jed's face as he looked up. 'Lukey's dead, Dad, he's gone.'

Alice breathed a sigh of relief as she saw Georgie girl and Harry huddled together. They were sitting on a grave crying. Desperate to find Jed, she ran past them. Sally was lying in a crumpled heap on the grass. 'Sally, where's Jed and Luke?'

Sally sat up in a dazed state. She'd vomited when she'd seen Jed covered in blood, then she must have passed out. 'Jed's been shot, Alice,' she whimpered.

'Jed! Where's my boy?' Alice screamed hysterically.

'Jed's OK. He's sitting up,' someone yelled.

Alice helped Sally up and, with the sound of sirens nearing, they both pushed their way through the crowd.

Spotting his wife, Jimmy stood up. Lukey boy had taken a bullet through his skull and he couldn't let Alice see him like that, it would crucify her.

As Jimmy tried to lead her away, Alice pushed him as hard as she could. 'I wanna see my baby. Jed, are you OK?' she yelled.

'Please, Alice, Sally, don't move any closer,' Jimmy warned.

Desperate to comfort both her son and Jed, Sally ducked under Jimmy's arm. 'Jed! Luke!' she screamed.

Weeping tears of pure pain, Jed was still sitting on the ground with Luke clutched to his chest. 'I love you, boy. I love you so much,' he wept.

Realising for the first time that it was her son who had copped the bullet, Sally let out a piercing scream. 'Let me see him. Let me hold my baby,' she shrieked.

The police and paramedics urged the crowd to move out of the way, and then witnessed a scene that would stay with most of them for the rest of their lives. Two hysterical parents sitting on the ground, cradling their dead son was a picture most of them had witnessed in the past. But the boy literally having had his brains blown out at a family funeral was a shock to virtually all of them.

In Whitechapel, Gary and Ricky were upstairs in Joanie's house. They were in the room they used for their meetings and, since Gary's return, they'd already necked half a litre of neat Scotch between them. Neither were drunk, just in a state of stupefied shock over what had happened.

Ricky glanced at his watch and then stared at the phone. Their dad was due to ring soon, and then the shit would really hit the fan.

Gary jumped as the phone rang a few moments later. His hands shook as he lifted the receiver.

Eddie immediately launched into their pre-planned code. 'Is Joanie OK? Has she sobered up?' he asked, fully expecting Gary to say yes.

'No, she's not OK,' Gary croaked.

Ed's heart skipped a beat. Surely Gary hadn't bottled it, or fucked things up. 'Do you want me to pop up and see her?' Ed asked. This meant, Is the coast clear?

'Yes, come up and see her,' Gary replied.

Gina was watching the episode of *Blind Date* she'd recorded the previous weekend. 'Where you going? You aren't driving, are you?' she said, as Ed snatched his keys off the coffee table.

'I've got to pop out. Joanie ain't well,' Ed lied.

'Be careful, you've had a lot to drink today.'

Ed pecked her on the lips. 'I'll try not to be long.'

'Oh, Ed, Raymond just rang on the landline while you were

upstairs. Says it's urgent, he wants you to call him back.'

Eddie slammed the front door. If Gary was at Joanie's he obviously hadn't got nicked, so what the fuck had gone wrong? Wondering if Raymond had heard something through the grapevine, Eddie got in the motor and punched in his number.

'Ray, it's me. What's up?'

'Have you heard what happened, Ed? At O'Hara's son's funeral?'

Eddie went cold. 'No, what?'

'Someone tried to shoot Jed, but killed his son, Luke, instead. Pat Murphy told Dougie, and Dougie rang me. Pat Murphy was at the funeral, said it was fucking chaos. The kid took the bullet straight through the head, apparently. Gruesome, eh?'

Ed dropped the phone in shock. What in God's name had Gary done?

Auntie Joan glanced at her pattern, then checked how many stitches she'd cast on. 'Shit,' she mumbled, as she realised she'd made a cock-up. Chucking her knitting on a nearby chair, Joan walked over to the TV and turned the volume up. Gary and Ricky were still upstairs and she knew by their mood and demeanour that something had gone dreadfully wrong.

Deciding to make herself a mug of Horlicks, Joan went into the kitchen. Seconds later the newreader's voice made her jump in shock.

'Police are hunting the killer of a four-year-old boy who was gunned down in a gangland-style shooting at Upminster Cemetery earlier today. Detectives particularly want to trace the driver of a white BMW, registration . . .'

Joan stopped listening as the doorbell rang. She turned the TV off and peeped through the net curtain. It was only Eddie, thank God.

'Where are they?' Ed asked, his face as black as thunder.

'Upstairs. Do you wanna cup of tea, love?' Joan replied.

Eddie ignored Joan's question and flew up the stairs. He ran into the room and grabbed Gary by the neck.

'What the fuck have you done?' he screamed.

Gary's face turned red with fury. 'Get off me, I ain't done nothing.'

Ed let go of his eldest boy, slumped on a chair and poured himself a Scotch. 'How could you be so stupid? You know how to shoot, so how the hell did you manage to kill the cunting kid?'

Gary looked at his father in total amazement. 'What kid? What you on about?'

'Jed's kid, Luke. The kid you fucking shot.'

'It weren't me. I was staring through the rifle waiting for 'em to get nearer to the grave when all hell broke loose. I heard the gunshots and then I saw Jed slump to the floor. I thought he'd been shot. I panicked and legged it.'

Eddie stared his son in the eyes. Gary wouldn't lie to him, so he had to be telling the truth. 'So, if it weren't you that fired the shot, who was it, then?'

Gary shook his head. 'I ain't got a clue, Dad, but I swear on mine and Ricky's life, it wasn't me.'

CHAPTER FORTY-NINE

After a sleepless night, Eddie got up at 6 a.m. The events of the previous day felt like a bad dream, and Ed found it difficult to understand how somebody else had turned up at the cemetery with the intention to kill at the same time as Gary. Perhaps Jed and the O'Haras had lots of enemies, but yesterday's coincidence was one that Eddie could have bloody well done without.

Ed made a mug of coffee and sat down at the kitchen table. Even though Gary had panicked when he'd seen what had happened, at least he'd had the sense to carry out the rest of the plan as though he'd fired the shot himself. The leathers and helmet had now been burned, and the bike had been crushed. The rifle was hidden where nobody would ever find it, but that didn't matter so much, as the police would know by the bullet what type of gun had been used to kill Luke and, providing Gary was telling the truth, it most certainly wasn't his.

Eddie thought about Frankie. Larry had managed to pull some strings behind the scenes at Chelmsford Crown Court, and it was looking highly favourable that she would be out on bail later this afternoon. The only problem now was, with Jed still alive, there was a chance she wouldn't get her kids back.

The shrill ring of his phone made Eddie jump. Nobody ever rang this early, which could only mean one thing – bad news.

'Ed, it's Larry.'

'What's up, mate?' Eddie asked.

'I've got some news for you. I'm just checking you're at home; I'm on my way over.'

Eddie ended the call, and put his head in his hands. If whoever had murdered Luke had ballsed up Frankie's chances of getting bail, he would personally fucking kill them.

Over in Holloway, Frankie was also suffering from insomnia. She'd tried counting sheep and all sorts last night, but her mind was full of worry, and sleep just wouldn't come. She sat up and hugged her knees. DI Blyth had paid her a visit yesterday and Frankie had tricked her into admitting the kids were with Jed. She'd pretended that Joey had told her the night before and Blyth had believed her. Frankie was furious with Joey and Kerry for lying to her. Finding out for sure that her kids were missing had tipped her fragile state of mind over the edge and Frankie had decided to banish both of them from her life from now on. That would teach them to tell wicked lies.

Thinking of the day ahead, Frankie sighed. Larry had come to see her again yesterday, and assured her once more that he was certain she would get bail. Frankie trusted Larry: trouble was, her luck was cursed at the moment and she could only hope and pray that he was right.

'You awake early, sister Frankie. Come scratch my back, Killer got a bad itch.'

Frankie obediently did as Killer asked. Larry had told her under no circumstances could she afford to get into trouble in prison while he was trying to sort out her bail.

'Wrong spot, Frankie. Scratch lower, by my ass.'

Feeling sick as Killer lowered her pyjama bottoms, Frankie shut her eyes as she carried on scratching. Since finding out that her kids had been snatched, she had wanted to smash Killer's ugly face in, but couldn't because of her bail application.

Sick of being taken for an idiot, Frankie opened her eyes and walked away.

'Where you going? I ain't said you can stop yet.'

'I have to start getting ready for court. They'll be coming to collect me soon.'

Killer grinned. 'You ain't going nowhere, sister Frankie. You'll be coming back 'ere to be Killer's slave for the rest of your days.'

Frankie defiantly shook her head. 'My solicitor has told me I'll definitely get bail. I'm going home to see my children.'

Laughing loudly, Killer propped herself up on her elbow. 'You got a lot to learn, sister. All solicitors are lying mother-fuckers. They tell you what you wanna hear. I bet you you be back here tonight, curled up in dat bunk.'

'No, no, I won't,' Frankie screamed.

Laughing even louder, Killer carried on taunting Frankie. 'Yes, yes, you will, and if you ain't, my name is Whitney fucking Houston.'

After ending the call to Larry, Eddie had rung Gary and Ricky and got them out of bed. 'Get your arses over here ASAP,' he ordered.

Gary and Ricky arrived within the hour. Larry lived in Sussex, and Ed was pleased to have some time with his sons so they could discuss things before Larry arrived.

'Maybe he's found out who did it. When you'd left last night, Auntie Joan mentioned the murder – she'd seen it on the news. She said police were hunting for a white BMW,' Gary told Eddie.

'Why didn't you fucking tell me this before?' Eddie shouted.

'Because you told us not to ring you. You said it weren't safe to speak over the phone in case we were suspects,' Gary shouted back.

Woken up by the shouting, Gina made her way downstairs and opened the kitchen door. 'Whatever's going on?' she asked.

'Nothing. Listen, babe, do you mind going back upstairs for a bit? Larry's on his way over and we've got some important business to discuss.'

Gina smiled. She understood Eddie more than any woman

probably ever had in the past. 'I'll go and have a shower, then I've got to pop to Tesco's. I need to do a big food shop,' she said brightly.

Ricky waited until Gina had shut the door before continuing the conversation.

'Look, there's no point us jumping down each other's throats. We don't even know what news Larry has got. It might be good news, for all we know.'

Eddie shook his head. 'It ain't. I clocked it in his voice.'

Joey and Dominic arrived at their grandparents' house at 8 a.m. Joyce had ordered them to arrive early so she could cook them a good English breakfast to set them up for the day. Both lads felt a bit worse for wear from Joanie's birthday bash, but they'd still made it on time.

'I can't smell no bacon, Nan. We're starving,' Joey joked as he walked into the kitchen. Even though he had to attend his sister's bail hearing later, Joey was in an upbeat mood. Yesterday, his dad had been adamant that Frankie was coming home and Joey knew his dad well enough to know that if he said something like that, he meant it.

'Raymond's on his way over. He'll be here soon, and then I'll make us some grub,' Joyce said.

'Where's Grandad?' Joey asked.

'Where do ya think? Outside playing with his cock.'

Dominic burst out laughing. Joycie had a way with words and he found her highly entertaining.

Joyce smirked, then put on her serious expression. 'We shouldn't be laughing and joking you know, not until we know we've got Frankie home safely and she's got them kids back.'

Joey hugged his nan. He knew that she and his grandad were worried about the outcome of today, which is why he and Dominic had come over early and offered to accompany them to the court.

'I spoke to Dad yesterday. Frankie's bail is a done deal, Nan, and she's getting the kids back,' Joey whispered.

Joyce grinned. 'That's brilliant news, Joey. Fan-bleedin-tastic!'

Gary and Ricky sat in silence as Eddie led Larry into the kitchen. Their father had been right to fear bad news. Larry's expression was sombre, and the look on his face said everything.

'Do you want a tea or coffee?' Eddie asked nervously.

'You'd best get the brandy out. You're going to need it when you hear what I've got to say,' Larry replied.

Sick of playing games, Eddie smashed his fist on the kitchen table. 'Just spit it out, Lal, will ya?'

'The police have made an arrest. They've got the guys who killed Jed's son.'

Eddie shrugged. He was just relieved that nobody had spotted Gary and suspected them of the dirty deed. 'So, what's that got to do with me?' he asked casually.

'Everything, Eddie. It was Paulie and Ronny that did it. They killed Luke and the police have apparently got them bang to rights.'

Unable to stomach listening to the ins and outs of Auntie Joan's birthday party, Stanley put his breakfast onto a tray and took it into the living room.

'Don't you turn my Eamonn off, Stanley,' Joyce shouted out.

Out of view of his wife's beady eyes, Stanley stuck two fingers up on both hands and poked his tongue out. Ever since GMTV had started earlier that year, his wife had a habit of turning the volume up and listening to the poxy programme while pottering about in the kitchen. As for that Eamonn Holmes, Joycie fancied him something rotten, and Stanley prayed that one day she'd meet Mr Holmes, run off with him, and leave him to live the rest of his life in bloody peace.

About to take a bite of his sausage, Stanley heard the news item and dropped his knife and fork in shock.

'Joycie, 'ere, quick,' he shouted.

473

Joey and Dominic stood open-mouthed behind Joyce as they listened to the reporter who was stood outside Upminster Cemetery.

'The murdered boy has been named as four-year-old Luke O'Hara.'

'That's Jed's little boy,' Joey said gobsmacked.

'What little boy?' Joyce asked perplexed.

'Jed had another kid with a bird called Sally. Frankie knew about it, but forgave him.'

As the newreader began talking about something else, Stanley turned the volume down. 'You missed the beginning of it. The reporter said that it was a murder that went wrong. He said that the police suspected the gunman was aiming for the child's father.'

'Who would shoot a poor, defenceless child? That's awful,' Dom whispered.

Stanley pointed at Joey. 'His father, that's who.'

Joey was furious. 'My dad had nothing to do with it. They said it happened yesterday and I was with my dad all day yesterday.'

'Don't say things like that to him, you wicked old bastard,' Joyce shouted.

For once, Stanley stuck to his guns. 'Yous lot need to take your rose-tinted glasses off. You mark my words, that killing has Eddie's name stamped all over it, and if it weren't him, you can bet he knows who did it.'

Larry left his car at Eddie's house and travelled to Chelmsford with Ed and the boys. There was lots to discuss and important phone calls to make. Because of Ronny and Paulie's arrests, Eddie had ordered Gina to go and stay with her friend Claire for a few days until the dust settled. Worried about Eddie's safety, Gina had flatly refused at first, but Ed had sat her down and had a heart-to-heart with her.

'Listen, babe. You and Jessica are the only two women I have ever loved in my life. Because of the O'Haras, Jessica is already dead, and I would never forgive myself if I also put your life in danger. Go to Claire's, at least until I know it's safe for you to come home.'

Out of his mind with worry, Ed had made sure Gina was gone before he left for the court. He was stunned by his brothers' arrest and furious at their interference and stupidity. If they'd have killed Jed and got away with it, he'd have shaken their hands with gratitude. But no, as usual, all Paulie and Ronny had done was balls things up and, now they'd been arrested, the O'Haras would be hell-bent on getting revenge for Luke's death, probably blaming Eddie in the process.

Larry ended his phone call and turned to Eddie. 'I've just spoken to Charlie. He reckons there is no chance that Frankie will get bail now, Eddie, not after everything that's happened.'

Eddie punched the steering wheel. 'I haven't had dealings with either of my brothers in fucking years. What happened yesterday is sod-all to do with me, or Frankie for that matter.'

'I'm sorry, Eddie, but this isn't my fault. I really did bend over backwards this week to get Frankie's bail assured. It wasn't easy, especially with Dickens' pals down at Chelmsford. Now this has happened, my hands are tied, I'm afraid. If anyone's to blame, it's your brothers, not me.'

'Sorry, Lal, I'm just so pissed off and upset. I was really looking forward to getting Frankie home. I could have got to the bottom of it, given time, found out what Jed really did to make her stab the bastard. Listen, I need you to do me a favour. Somebody has to inform Frankie what's happened and I want that person to be me. She already has her suspicions that Jed's got the kids and I don't want anyone else telling her. She also needs to know that her uncles have shot Luke.'

Larry shook his head. 'I don't think I can wangle that one. I can go and see her myself and tell her for you if you want.'

'No, I have to see her myself. Please Larry, this is important to me.'

Larry picked up his phone. 'OK, I'll do my best.'

*   *   *

475

Back in Rainham, Jimmy O'Hara was climbing the walls. Years ago, when he was in his prime, he'd been one violent son-of-a-bitch, but splitting up with Alice that time had changed him as a person. To win back his beloved wife, he'd sold his Rolls-Royce, lost his flashness and settled for the quiet life. Today, however, Jimmy felt differently. His favourite grandson had just been brutally murdered and, when he found out who was responsible, he would personally rip their fucking throats out.

'Jimmy, please sit down. You're making my nerves bad,' Alice pleaded.

Jimmy stormed out into the kitchen and urged Billy, Sammy and Jed to do the same. The police had popped round that morning to inform them that they had arrested two men in connection with Lukey boy's murder. They wouldn't say who they were, said they had been told not to release any names until the suspects were formally charged.

Seeing Jed break down again, Jimmy held his son in his arms. 'Where did Sally go?' he asked.

'She went home with her dad. I think he made her,' Jed wept.

Jimmy led Jed out the back and sat him down on the step. 'Listen, boy, you've gotta be strong for Georgie and Harry's sake. Them chavvies of yours have barely said a word since yesterday. They saw what happened, remember, they were standing near Luke. You need to comfort 'em, let 'em know everything's gonna be all right. Harry ate some cornflakes this morning, but Georgie girl still ain't touched a morsel. You need to be there for 'em, Jed. I know how much you loved Luke, but you've got another two that need you as well.'

Jed nodded and stood up. 'I'll go and talk to 'em now, but before I do, can you promise me something?'

'Go on,' Jimmy said.

'I know you've spoken to Pat Murphy and he reckons what happened is fuck-all to do with Eddie Mitchell, but deep down I know it is. When the gavvers tell us who did it, if there's a link with Eddie, will you help me kill him?'

476

Jimmy stood up and put an arm around Jed. 'With pleasure, son.'

Larry had had no joy in allowing Eddie to speak to Frankie. Instead it was DI Blyth who came up trumps.

'I can't leave the pair of you alone, but I'll stand a few feet away and cover my ears with my hands,' Blyth said kindly. She liked Frankie, felt sorry for the girl because of the family she'd been born into and the life she'd subsequently endured.

Eddie felt nervous as Blyth led him towards the cells. He'd never liked the Old Bill – there were too many bent bastards among them – but he had to give credit where it was due.

'Thanks for this. I appreciate it,' he said awkwardly.

'Frankie's along there on the right. I'll leave yous two to it, but you've only got five minutes,' Blyth replied.

Frankie was gobsmacked to see her father standing a foot away from her. She knew that he would turn up at court and she also knew that he was paying for Larry to represent her, but she hadn't been in close contact or spoken to him since that night in the restaurant when she'd found out about Gina.

As stubborn as ever, Frankie glared at him. 'What do you want?'

Eddie took a deep breath. He wasn't good at explanations, and over the years, when it came to the twins, he'd always left that duty to Jessica.

'Look, I know you're still pissed off about Gina, but I've only got five minutes and you need to listen to me, Frankie. Jed's got Georgie and Harry – he's had them since you got banged up. Sammy turned up . . .'

Frankie interrupted him by laughing. 'And you thought I didn't already know that? I ain't stupid, I worked that out last week when I kept ringing Kerry and Joey asking to speak to them and they wasn't there. Is that all you've come to tell me?'

'No, there's more. Listen, I ain't good with speeches, so I'm just gonna say this bluntly. Did you hear that Jed's brother Mark got killed in a road accident?'

Frankie shook her head, so Eddie explained what had happened. 'Well, yesterday at his funeral, Luke, Jed's son, got murdered. The police reckon the bullet was meant for Jed and, before you ask, it was fuck-all to do with me. I was out with the rest of the family celebrating Auntie Joanie's seventieth birthday. Then this morning I had Larry turn up at my door informing me that the police have arrested your uncles, Paulie and Ronny. And I'm sorry to have to tell you this, sweetheart, but because of what those two prized pricks have done, I don't think you're gonna get bail today.'

Frankie sat in silence for what seemed like ages.

'Hurry up, Eddie. We have to go soon, otherwise my job will be on the line,' Blyth shouted out.

Eddie leaned towards Frankie and urged her to do the same. He grabbed her hand. 'Make sure you get rid of it,' he whispered.

'Eddie, we must leave now,' Blyth ordered, marching down the corridor.

Winking at Frankie, Ed walked away.

CHAPTER FIFTY

Alice saw the police car pull up outside and quickly ushered Georgie and Harry upstairs.

'Jimmy, the gavvers are 'ere again. I don't wanna see 'em, I can't handle it,' Aliced yelled.

Georgie sat on Alice's bed and put her arm around Harry. Both children were traumatised over the previous day's events and Georgie knew, being the oldest, it was up to her to do something about it. 'Nanny, me and Harry don't want to live here any more. Can we go home to Mummy?'

Alice put her head in her hands. Luke and Marky's deaths had not only broken her heart, but spiralled her back into the depths of depression and she couldn't take much more. She looked up and stared at Georgie as though she were a complete stranger.

'No, you can't! You ain't never gonna see that old shitcunt of a mother of yours again. This is your home now, with me, your dad, and your grandad, so best you fucking get used to it.'

Downstairs, Jimmy, Sammy, Jed and Billy were standing in the living room opposite the Old Bill.

'For fuck's sake get to the point. Who's been charged?' Jimmy shouted.

DS Shreeves glanced at his colleague. The whole of the Essex Murder Squad were aware that once the names of Luke's killers were disclosed, a bloodbath would be sure to follow.

'The two men that we've charged are Paul and Ronald Mitchell.'

Jed immediately went berserk. 'The fucking cunts! I'm gonna kill 'em. I'll burn the whole family alive while they beg for mercy!' he screamed, smashing his fists against the wall.

Not wanting his son to get himself nicked, Jimmy pushed the coppers out of the room. 'He don't mean nothing he says. Jed's just upset, I'll keep him in order.'

Shreeves nodded. He had no intention of arresting Jed. Years ago he'd been attacked by a gang of travellers and had been extremely wary of them ever since.

'If you need to speak to us, or you want some counselling for your family, you know where we are,' he said, as Jimmy opened the front door.

Slamming the door behind Shreeves, Jimmy leaned against it and caught his breath. He'd really enjoyed the quiet life. Retiring from the underworld and spending time with Alice had been a blessing in disguise. Now Luke had been murdered, everything was different. Respected in the travelling community, Jimmy was now left with only one option. He had to come out of retirement and get revenge.

Over at Chelmsford Crown Court, Joyce sat in the gallery next to Joey and Dominic. She and Stanley had had an enormous row earlier over what he'd said to Joey about Eddie and, like a sulky child, her husband had then refused to come to the bail hearing. Joyce was furious over Stanley's behaviour, but still managed a wave and a smile as Eddie, Raymond, Gary and Ricky walked in. All that mattered today was getting Frankie home where she belonged, Stanley could be dealt with later.

Eddie sat directly behind Joyce and Joey and put an arm round each of them. He had been hoping to arrive before his son and mother-in-law, so he could speak to her outside but, due to an accident on the A130, and his insistence to speak to Frankie personally, his good intentions had been hampered.

'I've got some bad news,' he whispered.

Joey turned to face him with a startled expression. 'What's the matter?'

'I don't think Frankie is going to get bail today. Did you hear about the murder in Upminster yesterday?'

Joyce nodded. 'We saw it on the news. Joey said the kid was Jed's.'

Eddie nodded. 'Well, it turns out that my stupid fucking brothers did it.'

'What, Uncle Paulie and Ronny?' Joey asked dumbly. His dad only had two brothers, therefore it couldn't be anybody else.

'What's that got to do with Frankie?' Joyce whispered.

'The family link, I suppose. She might still get bail, but because of those two imbeciles, it now looks extremely doubtful,' Ed explained.

'Does Frankie know all this? I spoke to her a couple of nights ago and she was upbeat about coming home,' Joey asked.

'Yes, I was allowed to have five minutes with her in the cell. She also knows that Jed has got the kids. There's no point in lying any more if she can't get bail.'

Joyce put her head in her hands. Frankie having to stay in prison was awful, but having to admit to Stanley that the murder had a link to Eddie was even worse.

Frankie had a manic expression on her face as she was led into the dock. She looked into the gallery and glared at her family. Locking eyes with Joey, she quickly averted her own. As for Kerry, she couldn't even look at her.

While her bail application was addressed, Frankie stared at the floor. There was no point in taking much interest when she'd already been told the outcome. Listening to her legal team drone on, Frankie clenched her fists. If she was heading back to Holloway, smashing Killer's face in was her first port of call.

When the words, 'Application for bail rejected,' were shouted, Frankie immediately started to laugh.

'Wankers! You're all a bunch of wankers,' she screamed.

481

The judge was appalled. 'Control your language, Miss Mitchell. This is a courtroom, please.'

Frankie ignored his obvious warning and continued shouting. 'I want everybody to know that I'm glad Jed's son got murdered. I've already lost my babies and now that bastard knows what it feels like to lose one as well. Jed is evil – he's a fucking traitor.'

The judge was disgusted by Frankie's behaviour. Red in the face, he turned to his colleagues. 'Take her down,' he bellowed.

When the officials tried to restrain her, Frankie let out a blood-curdling scream and DI Blyth jumped out of her seat. 'Be gentle with her, she's eighteen weeks pregnant and she isn't well,' she said, voicing her concern.

'Oh, my gawd! She's gone off her rocker, Eddie. Do something,' Joyce pleaded as Frankie was bundled off.

Eddie gave her shoulder a comforting squeeze. 'She'll be fine, Joycie, I know she will.'

Joey was in tears and being consoled by Dominic and Kerry. 'I love you, Frankie. Please ring me as soon as you get a chance. I'm sorry for not telling you about Georgie and Harry, so is Kerry. We're sorry for everything,' he cried.

When Frankie disappeared out of sight, Eddie led his family outside the court.

'I don't think she's gonna cope, Dad,' Gary said bluntly.

Ricky and Raymond both agreed, but Eddie saw things differently.

'My Frankie's made of strong stuff. She has the Mitchell temperament and my blood running through her veins. Of course she'll cope,' he insisted.

Ricky tapped his father on the shoulder. 'Dad, Larry wants a word with you.'

Eddie walked towards him. 'What's up?' he asked, as he saw the bleak expression on Larry's face.

'I've just had another phone call. Your not-so-bright brothers have also just been charged with killing Jimmy O'Hara's son, Mark.'

'What?' Eddie said in absolute astonishment.

'A witness came forward, Ed. Ronny and Paulie apparently used the same car to run Mark O'Hara off the road as they used when they shot Luke.'

Eddie crouched down with his head in his hands. Luke being murdered by Paulie and Ronny was bad enough, but Mark being topped by them as well was going to cause the type of repercussions he'd never had to deal with before. This would create the feud of all bloody feuds.

Seeing their father crouched down, Gary and Ricky ran over to him. 'What's wrong?'

Eddie looked up and shook his head. 'Everything's wrong. Fucking everything! We're in big danger now, boys, all of us are.'

Unaware that her uncles had also been charged with the murder of Jed's brother, Frankie was in the back of a meat wagon on her way back to Holloway. Feeling her baby move again, she put her hand on her tummy. When she'd lost her rag in court, her baby had been kicking her good and proper, and she wondered if he or she was going to be a fiery one like she and her dad were.

Seeing one of the screws looking at her, Frankie poked her tongue out and started to sing. She smiled as the officer looked away. The bloke obviously thought she was loopy, and that was the bloody plan. Her dad handing her that folded-up letter in the cell had not only meant the world to Frankie, but had also given her hope for the future. Obviously, she was gutted that she hadn't got bail and she was also concerned over Georgie and Harry's welfare, but knowing Jed had now suffered the same kind of heartbreak that he'd put her and her family through made her feel a whole lot better.

Finding out that Jed had murdered her grandfather had been the worst moment of Frankie's life. Even Killer's brutal assault didn't match up to that, and what she had shouted in court, Frankie had meant. She was really glad that Luke was dead. It

483

was payback for the evil bastard that had fathered him.

Thinking of her own dad again, Frankie wondered if she should tell him the truth now. Apart from Kerry, nobody knew the real reason why she'd stabbed Jed, and now she hadn't got bail and was looking at a long stretch, it might do her a favour to let the cat out of the bag. Her dad would definitely sort things out once he knew the truth, but he might do something rash and she didn't want to see him get banged up again.

Seeing the same prison officer glance her way again, Frankie began to giggle. 'You are a bunch of cunts, doo-dah, doo-dah. You are a bunch of cunts doo-dah, doo-dah day,' she chanted.

Hearing the words, 'Hospital wing,' whispered, Frankie smiled inwardly. She thought of her father's letter again. Three times she'd read it before she'd chewed it up and she had memorised every sentence.

Dear Frankie,

I am not very good with words, so I thought I'd speak to you by letter instead. I know you were pissed off about me and Gina, and I'm sorry you found out the way you did. I should have been more of a man and told you, but because I know you have a temper like me, I didn't have the guts. I need you to know that even though Gina is special to me, nobody will ever replace your mother in my eyes. I loved your mum from the day I first met her and I will never love another woman like I loved her.

Now that's been said, I have things to say to you, Frankie. From the day you were born you have always been the apple of my eye. You are my only daughter and I love you more than you will ever know. Out of all my children, you are the one that is most similar to me. Don't get me wrong, I love your brothers just as much, but me and you have that special bond. We always have, and we always will.

Which brings me to Jed. Do not worry or fret, because your dad will see to things, I promise you that. Georgie

484

and Harry will be fine, trust me, and even though you haven't got bail today, your QC will get you off with this, I know he will.

I need you to be strong for me, Frankie. I don't know who your cellmates are, but if you don't like them, act like a loony and get yourself put in the hospital wing. You'll be safer in there and so will your baby.

I think I've said everything I need to say for now. Chin up, and I'll see you soon, darling. Ring me, and send me a visiting order and we can talk more.

Love always,

Dad

PS CHEW THIS PAPER UP AND TRY TO SWALLOW IT. IF YOU CAN'T, MAKE SURE IT'S UNREADABLE.

Clocking the screw staring at her yet again, Frankie broke into song once more. 'God save our gracious Queen, long live our noble Queen, God save our Queen. Send her victorious ...'

'Please shut up,' the screw said.

Frankie shook her head and stared at him with a psychotic expression. 'Happy and glorious, long to reign over us, God save the Queen.'

As the screw glanced at his female colleague, Frankie smirked. She wasn't mad – anything but. She was cleverer than most people and so she should be.

After all, she was Eddie Mitchell's daughter.

DISCOVER
MORE FROM
Kimberley
CHAMBERS

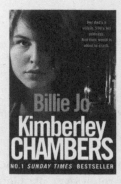
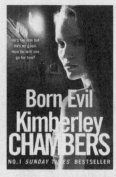

The Mitchells & O'Haras Trilogy

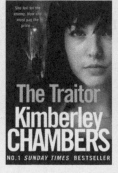
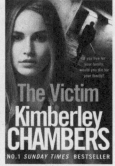